"THIS SEEMS LIKE A GOOD PLACE FOR A COP TO DIE."

"Go ahead and get it over with," Horn said calmly to Zamora, feeling his mods jerk crazily.

The Colombian looked momentarily confused. "All right, then die."

Horn's foot was already slamming into Zamora's midsection when he pulled the trigger. The bullet ricocheted off Horn's modified shoulder, its fiberglass tip exploding in a shower of splinters. One of the shards drove nearly an inch into his right eye, and his head filled with an excruciating pressure. He hit the catwalk, fighting the pain and forcing his left eye open.

Zamora staggered closer, the automatic in his hand zeroing in on Horn's chest. He was clutching his side with his other hand, and his chest was heaving. "You son of a bitch. I hope that hurts."

Horn was conscious that his 9 mm was no longer in his hand and looked around desperately. His stomach dropped when he spotted it lying directly between his opponent's feet.

Zamora sneered. "Too late, cop. You're dead—"

HORN
OUTLAND STRIP
BEN SLOANE

A GOLD EAGLE BOOK FROM
WORLDWIDE.

TORONTO • NEW YORK • LONDON • PARIS
AMSTERDAM • STOCKHOLM • HAMBURG
ATHENS • MILAN • TOKYO • SYDNEY

First edition February 1991

ISBN 0-373-64003-X

Special thanks and acknowledgment to
Stephen R. Cox for his contribution to this work.

OUTLAND STRIP

CHAPTER ONE

POLICE CAPTAIN DICK KELSO leaned forward in the back seat of the unmarked cruiser and ordered, "Up the AC, Murphy. I'm sweating like a bull." He ran a finger around the inside of his shirt collar, then tugged unconsciously on his already loosened tie.

It was the second time in less than ten minutes that Kelso had given the order. Murphy cringed behind the wheel and barked over his shoulder, "That's it, Captain. It's up as far as it'll go." The big plainclothes sergeant tapped a finger on the digital panel that controlled the temperature of the car's interior.

Kelso flopped back in his seat. He pulled a handkerchief from an inside pocket of his worn sport coat. "I'm too old for this," he said, wiping the front of his balding head with the wadded cloth.

"I've got a bad feeling about traveling crosstown in a goddamn po-lease car."

Kelso turned toward Jack Rohde, whose huge form was hunched over slightly in order to keep his smooth, bullet-shaped head from touching the roof of the car. The big man's hands were cuffed in front of him and in one he held an unlit cigarette. Kelso had told him he couldn't smoke in the car, but Rohde had pleaded, "Just let me hold one in my hand. It'll steady my nerves."

"You think we should have taken you in a helicopter?" Kelso asked sarcastically, staring at his prisoner. Rohde's long face reminded him of a beagle his first wife had owned.

Rohde did look like a sad hound dog. His cheeks sagged, a feature emphasized by the bags under his pale green eyes that resembled his huge, floppy earlobes. His voice matched his face—a maddeningly slow Texas drawl.

"That would have been a damn sight smarter than doing this dance through...where the hell are we?" Rohde peered around Murphy's head and squinted through the windshield.

"Seventh Avenue," Kelso answered as he watched the black-and-white in front of them inch forward, its red lights flashing uselessly in the bogged-down traffic. "Get that son of a bitch on the horn and tell him to off that goddamn light," he barked at Murphy.

"Are we in Manhattan yet?" Rohde asked, grimacing as though waiting for someone to give him an injection.

Kelso grunted a half laugh. "What do you mean, *in* Manhattan? Shit, we never left it. I told you, we're going to the Justice Center Annex for your prelim—"

"Don't remind me," Rohde interrupted. "If I'm lucky, my lawyer's stuck in this same traffic. If I'm real lucky, the son of a bitch won't make it at all."

Kelso leaned against the door and grinned, his raggedly trimmed mustache sliding crookedly to one side like a caterpillar. "Hell, your lawyer probably flew there in his private helicopter. I'm sure he could afford one with the retainer you had to pay."

Rohde's glistening face broke into a smile. He raised his cuffed hands and shoved the unlit cigarette between his teeth. "You got that right, Captain Kelso." The smokeless tube bounced around as he spoke. "The bastard is probably sittin' in the courtroom right now, hopin' I don't show. It'll give him another chance to stretch his goddamn bill."

Kelso noticed that the big Texan seemed to have relaxed a bit. "Tell me something, Rohde," he said. "Are you going to cut a deal with the D.A.?"

"Shit," Rohde replied with a chuckle. "The only deal I'm gonna cut is on a felt-covered table."

"Come on," Kelso coaxed, "are you going to roll over on the Colombian?"

Rohde's expression changed suddenly to show frustration and anger. "I'm not in bed with the son of a bitch. How the hell can I roll over on him?"

"Okay." Kelso held up a hand. "Bad choice of words. Are you...how should I say it, going to cut the asshole's throat?"

Rohde stared at Kelso for several seconds before his face began to relax. A smile curled up the corners of his mouth and his eyes glinted. Kelso thought for a moment that Rohde looked like a python eyeing its prey.

"If I can," Rohde said, his voice nearly a whisper, "I'm going to cut the evil fucker's head clean off." He snapped out of his deadly stare, leaned against the rear doorpost and studied Kelso almost curiously. "I wish I could take the bastard's head off, literally, because I'm sure that's what he intends to do to me."

Kelso cleared his throat. He hadn't expected his prisoner to be so candid. Over the past several weeks the newspapers had been speculating full tilt about the question he'd just asked Rohde. Now he had the answer. For a moment he wished he was a reporter instead of a cop. People all across the United States—the world, for that matter—wanted to know if Jack Rohde was going to spill his guts and send Ruben Zamora to prison for the rest of his life or, if the D.A. had his way, send him to see the Black Nurse, who would pump enough poison into his veins to kill a herd of cattle.

"Uh—" Kelso started to speak, but cleared his throat again. "I guess you know they didn't find Zamora on that little island near Australia like they thought they would."

"Shit, I know that." Rohde gave a hollow laugh. "Why the hell do you think I'm so nervous? That son of a bitch has got a ten-mil bounty on my head, and that's in gold. He knows he has to nail me before I go to trial." The humor dropped from his voice. "The bastard knows he's going to get caught sooner or later. He also knows I'm the only swingin' dick on this planet who can do him any real damage."

Kelso had heard that Zamora, the Colombian heir to one of the largest South American drug dynasties of the late twentieth century, had put a bounty on the Texan's head, but one to two million in untraceable electrocash were the figures he'd been privy to. He figured Rohde, whose occupation for the record was gambler, was just adding to the theatrics of the moment by exaggerating the price on his head.

"They must think they can nail him with your testimony," Kelso said. "I guess they're betting on the outcome. They must think you're serious."

"Look at it this way, Kelso," Rohde drawled, emphasizing the *O* of Kelso's name. "They must think I'm a heart attack for them, or why did they assign a po-lease captain to escort me around this sinkhole you call a city."

Rohde broke out in a fit of laughter that turned into coughing and choking. The cigarette fell from his mouth and dropped between his legs. The big man squirmed a couple of seconds, then apparently remembered it wasn't lit.

Kelso couldn't help but smile. He also couldn't help but like the big Texan. However, he felt obliged to straighten him out about one thing. "The only reason I'm stuck with this dismal assignment is because one of my detectives managed to weasel out of it at the last moment. Unfortunately for him, I was the only one available to cover." Kelso smiled to himself as he thought about what kind of assignment he was going to dump on Max Horn in retaliation, once he got back to the precinct.

"I might say I'd hate to be in his shoes," Rohde said, shifting his bulk in the seat, "but you don't look like a vindictive asshole. As a matter of fact, you don't even look like a cop. You sort of remind me of a professor I had back at the University of Texas." Rohde snickered and grinned at Kelso as though they were old buddies.

"The cop that stiffed me with this knows I'm retiring in September," Kelso said, nodding, more as though he were thinking aloud than talking to Rohde. "This is probably his idea of a joke."

Kelso thought of the call he'd gotten less than two hours earlier from Stu Winger, Horn's partner. The young detective told him that Horn had gone into the outskirts of the Bronx to meet one of his snitches, who supposedly had a line on a big shipment of needle track. Winger, naturally, was stuck on standby, waiting at some rattrap off Harlem Drive in case Horn needed backup.

"I'm going to have both their asses on wino patrol for the next six weeks," Kelso muttered. The thought made him feel a lot better.

"Both their asses?" Rohde had managed to pick up the cigarette from between him legs and had returned it to his mouth. He unconsciously squinted his right eye as though protecting it from the nonexistent smoke.

"Yeah," Kelso said, "Horn and his partner. They think they're free agents, and that all of this shit—" he gestured with his hands as though to indicate the city "—is a goddamn baseball game."

"If this is a baseball game," Rohde wheezed, "then I think both teams are losin'."

"You got it," Kelso said. For some reason he suddenly felt great. In less than three months he'd be sitting in his stilt house on Mexico Beach, listening to the waves roll in instead of traffic noise, sirens and the incessant gurgling of humanity as it flushed down the inner-city drain.

Kelso leaned forward and tapped Murphy on the shoulder. "Give me your lighter."

"Huh?"

"Give me your lighter," Kelso repeated. He stretched out his hand over the sergeant's shoulder.

Murphy mumbled several profanities as he fished around in his jacket pockets, finally extracting a disposable lighter. "There," he barked, slapping it in Kelso's hand.

Kelso turned toward Rohde and struck a flame. He held it up to the end of the Texan's cigarette and watched something akin to awe spread across the man's face.

"Well, I'll be damned," Rohde drawled before shoving the end of the cigarette into the flame and firing it up. He inhaled deeply, then blew the smoke out his flared nostrils. "I sure as hell appreciate this, hoss," he said finally, squinting both eyes this time as real smoke wreathed his face.

Kelso felt a flash of embarrassment. Rohde sounded as if Kelso had just saved his life instead of lighting his smoke. The police captain pushed a button on the armrest and rolled down the window a couple of inches. The noise from the street poured into the car along with the stench of exhaust fumes, and he quickly rolled the window almost all the way up again, grimacing at the sound and smell.

"No problem," he said. "If you nail the Colombian, you'll be the hero of every cop in the city."

"She-it." Rohde smiled and thrust the cigarette from one corner of his mouth to the other with the tip of his tongue. "I sure as hell ain't tryin' to be no goddamn hero. I'm tryin' to save my ass, that's all!" The big man laughed loudly and raised his eyebrows. He looked like someone trying to wake up.

"How did you manage to get on his death list?" Kelso asked, wondering how much Rohde would tell him. The idea of selling this story to the *Times* crossed his mind.

"It's a long story," Rohde answered, glancing at the cigarette, which was burned nearly to the filter. "Maybe I'll unreel it over a bottle sometime under different circumstances." Rohde plucked the smoldering butt out of his mouth and held it out to Kelso. "Here."

Kelso tossed it into the street through the open crack of the window. A mild disappointment tugged at him. He was just about to ask Rohde what Zamora looked like when he found himself slammed against the back of the front seat. Murphy let loose with a string of oaths.

"What the hell's going on?" Kelso asked, pulling himself back into a sitting position.

"Look at this son of a bitch, Captain." Murphy gestured to a short tractor-trailer rig that had knifed its way from a side street directly in front of their car, blocking all four lanes of Seventh Avenue. Murphy laid on the horn. "Come on, you mother-humpin' asshole, get that goddamn thing outta the way."

Kelso felt a pang of anxiety as he realized they were cut off from the black-and-white that had been driving point. He craned his neck, looking for a way out of the plugged mass of automobiles.

"Cut over the curb and head down Charlton," Kelso ordered, pointing down the street from which the truck had emerged. "Call up the black-and-white and tell them what the hell we're doing. Maybe Westway is better than this parking lot."

Cursing under his breath, Murphy yanked the wheel over hard. The car jolted over the curb and mounted the sidewalk, causing two ragged men to stumble over each other as they fled from its path.

"You sombitch," one of them half screamed, half slurred as he lurched to his feet. He leaned over the front fender and banged both hands on the hood.

"Blow it out your ass," Murphy snarled as he steered slowly among the other pedestrians. He punched a button on the touch-screen commo panel, then growled, "Mary Six, this is Murphy, copy?"

Nothing but static rolled out of the speaker on the dash.

"Mary Six," Murphy repeated, "copy, please. Shit." He took his finger off the button and barked over his shoulder, "Either their radio is broke or Barnes is asleep at the wheel."

Kelso's stomach sank as Murphy wheeled the cruiser off the sidewalk and onto Charlton. There was something wrong with the street. At first he couldn't put his finger on it, but then he realized what it was: there was hardly any traffic. The street was nearly deserted. He whipped his head around. Helpless fear clenched his gut as he watched the tractor-trailer rig back out of Seventh Avenue and jink sideways, effectively blocking them from the rear.

Kelso leaned over the front seat and punched the call button on the commo panel. "This is Mary Niner calling any listening officer, copy." The same static poured from the speaker as when Murphy had tried to hail the black-and-white.

"Holy shit!" Murphy yelped, and slammed on the brakes, nearly throwing the police captain into the front seat.

"What the hell are you doing, Murphy," Kelso shouted as he pulled himself up.

"We got problems, Captain," Murphy answered, nodding down the street.

Kelso looked ahead and saw two garbage trucks pull off Hudson Street, forming an ugly barricade across their path.

"What's wrong with this goddamn radio?" He punched the call button again, his heart pounding like a hot mambo.

"I'm sure they jammed it."

Kelso turned toward the source of the voice. He'd nearly forgotten about his prisoner.

"Take these off, hoss." Rohde held up his cuffed hands, his voice grim, sober. "I ain't gonna die trussed up like a goddamn animal."

Kelso released the commo button. He slid his hand to the bottom of the dash and flipped up a lever, causing an ugly black 12-gauge Street Combat autoloader to pop from its hiding place. He grabbed it and fell back into the seat next to Rohde. "Try the alley," he ordered Murphy. He pulled back the slide on the weapon, ensuring that one of the caseless rounds was in the stainless-steel chamber.

"Come on, Captain." Rohde's voice carried a mixture of urgency and fear. "Get these sons of bitches off me."

As Murphy burned the tires and aimed the cruiser toward a narrow opening between a private dance club and an abandoned flophouse, Kelso's left hand punched a code into the digital cipher on Rohde's cuffs. They popped open with a click, and Rohde seemed to shift into hyperstate. "Gimme a weapon," he yelled as the police car bounced into the trash-strewn alley.

"You're crazy," Kelso yelled back. "How do I know you're not in on this?"

"They're not tryin' to help me escape, for God's sake!" Rohde screamed. "Look at me! They want me dead. Goddamn, man, wake up!"

Kelso reached inside his coat and extracted an ancient snub-nosed .357. He handed it to Rohde, whose face was the color of a fish's underbelly.

"Shit!" Rohde cried. "Is this all you—"

The sound of an automatic weapon firing cut Rohde off in midsentence, and a half second later the windshield ex-

ploded in a shower of glass. As Kelso watched, events unfolded in a crazy jinked-up motion. Murphy raised his
hands, turned his head sideways in a futile attempt to shield
his face from the jagged shards. Tiny flecks of red appeared across his cheeks and forehead as the glass drove into
his flesh like shrapnel. The side of the car slammed into a
graffiti-covered brick wall and ground ahead, sparks flying
as metal peeled from the fender. Kelso, too, had his hands
up, and closed his eyes briefly. He felt himself rammed forward as the cruiser hit the corner of a dumpster and jerked
to a stop against the cement-block wall at the end of the
blind alley.

"Goddamn!" Murphy screeched as the engine chugged
twice before dying.

Kelso dropped his hands and opened his eyes just in time
to see Murphy's head snap sideways and half his skull blow
out.

"Come on, you fool!"

Kelso felt Rohde's spit hit the side of his face as the big
man grabbed his arm and jerked him out of the car. He felt
numb, as if his entire body had been injected with a big shot
of Novocain. He hadn't even heard the shot that had taken
out Murphy. This couldn't really be happening, it had to be
a bad hallucination.

"Get down, goddamn it!" Rohde shoved Kelso to the
asphalt as a hail of lead rained down from the top of one of
the surrounding buildings. Before Kelso could react to the
voice, he found himself facedown in the dirt. He was surprised he still had the riot gun in his hands. As if it were the
natural thing to do, he rolled under the police cruiser. Bullets slammed into the dead machine, sounding as though
someone were beating it with a sledgehammer.

Kelso managed to twist his head sideways. He saw Rohde
scramble to a doorway opposite the police car. The hulking
man crouched, holding the .357 in one hand, peering up-

ward as though he expected to get hit by lightning any second. He grabbed the knob of the battered steel door and twisted it. His lips moved in an obvious curse at the securely locked door. Kelso started to yell, "Shoot open the son of a bitch," but before he finished Rohde had already raised the Magnum and pointed it at the locking mechanism beneath the knob.

Startled by the sound of something heavy landing on the hood of the car, Kelso raised his head and banged it on the automobile's frame. The next thing he knew a pair of hybrid street boots landed on the dirty asphalt between him and Rohde. Almost automatically Kelso slid the shotgun from his side, pointed it at the gray Gore-Tex boots and pulled the trigger.

The sound and pressure of the autoloader cooking off underneath the car made Kelso bang his head again. The recoil of the loosely held weapon sent it sliding backward into the side of his head, bending his trigger finger nearly double.

Kelso blinked. He watched one of the boots fly off a leg as though its owner had kicked it off. A hideous scream of pain erupted in the alley as blood spewed from the stump. The shortened leg jammed down, and its owner tumbled over, dropping a weapon with a huge, curved clip, which clattered to the pavement.

Cursing out loud, Kelso got the autoloader into firing position again. He suddenly realized he was no longer scared. He was no longer in that slow-motion nightmare over which he had no control. He felt different, but he recognized the feeling. He felt like a real cop again. He almost laughed, a giddiness welling up in his chest. All the dull years he'd spent behind a desk, going through the motions by rote, were gone. He was a cop, and all his training came back to him in a flash, as though it were in his genes. If he got out of this alive, he thought, he'd kiss Horn for stiffing him with the job of delivering Rohde.

The sound of Rohde firing his .357 into the steel door brought Kelso back from his moment of insight. He saw the lock fly apart in pieces as Rohde shielded his face with one hand. With a wave of shock he realized that the man on the alley floor, who had been groaning like crazy, had retrieved his weapon and was aiming it toward Rohde, who was yanking on the doorknob. Kelso willed his throbbing hand to move. He squeezed the trigger this time instead of jerking it as before. The deadly circular pattern of number four shot drove into the small of the man's back like a swarm of supersonic bees. A scream jerked out of his gaping mouth and echoed in the alley as though a door to hell had been opened briefly, then slammed shut as the scream subsided and the man gurgled his death.

Rohde whipped his head around at the sound. His jaw dropped as he took in the grisly scene and understood what had happened. His eyes darted to the place where Kelso was hidden under the car. The big Texan gave a crooked grin and disappeared into the black hole of the open door.

Something like joy sprang into Kelso's soul. They won't get that crazy Texan son of a bitch, he thought, surprised at how fast the gangly-looking man had moved. Suddenly he froze. A voice echoed down from the top of the one of the surrounding buildings in the trash- and death-strewn alley. It sounded like a chain saw with dry bearings.

"Kringa! Where the hell is the target?"

A cold shiver ran down Kelso's spine. He was going to have to take a stand. He thought about crawling from beneath the battered cruiser and sprinting for the rabbit hole into which Rohde had disappeared, but he knew he'd be cut down like a stray dog—probably before he ever got half his aging body out from under Murphy's riddled coffin. Kelso felt like a cop, but he didn't feel like a fool.

"Kringa!" the man above boomed again in a bass so deep that the words seemed to have been filtered through coarse gravel. "What the hell's going on down there?" It sounded more like an order to report than a question.

"Yeah, yeah" was the response from the person called Kringa. "That stupid LeRoy Childress is deader than dead, and I think the target has escaped."

The voice of Kringa was as distinctive as that of his master, ringing with a pronounced backwoods-hillbilly twang. Yet it was calm, betraying no anxiety.

"It looks like Childress got zapped in the back," Kringa reported to the man above. "I know I got the big redhead who was drivin', but there was another cop with Rohde in the back." There was a pause of several seconds before Kringa continued. "I think that son of a bitch is under the fuckin' car."

Kelso's blood went cold. He'd thought he was invisible under the crashed cruiser, in a safe haven. His finger fidgeted nervously on the sweat-slick trigger, and he licked his dry lips. But in spite of the dismal situation he still felt invigorated, charged with a youthful energy that kept a crazy smile etched across his face.

The gravel voice rumbled again from above, like the voice of a god in an old movie. "Take care of him."

Kringa gave no answer, but Kelso heard a bang as feet landed on hollow metal. He figured someone had jumped onto the remains of the dumpster, and he waited for a pair of boots to land on the filthy alley floor, which was stretched before his eyes like the landscape of the moon.

"Fire in the hole!" Kringa's voice rang out like a cracked bell.

Kelso stared in amazement as a dull green, egg-shaped object came bouncing down and under the car. He knew what it was even before it rolled to a wobbling stop in front of his nose.

"Shit!" Kelso breathed. He released his grip on the shotgun and grabbed the smooth death egg. Time went south, and Kelso's mind stumbled into the crazy gap between the present and the future. He pulled the grenade toward his head to gain the leverage necessary to fling it from beneath the car. His eyes happened to latch onto the grenade, and for an insane moment he admired its simple beauty: it looked as if it were built to fit in a slot somewhere, as if it had been made to perform some clean and extraordinary act. It felt cool in his hand.

Kelso wondered what Horn would do when he found out what had gone down in this alley. Then somewhere in front of him a bright flash erupted, and Kelso was conscious only of his life being sucked into a blinding white void.

CHAPTER TWO

HORN WHEELED the unmarked Chrysler Elint off Broadway onto Fairview Avenue. He looked over at his partner, Stu Winger, who was in the process of stuffing the last morsel of a cheese-and-salami hoagie into his mouth.

"Where to?" Horn asked, idly noticing Winger pull a plastic foam cup out of a sack on the floorboard.

"Go down to Audubon and cut back south a couple of blocks. He's supposed to meet us in front of an abandoned grocery store somewhere around there." Winger peeled the lid off the cup and sipped the steaming coffee.

"You know, it's probably 106 in the shade and you're drinking hot coffee," Horn chided. But he wasn't surprised. Winger's behavior didn't always adhere to the norm.

"I need my caffeine fix." The young cop grinned. The car's air conditioning blew back the short, sandy hair that topped his head like a sheaf of cut straw. Except for his ever-present five o'clock shadow, Winger looked more like a high school kid than a detective in his mid-twenties. But appearances could be deceiving. Horn knew from experience that his young partner was one of the best cops he'd ever worked with.

Horn pulled off Fairview onto Audubon. The pavement on Audubon was pitted with so many crater-size potholes that it resembled a bomb site, and the car immediately slowed to a crawl. Abandoned and burned-out vehicles lined the trash-strewn avenue, as if it had been a training camp for rioters. Across Highbridge Park and Harlem Drive, Horn could see the stagnant green water of the Harlem River. Beyond that lay the Bronx, a modern-day no-man's-land that had been literally abandoned by New York City since 2020. Now, six years later, it thrived as a sinkhole and refuge for criminals, gangs and those who had chosen to stay and live among the desperate.

"This must be the place," Horn said, turning into a junk-littered parking lot. Set back among the debris was the shell of an old grocery store. Someone had torn down half the big red letters from the sign on the front of the building and it now read SH IT. It seemed appropriate.

"There's Lenny." Winger pointed to one side of the building.

"Where?" Horn couldn't see anything except trash.

"There, next to what's left of that telemonitor booth."

Horn drove straight toward the booth, whose folding door hung by one rusting hinge. "I still don't see him."

"Right there. Sitting on that bucket."

Finally Horn spotted Winger's skinny street connection. He blended into the surroundings as if he belonged there— another piece of junk abandoned as humanity rolled on in search of progress.

The little guy, no taller than five-two, stood as the cop car pulled up to the sidewalk in front of the store. In the sparse shade of a tattered canvas awning that hung over the sidewalk, he looked like a rat that had just crawled out of a sewer. In fact, he probably had, because the shrunken homeless man was known to frequent the maze of pipes beneath the city. Winger called Lenny his "human key," which was synonymous with break-in artist. Winger and Horn had used his services on a number of occasions when time or circumstances necessitated clandestine access to certain well-secured locations.

As Horn and Winger got out of the car, Lenny shuffled toward them. He was wearing fluorescent-green mirror-finish sunglasses, a ragged New York Yankees T-shirt and a pair of shorts made from old olive drab fatigues. Unmatched combat boots adorned his feet, one a canvas jungle type and the other a thick-soled jump boot. Horn could see the smooth handle of a knife sticking above the top of the jump boot.

"Lenny!" Winger said enthusiastically, holding out his hand. "Long time no see."

"No shit," Lenny said in a sort of nasal squeak. He slapped Winger's palm and half nodded toward Horn.

Lenny stuck his hands in his pockets and walked over to the dirty Chrysler. "Is this the same dog turd you tried to palm off on me the last time I did a job for you?" He spit on one of the tires, then turned back toward Winger as though waiting for an answer.

Winger laughed. "No, they sent that old horse to the glue factory. Besides, I was just—"

"I know, you were just joking," Lenny interrupted. "Got a smoke?"

"You know I don't smoke," Winger answered.

Horn smiled. Every time they met, Winger and Lenny went through the same routine.

"Just checking," the little man said as he pulled a half-smoked butt from behind one ear. He lit it with a worn old Zippo and inhaled deeply.

Winger crossed his arms and stared at Lenny. "Take off those goddamn glasses, will you?"

"What's the matter, Winger?" He smiled. "Can't you stand to look at your own face?" Lenny took another drag on his cigarette and blew the smoke through his nose. "You didn't ask me here to bullshit about my glasses. Now what gives? I'm a busy man, you know." He turned his head slightly and spit on the sidewalk, then faced the young cop and took off his sunglasses, hanging them by hooking an earpiece into a hole in the front of his shirt.

"I know you're busy." Winger grabbed Lenny by one arm and patted him on the back. "Horn and I need to get into a warehouse not too far from here and we need your help."

"Naturally," Lenny said, his voice a mixture of boredom and sarcasm. "Which warehouse you talking about?"

"The one that looks like a giant bunker at the corner of Ninth and 216th." Winger nodded toward the north.

"You mean on the other side of the subway yard?"

"Yeah, the big one with razor wire running around the top."

"Shit!" Lenny whistled. "I started to top that place one night. There's a twenty-four-hour traffic jam of armed guards in and around there. Why the hell do you two want to get in—"

Winger cut him off. "Is there a way in?"

Lenny grinned, exposing a crooked set of nicotine-stained teeth. "You show me a place I can't get into and I'll kiss your ass." The smile suddenly dropped from his face, and he lowered his voice to a serious tone. "I can get you into the place, but after that, it's your funeral." He took a last drag on his smoke and flipped it into the street. "I'm not shitting you, there's guys walking around in there with shotguns, automatics, you name it. I'll get you in there, but it'll cost you two hundred up front."

"Did you see what was in the place?" Horn interjected. He and Winger had been tipped that the warehouse was a holding point for one of the largest stolen car rings in the United States. Over a period of several weeks they had observed several large tractor trailers moving in and out of the hangar-size building, which was supposed to be owned by a ceramics exporting business. The tip they'd received said the operation was getting ready to move to New Jersey.

"No, I didn't," Lenny answered Horn. "All I saw was a bunch of mean-looking bastards with guns. I figured it wasn't worth satisfying my curiosity at the risk of getting drilled." He turned back to Winger. "Two hundred," he said, "not a dime less."

"One hundred." Winger pulled a stack of disposable credit wafers from his pocket. He counted five of the thin pieces of plastic and held them out to Lenny. "Take it or leave it."

"You're an asshole, Winger," Lenny said, grabbing the eletrocash and stuffing it into his pocket. "You're lucky I'm hard up this week or I'd tell you to go knock on their door like you were selling encyclopedias or something."

"Yeah, sure," Winger said, stepping off the sidewalk and opening the back door of the Elint. He motioned for his human key to get in. Lenny ran over to the bucket that had served as his chair and picked up a small canvas pack. He walked back to the car and climbed into the back seat. Winger closed the door and said to Horn, "Let's go, partner."

Horn got behind the wheel, drove out of the parking lot and headed back the way they'd come. When they turned up Tenth Avenue, Winger said, "I'm killing the radio," and he punched off the master switch on the commo panel. Horn glanced over, but didn't say anything. He knew he and Winger were sticking their necks way out by hitting the warehouse without a warrant and without uniformed backup, but it didn't bother him; he knew if they waited for the system to work, the perps would have had time to move to another country, let alone another state.

Winger drew a wicked-looking machine pistol from a holster attached to a webbed harness hanging from his shoulders and strapped around his chest. Pulling back the slide on the side of the odd weapon, he checked the chamber. Then, to explain his switching off the radio, he said with a laugh, "I'm sure you don't want Kelso tracking down your ass since you stiffed him with chasing that prisoner crosstown."

"He deserves it." Horn smiled. "It's kind of a retirement present." He knew Kelso would be hot, but he'd take him down to Kelsey's tonight and fill him with cold beer and they'd laugh about it. Horn liked Kelso. The little Irish police captain was always riding his and Winger's butts, telling them, "for God's sake," to learn to read and follow P-cubed—Proper Police Procedure. Kelso reminded Horn of someone who should have been smoking a pipe or shuffling around a library instead of winding up his career as a New York City police captain. The image of the fatherly-looking Kelso dragging a handcuffed prisoner up the steps of the Justice Center Annex made Horn chuckle.

Lenny spoke up from the back seat. "Turn here." He directed Horn to drive down an alley along the edge of the river. After half a block, he said, "Park here. Once I get you guys in, I'm splitting. Agreed?"

Horn stopped the car and cut the engine. Farther up the alley he could see the tall block warehouse, its skirt covered with graffiti and territorial gang markings.

"Agreed," Winger answered. "Let's go."

The three men got out of the car, and Winger put on a light windbreaker to conceal his webgear. In addition to the machine pistol, he was carrying a big .44 automatic, three throwing knives, a penlight, two concussion grenades, two smoke grenades and several clips of ammunition.

"How can you stand to wear all that shit in this heat?" Lenny asked as he pulled one of the straps of his pack over his shoulder.

"I like to sweat," Winger said, smiling crazily. "Now how do we get into this castle?"

"This way." Lenny took off toward the riverbank.

Horn removed his laser-sighted 9 mm automatic from its shoulder holster and pulled back the slide, charging the chamber. He followed Lenny and Winger down a debris-covered bank toward the stagnant river, which stank of sulfur.

"Here," Lenny said, stopping just before they reached a mound of rusted tin siding and rotting boards. "Give me a hand." He reached down to lift a panel of tin and wood that looked as if it had once been the wall of a skid row shack.

Horn grabbed its edge with his gloved right hand and raised it easily. He moved it to one side, revealing a slime-lined pipe two or three feet in diameter. It dropped approximately six feet and opened into a tunnel running back toward the alley in the direction of the warehouse. Footholds were welded onto the interior of the steel pipe, and Lenny wasted no time hopping into the hole and scrambling to the bottom.

"Come on," he said, looking up. "And the last one in should pull some of that shit back over the hole so no one knows we're in here."

"Yeah, right," Winger said as he climbed down after Lenny. "Jesus...what the..." The young cop coughed, then went into a fit of gagging. "Goddamn, Lenny! The stink!" he gasped, finally bringing his gagging under control. "It smells like the breath of a dead man down here. How the hell can you stand it?"

Horn could hear Lenny's high-pitched laughter floating back from somewhere down the tunnel. He pulled a piece of loose tin over the hole and stepped into a pool of sticky mud that served as a welcome mat to the foul tube that lay ahead. Winger's light shone up ahead in the darkness like a dim candle, and he moved toward it, bending nearly double in order to keep his head from scraping the top of the pipe.

They hadn't traveled for more than ten minutes when Horn heard Lenny give the order to stop. He moved next to Winger, who was directing his light up into a pipe similar to the one through which they'd entered the tunnel.

"There you are, gents," Lenny said as he tried to squeeze around Winger.

"Wait a second." Winger stuck out an arm and blocked the little man's exodus. "What the hell do you mean, 'there you are'? Exactly where does this piss tube lead?"

"It takes you into a sort of crawl space." Lenny sounded nervous, and he spoke quickly, obviously anxious to get going. "There's grates. You'll see them. They're like drains for when they wash the floors, no shit."

Winger shone the light on Horn's chest. "What do you think, partner?" he asked.

"Let's take a look," Horn answered.

"See you around, Lenny." Winger dropped Lenny's arm, and without saying a word, the little guy scurried off like a rat in a drain. "Who's first?" the young cop asked, directing the penlight's beam up the vertical pipe.

Without answering, Horn grabbed one of the metal footrests and pulled himself up. He climbed in darkness for three steps before his head emerged into an opening that was, as Lenny had promised, a crawl space. A cool breeze that smelled of mold washed over his face, and he could see several thin shafts of light scattered in the gloom. He assumed these marked the grates Lenny had referred to. Every ten feet or so a massive concrete floor support stuck out of the dirt.

Horn hoisted himself up into the three-foot-high space and moved to one side. He helped Winger over the edge, then motioned for him to follow.

The two men crawled to one of the light sources, which turned out to be a drain covered with heavy wire mesh. Through it Horn could see the ceiling of the warehouse and a sort of elevated walkway that he assumed ran around the walls of the structure. He heard voices and a radio playing somewhere in the background.

"Can you get through it?"

A tightness in Winger's voice caused Horn to turn his head. In spite of the dank coolness of the crawl space, the young cop was sweating heavily. There were big dark circles under the arms of his windbreaker, and his hair was wet and plastered to his forehead. "Are you all right?" Horn asked.

"Yeah," his partner answered. "Just a little nervous, that's all. This place gives me claustrophobia."

Horn reached up, tested the mesh and found that it was welded to a steel ring embedded in the concrete floor. "It's welded," he whispered to Winger.

"That son of a bitch Lenny," Winger muttered disgustedly. "I'll kill the little bastard. This isn't exactly getting us into the place."

"Come on," Horn said, "let's try another one."

The two cops crawled to another grilled opening, and once again Horn tested the mesh grating. "Same thing," he announced.

"What the hell do we do now?"

"I'm going to tear it off," Horn said matter-of-factly. "It's the noise that I'm worried about."

Winger looked puzzled for a couple of moments, then his eyes moved to Horn's gloved right hand. "Oh," he said almost sheepishly, as though he'd just been reminded of the obvious.

"Let's see how much racket this makes." Horn reached up and stuck the fingers of his right hand through the wire mesh. He gently flexed his modified hand, and three welds popped, sounding like the snapping of guitar strings. "Damn," Horn said, wincing.

"Holy shit," Winger hissed, his face pasty and dripping sweat.

Horn held a finger to his lips. "Listen," he whispered.

The two cops stared at each other, their ears tuned in on the hole above their heads. Nothing happened. They heard no running footsteps or alarmed voices. The radio Horn had heard earlier was playing some type of Latin bop music. He hoped it drowned out the sound of ripping metal.

Licking his lips, Horn grabbed the mesh again and pulled. The welds broke loose, one by one, popping and echoing in the crawl space like shots from an air rifle. Finally he held the mutilated screen in his hand.

"Can I go first?" Winger asked, anxiety hanging on his words.

"Take a look around before you show yourself," Horn said, crawling out of the way. He tossed the torn screen aside and pulled the 9 mm from its holster.

Winger appeared relieved. Horn watched the young cop peel off his windbreaker and remove the deadly little machine pistol from its holster. Slowly he poked his head through the drain hole. He looked from side to side, then turned his body to get a three-sixty view.

"The hole's right in the middle of a bunch of cars," Winger informed Horn as he leaned back into the crawl space. "They're all expensive bastards—Mercedes, X-Pacs and the like. There's some activity down at the far end of the warehouse. From what I could see they might be crating them up."

"Maybe they're getting ready to ship them overseas. How many heads did you count?"

"I saw four sets of legs under the cars and one guy on the walkway," Winger answered. "He was carrying some kind of weapon. It looked like pictures I've seen of the H&K Autodart."

"What the hell's an Autodart?"

"Only the military are supposed to have them." Winger wiped the sweat from his forehead with the back of one hand. "They're little carbon fiber machine guns that shoot darts."

"What kind of darts?"

"Exploding darts, poison darts, razor tips, you name it."

Horn noticed that Winger seemed his old self again. He was glad about that, especially if things in the warehouse went south. "Still want to go first?" Horn asked, nodding toward the hole.

"You bet!" Winger stuck his head through the hole, paused briefly, then slithered out like some sleek animal.

Horn followed and found himself on his stomach next to a charcoal-gray Porsche X-Pac that resembled a jet airplane without wings. Winger had crawled across the smooth concrete and was crouched at the front of the machine, staring intently at something. Horn followed his gaze to a man on the walkway who was leaning on the railing and lighting a cigarette. A dull black rifle with a circular clip was cradled in one arm. Horn assumed it was the Autodart.

Winger glanced back at Horn, who motioned him toward the far end of the warehouse where the radio played. The music was almost drowned out by the banging of a nail gun, which echoed in the cavernous building. Winger duckwalked, and Horn followed in a winding path among exotic, high-priced sports cars—almost every model that had been built during the past decade. Winger came to a stop behind a Nissan-Marx Turbo and assumed a prone position.

Horn crawled up next to him and peered beneath the low-slung machine. He counted four burly Hispanic males who were busy crating up a bright red Mercedes coupe. As well as the tools and crating material, Horn could see two shotguns and a long-barreled handgun on a bench near the men.

"What's the plan?" Winger whispered, leaning toward Horn.

"I want you to go over and cover the dart gun. I'll take care of these guys," Horn answered, nodding toward the men working on the crate. "When you hear me take them down, stand the guy up and bring him down here."

"Take this then," Winger said, holding out the machine pistol. "I'll use my Mag."

Horn shook his head. He watched Winger look down at the old 9 mm in his hand and grin. "Don't say it, asshole." Horn knew his partner was getting ready to cut some smartass comment about his ancient weapon. "Get moving."

Winger looked up at Horn, still grinning. Horn thought he detected a degree of madness in the young cop's eyes. He wondered what could be seen in his own eyes. Madness? Maybe something darker. Horn had drawn criticism from the precinct as well as the D.A.'s office for being a rogue, a free agent. "Sometimes I think you're *trying* to get blown away," Kelso had once said. Horn had laughed it off, but the police captain's words had struck a chord that sounded along the periphery of his consciousness like a cracked bell. But Horn refused it, refused to listen to anything that called up hopeless memories of the past. There was only the present for Horn, and that meant action.

Horn stood up and glanced toward the far side of the warehouse. He could see Winger moving in a crouch, covering the man on the walkway, who was heading slowly toward the opposite end of the building, his back to the young cop. As Horn began walking toward the crate builders, he pulled his badge holder from his belt and flipped it open with his left hand. Adrenaline began to course through his body.

Horn stopped within fifteen feet of the crew gathered around the nearly completed shipping crate. He held the 9 mm loosely at his side. His enhanced modifications twitched slightly as he raised the badge shoulder-high and asked, "You boys got anything in here that gets good gas mileage?"

All the crate builders jerked their heads up at once, their mouths dropping open. One long-haired guy with a Fu Manchu and a body the size of a weather balloon yelped something in Spanish that Horn didn't catch. He stared at the badge as though it were a ghost, his bloodshot eyes bulging in disbelief.

"Everybody raise your hands very, very slowly," Horn ordered calmly. He could hear Winger at the far end of the hangar telling the guy on the walkway to toss his weapon over the railing. "You're all under arrest on suspicion of harboring stolen property."

A skinny guy with stringy hair and a goatee cleared his throat. "Bullshit," he said tentatively. "I want to see my goddamn lawyer." He was holding a big nail gun, which was hooked to a red rubber hose hanging from a spring above his head.

Horn raised the 9 mm and pointed it at a short man whose head was covered by a bandanna and who had sidled toward the bench where the shotguns and pistol lay. "One more step and I'll blow the scarf off your head."

The little man froze in his tracks and licked his lips nervously.

Horn moved closer and barked, "Put your hands up now, then put them on your heads and lock your fingers."

At the sound of Winger's machine pistol cooking off, Horn jerked his head around. He caught sight of Winger firing point-blank into the chest of a tall man carrying an old Charter Two-Twenty who had walked in through a door directly beneath the walkway. As he went down, the short-barreled machine gun fired in an uncontrolled arc across the roof of the warehouse, causing dust to rain down and blowing apart several mercury vapor lights that hung from the rafters.

"Goddamn it!" Winger screamed as the sound of gunfire died down. "Horn! I lost the Autodart!"

Horn twirled around just in time to see the little man with
the bandanna lunge for the weapons on the bench. Horn
swung the 9 mm toward the man and tracked the red beam
of the laser sight to his right shoulder. He pulled the trigger. The big automatic bucked violently. Bandanna was just
lifting one of the shotguns when the Teflon-coated bullet
slammed into his shoulder and blew his body sideways like
a leaf dropped into jet exhaust.

The shotgun clattered across the concrete floor and slid
to a stop next to a pair of fluorescent-pink tennis shoes worn
by a slender, shirtless man wearing round sunglasses. His
chest and arms were covered with tattoos and his long hair
was tied in a ponytail with a piece of parachute cord. He
looked down at the shotgun and went for it like a bum going
after a credit wafer dropped on a crowded sidewalk.

"Don't even think—" was the only part of the warning
Horn managed to get out before his finger squeezed the automatic's trigger. Tennis Shoes was halfway up with the old
gas-operated autoloader when Horn's bullet struck him
square in the forehead, jerking his head backward.

"Shit!" Horn grunted as something hard and flat sliced
across the side of his head. The next instant the weather
balloon with the Fu Manchu slammed into his chest like a
wrecking ball. Horn managed to extend his right leg backward and countered the body block. Flexing his modified
knee, he lowered his head and rammed it into the man's chin
and shoved hard. The weather balloon stumbled backward
several steps before tripping over a box of nails. As he fell,
Horn was right on top of him.

The two men seemed evenly matched for a while in their
struggle until Horn raised his right arm and discovered he
no longer held the 9 mm. When he turned his head in an effort to locate it, he was met with blinding pain as the balloon jammed his fingers into Horn's eyes.

"You son of a bitch!" Horn swung his right arm in front of his face, allowing his mod to release totally. A helpless, pain-filled scream immediately erupted from the balloon as the edge of Horn's gloved hand slicked into his lower forearm, nearly taking the man's hand off at the wrist. Limp and bloody, it dangled from the end of the fat, tattooed arm like a dead fish.

Blinking his stinging eyes to clear his vision, Horn rolled to one side and looked up to see a blurred form lunging toward him from the end of the crate. The object the man wielded awkwardly in his right hand was the nail gun.

"I'm on you, cop!" the skinny, wild-eyed man screeched. "I am your death!"

Horn raised his right arm just as his attacker brought down the ugly blunt head of the nail gun. It hit his biceps, and a loud explosion of compressed air escaped as the man pulled the trigger. The spike-driving weapon recoiled, nearly ripping itself from the man's hand as the steel nail slammed violently into Horn's titanium arm.

A look of fear and amazement spread across the man's face. His jaw dropped and his eyes widened. He yelled something in Spanish that Horn didn't understand and lunged forward desperately, aiming the nail gun straight at the center of Horn's forehead.

Horn's right hand moved in a blur and grabbed the head of the gun. He turned it back toward the attacker's chest and heard the man's trigger finger snap as it was twisted 180 degrees. A howl of pain escaped from between his thin lips. His skinny body flopped down on the head of the gun, and Horn felt the compressed air blow out between them as a four-inch steel nail drove into the man's chest.

"You stinking..." the man gasped, raising himself slightly. Surprise and extreme pain were etched across his face. His bulging eyes suddenly rolled in his head and he fell back onto the gun. It bucked violently once again. Over the

dying man's shoulder Horn could see the nail blow out
through his back like a tiny missile and bounce off the ceiling of the warehouse.

Horn rolled the limp body off his chest. The nail gun
flopped harmlessly onto the concrete, still hanging from the
man's twisted, broken finger. He stood in a crouch and
spotted his 9 mm on the floor next to the weather balloon,
who was moaning and holding his mangled hand to his
chest.

Horn took one step over the fat man's legs, and a searing
pain spread through his groin. One of the balloon's log-sized
legs swept into Horn's ankles, and Horn found himself
facedown on the floor. He reached out toward his automatic, but suddenly felt as though someone had dropped a
safe onto his back. The breath was forced from his lungs,
and he thought he heard several of his ribs crack. Moving
his right arm beneath him, he took a deep, painful breath
and attempted to roll the weather balloon from his back.
Just as he started the levered motion, a single shot rang out.
Horn twisted his head and upper body around and could see
a metal-finned silver dart sticking into the fat neck of the
man on his back. The man howled like a moonstruck animal. A millisecond later the cigar-size dart in his neck exploded. Horn, still looking up and back, was sprayed in the
face with blood. The fat man slumped and died, still on
Horn's back.

Ignoring his pain, Horn heaved off the deadweight and
scrambled for his weapon. Winger, where the hell are you?
he thought. Horn swung the 9 mm in the direction from
which he figured the dart had come and tried to wipe the
blood from his eyes with his sleeve.

Like metal to a magnet, Horn's eyes were drawn to the
walkway. He stared at the barrel of the Autodart, which was
trained straight at him. He figured the guy holding it must
have shot the weather balloon from his back in order to get

a clear shot at him. Even in his modified hand, the 9 mm felt like a massive block of lead. Horn could have sworn he saw the man glance up from behind the scope and grin.

"I'm a dead man," Horn said aloud, wondering if Winger had already bought it. Time seemed suspended.

Horn stared steadily at the elevated killer, preferring to face his death instead of catching its dark message blind. But suddenly the walkway beneath the gunman's feet disintegrated in a shower of wooden splinters and lead. Winger was firing his machine pistol up through the floor of the walkway into the legs and lower body of the would-be assassin, who did a death dance as Winger emptied his clip.

Time returned to normal. Horn felt his modified hand, seemingly on its own, squeeze the trigger and send its own death message into the middle of the man's chest. The slug knocked him backward into a wall, pinning him briefly against the blood-spattered cinder block before he staggered forward, tipped over the metal railing and crashed into the sloped windshield of a bright red X-Pac.

Horn stood and stepped over the fat man's body. He weaved among the cars toward Winger, who was leaning against the wall, looking as if he'd just spent ten hours in a steam bath. The machine pistol hung at his side. Slowly it slipped from his sweat-slick fingers and banged to the floor. He didn't seem to notice. Tiny rivers of sweat streamed down his face.

"Are you all right?" Horn asked, suddenly conscious of the fact that he felt the exact opposite of the way his young partner looked. He could still feel the adrenaline flowing through his body.

"Yeah, I'm all right. I'm fine." Winger gave his head a shake to banish the vacant stare and focused his eyes on Horn. "The son of a bitch slipped into a closet or something up there." He nodded upward. "I had to wait until he moved to the rail before I could be certain of hitting him."

"Go and bring the car to the front," Horn said, picking up the machine pistol. He slipped it into the modified holster hanging from the young cop's webgear. "Call in our location and tell them what we've got. I'll check out the rest of the building."

As Winger walked zombielike toward the doors and loading docks at the far end of the warehouse, Horn returned to the grisly scene around the partially crated Mercedes. He examined each body for signs of life and found none. The waist and legs of the Autodart man were hanging out of the Porsche's broken windshield as though the machine were in the process of eating him.

Horn checked out the guy Winger had initially shot, who was sprawled in the doorway that led to a cluttered office area. He pulled the glove off his left hand and placed his fingertips on the man's neck. He was dead, his skin cold. Horn put the glove back on, then stuck a fresh clip in the 9 mm before stepping over the dead man and moving into the offices.

What had once been the business center of the huge warehouse was now a dust-covered collection of desks, credenzas, chairs, filing cabinets and ancient PCs. Papers, printouts and trash littered the room. Empty beer cans, fast-food wrappers and skin magazines were scattered across the desktops. Horn figured the crate builders had used the room for their meal breaks. He noticed several spent spools of string, the cheap, nasally ingested amphetamine whose use was an epidemic in the streets of the city.

"Max," Winger said as he walked into the room.

Horn turned toward his partner. "Did you call the precinct?" he asked, noticing Winger was carrying a hand-held commo set in his hand.

"Yeah," the young cop answered. "Christina Service wants to talk to you right away." He was referring to the assistant district attorney. "She's waiting for your call."

Horn could see that Winger was upset about something. He took the commo set from Winger, a sense of foreboding sweeping over him like the breath of an undertaker. Winger immediately left the room.

Leaning against one of the trash-covered desks, Horn punched up dispatch and asked to be patched through to the D.A.'s office. Seconds later the crisp, businesslike voice of Christina Service echoed in the room. "Is this Detective Horn?" she asked, an edge of impatience hanging from her words.

"This is Horn."

Christina lowered her voice to a somber, almost whispering tone. "Listen, Max..." She paused. Horn knew she was about to say something he didn't want to hear. For some crazy reason he was reminded of the time when Dan Riddle, his previous partner, had broken the news that Horn had lost his arm and most of one knee. A shiver ran down his spine, and he shook his head to dismiss the thought.

"What is it?" he asked.

"Dick Kelso's dead."

Horn stared at the commo set as his mind fought to take in what she'd said. "No," he whispered, his heart beating somewhere in a vacuum a thousand miles from his body.

"Max?" Christina's voice filtered through the RF static. "Are you okay?"

Horn swallowed. "Yeah," he said hoarsely. "How did it happen?"

"They were apparently cut off from the escort and got hit. Jack Rohde's missing, so it seems likely it was a planned escape."

Horn didn't want to ask, but he found himself asking, "Did he suffer?"

Christina hesitated for several seconds, then answered, "I don't really know. The report I got just said it was pretty violent."

Without saying anything else, Horn punched off the commo set and laid it on the desk. Three words formed a maddening loop in his head: *It's your fault.* The whole sad scenario hung like a dirty bloodstained curtain behind the self-indictment. Horn's idea of a joke had wound up with his boss dead. Kelso dead instead of Horn. And to Horn, Kelso was more than just a boss; he was one of the few people on the face of the earth Horn could call a friend. Kelso had stood behind him when his wife, daughter and partner were killed. He had argued on Horn's behalf to get Horn mustered back into an active Crime Suppression Unit in spite of the electromechanical appendages that had replaced his entire right arm and knee. And Horn knew that Kelso knew he'd gone underground and gotten state-provided modifications enhanced, replaced with hardened multiplexed servos and covered with combat titanium. Kelso knew, but he never said a word, in spite of the fact that it was a felony to wear the weaponlike limbs.

Horn leaned back his head and howled. It was an animal groan of sheer anguish. Tears welled up in his eyes, burning and blurring his vision. He choked back a sob.

Shoving the 9 mm back into its shoulder holster, Horn pulled off the black leather glove covering his modified hand. He looked down at what the techno-doc had called his best effort, his masterpiece. He flexed the fingers, turned the palm up. Most of the dull combat-green plating had been worn away, exposing the smooth silver gleam of the titanium. He stared at the hand as though it were the first time he'd seen it. It was alive. It was tapped straight into his spine. Horn thought for a moment that instead of the arm being a part of him, he had become a part of it . . . a killing machine. Everything around me dies, he thought.

"You okay, partner?" Winger's voice floated into Horn's consciousness, bringing him back to reality. He turned and saw the young cop staring at him from the doorway.

"I did it," Horn said flatly. "I killed Kelso."

"That's bullshit," Winger told him, taking a step into the room.

Horn held up a hand to silence Winger. He walked toward the doorway, thinking it ironic that he would now use this killing bent of his to track down whoever had murdered Kelso. Numbness replaced the grief that had gripped him, and for that he was glad. He looked at Winger, who had moved to one side to let him pass. He wondered how long it would be before the young cop's face stared at him from a coffin.

CHAPTER THREE

THE HUNTERS CLUB STOOD like a faded piece of furniture among the mismatched businesses and run-down buildings on Crosby Street near Chinatown. The old restaurant had once been a showplace, a classy affair whose decor featured red leather and polished wood and whose waiters, clad in freshly pressed tuxedos, went out of their way to please the diners. Like its clientele, however, the club had grown old. The leather sagged and cracked, the wood had become worn and faded, and the gray-haired waiters crept about in tuxedos that were frayed and wrinkled.

The Trophy Room was a private dining area at the back of the restaurant, its walls festooned with dusty animal heads. At the head of a long mahogany table sat Ruben Zamora, smoking a cigarette and sipping a glass of white wine. On the plate in front of him was an as yet untouched broiled trout, its dead eyes staring sullenly at the ornate chandelier that hung over the table.

To the right of the Colombian was Tucker Moore, an impeccably dressed man in his mid-forties. Erwin Rust, a white-haired, heavyset man with a bulbous nose and a perpetual frown carved into his ruddy face, sat beside Moore. The man on Zamora's left, Sam Taylor, had also chosen fish for his entrée, and was busy tearing it apart, talking between bites. He had shiny jet-black hair, a potbelly that threatened to pop the buttons of his too-small shirt and was wearing an old pinstriped suit that looked as if it had never seen the inside of a dry cleaner's.

Zamora took a deep drag of his cigarette and inhaled the thick smoke, his eyes squinting behind wire-framed glasses. He was in his late thirties, light-skinned for a South American. His short black hair was combed straight back, and patches of gray at the temples made him look like the curator of a museum or a professor of archaeology; however, Zamora looked like anything but what he was, a man without conscience and the only son of Jesus Zamora, the infamous leader of the largest drug cartel of the late twentieth century.

"Listen, Zamora," Taylor said as he removed a bone from his mouth and placed it on his plate, "I was sorry to hear about your father dying in prison and all." Taylor took a healthy swallow from his wineglass. A trickle of the clear liquid ran from the corner of his mouth, and he wiped it with the back of one hand. "I mean, it's too bad you couldn't get him out of there before he..." Taylor paused to burp into a clenched fist and appeared to be searching for the correct word. Finally he held up his hands and shrugged, as if there were no other way to say it. "Before he died. You know, these things happen." The slovenly man's eyes, which looked like black beans, shot around the table as if seeking confirmation of his trite words.

Rust and Moore avoided making eye contact. Zamora, however, leaned over and patted Taylor on the arm. "I appreciate your condolences, Samuel. Believe me, it means a lot to hear you say what you just did."

Zamora was indeed sorry he hadn't been able to get his father out of the maximum-security prison in Pennsylvania where he'd died three weeks earlier, eaten up by cancer. His principal regret, however, was that he hadn't been able to find out where his father had hidden his fortune, which was estimated to exceed ten billion dollars, half of which was in gold. Zamora's only hope was that his father had told one of Zamora's two surviving uncles the location of the lucrative holdings before he died. They were in the same prison, after all. Knowing how secretive his father had been, Zamora knew the chances were slim, but better than no chance at all. The Colombian needed money. He hadn't quite figured out how to spring his uncles from prison, but he knew it would take cash and lots of it. That was why he was now sitting with the three men who controlled the majority of the casinos in Las Vegas and Atlantic City.

"I don't understand why you didn't accept my invitation to have this meeting in Atlantic City," Moore said, wiping the corners of his mouth delicately with his napkin. "Nothing against this place—" he gestured around the gloomy room "—but I would gladly have provided a more luxurious setting." He ran a hand over his neatly trimmed beard and smiled, his dark eyes twinkling like tiny jewels.

"And I'm sure you would have been a most gracious host," Zamora replied. "But I wanted to have this meeting on what all of you might consider neutral ground. Mr. Taylor and Mr. Rust might not have felt comfortable in the main camp of one of their largest competitors." He nodded toward the other two men. "Likewise, I didn't want to hold the meeting in Las Vegas, even though Mr. Rust was kind enough to offer." Zamora turned his head as if to look around the room, but his eyes never left Moore's. "It's certainly not the Taj Majal, but it's safe and holds many fond memories for me. My father and my uncles met many times at this very table."

"When they weren't hiding in the jungle, right?" Taylor laughed loudly and drained the last of his wine.

Zamora turned toward Taylor. "More wine, my friend?" he asked, smiling warmly. "Perhaps some brandy?"

"Sure," Taylor answered, belching again. This time he didn't bother to cover his mouth.

"Gentlemen?" Zamora glanced toward Rust and Moore, who both nodded. "Leonard, send the waiter in, please."

A burly South American who had been standing just inside the entryway looked up. He was wearing a leather sport coat and sunglasses. Nodding, he left the room, and moments later an aged, gray-haired man in a faded black tuxedo appeared.

"Yes, sir?" he said, picking up the used plates and placing them on a tray.

"Coffee, cigars and brandy," Zamora said, gesturing around the table to indicate that everyone was included.

As the waiter finished clearing the table, Zamora leaned toward Taylor and said softly, "Your voice, your eyes, make me think you may have Hispanic blood in your veins, Samuel. Am I correct?"

Taylor made an abrupt choking sound, his face flushing red. "No goddamn way," he blurted. "My family immigrated to the United States from Canada. You think I look like a spi—" He suddenly chopped off the word, apparently realizing he had almost insulted his host. His face seemed to turn a brighter shade of red. "Not that I've got anything against you people," he said awkwardly. "I'm just surprised you might think I was one."

"Of course," Zamora said, his smile never wavering. "Maybe it's your hair." He leaned back in the chair and chuckled.

Rust and Moore looked puzzled by the exchange, but laughed tentatively, while Taylor's embarrassment turned into obvious irritation. He glared at Zamora as the waiter returned and placed a coffee service, snifters of brandy and a box of cigars on the table.

"Never mind," Zamora said to the waiter, who was about to pour coffee. "I'll do that."

The waiter left the room. Zamora stubbed out his cigarette in a glass ashtray and served each man coffee and brandy, then offered the cigars, recommending them as among Cuba's finest. Rust accepted one of the long, dark Havanas, and Zamora was quick to light it for him.

"Come on, Zamora," Taylor said impatiently, downing his brandy in one swallow. He glanced at the other two guests and snapped, "Let's get on with the meeting. I've got other shit to do today."

"Of that I'm certain," Zamora said, returning to his seat. His voice was flat and businesslike. He leveled a stare at Taylor and watched the man shift uncomfortably in his seat, avoiding the Colombian's eyes. Finally Zamora glanced at the others.

"Gentlemen," he began in a calm and measured tone, "I'm sure that all of you are aware that we four represent the controlling interest in the majority of the casinos in Las Vegas and Atlantic City. Mr. Taylor and Mr. Rust from—"

"Wait a goddamn minute," Taylor interrupted. "I know *we* own the controlling interest in the Vegas and Atlantic City houses—" he gestured across the table toward Moore and Rust "—but where the hell do you come in? I mean, you said 'we'.... What the hell controlling interest do you own?" Taylor laughed as though he'd just told a joke and hoped to drum up a reaction, then loosened the large knot in his tie and poured himself more brandy.

Moore and Rust didn't join in the laughter. They did, however, look at Zamora questioningly. Moore raised his eyebrows.

Zamora smiled to himself, knowing it was time for his sales pitch. "I'll have to ask Mr. Taylor's pardon," he said, speaking directly to Moore and Rust, "but I own nearly five percent of the Nugget's holdings in Vegas and approximately 6.5 percent of Bally's Grande on the Boardwalk." The Colombian was lying. His holdings in either organization amounted to less than one percent, but he figured if they went for his scheme—and he intended them to make that decision before they left the restaurant—they wouldn't bother checking out his claim.

"Still," Taylor said, his voice devoid of the humor he'd enjoyed moments earlier, "five and six percent isn't much."

"Five and 6.5 percent," Zamora corrected. "And I take exception to your statement. My holdings are significant." He looked at the other two men, who nodded their heads.

"He's right, Sam," Rust said, looking at Taylor. "At least it's enough that we ought to hear his proposition."

Taylor's face flushed and he leaned back in his chair. "What the hell," he said. "As long as it doesn't cost anything."

"Thank you." Zamora nodded, his facial expression unchanged. Again he stared at Taylor until the man squirmed uncomfortably.

"The Outland Strip," Zamora said, looking at each of the three men in turn, "is turning Las Vegas and Atlantic City into a couple of ghost towns. Pretty soon—" he directed his attention to Taylor "—the only people you're going to see on the Boardwalk are those old people they bus in from New York." Zamora gestured in a helpless manner and addressed Moore and Rust. "And Vegas, well, Vegas was having a hard time even before the Strip was launched."

The three men remained silent. Zamora had done his homework. The revenues from the casinos of Atlantic City and Las Vegas had plummeted drastically since the Outland Strip had opened for business a brief four years before.

The Outland Strip, often referred to as just the Strip or the OS, was nearly one hundred square miles of casinos, hotels, luxurious brothels, sensory theme parks, artificial beaches and a substantial supporting colony, all of which orbited Earth some ten thousand miles outboard of the moon. The structure, shaped like a giant shallow bowl, was covered with a clear, glasslike material laid out in diamond-shaped grids. This served as the edge of the sky for the neon-bathed surface of the Strip, which had become *the* number one resort of the twenty-first century.

Since its opening, the orbiting gambling resort had attracted a steady stream of high-rolling elite who thought nothing of flying up in their private shuttles and dropping half a million over the course of a sensation-filled week that gave new meaning to the old adage *anything goes*. And it was the absence of this steady stream of high-rolling, electrocash cows that had turned the Atlantic City and Las Vegas casinos into something resembling bingo parlors for senior citizens. The cash cows grazed happily on the Outland Strip, gambling, whoring and supporting an underlevel of drug dealers, pleasure brokers and fortune agents that had formed like a fungus, created by the sound of money being dropped into a sinkhole.

"My plan involves the consolidation of the Las Vegas and Atlantic City operations." Zamora pulled single-page briefing sheets from a folder on the table and passed them to the three men. "We would call this consolidated operation the VAC, the Vegas-Atlantic City connection. Instead of competing with one another, we could use the...how shall I say it?" Zamora allowed his Spanish accent to creep into his voice. "We could cooperate to lower overheads and regain some of the business lost to the Outland Strip."

"How would you propose to regain this lost business?" Moore asked, his eyes sparkling like crystal.

Zamora smiled to himself, pleased to see that Moore was interested.

"Yeah." Rust leaned across the table. "The Outland Strip ain't got no taxes, they got their own law and they ain't regulated by no goddamn government. How the hell are you going to overcome those advantages?" Rust sat back in his chair, scratching his head. "I mean, it's getting where it don't cost shit to travel up there. Pretty soon everybody's mother'll be up there playing slot machines, for chrissake." He looked at Moore and Taylor. Both men nodded.

Zamora lit a cigarette and inhaled deeply. He took a healthy swallow of his brandy before blowing the smoke through his nose. "The salient points of my plan are on the sheet in front of you." Zamora gestured toward the paper in front of each man, on which were listed the advantages of consolidating the two gambling factions.

VAC ADVANTAGES
- Estimated overhead reduction of 10-15 percent
- Consolidated purchasing/Economy of scale
- Dilution of union bargaining positions
- Geographic specialization
- Oddsmaker coordination
- Consolidated control of spin-offs

Zamora went through a detailed explanation of each point, stressing the savings that could be achieved by combining control of the two gambling venues.

"What the hell does 'spin-offs' mean?" Rust asked, looking over the half-lensed reading glasses he'd donned in order to study the sheet. "I don't think I understand what you're saying."

"It's pretty simple," Zamora said, lighting a fresh cigarette from the butt of his old one. "The VAC takes a more active hand in managing the drug and prostitution trade. Or at least we place a heavy tariff on its operation."

"How the hell do we do that?" Rust asked, taking off his glasses and shaking them at Zamora to emphasize his point. "We've tried for years to cut ourselves into that action, but it's not like the old days...." Rust's voice trailed off and he slumped in his chair.

"What do you mean, 'the old days'?" Zamora asked between drags on his cigarette. "It is my turn not to understand."

"Well, there ain't no real organization controlling the dope dealers and the whorehouses," Rust answered, shaking his head. He reached out and picked up his brandy, but didn't drink. "At least in the old days you knew who you were dealing with."

"You mean the Mafia?" Zamora asked.

"Yeah. Nowadays it's just a long line of punks and zipper-headed freaks hustling like rats in a gutter. They change faces on a daily basis."

Zamora smiled. "That's where my connections can help you out. If I have standing business arrangements with several organizations who—"

"We don't really want to hear about your underground network of thugs, Zamora," Taylor interrupted. He tossed the sheet of paper toward the center of the table. "All of this—" he nodded toward the list "—is just bullshit rhetoric. Sure, it might save us a couple of points, but I don't see how any of it's going to get the Outland Strip off our backs." Taylor glanced at Moore and Rust before staring truculently in the direction of the Colombian.

Zamora felt a pang of anxiety and at the same time gained a measure of respect, albeit small, for the squat, big-mouthed Taylor. He had wondered if any one of the men would perceive he had failed to ask and answer the real question: how do we avoid going down in the quicksand created by the Outland Strip? Zamora knew his VAC proposal only slowed the sinking and was surprised that it was Taylor who called him on it. He'd figured Moore would be the one to see through his thin veil.

"More brandy?" the Colombian asked, sliding the decanter of amber liquid toward Taylor, who was eyeing him warily.

"No thanks," Taylor looked as though he suspected Zamora of cheating in a poker game.

"Does anyone need to take a break before I answer Mr. Taylor's question?" Zamora stalled, knowing his explanation would need to be halfway plausible.

In truth, Zamora didn't know how the hell he was going to recoup the portion of the market that the Outland Strip had captured. And actually, his concern over the matter extended only as far as being able to convince the three fools at the table that he could discount the Strip's holdings and pump the business back into the VAC. His problems were more pressing. He needed the operating capital, however meager, that the VAC afforded. His own drug-related operation, the remnants of his father's cartel, had dwindled to where it was more of a liability than an asset. The United States' halfhearted war on drugs, launched in the late twentieth century, had put a minor dent in the operation's profitability.

However, the decline of the South American drug heartland was caused, ironically, by the advent of other drugs. Synthetics had replaced the organics. Amphetamines, cheap and easy to produce, had replaced the expensive white powder that had to be soaked out of plant leaves and processed scientifically. Hallucinogens chemically bonded with the so-called designer drugs were now preferred over the bulky and inconvenient opiates, hashish and marijuana. These new drugs had evolved with a generation of users who looked upon their fathers' concept of life in the fast lane as a ride down the sidewalk in a wheelchair.

The thin plan that had been sprouting like a weed in the back of the Colombian's mind involved raising enough capital to buy his uncles a pardon or at least to put together a small army that could take the prison by force. The last scheme he'd had to ransom his father out of prison had turned to garbage and cost him most of his cash reserves.

Now his father was dead and all he had left was the weak hope that one of his uncles had been made privy to where the senior Zamora had stashed his wealth. Zamora's moods fluctuated between overwhelming desperation and calm assurance. Sometimes he felt like a man on death row awaiting a pardon, or like a rat dropped onto a rush-hour freeway. But if he forced himself to concentrate on the task at hand, as he did now, he immediately felt calm, dangerous.

Moore and Rust remained silent, and Taylor answered Zamora, "I don't think so, Ruben. Get on with your pitch. I've got a shuttle standing by at JFK to take me back to Vegas. I don't have all night."

"Certainly," Zamora answered, resisting the urge to slap the man across the face. He'd known from the start that Taylor would oppose his plan, but before he played his hole card he wanted to give Moore and Rust the opportunity to vote yes of their own volition. "Once the VAC is established, it's my plan to undermine the Outland Strip by making it an unsafe place to vacation." Zamora was actually just winging it, but the idea amused him. It might even be worth trying.

"What do you mean?" Rust asked.

"I mean there will be a wave of robberies, hijackings and killings there that will make the Bronx look like a nursery school." Zamora snapped his fingers, pleased with the way his mind was building on the idea. "All of which, naturally, will receive more press coverage than normal." Zamora gestured as though framing a newspaper headline. "The Outland Strip—lose your money, lose your life. I've already got a contingent of...'thugs—'" he nodded and smiled at Taylor "—standing by to initiate this part of the plan."

Rust leaned over and picked up the decanter. "It doesn't sound too bad," he said, pouring himself more brandy. "What do you think, Tucker?"

Moore stroked his beard. "It could work. I wonder—"

"Bullshit!" Taylor interrupted, his voice revving up like an out-of-tune chain saw. He directed his speech toward Moore and Rust. "This son of a bitch can't even take care of his own dirty work."

"What are you talking about?" Moore asked.

Without taking his gaze off Zamora, Taylor answered, "Shit, he tried to take out the guy who could send his ass to the slammer and screwed that up. What makes you think he could run this kind of operation?" Taylor picked up one of the briefing sheets and turned to Moore, tossing it toward the man's chest.

"You're talking about what happened to Jack Rohde, aren't you?" Rust asked, making the connection. "I read about that in yesterday's *Times*."

"I'm talking about what *didn't* happen to Jack Rohde," Taylor said, turning back to Zamora. "I assume you meant to kill him and instead he escaped. Correct?"

Zamora stared at Taylor without answering. He watched the little man shift his eyes wildly in order to avoid making contact.

When it was clear that Zamora wasn't going to respond, Taylor continued his diatribe. "Instead of killing his old buddy Rohde," he said, a high-pitched chuckle woven into his words, "he offed two city cops, one of them a goddamn captain!" Taylor's chuckle turned into cackling laughter.

Zamora lit another cigarette while he waited for Taylor's laughter to run its course. Finally it died out. "Jack Rohde has no relevance to this discussion or to my proposed plan," he said calmly.

"The hell it don't," Taylor blurted. "It ain't on your briefing sheet, but I assume you're proposing that *you* head this so-called VAC, right?"

"That was to be a matter for discussion once the plan was approved," Zamora answered.

"Sure," Taylor said, his voice edged with sarcasm. "Whatever you say. But look at it this way." He turned toward Moore and Rust. "If he managed to screw up when he was taking care of his own problem, I sure as hell don't think he could run the kind of operation he's proposed. Besides—" Taylor looked at Zamora again "—I think his plan sucks. I vote no." He leaned back in his chair and scratched the area beneath his chin.

Zamora looked at Moore, who showed no reaction to Taylor's speech. Moore glanced at Rust for a moment, then smiled as though they'd been discussing something totally innocuous. "Speaking for myself," he said, "my holdings in Atlantic City have done nothing but cost me money ever since the Outland Strip opened." He made a little rolling gesture with one hand. "I can't even sell because no one wants to buy an opportunity to lose his ass." He laughed.

"Come on," Taylor interjected, obviously irritated by the casual pace of Moore's speech, "get to the goddamn point. I ain't got all night."

Moore turned and looked at Taylor, the smile dropping from his face like a flag being lowered. "Very well," he said. "I vote yes."

"You're out of your fucking mind," Taylor snapped, obviously surprised at Moore's answer. "How about you?" he asked Rust.

"I'm voting for it," Rust answered simply. "I think it's a good idea, especially the part about making the Strip look like a snakepit."

"You dipshits." Taylor raised his hands and then dropped them to his sides in an exaggerated gesture of frustration. He tilted back his head and stared at the ceiling for several seconds. "It really doesn't make any difference," he finally said, glancing around the table. "If I don't vote for it, you bastards are shit out of luck." He smiled at Rust. "Don't forget, I own more of Vegas than you do, Erwin. And that little shitheel operation of yours, Tucker, isn't big enough to make a difference."

"I appreciate your votes of confidence, gentlemen," Zamora said, nodding at Moore and Rust. He held up a hand as if to silence Taylor, then raised his voice slightly to say, "Leonard, would you come in here please?" A moment later Leonard's massive form was standing behind him, slightly to his right. "And I want to thank you also," Zamora said, smiling at Taylor.

"I don't know what the hell you're talking about." Taylor looked confused. "I vote no, *comprende?*" He touched his thumb and index finger together and shook his hand in front of his face. "Don't you understand English?"

The smile vanished from Zamora's face, and he took a long drag on his cigarette. "Let me explain. Mrs. Taylor has already voted yes . . . for you."

"Mrs. Taylor?" Surprise and puzzlement spread across Taylor's face.

"It is somewhat difficult to explain, but bear with me." Zamora glanced at Rust and Moore, who looked as confused as Taylor did. "I had a meeting with Marjorie last week and she agreed that your Las Vegas holdings would be better managed under the VAC."

"W-wait a goddamn minute," Taylor stuttered, blinking rapidly. "What the hell are you doing meeting with my wife? Goddamn it, that bitch can't fork over control of the operation unless I'm de—" Taylor's speech ended abruptly as though it had been chopped off with a cleaver.

Zamora leaned back in his chair and laughed heartily. He snapped his fingers several times as Taylor's mouth dropped open like a trapdoor.

"What the hell's going on..." It was more a statement than a question. He started to get up from his chair, but Leonard shoved him back down. "Hey, goddamn it!" he yelled, looking up at the huge South American bully's expressionless face.

"Shut up," Zamora said as his laughter subsided. He took off his glasses and wiped the tears from his eyes with his fingertips. "Marjorie is a nice lady." He put his glasses on again and focused on Taylor, whose skin had turned the color of pale cheese. "She said you had the sense of a goat, and frankly—" Zamora paused to light another cigarette "—after our conversation this evening, I think she overrated you."

"You can't kill me," Taylor stammered, his dark eyes wide with disbelief and fear.

"I think it's time we got out of here," Rust said uneasily, rising from his chair. He tapped Moore on the shoulder and nodded toward the door.

"Not just yet, gentlemen." Zamora held up a hand. "Take your seat, Mr. Rust. This business with Mr. Taylor is the VAC's business, and therefore partly your business. Mrs. Taylor will sign over his holdings as soon as he is...er...eliminated. Apparently their marriage has left a lot to be desired."

Rust slowly settled back into his chair, his expression grim.

"You're insane," Taylor gasped. To Moore and Rust he added, "Don't let him do this. You'll both be accessories—"

At Zamora's nod Leonard slapped Taylor across the right side of the head. A howl of pain spilled from the man's throat. With his left hand Leonard grabbed a handful of hair and jerked back Taylor's head. He then picked up a napkin from the table and stuffed it into his mouth. Taylor reached up in panic and tried to grab one of the South American's arms. Muffled choking sounds escaped through the gag.

Leonard seized one of Taylor's wrists with his free hand and jerked it away from his arm. He raised it as though signaling Taylor was the winner of a boxing match, and then suddenly twisted it backward. The forearm snapped like a rifle shot, and Moore and Rust jumped in their seats. All of the color faded from Taylor's face as though it had been sucked down a drain. His eyes rolled back in his head and he went limp.

"You see, gentlemen," Zamora said to Moore and Rust, who were staring at Taylor, their expressions a mixture of fear and morbid fascination. "Mr. Taylor's slick little Astrocraft is going to go down somewhere in northern New Mexico. They won't find much of the airplane, let alone who was in it." He turned to address Leonard. "Finish it," he said simply.

Taylor chose that moment to recover consciousness and managed to pluck the gag from his mouth. "No! Don't do this…" he wheezed as Leonard snaked a big arm around his neck and grasped him in a modified headlock.

"Now, goddamn it," Zamora ordered.

Taylor emitted a hoarse scream as Leonard hoisted him, twisting and kicking from the chair. In one swift, violent motion the huge South American leaned back slightly before jerking the man's body down as though he were cracking a whip. Taylor's neck snapped like a stalk of celery, and his body went slack as though his bones had dissolved. Leonard released his grip. His victim's body flopped into the chair like a rag doll.

Zamora picked up his brandy glass and held it in front of him. "Here's to the VAC," he said simply.

Moore and Rust picked up their glasses, glancing nervously at each other. "To the VAC," they said in unison before raising the brandy to their lips.

Zamora downed what was left in his glass and lit a cigarette. He leaned back in his chair, feeling sublimely confident, and oblivious to Taylor, whose eyes stared at him like clumps of cold, wet ash.

CHAPTER FOUR

HORN SAT at the card table in the dining area of his cramped apartment. On the table was a nearly empty liter bottle of Red Square vodka, a glass half-filled with the clear liquid and Horn's 9 mm automatic, the hammer cocked, the safety off. Next to the battle-scarred weapon was a cracked hand mirror, propped against an empty beer bottle.

Picking up the glass of vodka, Horn drank, never taking his eyes off his reflection. Dark circles ringed his bloodshot eyes, and a week's worth of beard shadowed his face, highlighting the scar that ran across his right cheek. Horn surveyed what he could see of his naked body in the mirror, running his eyes along the worn combat titanium that covered his right arm. The area around his shoulder where the E-mod joined his body was an ugly mass of scar tissue. Horn looked down at his 9 mm, then back at his modified arm, and it occurred to him that they were strangely similar. The similarity went beyond the battered appearance; both were machines, both were weapons. His modified arm, as well as the mod that had replaced his right knee, twitched involuntarily as if the thought caused them to react. The glass of vodka slipped through his fingers, and he cursed as it hit the floor, spattering booze across his bare feet.

"Goddamn," he muttered, pulling his worn flannel bathrobe from the back of the chair. Bending over, he used the robe to wipe his feet, then tried to hang it on the back of the chair next to the one in which he was sitting. It slid off and landed in a heap next to a stack of yellowing newspapers.

"Who needs a glass...?" Horn grabbed the bottle, tilted it and downed half of the remaining liquor. A shiver ran down his spine as the alcohol trickled down his throat. He stifled a cough and swallowed hard, forcing down the vodka that had tried to surge back up his gullet.

Horn took a deep breath and exhaled, a whistling sound escaping between his lips. Once again his eyes wandered back to his laser-sighted automatic. It was big and ugly—an ugly old friend, he thought. He set the bottle on the table and picked up the weapon. He aimed it at his reflection in the mirror and squeezed the trigger just enough to activate the laser sight. The pencil-thin beam struck his image between the eyes and bounced off, its red light shining into the apartment's gloom like a crazy searchlight.

Half closing his eyes, Horn watched the red beam of the weapon dance on the surface of the mirror and contemplated the hand he'd been dealt. It seemed as though everyone who meant something in his life died through their association with him. Only it doesn't just seem that way, he said to himself, it's true. Horn's thoughts flashed briefly to his wife and daughter, and immediately his mods glitched, jerking violently. He forced the memory back into the darkness, knowing if he entertained the vision too long he would be absorbed into it.

Horn downed what remained in the vodka bottle and wiped his mouth with the back of his hand. He looked at the mirror again, and instead of his own face, he stared into the dead eyes of his former partner, Dan Riddle. Blood covered one side of the boyish-looking face in a crazy-quilt pattern that seemed to glow. Horn could see the young cop's lips moving and he bent forward, trying to hear.

"What? I can't hear you." Horn jerked back at the words. Now he saw his own reflection in the mirror; he was watching himself speak. "What is this shit?" he heard himself ask, his voice echoing through the apartment. "Who's next?" But he knew who was next. He waited for Dick Kelso's picture to come up in his mind.

When Sharon and Julie were killed, when Riddle was killed, there had been one fact that had kept Horn sane: their deaths had been beyond his control, outside the realm of what he was meant to control. But in Kelso's case that wasn't so. Horn figured he might as well have put a gun to the police captain's head and pulled the trigger himself.

"I killed him," Horn said, louder this time, his voice hoarse from the booze. Some joke, he thought. A hell of a retirement present to give one of the few friends I had.

Horn shivered, suddenly becoming chilled. He realized his thoughts were sober. The fog caused by the vodka had rolled away, forcing him to face the music his conscience was playing. "I killed him," Horn whispered.

He stared at the 9 mm cradled in the palm of the machine that served as his hand. He watched with a strange fascination as his modified hand fingered the trigger, activating the laser sight over and over. Horn knew it couldn't be, but he had the sensation that the mod was functioning on its own, free from his conscious control. "Right," he said softly, "my turn." The titanium hand slowly turned the gun toward Horn and stopped, its ugly, dark barrel pointed directly above his right eye. He watched the beam come on and felt a crawling sensation sweep across his scalp. A strange comfort settled in his chest and he realized he was no longer cold. He smiled to himself.

From somewhere, from some immeasurable distance, came a faint thumping, a pounding. At first Horn thought it was his heart, then realized he could also hear a voice. Suddenly his focus on the weapon, on the moment in which he'd been suspended, snapped. He was jerked back into the gloomy environment of the littered apartment. The vodka fog rolled back in, and Horn reared his head away from the barrel of the 9 mm as though it were the first time he'd seen it.

"Goddamn it, Horn! I know you're in there. Open up the door before I break the son of a bitch down!" Winger's words were followed by a loud pounding as he beat on the door.

Horn continued to stare at the automatic for several seconds, then shakily placed it back on the table. He got up and staggered to the door, amazed he could walk on legs that felt like chunks of ice. When he'd unbolted the door, he swung it open and stared at Winger, whose fist was raised in preparation for another drumroll on the scarred wood.

"Holy shit," the young cop said, more to himself than to his partner. He looked Horn up and down, an expression of amazement and disgust spreading across his face like a cloud. "You look like—" Winger searched for the proper descriptive for several moments before simply adding "—Shit."

"Thanks," Horn slurred before turning and walking back to the table. He flopped into the chair, nearly tipping it over, and looked around, wishing he had a drink.

Winger followed Horn over to the table, "No, partner," he said in anger and disgust. "I mean it. You look like shit." And then, as if to drive home his simple point, he added, "Hammered shit."

Kicking the empty Red Square bottle out of the way, Winger pulled a folding chair away from the card table and straddled it, facing Horn, who belched loudly and pointed toward the refrigerator. "Get me a beer, will you?" he said. "Help yourself, too, I think there's some left."

"Go to hell," Winger answered. "I figured I'd find you like this. At least I'm not disappointed." He looked around the tiny apartment, which was littered from wall to wall with empty beer bottles, dirty clothes, newspapers and trash.

"Your absence at Kelso's wake was noticeable," he said, turning back toward Horn, who had his elbows on his knees and was leaning forward, face in hands. "I wasn't surprised, though."

"Fuck you," Horn said, standing now, his legs wobbly. He walked the three steps it took to get to his kitchen, which consisted of an ancient refrigerator, a microwave and a sink overflowing with dirty dishes. He took a bottle of beer from the refrigerator and twisted off the cap. Raising the bottle to his lips, he took a healthy swallow before staggering back to his chair.

"You're disgusting," Winger said, glaring at Horn. Horn just tilted the bottle, chugging a third of its contents in a matter of seconds.

"So," Horn replied, "why don't you go down to the mission and berate some other bum?"

Winger laughed. "You got that right...bum. Look at you." He picked up the mirror and held it in front of Horn's face. "You're naked, for chrissake, and you stink. You look like you just crawled out of a goddamn sewer."

"I did." Horn laughed grimly. "It's called my mind."

"You self-serving bastard," Winger said, his voice returning to its normal tone. "We just buried one of your friends, not to mention a fellow cop, and you're holed up over here, drinking your brains out and wallowing in self-pity."

"I killed him," Horn said simply, looking up at his partner. "If we stay partners, it's only a matter of time before I kill you, too."

Winger leaned back in his chair without responding. Finally he said in almost a whisper, "You didn't kill him, Max."

"All right, now the speech," Horn said, resting the beer bottle on the combat-green titanium covering his right knee. It slipped off and he nearly fell out of his chair. "Goddamn it, hold on just a minute." He downed the rest of the beer and placed the empty bottle on the table. "There," he said, "now you can go ahead. Give me the speech about how it's not my fault. How it's one of the risks of being a cop. And how it could have happened to any one of us." Horn's voice had risen almost an octave, and his nostrils flared as he worked himself into a verbal frenzy. "Tell me that crap and I'll puke, Stu. And not because I'm drunk, either. You know as well as I do that it should have been me chasing that prisoner over to the annex, that my little idea of stiffing Kelso with the dirty work got him killed. For God's sake, it was me!" Horn rose from his seat and touched his chest with the tips of his fingers. "I killed him!"

Suddenly Horn flopped back into his chair as though someone had pulled his plug. "Listen, Stu," he said in a low, sober tone. "I didn't really stiff Kelso with the shit detail in order to play a joke on the guy."

Winger looked puzzled. "I don't understand. What are you talking about?"

"I mean, I did it so we could cowboy the stolen car warehouse. I wanted the action. I wanted to use this." Horn suddenly raised his right arm and brought it down on the flimsy table, which shattered as though it had been hit with a pile driver.

Winger almost jumped out of his chair. "Goddamn it, Horn," he said nervously, a look of concern dropping over his face like a shadow. "You're not making any sense."

"You know exactly what I'm talking about." Horn stared at his E-mod, flexing its fingers slowly. "I look for it...."

"Look for—" Winger cut off his sentence, apparently changing his mind about what he was going to say. "That's still no reason for you to blame yourself for Kelso's death." His voice had dropped to a funereal whisper.

"Don't forget about Murphy," Horn reminded him. He leaned over and picking up the hand mirror, which was now completely shattered. "He's dead, too." He stared at the broken glass for several seconds before tossing it onto the floor. "Seven years of bad luck."

"Listen, partner," Winger said, "you're still a cop."

Horn looked up, wondering what kind of bullshit his partner was going to deliver next.

"One of my snitches got a line on Jack Rohde. Seems he caught a shuttle the day after the escape and left the planet." Winger spoke in a businesslike manner. He pulled a small notebook from one of his jacket pockets and flipped it open.

Horn was a little shocked at his partner's shift in gears. Something like interest stirred in his mind. He fought off the dulling effects of the vodka and focused on Winger's words. Anything was better than the dark limbo in which he'd been floundering. But there was something more than interest flickering in the graveyard reaches of his thoughts. It was an old, old friend, comforting in its dark and dangerous way...ugly like his 9 mm...like his E-mods. It was the shadow offering of revenge skulking there, telling Horn it was all that was left. All that could be had. Telling him the lie that it would fill the black hole that his soul had become. Horn knew it wasn't true, that it was a placebo cure for the disease that ravaged him like a hungry demon. But, he thought wearily, it's better than nothing.

"Where did he go?" Horn asked.

"Here it is," Winger said, finding the page containing his notes. "He transferred to one of those intercolony ships and is supposed to be on his way to the Outland Strip."

"The gambling resort?"

"That's correct," Winger answered, closing his notebook.

"Before, you said he caught a shuttle the day after the escape," Horn said. He leaned over and picked up his bathrobe, then made a vain attempt to put it on.

"That's right," Winger answered as he reached over and helped his partner pull the sleeve over his modified arm.

"What makes you think it was an escape and not a hit?" Horn stood shakily and finished donning the robe. He tied the belt before sitting back down.

Winger stared dumbly at Horn for a few moments, then said, "I don't know. I suppose they could have been trying to kill him, but the fact that he got away seems to point to an escape. At least that's what the newspapers are saying."

"I've got a feeling they were out to kill Rohde before he nailed them," Horn said. "He turned out to be a little bit more slippery than they bargained for. If my hunch is correct, they'll go after him wherever he goes."

"And when they do—" Winger held up his hands "—you'll be there, right?"

"Something like that," Horn answered, conscious of a monstrous headache creeping into his skull.

"Before I forget, the Barracuda wants to see you at 7:30 in her office," Winger said, referring to Christina Service, the New York City assistant district attorney. He stood up and returned the notebook to his jacket.

"When...today?" Horn realized he didn't know what day it was, let alone what time it was.

"In the morning," Winger answered. "Tomorrow." He looked at his watch and shrugged. "I guess I should say today."

"What time is it?" Horn felt his bare wrist and wondered what he'd done with his watch.

"It's almost 2:00 a.m." For the first time since he'd walked into the apartment, Winger smiled crookedly.

"Shit," Horn croaked. He pulled himself up and weaved his way to the refrigerator. He pulled a plastic tray of ice cubes from the freezer section. Shoving aside some of the dirty dishes on top of the counter, he spread out a dirty towel that was hanging over the sink, dumped the ice into it and wadded it up. He applied the sloppy cold pack to the back of his head.

"I'll pick you up at seven," Winger said, walking to the door.

"Fine," Horn said as he moved toward the tiny bathroom. Then he turned toward his partner, who was already in the hallway. "Listen, Stu, I appreciate you coming over here and everything—" Horn didn't quite know what he was trying to say or why he was trying to say it. He felt relieved when Winger cut him off.

"Forget it," the young cop said as he closed the door.

Horn staggered into the closet-size bathroom just in time to throw up.

HORN FOLLOWED Winger through the glass doors of the Justice Center. He stopped at a fountain and popped four headache tablets into his mouth before taking several swallows of the cold water. His head felt like a giant thumb that had been smashed by a hammer. It was throbbing painfully in time with the beating of his heart. Horn had read that the brain itself could feel no pain. The thought almost made him laugh. He would have laughed, but he was afraid it would cause him to throw up again.

"Come on, partner," Winger said, motioning for Horn to move it. "The Barracuda wants her breakfast."

"Very funny," Horn said, following his partner down the long marble hall. There was a dull burning sensation in his stomach as though he'd swallowed a dozen or more live coals. A constant tickling at the back of his throat gave him the urge to cough every few seconds, but he resisted for the same reason he was afraid to laugh.

The two cops got on an elevator, and Winger pressed the button for the floor occupied by the district attorney and his staff. As the door closed and the elevator started upward, Horn once again became aware of the torturous pain in his head. It felt as if some hideous monster had strung razor wire between his ears and was flossing his brain.

"Here," Winger said, holding out a package of breath mints. "Take a couple of these. Your breath smells like an empty bottle of—" the young cop grinned "—what was that cheap shit you were drinking?"

"Don't remind me," Horn said, taking two of the mints and popping them into his mouth. He hoped they wouldn't make him throw up.

"Wasn't it Red Flag or something like that?" Winger grunted a laugh as the doors opened. "Now I know why you feel so bad," he said as they stepped into the hall.

"Don't press your luck," Horn said weakly as beads of sweat walked across his forehead.

"That was bug spray you were drinking!" Winger laughed loudly as they walked up to a receptionist who was staring blankly at the flat panel data screen in front of her.

"May I help you?" the woman asked without looking up. Her voice was so nasal that Horn half expected to see her nose pinned.

"Detectives Winger and Horn to see Ms. Service," Winger answered, drawing out the *Z* sound at the end of the word *Ms*.

The haggard-looking woman behind the screen raised her eyes and glared at the young cop. "Just down the hall on your right. She's expecting you."

"Thanks, honey," Winger said, grabbing Horn by the arm.

Horn allowed Winger to guide him down the hall until they stopped in front of the assistant district attorney's office. "Wait a minute," he said, pulling his arm away from the young cop's grasp. "What the hell is the subject of this meeting?"

"She wouldn't tell me," Winger answered, pausing between each word. "I think she wants to surprise you."

"Did you ask?"

"Ah, come to think of it—" Winger rubbed a hand over the stubble on his chin "—I didn't." He grinned and pointed a thumb toward the receptionist's area. "I'll wait for you back there next to Miss America."

It was Horn's turn to grab his partner's arm. "Wait a second! You're not going anywhere but in there with me." He nodded at the nameplate on the door.

"Bullshit." Winger laughed nervously. "She specifically said you, not me." He tried in vain to pull his arm away.

Horn shrugged and, in spite of his massive hangover, he smiled. "You're going in with me, partner. If she doesn't want you in there, I'm sure she'll ask you to leave."

"I'm sure," Winger said with a sigh. He looked as if he'd just been told the IRS was going to audit his tax return.

Horn knocked once on the door and waited. He was just raising his hand to knock again when he heard Christina Service order them into the office. Horn swung open the door and motioned for Winger to enter first.

"Thanks a lot," his partner whispered sarcastically as he stepped into the carpeted room. Horn followed and pulled the door closed behind them.

Service was standing behind her desk, arms folded, looking still and expectant. Horn glanced about her sparsely furnished office, which hadn't changed from the last time he'd been there. Bookshelves lined the windowless walls and her large wooden desk took up the center of the room, facing the door. Neatly arranged stacks of papers covered the polished wood, reflecting the organized manner in which the woman conducted her business.

The assistant district attorney's bent toward neatness and organization extended to her appearance. She was immaculately dressed in a gray suit, high-collared blouse and black heels. In spite of the conservative cut of the suit, her lean, well-built body wasn't totally camouflaged. Her blond hair was cut medium-length, curling under just above the top of her collar.

"I really only wanted to see you, Detective Horn," Service said, her pale blue eyes locking onto his. "But since you're both here, have a seat." She gestured toward two modest chairs in front of her desk before sitting in the red leather armchair on the working side of the desk.

Horn thought he heard Winger groan slightly as they took their seats. He turned his attention toward the Barracuda, referred to as such by the street cops, and waited for her to begin. He didn't have to wait long.

"The bust you two made at the warehouse has to rank with the most moronic stunts of all time. You even turned off your radio!" She let her voice carry a sharp edge and gestured in a frustrated manner with her hands. "I mean, who the hell do you think you guys are?" Service shifted her glare to Winger, who shrank several inches into his chair. "You must think you're some sort of super cops, right?" she said, returning her attention to Horn, who was surprised to hear Winger speak.

"We had information that the perps were monitoring the net," the young cop said. "We didn't want to chance losing our cover."

Service looked at Winger and nodded slowly. "They're all dead," she said calmly before focusing her ice-blue eyes on Horn. "This isn't the first time you guys have pulled this sort of mindless stunt." She raised her voice. "I've told you before, I can't prosecute dead people."

Horn didn't respond; he simply stared at the woman's face, not really hearing what she was saying.

"Don't you have anything to say?" she asked, directing her question to Horn, who slowly shook his head, his expression neutral.

"Okay, that's enough." Service suddenly stood. "You may leave now," she said, crossing her arms across her chest.

Horn started to rise from his chair, but Service held out her hand. "Not you, Detective Horn," she said. "I still need to talk to you." Service nodded toward the door and looked at Winger, who had stood. "You may leave, Detective. Close the door behind you."

As soon as the door closed behind Winger, Horn looked up at the assistant D.A. and said, "Rohde wasn't snatched by his pals. They were trying to kill him and he escaped."

"How do you know that?" Service asked, a look of mild surprise flushing her pale cheeks.

"It was Zamora, the Colombian," he said, ignoring her question because he didn't have an answer. He couldn't tell her that it was a feeling in his gut, his cop sense that made him certain the Colombian had tried to take out Rohde and, more important, had killed Dick Kelso.

"I've thought the same thing," Service said, causing Horn to raise his eyebrows. It was his turn to be surprised.

Horn watched the woman take her seat and realized the pounding in his head was gone. He felt calm, even relaxed.

"I was certain Rohde was going to provide the hard connection between Zamora and the hostage situation at last year's Super Bowl," Service said, shaking her head in disappointment.

"Hell, it was the guy's father and a couple of other relatives he was trying to ransom out of the pen," Horn said. "How much more of a hard connection do you need?"

"More than that," Service answered. "It could have been any one of the other relatives' kids who initiated the scheme."

Horn started to speak, but Service held up her hands. "I know and you know it was Zamora. However, the evidence against the man was circumstantial."

"How was Rohde connected to the Colombian?" Horn asked.

"He kept Zamora's books," Service answered. "Rumor has it he embezzled almost four million dollars from the Colombian's operations before he was found out. Rohde's a gambling addict, bets on anything. He was apparently using Zamora as his bankroll."

Horn looked hard into the assistant district attorney's eyes. He wondered if she knew he had set Kelso up, however unintentially, to meet his death.

"Listen, Max," Service said, her voice low and soft, "I'm sorry about Dick Kelso."

Horn felt his skin prickle. His mods glitched mildly, and he wondered for an instant if she could read his mind. "We've already got a line on Rohde," he said, wanting to get off the subject of Kelso's death. "Give us a couple of weeks and he'll be standing right here in front of your desk."

Service nodded slowly. "On one condition."

"What do you mean?" Horn was puzzled.

"I mean you get the assignment only on my terms."

"Go on," he said.

"We work together on this one," Service said. "No dead radios, no cowboy crap. Understand?"

"You've got it," Horn answered, rising from his chair.

"One more thing," she added. "I know you're going after Rohde in order to bring down whoever killed Dick Kelso."

Once again Horn felt his skin prickle crazily. He didn't say anything, even though it was clear Service was giving him the opportunity.

"Don't let that cause you to ignore my conditions," she said, her eyes boring into his like two cold-beam lasers. "Is that clear?"

Horn nodded before turning and walking to the door.

"And one more thing, Max."

Horn paused, his gloved hand on the doorknob. He looked at the woman. "What is it?"

"Don't underestimate the Colombian."

CHAPTER FIVE

THE WHITE HONDA LIMO purred smoothly along the road as Ruben Zamora pressed a button on his armrest. The glass between the passenger and driver sections slid quietly down. "Pull over there," the Colombian said to Leonard, who was behind the wheel, "but don't drive in just yet." He pointed to a trash-strewn parking lot across the pitted street from an airplane hangar whose huge doors were opened just wide enough to admit a car.

"Look at this place," Zamora said with distaste, resting an elbow on the seat at Leonard's back. "Ever since Grumman went out of business this part of Long Island has been like a ghost town. Kind of spooky, no?" He slapped Leonard's shoulder with the back of his hand and laughed.

The place did look like a ghost town. The streets, the grounds, the sidewalks were all covered with windblown trash. The buildings that had once housed one of the major military aircraft companies in the United States were now shells with peeling paint and broken windows. Several abandoned and stripped-down cars lined the streets and littered the parking lots. It was getting dark and the giant hangars cast huge, blanketlike shadows over the smaller buildings of the abandoned facility.

"Make sure your *compadres* are set up," Zamora said. He pulled a pack of cigarettes from his jacket pocket and shook one into his hand. "I don't want to drive into that goddamn place with just you and me, eh?" He nodded toward the hangar and once again laughed. Placing the cigarette between his thin lips, he lit it and inhaled.

Leonard picked up a flat, hand-held communications module from its cradle on the dash and punched a series of numbers into its tiny keyboard. Seconds later a Spanish-accented voice whispered out of the module's speaker, "*Sí*, Escobido here."

Leonard asked a number of quick questions that Escobido answered succinctly, both speaking Spanish. Leonard placed the module back in its cradle and spoke to his boss out of the corner of his mouth. "They're in position," he said. "Both men have rifles with night vision scopes."

"Good." Zamora nodded. "Do they know the sign?"

"*Sí*," Leonard said, pulling a huge .44 Magnum from inside his jacket and placing it on the seat next to him. "You touch someone on the left shoulder, and they'll be dead as soon as you move away."

"Good," Zamora said once again. He looked at his watch. "Are our friends in there yet?"

"They're at the far end of the hangar," Leonard answered. "Juan said they have been there for almost thirty minutes."

Zamora sat back in the black leather seat. "Then let's go," he said.

As Leonard pulled the Honda into the gloom of the hangar, Zamora could see the outline of a car at the far end. Junk, abandoned tooling and piles of debris covered the floor of the huge building, except for an aisle just wide enough for a car to pass through that ran from Zamora's idling Honda to where the other car crouched like an animal in a jungle of outdated technological garbage.

Leonard flashed the Honda's lights twice, and moments later the other car did the same. "Go on," Zamora ordered, leaning over the seat and peering through the windshield.

The two automobiles approached each other slowly. When they were twenty or so yards apart, they stopped as if on cue. "Look at the freaking tub they're driving," Leonard said, his low voice displaying a degree of amazement.

Zamora was surprised by his bodyguard's comment, for the big South American seldom spoke unless he was spoken to, and rarely offered an opinion. Zamora understood what had caused Leonard's outburst, however, when his eyes took in an old 2008 Cadillac Park Square, painted flat black from tip to stern. Even the wheel covers were black. The windows of the once-classy sedan had been tinted to the point that they blended in with the rest of the body. The big car had been lowered, and its chrome bumpers had been replaced with sections of four-inch steel pipe, painted, of course, flat black. The vehicle looked like a Stealth bomber on wheels.

"Let's go," Zamora said, opening the door. "They're getting out." He stepped out of the limo and walked slowly into the area between the automobiles. Leonard followed, sticking the .44 into his waistband.

Three doors on the Cadillac opened. Zamora turned toward Leonard and spoke loud enough so that the men getting out of the car could hear him. "Turn on the lights, Leonard. We need to be able to see one another."

Leonard went back to the driver's window, reached in and turned on the lights. The area between the two machines was illuminated in a blue-white hue that spread out in the hangar, casting weird shadows on the high walls and enormous ceiling.

"Ah, Domino Jones. How are you this evening?" Zamora addressed a huge black man who stood nearly seven feet tall. He was wearing a purple silk body shirt that was tucked into green multipocketed parachute pants, stretched tightly across the man's meaty thighs and tucked into polished black jump boots. A single holster carrying a big, exotic-looking automatic pistol hung from a web belt cinched around his slender waist. The man responded to Zamora's greeting with a grunt.

"You look like you've been working out," Zamora said, lighting a cigarette. "You probably don't want one, but I'll ask you, anyway—smoke?" He held out the pack.

Jones tilted his head at an angle and peered at the Colombian through milky eyes. No pupils were visible which gave the big man's face the look of a zombie. He shook his head slowly and ran his hand, in a glove without fingers, through his closely cropped hair. The imprint of fear was stamped into his ugly face as though it had been struck there with a steel die.

"You know Leonard." Zamora nodded toward his constant companion. "But I'm afraid I don't know the gentlemen you're with, or—" he paused briefly, smiling "—who are with you." Zamora laughed. He had let the accent of his native country seep into his speech.

The black man's expression didn't change. His look reminded Zamora of a horse caught in a burning barn. "These are the Sthil brothers," Jones said without turning toward the two men who were standing on either side of and slightly behind him. "I brought them along so they could explain how they fucked up the hit."

"Now wait a goddamn minute, Jones," one of the brothers said, grabbing Domino by the arm. "We were just following your dicked-up plan. It wasn't our idea to go after the bastard in the middle of the street, for chrissake—"

"Shut the fuck up!" Jones yelled, jerking his arm out of the man's grasp.

"He's the one who masterminded the goddamn joke," the brother who had been holding on to Jones's arm muttered.

Zamora held up a hand. "That's enough." He raised his voice to emphasize the order. "I will calculate who is to blame here. Maybe no one is to blame, so there's really no need to start jumping on each other's backs."

The Colombian eyed the brothers. He'd heard of the two contract killers; they were a strange pair, but considered to be good at their work. They had a reputation for overkilling their assigned victims. When using explosives, they always applied at least twice as much as was required; if they were simply to shoot someone, the victim ended up with enough lead in his body to shield a pound of plutonium.

"You must be Luther," Zamora said, directing his speech to the man who had defended his own and his brother's honor.

"That's right," Luther answered gruffly. "And that's my brother, Kringa, on the other side of Mr. Jones."

Although he looked like a dwarf standing next to Jones, Luther Sthil stood well over six feet and weighed close to 250 pounds. His barrel-chested body was dressed in paramilitary garb—jump boots, desert camou trousers and an old bush-style jungle jacket that hung open, exposing his hairy chest. An ugly little Stoner machine gun was quick-clipped to a web belt, its characteristic box-shaped clip looking out of place in the death-dealing design. What Zamora found the most fascinating about Luther, however, was the man's hair and eyes. His rather long, graying hair stuck out, clownlike, from the sides of his head, around a bald crown. It was wiry in texture, as was the hair of his goatee, which covered the lower part of his face like animal fur. Luther's eyes were fluorescent-green, and Zamora could have sworn they glowed.

Kringa Sthil suddenly spoke up. "Yeah, mister, we're professionals. We sure wouldn't have come up with the unfortunate setup we were saddled with."

Zamora was somewhat taken aback by Kringa's accent, which didn't match his words. The tall, wiry man spoke more like an Arkansas chicken farmer than a hired killer. His voice was nothing like Luther's rumbling bass, which identified his hometown as Detroit or Chicago.

"Are you two really brothers?" Zamora asked, pointing the two fingers holding his cigarette first at Luther, then at Kringa.

Kringa broke out in a goofy-looking grin, his eyes slightly crossed and his head tilted. He scratched the top of his head, which had been shaved in a burr style, giving it the appearance of a bare skull. Kringa's clothes were similar to his brother's, and he had a sawed-off, autoloading 12-gauge hanging from a leather strap over one shoulder.

"I hate to admit it," Kringa answered, "but, yeah, we're brothers. The reason we talk different is we were separated when we was kids and just got back together six or eight years ago." He turned toward his brother. "Ain't that right, Luther?"

Luther grunted as though he didn't want to acknowledge what Kringa had said. He pulled a pack of cigarettes from his jacket pocket and lit one with a lighter that had been stuck under the strap on the back of one of his gloves. He took a deep drag before speaking. "You didn't come here to discuss our heritage. Let's get on with the meeting." Luther glanced at Kringa, and Zamora noticed the grin drop from Kringa's face like a stone down a well.

"You are correct," Zamora said, then returned his attention to Jones. "You, Mr. Jones, guaranteed that Rohde would be dead. I believe your words were 'piece of cake,' or something to that effect." Zamora paused and lit a fresh cigarette from the butt in his hand. "Well?" he asked.

Jones held out his huge hands, palms up, as if pleading for the Colombian to lend a sympathetic ear. "Like I said, these two guys were supposed to be the best. I didn't know I'd hired a couple of wet-dicked rookies.''

"Why, you son of a bitch!" Luther spit, and his hand moved toward the automatic hanging from his waist.

"No, no, no, no need for that," Zamora said quickly. "You'll get your turn soon. Please." He held up his hands and lowered them slowly in a calming gesture. Luther's hand dropped to his side, and he shifted his stance.

"When I hired you, if I recall," Zamora continued, addressing Jones once more, "I didn't authorize you to subcontract the job. As a matter of fact, you gave me the distinct impression that you would be handling the job personally.''

"Well, there must have been a misunderstanding," Jones said. He was trying to sound tough, but fear leaked through his voice. "I...I had another job that took priority."

"Oh?" Zamora raised his eyebrows.

After several seconds of silence, Jones realized he was expected to explain. A silly smile spread across his face. "It was a job I'd already signed up for. I can't discuss it...customer privilege, you understand." He hesitated, then added, "You wouldn't want me discussing *our* deal with nobody, right?"

Zamora didn't answer immediately. Finally he nodded and softly said, "Right." He put his hands in his suit coat pockets and rolled his head around on his neck as though trying to work out a stiffness. "Well, what about this plan of yours, delegated, as it was to the Sthil brothers?"

"Yeah, well, it should have worked." Jones turned his head and spit on the concrete.

Jones was becoming more confident, Zamora noticed, probably because he was still standing rather than lying on the floor with a hole in his head. Zamora figured that Jones's fear was abating also because he and the brothers outnumbered Zamora and Leonard. The Sthil brothers seemed confused by the change in Jones's attitude. They glanced at each other and fidgeted nervously.

"Well, you did manage to kill a New York City police captain," Zamora said.

"Listen," Jones said, "I'm getting a little bored with this shit. Let me tell you what I've got."

"By all means," the Colombian said calmly.

"I've got a contact in the Bronx who can give me a lead on Rohde." Jones hitched up his belt and looked down at Zamora. "As a matter of fact, I was on my way to see the cat when you called this little meeting. I'll get that son of a bitch Rohde, but I'll do it my way."

"That sounds good, Domino, real good." Zamora tilted his head back and stared at the eerie shadows cast across the cavernous ceiling.

"Yeah, damn right. You hired me to do a goddamn job, and I'd appreciate it if you'd get the hell out of the way and let me do it." Jones had obviously taken Zamora's calm demeanor as a sign of weakness or apathy. "And I'll tell you one thing I don't need. I don't need a goddamn meeting fucking up my schedule." Jones shuffled a few steps like a boxer. "After all, I *am* a professional. You dig?" He pointed a long finger at Zamora's chest.

The Sthil brothers were wearing out their necks looking at each other. Their facial expressions said something weird was going on; their body language said they didn't have the slightest idea what it was. The two killers were acting like a couple of range animals anticipating a lightning strike.

"Ah, yes," Zamora answered, "I see your point. Please believe me when I tell you that I didn't mean this meeting to be an inconvenience." The Colombian walked slowly toward the big killer. "And just to prove that I have confidence in you and trust you to keep your word, I want to give you the other half of your payment." Zamora reached into his jacket with his left hand and pulled out five ten-thousand-dollar credit wafers. "These can't be traced, my friend," he said softly, holding them out.

Jones looked at the wafers for several seconds before shifting his wary gaze to Zamora's face. "You serious?" he asked, cocking his head, his eyes flared wide.

"Certainly. Think of it as my way of apologizing for the way the meeting got started." Zamora took a half step toward Jones, who reached out for the wafers. "I didn't mean for it come off like some kind of third degree."

Zamora placed the wafers in the man's huge hand. "No bad feelings, right?" he asked softly, placing his free right hand on Jones's left shoulder.

For the first time that evening Jones smiled, exposing huge polished teeth. "Right, Mr. Z.," he said, pulling the wafers out of Zamora's hand.

The Colombian patted the huge assassin once on the shoulder and backed away slowly. As he took his third step, two sounds like the popping of champagne corks echoed in the hangar. One side of Jones's head disintegrated as though a small explosive had been embedded in his skull. Almost simultaneously, on the opposite side of his body, a shower of blood gushed from his neck. The man's large head, opaque eyes staring wide with surprise, flopped over ninety degrees. Less than a second later two more corks popped, and Jones did a little dance step as a pair of Teflon-coated lead missiles drove into his massive chest. The sleek little projectiles burned through his lungs and destroyed his heart. Jones's body toppled forward like a felled tree and hit the concrete with a sickening thud.

"Jesus!" Kringa screamed. He threw himself onto the dirty floor of the hangar, the autoloading shotgun in his hands, and peered intently into the shadows of the hangar. Lightning had struck, and he was waiting for the next bolt to come ripping out of the darkness.

Luther reacted in a nearly identical manner. He was on one knee, holding the Stoner machine gun chest-high, looking for something at which to aim its short, ugly barrel.

"If either of you fires a single shot, you'll look exactly like Mr. Jones here," Zamora told them calmly as he walked to the corpse. Blood had spread in a huge crimson stain on the concrete around the dead man. He stepped on Jones's wrist, then leaned down and pulled the credit wafers from his hand. "Put your weapons away now, gentlemen," Zamora said as he straightened and pocketed the thin plastic cards. The Sthil brothers glanced tentatively toward Zamora, but neither moved out of the defensive positions they'd taken.

"Trust me, gentlemen," Zamora said, a half smile wrinkling the corners of his eyes. "If you wait ten seconds longer to follow my orders—" the Colombian glanced at his gold wristwatch "—you will...well, you'll be dead." He shrugged.

Luther rose first, then motioned for Kringa to follow. Both men slowly returned their weapons to their carrying positions.

"How come you're sparing us?" Luther asked. He turned his head slightly without taking his eyes off the Colombian and spit. "After all, we're the ones who screwed up the hit."

"Jesus, Luther," Kringa interjected, "don't say shit like—"

"Shut up!" Luther growled.

"You are a wise man," Zamora told him. He took the cigarettes out of his jacket pocket and placed one between his lips. Luther immediately pulled the lighter out of his glove and struck it, holding up the flame. Zamora stuck the cigarette tip into the fire and eyed the wild-haired man. "This Rohde, think you and your brother can track him down?"

"Damn right we can," Kringa said over Luther's shoulder, relief obvious in his voice.

Luther turned his head slightly and snarled, "Shut the fuck up, Kringa. I'll do the goddamn talking." He turned back to Zamora. "Sorry about that. My brother is good at what he does, but he ain't no businessman."

Zamora smiled warmly. "I understand."

"To answer your question, there ain't no one we can't find. My brother and I are the best goddamn bounty hunters in the business."

"Bar none," Kringa added.

Luther glared menacingly at his brother, then seemed to relax slightly. "Like I was saying, we can find the man. You want him killed?"

Zamora nodded. "That was the arrangement I had with Jones. You want the contract?"

"How much?" Luther asked, rubbing his scraggly beard.

"One hundred." Zamora pulled the five wafers out of his pocket. "Five now, the balance when you bring me Rohde's left hand."

"Hand?" Luther grunted, looking slightly puzzled.

"Yes, his left hand," Zamora answered. "He wears a big gold ring on his little finger. We'll say it's sort of a symbol for the rest of his body."

Luther laughed, a hollow sound like that of a demon at the bottom of a well. It echoed through the cavernous hangar. "I like it," he said, and took the wafers from the Colombian. "You got yourself a deal."

"You won't be sorry, Mr. Zamora," Kringa put in, his voice twanging like an out-of-tune guitar. He craned his neck to see over Luther's shoulder.

"I'm certain I won't be," Zamora said, nodding at Kringa. Then he asked Luther, "You know this contact Jones was talking about?"

"Yeah, we know the flake." Luther pulled out his cigarettes and lit one. "He goes by the name of Bonefish. Runs a high-stakes card game up north. Jones told us Rohde was a regular."

"I suggest you start there," Zamora said.

Luther stroked his beard and looked at the Colombian through half-closed eyes. He appeared to be lost in thought.

"That's exactly what we were thinking," Kringa said nervously when it was clear Luther wasn't going to respond. "Right, Luther?" He slapped his brother on the shoulder.

"Huh?" Luther turned toward Kringa, his voice thick, as though he'd just awakened from a deep sleep.

"The man says we should check out Bonefish."

"Ah, right..." Luther said, his eyelids fluttering.

"You gotta excuse my brother," Kringa said, an embarrassed grin painted on his face. "He gets sort of...lost in his own mind when he's concentrating."

"Like Socrates," Zamora said, smiling.

"Who?" Kringa looked blank. He grabbed Luther by the scruff of the neck and gave his brother's head a couple of vigorous shakes.

"Oh, yeah," Luther said, coming out of his trancelike state. He stared at Zamora for several seconds, however, before speaking. "You won't be disappointed. We'll bring you his hand...hell, we'll bring you the son of a bitch's head if you want it." Luther broke into another mad laugh. He seemed to be his old self again.

"Just his hand. His left one. And, gentlemen—" he looked into Kringa's eyes, then locked onto Luther's fluorescent-green ones "—if you screw up... well you can see what happened to that incompetent fool, Domino Jones. Need I say more?"

CHAPTER SIX

WINGER STOOD on the accelerator and rammed the Elint through a flimsy barricade of wooden sawhorses, trash cans and bags of garbage. The six armed men behind the makeshift roadblock scattered like a covey of spooked birds. One of them managed to get off a shot with a small-caliber rifle, and Winger heard it slam harmlessly into the trunk. He aimed the machine up Willis Avenue and kept the foot feed pressed to the floor.

"Now that was disappointing," Winger said as he maneuvered around the burned-out shell of a bus blocking the right lane. "Remember the first time you brought me here?" He looked over at Horn, who was staring through the windshield as if they were in a funeral procession.

The two cops had just crossed the Harlem River and entered what was called the country's largest urban war zone—the Bronx. The once ethnically rich borough of New York had been literally abandoned by the city government and for nearly six years had been left to its own devices. Services were sporadic or, in certain areas, nonexistent. There was no law in this inner-city badland; it was ruled by gangs and factions of organized crime who exploited the few normal citizens who clung to the vestiges of a former fading way of life. In general, once you crossed the boundary that separated the Bronx from the rest of the city, you were on your own. Survival depended on who you knew or, in many cases, on how much firepower was at hand. As Winger wheeled the Elint across East 149th, he had the feeling they had passed the point of no return. Whether he and Horn made it out would depend on their wits as well as their weapons; here their badges were worthless. But what the hell, he thought, we've done it before.

"If you're not up for conversation," Winger said, glancing at his partner, "let's talk about the task at hand." For the first time since they'd been tagged partners, he was worried about Horn. Dick Kelso had been one of the few people Horn considered a friend, and Horn blamed himself for Kelso's death. Winger didn't agree. Dying was one of the risks of being a cop. It could come anytime, Winger figured, and the day it came to Kelso was Kelso's time.

Winger decided the best way to get his partner out of the dark groove he was tracking would be to get him to focus on nailing whoever had done Kelso. "You ever meet this guy I'm taking you to see?"

"He's *your* connection," Horn answered, his voice flat.

"Damn it, Max," the young cop snapped, "get your head out of whatever hole you've got it in and tune in to what the hell we're supposed to be doing. You're not going to do a damn bit of good the way you are. Goddamn it, we got a job to do."

Horn slowly turned his head and stared at Winger, who was looking at Horn. His partner's appearance gave Winger the creeps. Horn hadn't shaved for several days, dark circles rimmed his bloodshot eyes and his face was gaunt. He looked like a zombie.

Winger was surprised when Horn responded. "You're right, Stu. We've got a job to do."

Mildly encouraged by Horn's response, Winger asked, "Well, do you know this guy Bonefish?"

"No, but I've heard the name," Horn answered, turning his gaze back to the street. "He's the one who told you Rohde went to the Outland Strip, right?"

Good, he's asking a question, Winger thought, his sense of encouragement inching up another notch. "That's right. I think old Bonefish can be a little more specific about where we can find the guy. The goddamn Strip's a big place. Ever been there?" Winger shot another glance at Horn before jerking the wheel over hard to avoid hitting a dumpster that had been abandoned in the middle of the street.

"No, but I've read about it. And you're probably right. We need a better idea of where he is before we head up there."

Winger felt a little more relaxed now that he'd gotten Horn talking about the investigation. "This place we're going to is supposed to be pretty raunchy. Bonefish said he wouldn't be responsible for our safety if we insisted on showing up."

Horn laughed. "That's funny. You say Rohde used to frequent this place?"

"That's right."

"I'd think Rohde would frequent a little higher-class place in a higher-class neighborhood." Horn gestured toward the crumbling buildings that lined the street. "The guy's supposed to be a high roller, right?"

"Yeah," Winger answered. "But remember what the Barracuda said. Rohde's a gambling addict. Bonefish supposedly runs a couple of games you can't find in Atlantic City or out west."

"Yeah, like what?"

Winger thought he detected genuine curiosity in Horn's voice. "I heard they have a game called Balls."

"Balls?" Horn said, puzzled.

"Yeah, you lose and they remove one of your testicles. I'm not kidding," Winger said with a laugh, noticing an incredulous look on Horn's face. "I guess you could, like, gamble your way to birth control, huh?" The young cop laughed again.

"You're full of shit as usual," Horn said, drawing his 9 mm out of its shoulder holster. He pulled back the slide and checked the weapon's chamber before returning it to the leather holster.

Winger turned off Webster Avenue and drove two blocks up East 184th before making a left onto Valentine. He brought the Elint to a stop in front of a low, flat-topped building that looked like a bunker. It was built from concrete blocks, had a single wide steel door facing the trash-covered sidewalk and was covered with graffiti. The ugly structure was apparently the only occupied building on the block, which was lined with burned-out brick shells and crumbling, long-abandoned businesses. Above its door a fading, unlit sign proclaimed it to be the Bonefish Lounge.

"Here we are," Winger announced, shutting down the cop car. He got out and adjusted the machine pistol under the light jacket he was wearing. Several battered cars and a couple of motorcycles were strung out on either side of the street. Night was beginning to fall, and the fading light added to the desolation of the place.

"Must be a popular spot," Horn said, closing the car door and joining Winger on the sidewalk.

"If you think the outside's great, wait until you see the inside." Winger grabbed the door handle.

"I thought you hadn't been here before," Horn said as he followed the young cop into the club.

Horn stopped just inside the door and took in the surroundings. One end of the huge room was set up around a horseshoe-shape bar, behind which rested an old computer-generated holograph of a naked woman stretched out in all her glory. To one side of the bar and in front of a low bandstand were several tables and a postage-stamp-size dance floor. A set of drums, a synthesizer and a couple of horns sat on the plywood-topped stage, waiting for the band to show up. The other end of the room held the card tables, slot machines, crap tables and other gambling equipment.

"Let's get a beer," Winger suggested, and headed for the bar. They ordered two drafts from a fat man with a crew cut who was sweating so hard that he looked as if he'd just come in out of the rain, and Winger tossed a credit wafer onto the scarred wood.

The two cops turned their backs to the bar and surveyed the lounge and its patrons. The crowd was about half capacity, a cross section of no-man's-land dwellers—bikers of both sexes, slick-suited dudes flashing fistfuls of thousand-unit credit wafers, tired-looking men and women hunched over the digital slots like droids. There were even a couple of people Horn judged might make the cut into normal status. He wondered what had brought them to this dive, this far into the Bronx, and whether they'd make it out again without getting their throats cut.

"That must be where the real action is," Horn said, nodding toward a door next to a row of slot machines. Private was stenciled across its faded blue paint, and a big guy wearing a wrinkled suit and mirror-finish sunglasses stood next to it, arms folded menacingly in front of his massive chest. The two cops watched a waitress with a short skirt carry a tray of drinks across the dirty red carpet. She paused at the door while Mirror Eyes opened it for her. They caught a glimpse of the inside of the room, which was bathed in an eerie red light. Some men were gathered around something that was out of sight, and they heard laughter just before the door closed.

"That looked interesting," Winger said. He glanced over Horn's shoulder, studying the people at the bar. "I don't see Bonefish." He turned to the man who was crouched behind the bar, grunting at the effort of sliding a heavy beer keg under the counter. "Where's Bonefish?"

The bartender looked up at Winger, an irritated expression on his round, flushed face. "How the fuck should I know?"

"You do work here, don't you?"

"No." The man stood and wiped his sweating hands down the front of his shirt. "I don't work here, I just died and got sent to this place. It was God's idea of a joke."

The fat man was so wrapped up in his insolent speech to Winger that he didn't notice Horn leaning over the bar. The cop's right hand shot out in a blur and grabbed him by the cheek. He jerked him off his feet and against the railing, and the man squealed in surprise. "Okay, okay. What do you want? Just leggo my goddamn face!"

Winger, too, was a little surprised at Horn's action. Horn seemed to have completely snapped out of his earlier apathy. He was still holding folds of the man's chubby face between his gloved fingers.

"The question was," Horn hissed, pulling the man's face to within inches of his own, "where's Bonefish?"

"In the back, I . . . I think. Lemme go, please!" The bartender wrapped his fat fingers around Horn's wrist and tried in vain to pull away the hand that was stuck to his face like a giant leech.

Horn stared into the man's bulging eyes, an expression of amused indifference on his face. He looked as though he were observing a fish he'd just pulled from the water.

Winger placed a hand on Horn's arm. "Don't you think that's enough?" he said.

"Huh?" Horn turned his head toward the young cop. Then he shoved the bartender backward, releasing his grip. The big man hit the keg he'd been trying to shove under the bar and flipped over, landing on his back. He groaned and rubbed the side of his face, where Horn's fingers had left angry red welts.

Winger glanced around and noticed the patrons were observing the scene as though it were the evening's entertainment. "Let's go find Bonefish," he said.

"You two come here to enjoy the place or screw with the barkeep?"

Winger turned toward the source of the voice, expecting to see Bonefish. Instead he found himself facing a young long-haired bruiser who looked as if he'd been lifting weights most of his life. He was wearing a skintight jumpsuit and slapping an ugly-looking aluminum bat into the palm of his hand. "Shit," Winger said, his voice rising slightly with surprise. "You're not Bonefish."

"You two boys here to see the Bone Man, huh?" The bouncer shook back his blond hair. Horn thought he looked as if he belonged on a California beach instead of a sweathole club in the Bronx.

"That's right. He's expecting us," Winger answered.

"Since when did the Bone Man start fraternizing with cops?" the man asked, a sneer turning up one corner of his mouth.

"What makes you think we're cops?" Horn felt adrenaline start playing that old familiar jazz in his body.

"Your goddamn car." The bouncer pointed his bat toward the door. "It sticks out like a whore in church."

"We're not here to arrest anyone," Horn said. He lowered his voice. "Now if you don't want to end up with that bat stuck down your throat, I suggest you direct us to Bonefish."

The muscle-bound kid looked into Horn's eyes. The arrogance on his face suddenly vanished and was replaced by fear. "Sure," he said, backing away from Horn. "He's right through that door." He pointed toward the door marked Private.

"Hey, Al." He waved at the man in the wrinkled suit. Holding his hand high, he pointed at Horn, then Winger.

"These two are okay." He then pointed toward the private door. The man in the suit nodded. "Be my guests, gentlemen," the bouncer said, pointing the bat in the direction of the door. Winger followed Horn across the room and through the door, held open by its guardian.

The two cops found themselves in a stuffy room that reeked of tobacco smoke and liquor. A couple of decks of cards were spread on a circular stainless-steel table that was raised just above waist level. Directly over the table hung a single red bulb, casting a crimson glow on the dingy room. There was another door on the other side of the room, with an illuminated exit sign above it.

It seemed obvious to Horn that there had been some variety of illegal gambling going on there, probably so corrupt that even in the Bronx, where very little law enforcement went on, its participants didn't wish to be identified as such. When Horn and Winger were spotted as cops, the game had broken up and the players had left the establishment by way of the room's exit to the outside. The bouncer had bought them time to get away, and the guy in the wrinkled suit had made it look as if he were still protecting Bonefish from unauthorized visitors, though he must have known the gamblers had flown the coop.

In the time it took Horn to figure this out, he realized the room wasn't empty of people as he had at first thought. A man was half sitting, half lying in a chair in the corner, an oldish guy with a stringy beard and an odd-looking earring made of feathers hanging from his left lobe. He appeared to be asleep, but Horn wasn't taken in by appearances. He activated the laser site and aimed it right at the man's nose.

"Put that gun down," the man said. "I've done nothing wrong. What do you want?"

"You've got five seconds to tell me where Bonefish is," Horn said.

"He...he's next door." The man jerked his head toward a wall with another door that neither Horn nor Winger had noticed previously.

Winger went numb with shock when Horn fired a round straight into the man's forehead. Blood flew in all directions, and the man slumped dead in the chair.

Winger grabbed Horn by his sleeve and pulled him around. He was taken aback by the look on his partner's face. Horn appeared relaxed and calm, as though he had just gotten up from a nap. "Listen to me, goddamn it!" Winger said. "I don't know what the hell's running loose in your head, but you better put a goddamn straitjacket on it. That son of a bitch was unarmed, for chrissake!" Winger pointed at the body in the chair. "What you did is too much. It's...extreme!"

A controlled anger flashed across Horn's face. He took two steps and leaned down, picking up the dead man's right arm. "You call this unarmed?" A small-caliber automatic stuck out of the dirty sleeve, attached to a sloppy-slide mechanism. Horn glared at Winger for several seconds before allowing the limp arm to drop back onto the floor. He straightened up. "You think I was going to turn my back on him and let him plug me? Like you said a half hour ago, partner, we got a job to do."

Horn strode across to the door the man had said would lead to Bonefish. It was locked. Horn took a short step backward, brought up his right knee and slammed it into the center of the thick wood, breaking the door in half lengthwise. He pulled away the knob side and tossed it onto the floor.

Horn could smell death wafting out of the room. He swallowed hard to keep the bile from rising in his throat as he stepped across the threshold.

Blood was spattered everywhere, even on the ceiling. Every piece of furniture in what appeared to have been an office had been destroyed. Wood, fabric, glass, paper were scattered about as though the contents of the room had been dropped through a giant shredder.

"Bonefish," Winger breathed. He stared at something hanging by its hands from a rope tied to one of the exposed beams on the ceiling. It looked like a chunk of butchered meat. Winger gagged as he realized the man hanging in front of him had been skinned.

The young cop raised his eyes and looked at Horn, who looked back at him. A chill ran down Winger's spine. It was as though Horn were speaking to him through his eyes, speaking to him in some strange new language. But Winger understood what he was saying, and it was a bleak understanding. He knew now some small measure—and he realized it was very small—of what Horn had felt when his wife and daughter had been slaughtered. Winger had just lost the threads that had linked him to his youth. A lonely feeling seeped through his spirit like a cold wind.

Horn walked around the dead body, studying it as though it were a sculpture in a museum. He looked at Winger. "Now *this* is what I would call extreme."

CHAPTER SEVEN

AN ITCH CRAWLED UP Kringa Sthil's back like a procession of fire ants on a search-and-destroy mission. He fought the urge to scratch it with the barrel of his all-composite Max-Lite assault rifle, in spite of the fact that it was driving him crazy. Any such movement might draw a passerby's attention to him on the roof. "What a shitty way to make a living," he whispered to himself, wishing he could light up a smoke.

Across the alley on another roof he could make out Luther crouched and peering through an ancient pair of night vision glasses. He wondered if his brother was as uncomfortable and miserable as he was.

From their rooftop perches the Sthil brothers were watching the rear door of a nondescript gambling parlor called Breakers, half a block from where they were staked out on what was called the Down Side of the Outland Strip. They'd been there for more than four hours, waiting for the target they'd tracked all the way from New York to come out of the club so that they could put a quick end to his life.

The thought of finally getting to pull the trigger on his compact little weapon was Kringa's only consolation. The entire scenario up to now was a blot on his record as a bounty hunter, mercenary and blue-collar assassin. From the beginning he had opposed taking the subcontract from Domino Jones, whom he considered a fool, and had cursed himself for not being more adamant about not taking the job. When he expressed his concerns about the Manhattan ambush to Luther, his brother had told him, as usual, that he worried too much, and had insisted they follow the plan laid out by Jones. Also, as usual, Kringa had in the end tagged along—number two dog in a pack of two.

Now they were working directly for Ruben Zamora, with no middleman. Up until their meeting in the abandoned hangar, Kringa had known nothing about the Colombian except what he read in the newspapers, but he did know the man had a sinister reputation. The Sthil brothers, in Kringa's view, were simple death dealers, but he had the feeling that Zamora would insist on the destruction of his victims' souls as well as their bodies. Kringa shuddered at the memory of Zamora's threat at the end of their meeting.

The more Kringa thought about the past several days, the fouler his mood became. He'd never been to the Outland Strip before, and this was only the second time he'd traveled through near-space. He'd hated every second of the long, slow ride, which had been made worse by a malfunction in the artificial gravity system of the dirty freighter when they were still ten hours from the orbiting resort. Luther had insisted on taking the outdated shuttle in order to cloak their tracking of Jack Rohde and to ensure a hassle-free trip, for they were taking with them a small arsenal of weapons, ammunition and explosives.

In addition to the nausea induced by weightlessness, Kringa was still feeling ill following the torture of Jones's former connection at the Bonefish Lounge. He disliked resorting to such extreme measures, but they'd been in a hurry and needed to know where Rohde had fled to. In any event, Luther, as always, had done the actual hands-on work. Kringa tasted bile at the back of his throat and swallowed it with the thought that such feelings were just part of the job.

When the freighter finally made its approach to the docking corridor of the space-based gambling resort, Kringa had actually been impressed to the point that for a moment he'd forgotten his space sickness. Through a transparent shell that covered the massive, curved structure, Kringa had had a magnificent view of the Strip proper, which curved across the resort's ten-mile width like a neon snake. The gambling theme park, complete with artificial beaches, luxurious hotels, high-class brothels and elaborate gambling casinos, made Las Vegas and Atlantic City look like Tobacco Road.

Kringa's initial impression of the place had changed quickly, however, as he and Luther had picked up the street information they needed to follow Rohde's trail to the seamy side of the Strip—the Down Side. It was a complicated maze of streets that covered the lower third of the Outland Strip's area, where the majority of the Strip's lower-class casino and hotel workers lived. It was also where the transients, fugitives, deal makers, drug peddlers, street hookers and fantasy hustlers wound up after the Strip's private police force ran them out of the so-called legitimate area—the area that had initially intrigued Kringa. The Down Side consequently sprouted dark aberrations of the glitzy establishments crowding the Strip. In the seedy alleys and rusting rattraps one could indulge in grim fantasies in games like Death Poker, Slide for Your Life and Bullet Bet. *I should feel right at home,* Kringa thought. *The Down Side reminds me of the Bronx.*

Kringa looked up and down the garbage-strewn alley that separated the two rows of modular, stackable buildings. The metal-sided, boxlike structures had long ago lost their painted finishes and were in a state of decay, rust-colored like the side of some great ship that had been beached and forgotten aeons ago.

Suddenly Kringa's discomfort vanished as Luther slowly raised one of his hands in its fingerless gloves. Kringa peered into the darkness, straining his eyes in an attempt to pick out what had prompted his brother's signal. He thumbed off the safety of his weapon. Then he heard voices and recognized Rohde's Texas drawl.

He glanced over at Luther, who had replaced the night vision glasses with an ancient 40 mm grenade launcher on which was mounted an infrared scope. Kringa chuckled to himself as his brother aimed the short-barreled blooper gun. The ugly weapon was Luther's favorite, and Kringa often kidded him about it, saying it matched his personality.

Kringa worked his body into a crouch and eased the barrel of his rifle over the edge of the roof. He felt adrenaline pick up his heart rate and course through his body like a sweet drug. Sending another glance across the alley, Kringa could see Luther's shadowy form backlit by the glowing Strip in the distance, frozen like a statue as he aimed the clown gun into the black trench of the alley.

Somewhere below and very close an automatic weapon sounded its loud, ugly death music. Kringa nearly jumped out of his skin. He could see muzzle-flashes strobing off the alley walls and caught a glimpse of Rohde diving behind an overflowing garbage container.

"Kringa!" Luther's booming voice drove its way through the din of gunfire. "Pop a flare!"

Kringa groped at the back of his belt and pulled off a hand flare the size and shape of a cigar tube. He immediately smacked one end of the device on the metal edge of the roof. The opposite end ignited in a bright white flame, and Kringa flung the flare backhanded in the direction of the gunfire as he looked toward Luther, who was standing now, aiming the 40 mm from the hip.

"There he is!" Luther yelled.

Kringa heard the sucking pop of the grenade launcher as it spit one of its smooth little death eggs into the alley, which was now lit up like the freeze-frame of a lightning strike. He ducked and felt the building under him shake noticeably as the grenade exploded, filling the alley with dust as thick as fog.

"Did you get the son of a bitch?" Kringa called out as he scrambled to his feet. He aimed the Max-Lite over the edge of the roof and stared wide-eyed into the cloud of dirt. The machine gun fire had stopped.

"How the hell should I know?" Luther growled. "I can't see a goddamn thing."

Just for the hell of it, Kringa fired a couple of rounds toward the garbage bin he'd seen Rohde dive behind. The sharp sound of his weapon firing echoed strangely and seemed too little too late, given what he'd heard just seconds before.

"Hold your goddamn fire," Luther ordered, frustration and disgust bubbling in his voice. "I'm going to be pissed if that son of a bitch got away again. Go on down. We gotta check it out."

Kringa wasn't too keen on checking out the alley, especially with some mystery man with a machine gun probably still lurking about. But he knew they had to check it out. Luther might have gotten lucky with the grenade launcher, although something in his gut told Kringa he hadn't. He slung the rifle over one shoulder. "Cover me," he yelled to Luther, and he crawled over the edge and dropped into the fog. Then he covered Luther, who also came down. The two men, with Luther in the lead, moved toward the area where Rohde and the other man had been standing before the machine gun had cooked off.

The smoky dust had thinned out somewhat, and Kringa could see Luther walking in a half crouch. He had replaced the blooper gun with his Stoner machine gun, which was deadly at close quarters.

The alley had grown deathly quiet except for the hissing of the flare, which had begun to wane. Its bright white light had dimmed to a weak yellow. Kringa, already edgy, felt his heart jump wildly as a low, gurgling moan filled the air. Crouching and aiming his Max-Lite toward the sound, Kringa methodically swept the desolate territory with his eyes in an attempt to locate the source of the sound. By the process of elimination, his eyes focused on the garbage bin.

He looked over at Luther, who had also crouched in a combat stance, and was slowly sweeping the area in front of them with the barrel of the Stoner. Kringa pointed toward the trash bin and Luther nodded. He moved away from Kringa in order to approach the bin from the opposite side.

Kringa moved forward, his finger on the trigger, primed. He nearly leaped out of his skin when the cry of pain once again broke the stillness. "Shit," he said aloud, thinking anyone who sounded like that couldn't put up much of a fight. He stood and rounded the large, square garbage container cautiously.

"Watch what you're doing there, Kringa," Luther snarled. "The guy could be baiting your ass."

Kringa silently agreed with him, but somehow he knew he wouldn't find some gun-toting ninja on the other side of the dirty, rusted container. What he did find was a smoldering lump that looked like a wad of shredded rags that had been fired from a cannon. Surmising that the form in front of him wasn't a threat, Kringa did the first thing that came to mind; he pulled a pack of cigarettes from a pocket on the side of his peg leg and lit one. Still, he kept the death-dealing end of the assault rifle pointed at what was left of the man in front of him.

Luther came around the far side of the garbage bin, looking like a mutant jungle cat ready to pounce. His green eyes literally glowed. He fanned the machine gun briefly before aiming it at the same target Kringa was covering. "Is this the guy with the automatic?" he asked, pulling a Chemlight from a pocket on his combat vest. Then bending the plastic tube with his teeth until it made a snapping sound, he tossed it next to the wounded man, and the immediate area became bathed in a blue-white chemical light.

"No," Kringa answered, inhaling deeply. He felt the calming effects of the strong tobacco in his head and lungs. "It ain't Rohde, either. This must have been the guy he was talking to."

The back door of Breakers suddenly opened, spilling yellow light around the doorway. Kringa and Luther immediately swung their weapons toward a long-haired man who froze on the threshold and stared at the gun barrels, his eyes the size of poker chips.

"What the hell do you want?" Luther growled, sounding like a chain saw starting up.

"Uh, n-nothing, man," the guy stuttered. "We just heard the . . . uh, n-nothing, no problem." He retreated inside.

The door slammed, and Kringa heard bolts being engaged. He turned back toward Luther and the man curled at their feet like a fried pork rind. Luther now lit a cigarette and went into a mild coughing fit when he inhaled. He cleared his throat, then spit on the body between them.

"See if he's dead," Luther ordered as his hacking subsided.

"Hell, you know he's not dead," Kringa said. "Look at him. He's still moving." The body was twitching slowly, and another low moan, quieter this time, slid from between the man's blackened lips.

Suddenly Kringa felt his heart bang to a stop as he caught sight of the small-caliber pistol the man was holding in one hand, camouflaged by the carbon from the grenade explosion. Luther saw it at the same instant and snapped, "Watch it!" He raised his weapon to a firing position.

"Hold it." Kringa put up his hand. "He's not movin' it. I think he don't even know he's holding it."

"Give the son of a bitch a head shot," Luther ordered.

"Wait a goddamn minute," Kringa whined nasally. He took a step forward and placed one of his boots on the gun hand's wrist, then bent and grabbed the short barrel of the weapon. "Holy shit!" he said disgustedly as he lifted the weapon. The man's blackened hand came with it. It hung from the pistol by its index finger, which was jammed through the trigger guard.

"Looks like something chewed it off, like maybe a dragon," Luther said. Then he broke into his deep, bellowing laugh. "Get it? Dragon...that bastard's, like, torched," he said, wiping the tears from his eyes with the back of one hand.

"Yeah, sure, Luther," Kringa said, examining the hand and the weapon for a couple of seconds before tossing them onto the pile of garbage in the bin. He looked at his brother, then nodded toward the body. "Why don't you see if he can talk?"

"Huh?" Luther looked puzzled.

"Him," Kringa answered impatiently, pointing at the man on the floor of the alley. "See if this piece of burned meat can tell us anything about Rohde or whoever that asshole with the machine gun was."

"Oh." Luther nodded, understanding replacing the befuddlement that had blanked his face. He lit another cigarette and bent over, staring at the man's charbroiled face.

At times like this Kringa sometimes wondered why they both assumed Luther was the leader of their two-man army. It wasn't that his older brother was slow, or even stupid, for that matter. But sometimes he just spaced out, as if some arbitrary word or question plunged him into a dull, hypnotic state. Kringa figured Luther had taken the lead first because he was older, but even more because the hulking, wire-haired man was the most cold-blooded person Kringa knew. Luther could kill or torture a man without batting an eye. However, Kringa had never seen him do in a man without a reason. He was cold-blooded, but not evil. At least not according to Kringa's standards.

"This son of a bitch looks like a chunk of burned ham," Luther said, the cigarette dangling between his lips. "Smells like one, too." He laughed again, the hoarse, chesty sound reverberating in the alley.

"Ask him something. Ask him where the hell Rohde's holed up." Kringa looked over his shoulder to check the entry to the alley, then back at Luther, who was patting the man's face gently with his left hand.

Both Kringa and Luther were startled when the man's eyes fluttered open and he spoke in an amazingly clear voice. "What the hell . . . Where am I? Is that you, Jack?"

"No, it ain't Jack," Luther answered. "But I'm your pal. What's your name?"

"Joey. Who . . . who are you?" the man asked, his eyes darting back and forth as Kringa crouched next to his brother.

"We're your friends, Joey," Luther said, apparently trying to make his sandpaper voice sound soothing. "We just happened to be out on the street—" he nodded up the alley "—and heard the commotion. We ran off the guy who was shooting at you and whoever it was you were talking to."

"Yeah, the shooter was that goddamn bounty hunter Sharkey," the burned man answered, his lips split and bleeding.

"Huh?" Luther's mind once again went into a holding pattern.

Kringa quickly picked up the line of questioning. "He means, who's this Sharkey? You said he was a bounty hunter. Who's paying him?" Kringa tried to make his voice calm and soothing, because Joey had begun to look around. Kringa was afraid he'd see the shape his body was in and go into hysterics, so he grabbed him by the chin and forced his face toward his. "No offense," he said, "but what did you mean when you called this guy who tried to nail you a bounty hunter?"

"I mean he's a goddamn bounty hunter," Joey answered, his voice growing raspy. "The Feds have put a price on Rohde's head." He licked his lips and swallowed. "That bastard Mark Sharkey has been trailing us for a week. The punk sure got lucky. He must have had a thermite grenade."

"That's kind of odd. The Feds would want the asshole alive. Why would this Sharkey cat try to gun him down?"

"He's not the brightest guy on the Strip," the burned man croaked like a frog as his eyes rolled back in his head.

"Hey, hold on." Kringa grabbed Joey's shoulders and shook him gently. "I need to know one more thing." The man's eyes rolled back into focus, and Kringa noticed that one pupil was much larger than the other. "Where can we find Jack Rohde?" he asked, speaking to the blistered side of the guy's face.

"You guys cops?" Joey whispered.

"No, we're not cops," Luther said, having snapped out of his mind lock. He moved Kringa away with the back of his hand. "We're friends of Rohde's. As a matter of fact," Luther added, smiling and glancing briefly at Kringa, "we owe him some cash . . . want to pay him back."

Joey's eyes grew suspicious. "How the hell do I know you're not another bounty hunter?"

Luther ignored the question and rose slowly to his feet. He turned Kringa, who had also straightened up and was lighting a cigarette. "I guess he really is a friend of Rohde's," Luther said, snatching the cigarette out of Kringa's mouth. He stuck it into his own and returned his attention to the burned man at his feet. "Just tell me where I can find Rohde," Luther said, placing one of his boots on the man's thigh.

"I thought you fuckers were cops," Joey answered, seemingly oblivious to the pressure on his leg.

"Cops!" Luther chortled, spitting on Joey's chest. "We ain't cops." He ground his foot on the guy's leg as though he were snuffing out a smoke. Still, Joey didn't react.

Kringa put a hand on Luther's arm. "Wait a second, Luther! For chrissake, can't you see the bastard's got burns all over his goddamn body?"

"So?"

Kringa sighed. "So when someone gets burned like that—" he gestured toward the victim "—it destroys their goddamn nerves. They can't feel nothing. He probably couldn't feel the therapy you were just giving him with your boot."

"Oh," Luther said with a manic grin. "Well, watch this." He shoved the little Stoner into Kringa's free hand and got down on one knee. "You're going to tell me where Rohde is, asshole." He grabbed Joey by his singed hair, but a big clump of it came away in his hand, crumbling like threads of ash. "Shit," he muttered, and clamped his left hand down over the burn victim's forehead. "I know one part of you that ain't burned." He pried apart one of the guy's eyelids with his thumb and forefinger.

"Wait! What the hell are you doing?" Panic rose in Joey's throat.

"You know, a good doctor could probably save you," Luther lied. "But what the hell good will it do if you can't see?" He leaned his right elbow on Joey's chest and pulled the cigarette from between his lips. "Now, where can we find Rohde?" He moved the glowing tip of the cigarette toward the guy's bared eyeball.

"Don't!" Joey screamed weakly.

"Where is he?" Luther breathed huskily. "Don't make me ask you again."

"You can probably find him at a place on the Strip called the Milky Way," he answered, jerking his head to one side as Luther flicked ashes off the cigarette into his eye. "Watch it, goddamn it!"

"Shut up," Luther snapped. "When does he go there?"

"Almost every Friday night, but not till late, real late."

"Thanks, chump," Luther said, using the man's chest to push against as he rose. He took a drag on his cigarette and turned toward Kringa, who held out the little machine gun. He took the weapon and growled, "As I was saying, I really don't understand why some fools insist on protecting people who…well, who are gonna die one way or the other. You know?" Luther actually looked and sounded as though he were trying to get a significant point across to his brother. "I mean, look at this—" he gestured around the alley with the Stoner "—a thousand years from now it'll all be meaningless."

"It's meaningless now," Kringa said, turning his head to one side and spitting. "Spare me your dismal philosophy. Save it for the next time you're a guest preacher."

Luther grinned, then broke out in his choppy, guttural laughter. "Put him out of his misery and let's check out the place on the Strip." He nodded downward at the scorched piece of flesh.

"Wait," croaked the man on the alley floor. Fear seemed to lend volume to his voice. "You said a doctor could—"

"Shut up," Kringa drawled, stepping next to him. He aimed the assault rifle at Joey's head. "This is the best treatment for the likes of you." Kringa pulled the trigger, figuring he was doing the poor bastard a favor.

CHAPTER EIGHT

ZAMORA STARED OUT at the lights of Atlantic City from the windows of his penthouse office in the thrice-renovated Taj Mahal hotel and casino. Behind him Eloy Baca stood before a bank of backlit LCD monitors, staring at the screens, occasionally touching one with his shaking index finger. The thin mustachioed man looked more like an aging waiter than a financial wizard whom Zamora often referred to as "my brain." Eloy was HIed into the computer; a thin fiber-optic cable ran from the console and was plugged into the back of his neck.

"Well, how does it look?" Zamora asked him. A cigarette dangled from Zamora's thin lips, and he stood with his hands in the jacket pockets of his loose-fitting suit.

"Not good," Eloy answered, "but I'll have a better cut at it in about ten minutes. Is that okay?"

Zamora waved a hand casually. "No problem," he said calmly. "Take your time. Why get in a rush to hear bad news, right, Leonard?" he asked, turning toward the ever-present bodyguard, who sat in a leather armchair next to the ornate double doors of the large office.

Leonard merely shrugged. Zamora knew he comprehended little, if any, of what was going on here.

"How about a drink?" Zamora asked himself more than anyone else. "Fix me a Scotch, will you, Leonard?" The big guard stood and moved toward a neat little bar tucked into one corner of the once-plush office. "Want a drink, Eloy?"

Zamora asked the tall, skinny man whose gestures betrayed a bad case of nerves.

Eloy turned his head, blinked and licked his lips. "Maybe in a minute, thanks," he answered.

Zamora ambled over to a round glass table flanked by a gray leather couch and two armchairs and snuffed out his cigarette in an ashtray on the table. He picked up a fresh smoke from an ornate box and a lighter shaped like a miniature slot machine. He had to pull its tiny handle to activate the flame. Then he turned toward Leonard, who was approaching with his drink. "Thanks," he said, taking it. "Fix Mr. Baca a tall Scotch, also. He'll be done in a few minutes."

"Certainly." Leonard returned to the bar, coming back with the drink just as Eloy walked over to the couch, loosening his tie.

Eloy thanked Leonard, and held up a sheaf of papers that had just been output. "I'm ready to talk about this," he said to Zamora. "And I think you want to talk about a couple of other things, as well." He tossed the papers onto the table and picked up the glass of Scotch.

Zamora held out the box of cigarettes and Eloy took one. The Colombian started to reach for the table lighter, hesitated, then reached into his pant pocket for a disposable. Striking the flame, he held it while Eloy lit his smoke.

"Thanks, Mr. Zamora," Eloy said. "You didn't have to do that." His voice was cracked and his black eyes darted wildly about the room.

"I know I didn't have to do it, *compadre*," Zamora said softly, "but you and I have been together a long time. I just want you to know that I appreciate your *fidelidad*." Eloy's face grew more flushed than it already was. Before he could answer, Zamora took a seat in one of the armchairs. "Now make yourself comfortable on the couch and tell me about the numbers first. How badly have my associates managed to screw things up?''

"Let's just say—" Eloy paused briefly while he sat down "—I've seen better managed rock fights.''

"That's good, Eloy,'' Zamora said, laughing, then the smile slipped from his face. "Now what's the real damage?''

"The VAC, if you will,'' Eloy answered, "is losing up to three-quarters of a million a week.''

"No wonder they were so willing to sign up for my plan,'' Zamora said, more to himself than Eloy.

"The only thing keeping it from going under completely is the weak hold Rust, Moore and the other guy managed to get on the drug and prostitution business in their areas.'' Eloy tilted back his glass and emptied it, his Adam's apple bobbing as he swallowed.

Zamora motioned for Leonard to refill Eloy's glass. "We will strengthen the spin-off activities, that's no problem, but what about the cash situation? I have someone who says he can put me in touch with a person who can arrange a pardon for my uncle, but it will cost ten to twelve million.''

Eloy took a long drag on his cigarette and choked, coughing out puffs of smoke. "Excuse me,'' he said when he had himself under control. "Are you talking about cash?''

Zamora smiled. "I certainly am.'' The smoke from his cigarette curled up and framed his face in opaque vapor.

"That may be a problem,'' Eloy said, accepting the fresh drink Leonard was holding out.

"Explain.'' Zamora already knew what Eloy was going to tell him.

"We're going to be lucky if we can glean five million at any given time from all the operations in both Las Vegas and Atlantic City. I'm not kidding you—both places are cash poor.''

"I'm not at all surprised." Zamora sipped his Scotch. "As I said, the others gave in too easily. They even admitted they had financial problems."

"They would have had a hard time hiding something of this magnitude." Eloy ground out his cigarette in the ashtray and immediately lit another from a pack in his pocket, using his own lighter.

"What else did your analysis reveal?"

Eloy spread the papers on the table in front of him. "Well, I did as you suggested and ran a simple regression of the combined financial performance of Vegas and Atlantic City against the activities of the Outland Strip. And it's as you suspected."

"You did it from the time the Strip opened?"

"Yeah, and even though the data was kind of sketchy back then, you can see the VAC start to spiral down as the Strip got wound up." Eloy made a little upward twirling motion with two fingers, the booze obviously enhancing his presentation. "Since then," he went on, "every time the Strip launches one of its big promos, you can see the VAC's revenue go down the shit can. Here, I graphed it." He slid a chart toward his boss.

Zamora waved a hand casually without looking down. "What about the assets, the capital?"

"Well, what the VAC does have has been written off, used to secure various lines of credit or both. Most of the land is also tied up one way or the other as collateral and that sort of thing. It would be hard as hell to get anything out of the casinos, at least in the short run."

"What about selling the whole damn conglomeration?"

"It would take too long. Anyway, the owners have been taking such a loss every year since the strip came on-line that it's no secret their operations are less than profitable."

"I figured as much," Zamora said, blowing smoke toward the ceiling. "Now I've got this loose cannon Rohde running around spooked as hell. I don't know whether he's going to roll over, sit up or self-destruct.''

"Huh?" Eloy used both hands to set his drink on the table.

"He's like a wild card. If the Feds or the locals get their hooks into him, my friend, you and I better head for the deep woods." The Colombian's voice was calm but deadly serious.

"Does he know that much?" Eloy shifted forward to the edge of the couch, his elbows resting on his knees.

"He knows as much as you do," Zamora said, lowering his eyelids to half-mast.

Eloy fidgeted noticeably and ran one of his bony fingers around the inside of his collar. "D-don't ever worry about me . . ." he stuttered.

Zamora chuckled softly. "No, friend, I would never question your loyalty. But the thing weighing heavily on my mind is whether the two men we hired can take care of Mr. Rohde. The man is not a fool. Aside from that little problem, I've got a consultant coming in from Los Angeles to see if he can help us with our cash problem." Zamora looked at his watch. "He should be here now, as a matter of fact."

"You want me to leave?" Eloy asked. It was obvious he didn't want to stay.

"I think so," Zamora answered. "This might prove boring."

Eloy gathered up his papers, rose to his feet, and said, "Oh, I almost forgot to tell you something else."

"What's that?"

"I found out that the NYPD has sent two cops after Rohde."

"So?" Zamora uncrossed his legs and picked up his drink. "I'm surprised they didn't send an army. We did kill one of their captains."

"That's not my point." Eloy waved his hand nervously. "The two cops are the same ones who undermined the Superplex operation last year."

Zamora pulled his head back slightly in a gesture of surprise. "You're kidding me," he said, setting down his glass without taking a drink. "Where did you hear this?"

"It's the word on the street. These guys are supposed to be like the ones they use to do the *trabajo sucio*."

Although facing Eloy, Zamora wasn't looking at him. Instead he stared into space beyond his hired brain, mentally digesting this unexpected news. He knew, of course, that his plan to obtain the freedom of his father and uncles by terrorism had been undone almost single-handedly by two New York City cops. He figured they had gotten lucky, very lucky. Thanks to them he was in his current predicament, trying to scrounge up enough money to buy a pardon for his dead father's brother with a bribe. The Superplex affair had left a bad taste in Zamora's mouth. He was dumbfounded now to hear that the same two cops who had spoiled the most brilliant scheme he'd ever put together were sniffing down the trail of the one man who could sound the death knell to Zamora's already weakened organization.

At last Zamora focused on Eloy's face. "That's interesting. Try to find out more about their itinerary—where they're staying, that sort of thing. Also, get hold of the Sthil brothers and have them contact me. Tell them I want to expand their charter."

"Anything else?" Eloy seemed anxious to leave the office.

"No, you may go." Zamora turned toward Leonard. "Has Sam Tripp arrived?"

Without a word, Leonard went to the door and looked outside. He turned and told Zamora, "He's out there. Want me to bring him in?"

"Eloy can tell him." Zamora nodded at Eloy, who headed for the door.

Moments later a tall, impeccably dressed man in a gray suit and striped tie entered the office. He glanced first at Leonard, who nodded toward his boss.

"Mr. Zamora, I assume." The man held out his hand, eyeing the Colombian warily.

"Yes, Mr. Tripp." Zamora smiled and they shook hands. "But you may call me Ruben."

"And please call me Sam."

Zamora evaluated the man with his eyes. Tripp was well built in a trim, muscular way. His clean-shaven face was rugged yet unscarred. His short, prematurely gray hair was combed straight back. He gave the impression that he would be equally at home in a boardroom or climbing the rock face of a mountain.

Zamora gestured toward the couch. "Have a seat. Would you like a drink?"

"No thanks." Tripp unbuttoned his suit coat, sat down and leaned back on the leather couch. "I understand you're looking for someone to... how should I say it, detune your competition."

"That's more or less correct," Zamora answered, lighting a cigarette. He remained standing. "But let's get to the point. You come highly recommended, and I'm told you do not compromise confidences. So I'd like to dispense with the preliminaries, if you will, and get right to the point."

Tripp smiled. "By all means. What's the problem?"

"The problem is simple. Our operations here in Atlantic City and in Vegas are losing money on a daily basis as a direct result of the Outland Strip. The Strip is hurting us badly." Zamora picked up his Scotch and took a healthy swallow. "Sure you won't have a drink?"

Tripp shook his head. "Have you thought about disinformation? Negative advertising?"

"Naturally, but I wouldn't have contacted you if I were interested in some type of ad campaign. I want the Outland Strip shut down completely."

Tripp looked thoughtful for several seconds, then responded. "Usually I take care of a client's *own* business. Fire, theft, some type of loss that results in a major insurance payoff."

"I'm aware of that. I know you masterminded the ARNCO refinery fire two years ago."

Tripp raised his eyebrows. "How did you hear I was connected with that job?"

"Let's just say I had my people check out your credentials before I asked you here. I have to admit they were impressive."

"Thank you," Tripp said. His jaw looked like a piece of machined steel.

"I understand two hundred people died in that 'accident,'" Zamora said, watching Tripp for a reaction.

"Two hundred twenty-eight," Tripp said without blinking.

Zamora was impressed. For all the emotion he showed, the man might have been telling him about his car's gas mileage. "Does that kind of work bother you?"

"Would I be sitting here talking to you if it did? I got six hundred thousand for that job. ARNCO got over a hundred million in insurance once the lawyers got finished. It's business. The only problem I had was I decided afterward I should have been working on a commission instead of a flat rate."

Zamora shrugged. "Torching a refinery is one thing. Disabling the Outland Strip is another. I want the place out of business totally. I don't care if you do it with paper or use some more...physical method. It's my understanding that all the electronically operated gambling devices are controlled from one central computer. We thought about sending a team up there and simply taking the system out."

"That's a possibility," Tripp acknowledged, "but I can see problems with it."

"That's exactly why we're considering the use of your services. Whatever you come up with, it must not be connected with the VAC, and it has to put the Strip out of commission for at least six months." Zamora sat down at last in the chair opposite Tripp. "Are you interested?"

Tripp didn't answer the question. "I understand you're now chasing down up there what could be considered a personal problem."

Zamora was surprised but didn't show it. "What is your 'understanding,' exactly?"

"It's on the street that some witness for the state is hiding out up there and you're trying to nail him before the Feds, or whoever, can get their hands on him. I heard you hired the Sthil brothers." Tripp shifted forward on the couch. "I mention it only because I might be able to use their services if we do make a deal. If they're already under contract to you, the business arrangements would be simpler."

"You know the Sthil brothers?" Zamora asked, wondering just how much of his activities was common knowledge "on the street."

"I'm familiar with their work. They get a little messy from time to time, but generally they're reliable. I'd like to be able to use them if I need to."

"What are you proposing?"

"Nothing yet." Tripp straightened the knot on his tie. "I'm interested in the job, but I'll need two weeks to put a proposal together."

"I'll give you a week," Zamora said, standing.

"Very well, a week it is." Tripp got to his feet and followed Zamora to the door. "Let me call you the day before and arrange for the next meeting. I've already got some ideas that might work."

"Very well," Zamora said, and the two men shook hands.

"And one more thing," Tripp said, pausing in the doorway. Zamora raised his eyebrows. "My fee will be substantial. If I'm successful, I expect to be rewarded."

Zamora placed a hand on Tripp's shoulder. "You'll be rewarded one way or the other, Mr. Tripp. Let's hope it will be for success."

CHAPTER NINE

"SO THIS IS THE STRIP," Winger mused, staring out the window of the taxi. "It must have cost a fortune to transport all this shit up here."

"This your first time here?" The toothless driver of the rickety electrically powered cab looked over his shoulder. "You need anything, I mean *anything*, I can show you where to get it."

"How about dope?" Horn asked, leaning forward.

"You name it," the cabdriver answered.

"Women?" Horn watched the man's face in the rear-view mirror.

The driver grinned. "You got it, Mack."

"How about a new cover for this?" Horn held his badge over the seat so that the driver could see it. He chuckled as the grin on the men's face changed to a cynical sneer.

"Cops, huh?" he grunted. "New York City cops at that." He pulled off the main strip into the entryway of the Orion Hotel and Casino, stopping in front of the bank of doors leading to the main lobby. "A word of advice to you two. Don't flash your goddamn badges on the Strip. They'll only get you an endless stream of problems. The Strip's own security won't even recognize you."

Horn just tossed a credit wafer onto the front seat. He grabbed his bag and crawled out the door that was being held open by a uniformed doorman. Winger was right behind him.

The two New York cops entered the plush lobby of the hotel, looking somewhat out of place in their paramilitary attire and field boots. It was obvious to onlookers that they hadn't come to the Strip to sample the varied recreation it had to offer.

"Who made us reservations in this posh place?" Winger asked as they approached the front desk.

"You think they should have found us something that was more of a match with your personality?" Horn asked. He dropped a credit voucher on the polished wood. "Something like a split-level roach ranch?"

"Who are you to talk, partner?" Winger handed his voucher to a tall, good-looking woman in a red blazer whose long hair was a rich auburn color. "I've been to your apartment, remember?"

"How long will you gentlemen be staying?" the woman asked, her smile revealing perfect teeth.

"Hopefully not long," Horn answered. "A week, two maybe."

"Have you stayed at the Orion before?" she asked, looking from Horn to Winger, then back to Horn.

"This is our first visit to the Strip," Winger answered, leaning against the long counter, "so we don't really know what the place has to offer. Maybe you and I can get together later, like when you get off work, and you could show me around."

"I'd really like to," the woman answered, "but the hotel has an escort service that can take care of you in that area." She handed him a brochure.

Winger took the pamphlet, while Horn picked up the slip of paper with the room numbers and key codes for the door locks printed on it.

"Do you gentlemen need a bellhop?" The woman's smile never wavered.

"No thanks," Horn answered.

"The elevators are at the far end of that hall." She pointed past a long row of electronic slot machines. "Have a lucky day."

"Look at this place," Winger said as they walked across the lobby. "It's like people can't wait to lose their asses."

The lobby, large though it was, was crowded with well-dressed people, most of the women bedecked with jewelry. Most were moving toward or away from the arched entrance to what Horn figured was the main casino. He could see long rows of crap and blackjack tables fanned out in the massive ballroom, people crowded around them like animals feeding at troughs. The walls were lined with slots as well as other types of electronic games that had been adapted to, or created specifically for, gambling. Several people were lined up to pull the oversize handle of a giant slot whose electronic sign promised a payoff of one hundred thousand dollars in electrocash every hour. In the center of the casino floor, like an offbeat religious artifact, was a glass sphere at least ten yards in diameter. It sat on a black onyx pedestal and was filled with what looked like gold dust.

Horn and Winger rode the elevator to the fifth floor and found their rooms, opposite each other at the end of a red carpeted hall. "Give me thirty minutes or so to clean up, then let's go down for a beer," Horn said, punching his code into the door's cipher lock.

"Thirty minutes," Winger repeated.

Horn tossed his bag onto the king-size bed and looked around. He smiled to himself, remembering what Winger had implied about the contrast between this place and what Horn was used to at home. The room was actually a suite complete with a small bar, wide-screen entertainment center, couch, desk and a bathroom that was as large as his living room at home. He walked to a wide picture window and looked out across a jungle of neon facades that pulsed in a stilted rhythm as though the Strip were a living, breathing thing.

It was getting dark, and Horn suddenly had the urge to hit the streets, right then. An irrational urgency filled his mind. He knew Rohde was hiding somewhere in that maze of casinos, bars and brothels out there, but he also knew he'd never catch up with his quarry if he allowed his emotions to override his training.

Horn went into the bathroom for a glass of cold water and was shocked when he caught sight of his face in the mirror. His skin was pale and his face was drawn as though he'd just been pulled out of an extended period of combat. Dark circles rimmed his eyes and matched the shadow of two days' beard. Horn stared into his own eyes and had the strange sensation that he was seeing himself for the first time. It was as though he'd just awakened from a dream that had lasted since he was born. And here he was, staring at himself—his own crazy, ugly ghostlike self, come back from the future, or from some place he couldn't actually remember being, to look at himself with an expression that seemed to say, I thought you were dead.

Unconsciously Horn looked down at his right hand and flexed his mod. The feeling of its servos and actuators functioning beneath his hard metal skin seemed to bring him out of the odd state into which he'd lapsed. At least this is real, he thought, slowly closing and opening his gloved hand.

He soaked a towel in steaming hot water and held it to his face for a few minutes, then repeated the process with ice-cold water. He looked in the mirror again and decided there was a little improvement to be seen.

Back in the living room, Horn punched on a flat-paneled telemonitor that was built into the desk, and looked at his watch. It was nearly midnight back in New York. What the hell, he thought, pulling a small notebook from one of his jacket pockets. He'd promised Christina Service he'd call her as soon as he and Winger got to the Strip, even if it was outside office hours, and she'd given him her home number. Horn punched in the ten-digit number and watched Please Stand By flash on the LCD panel. Less than ten seconds later Service's image appeared on the screen.

The assistant district attorney was sitting in front of a telemonitor that Horn guessed was in her study. In the background he could see a desk on which sat a computer, its monitor filled with text of some sort. Bookshelves lined the walls, reminding Horn of her office at the Justice Center. It figured, he thought. She seemed the type who would think nothing of working every waking hour.

What particularly struck Horn, however, was what she was wearing. Her lean body was clad in loose-fitting black pajamas that revealed more than a hint of the smooth valley between her breasts. The blond hair that she normally kept pinned up, pulled back or tucked into a bun hung loosely around her shoulders. Horn thought she looked like a model for perfume or lingerie—not at all like the woman he'd become accustomed to.

"Well, I see that you made it," she said, scrutinizing Horn with her intense blue eyes.

Horn got the feeling that Service was unaware of her sexy appearance as she shifted her weight and brushed back the hair from one side of her face. "Sorry about the time," he said, pretending to look at his watch.

"It doesn't matter. I was just catching up on some things I can't seem to get done at the office." She sent a quick glance to the computer screen. "I've found out a couple of things since you left that may or may not help you. The Colombian has hired a couple of dedicated headhunters to find Rohde and get rid of him."

"Do you know who they are?" Horn asked. His eyes felt trapped by the woman's stare.

"They're a couple of brothers. Their last name is Sthil. Zamora had the guy killed who botched the job in which Captain Kelso was..." Christina's voice trailed off, then she continued in a soft tone that suggested she was sorry she had mentioned Kelso's being killed."

Horn didn't react, although he sensed Service expected him to. He had put Kelso's death as far out of his mind as he could, which was about as far away as he could get from his own shadow. Still, he returned her stare, his face expressionless. "The name doesn't ring a bell," he said soberly. "Anything else?"

"Yes," she said, her voice returning to its all-business tone. "You're probably going to have some competition finding Rohde, in addition to Zamora's hired killers."

"How so?"

"The Feds put out a reward for Rohde. I don't remember how much exactly, but it's enough to attract the usual crew of..." Christina paused, searching for the right term.

"Lowlife," Horn said, filling in her blank. "Why the hell did they do that?" he asked, irritated that he might have to contend with any number of self-proclaimed bounty hunters, who were more apt to screw things up and get Rohde killed than bring him in alive. At least Horn knew where he stood with the likes of Zamora's hit men: their mission was simple and straightforward—to kill. With the federal reward seekers, however, he was dealing with unknowns. They would make his job harder.

Christina shrugged. "I tried to get it stopped, but they were adamant. They said something to the effect that we'd had our chance. They also said they had to go after him since it was highly unlikely he would turn himself in, especially after what happened."

"Don't worry about it. I'll get him one way or the other."

"Detective Winger is with you, isn't he?" Service asked, raising her eyebrows, obviously ready to change the subject.

"Yeah, he's here. We're supposed to go have a beer in a few minutes."

Horn looked hard at the woman. He couldn't deny he was physically attracted to her. But there was something beyond the physical attraction, and it puzzled him. He knew what it wasn't. It wasn't the beginning of what he'd known in the past as love. He didn't long for her company, and his heart didn't skip a beat when he looked at her. The woman had a mysterious presence. She always had her act together, even when things got tight. And she was tough. He felt that she was one of the few remaining connections he had to normalcy, and he laughed sardonically to himself when he thought of the other links: Winger, his 9 mm and the metal scars on his body called E-mods.

"Just checking," Christina said, a smile flashing briefly across her face.

Horn laughed genuinely this time, knowing what she was implying. "Don't worry. I didn't dump Winger somewhere so I could come up here and play myself like a silver bullet."

Christina's smile returned and held this time. "Sometimes I wonder. And it probably doesn't matter one way or the other. I really don't know if the two of you are more dangerous together or apart."

Horn motioned around the room. "Explain this to me. I assume you had someone make our reservations here. How can our per diem handle a place like this?"

"I guess you're not used to such luxury," Christina said. "It must be quite a shock to your system."

"Winger said the same thing." Horn felt something like relaxation sweep over his tired body.

"To answer your question," Christina said, "you'd be surprised at how inexpensive those places are. They figure you're going to lose enough money in the casinos to compensate for the big discount they give you on the room. I also thought you might enjoy staying in a nice place."

"I do appreciate it," Horn said sincerely. "And hopefully we won't be here long enough to run up too big a tab. Anything else?" He looked at his watch. "I'm due to meet Winger now."

"No. Just stay in touch. I'm trying to keep tabs on Zamora so that when you do bring in Rohde we'll be able to pick him up right away."

"Right," Horn said.

But he had a feeling it would be easier said than done. He knew if he could find Rohde, he could make the connection to the Colombian, though whether through Rohde himself, or through the hired killers that were after him, Horn didn't know. But if the others got to Rohde before he did, Rohde would be dead and the man responsible for Kelso's death would disappear into the woodwork like a cockroach. Horn acknowledged a dark corner of his mind that was telling him he could go after the Colombian one way or the other, solo—throw away the badge, give in to the power he really had. His mods glitched a little and reminded him that the woman was still on the screen in front of him. "I'll stay in touch," he said, and punched off the monitor. The screen darkened to the color of her pajamas, and she was gone.

A short time later Horn and Winger were sitting in one of the many bars of the large hotel, which was nearly a city unto itself. There were restaurants, a movie theater, a mini-shopping center and almost any type of sales or service establishment one might need. The bar was called the Jungle Room, a name not quite in keeping, Horn thought, with the astral theme the hotel had chosen for most of its labeled facilities. But at least Horn felt more at home in the bar decorated like a safara trophy room than in more celestial surroundings.

The stuffed heads of lions, wildebeests and other horned and game animals adorned the walls of the Jungle Room. Zebra skin rugs were laid out across an acrylic floor under which soft lights flashed in time with a primitive yet ethereal music that flowed through the room like a breeze. A bamboo-trimmed bar ran the length of one side of the room, and tables were fanned out into the shadows. The two cops had chosen a table next to the wall and farthest from the entrance. They were bathed in an orange light produced by simulated burning torches fixed in holders on the walls, which created a lighted perimeter as though the table were in a clearing.

The place was sort of tacky, Horn had to admit, but even more than the decor, it was the patrons who made him feel most at home. There were no formally attired people in the Jungle Room, no tuxedos or ball gowns. The patrons appeared to be the same cross section of people he might see in a bar in the Village or in one of the blue-collar lounges on North Broadway. There were zip-suited dudes with outrageously dressed women hanging on their arms like costume jewelry; tough guys wearing dark suits, hunched over their drinks, speaking low; prostitutes dressed like dragon slayers, whispering into the ears of prospective clients or surveying the crowd for potential fire breathers; and a number of other mismatched souls. Horn suspected the bar was frequented by hotel employees as well as tourists weary of the formal glitz that was pumped through the rest of the complex.

Winger ordered their beer from a long-legged waitress wearing an ultrashort leopard skin outfit that would have looked ridiculous anywhere else but was just right for the Jungle Room. ''This place sort of reminds me of that joint in the Bronx you took me to last year," Winger said after handing the waitress a five-credit wafer. He grinned. "The place where your Mexican buddy tried to drink that jet fuel he called mescal through his ears." The young cop laughed heartily and slapped the top of the table.

"You're so full of shit you should be selling it as fertilizer," Horn said, smiling. The relaxed feeling he'd experienced while talking to Christina Service had stayed with him, and he was enjoying it. "This place is nothing like the Red Worm."

Winger picked up the tall mug the waitress had placed in front of him. He took a healthy drink, wiped the foam from his lips with the back of his hand and said, "That's it. I knew the goddamn place had some kind of an insect in its name."

Horn laughed and picking up his beer. "A worm isn't an insect."

The young cop looked confused for a second, then his crooked grin spread across his face. "Insect, bug, worm, whatever the hell you want to call the damn things. I can think of better things to drink than jet fuel. Like this." He held up the mug of brew, then tilted it, downing nearly a third of its contents in a large gulp.

Horn started to say something, but stopped as Winger's eyes locked onto someone who had just entered the bar. "Holy Mother," the young cop said, suppressing a belch. "What the hell's she doing here in the freaking jungle?"

Horn followed Winger's gaze and was surprised to see the tall redhead who had waited on them at the front desk. She was no longer in uniform, but sported a skintight black dress with a skirt that ended midthigh. The low-cut dress accented her hair, which flowed around her shoulders like flaming water. She was with another woman, an athletic-looking brunette wearing a bright orange jumpsuit and spike heels.

"I think I'm in love," Winger said, staring at the two women.

Horn laughed as he watched them take a table across the room. "Maybe the jungle's looking a little better to you now?" he asked, amused that his partner's stare hadn't left the women since he'd first spotted them.

"It's looking a whole lot better," Winger answered, finally wrenching his eyes away. "Do you mind if I go ask them to have a drink with us?"

"I don't mind," Horn answered, rubbing a gloved hand over the stubble on his chin. He wished he'd taken the time to shave, but then he hadn't planned on meeting anyone but Winger.

"Don't worry about it," Winger told him. "So you're ugly and you look like you just crawled out of a ditch. We can only hope they're partially blind."

Before Horn could offer a retort, Winger was up from the table and halfway across the room. He watched his boyish-looking partner lean over the women's table, talking, smiling and gesturing with his hands. After two or three minutes he straightened up and pointed toward Horn, who was somewhat surprised when the women picked up their drinks and followed Winger back through the maze of tables.

Horn stood as the trio approached, and pulled out a chair for the woman in the orange jumpsuit, who was closest to him. It was obvious that his partner had his eye on the redhead. Horn smiled to himself as Winger nearly tripped in his rush to pull out a chair for the woman.

"This is Max Horn," Winger said, gesturing at Horn. "This is Roxy Corner—" he nodded at the redhead "—and this is, uh . . ."

"Carol Ford," the brunette said, bailing Winger out of his short-term memory loss. She had a distinctive British accent and smiled warmly at Horn, holding out her hand.

Horn watched the woman's expression change to one of mild puzzlement as he shook her offered hand. She looked down at the black glove, then toward Roxy, who had her hand out in Horn's direction. What the hell, he thought, and grabbed the redhead's hand firmly. Roxy, too, did a double take.

"Ready for another drink?" Winger asked when they were all seated. He put one arm on the back of Roxy's chair and waved at the waitress with the other. "Two more beers," he told her, "and a . . ." He looked at Carol.

"Gin on the rocks with a twist of lemon," she said, although the glass in front of her was still nearly full.

"And what are you drinking?" Winger asked Roxy.

"I'm fine, thanks," she said, looking across the table at Horn. Her dark green eyes fixed on his.

A warm feeling fluttered in the lower part of Horn's abdomen. He smiled at her. She stirred something in him that he hadn't felt for a long time.

Horn glanced at Winger, who was staring at him, the expression on his face telling Horn that he'd noticed the subtle exchange between Horn and the woman. Horn shrugged and flashed a grin, and Winger rolled his eyes in a look of mock disgust.

"You two guys are a little bit off your beat, aren't you?" Roxy asked, directing her question at Horn.

"What do you mean?" he answered.

"You're cops—New York City cops at that." She laughed. "It's no secret. I ran a trace on your reservations."

"And pretty scruffy cops at that," Carol said, tipping back her head and nearly emptying her glass in one swallow. She placed two fingers over the lip of the glass in order to hold back the ice and poured the little gin that remained into the fresh drink the waitress had just placed on the table in front of her.

"We're just up here for a little R and R," Winger explained.

Roxy gave a musical, lilting laugh that reminded Horn of someone strumming a harp. "Is that why you're both carrying guns under those jungle jackets you're wearing? Honest to God, you look like a couple of big-game hunters."

"We are," Winger said with a leer. "What kind of animal are you?"

Horn couldn't help noticing a look of embarrassment and disappointment spread across his partner's face when Roxy ignored his attempt to capture her attention. Instead, she looked at Horn, her eyes dancing, and asked, "What are you two really up here for? Everyone knows that Earth cops have no jurisdiction here."

"Maybe they really are here for a vacation," Carol slurred. She took another healthy belt of gin.

"Let me get you another drink, sweetheart," Winger said, waving at the waitress again. "You sound like you could use it."

"Actually we're looking for someone who came up here a week or so ago," Horn said to Roxy, thinking there was no reason to hide that much of their mission. "He's a gambler named Jack Rohde. Heard of him?"

Roxy's musical laugh spilled from her lips once again. "If you're looking for a gambler, good luck. There's only about three or four hundred thousand here at any one time. But—" her voice dropped to a more serious tone "—I might know someone who can help you."

"We'd appreciate all the help we can get," Horn said as he watched the woman fish a piece of ice out of her drink with her long fingers, then slip it between her lips.

"Well, you need to talk to Dartt," Roxy said.

"Who?" Winger asked. Horn was pleased to see that his partner had taken out his notebook and pen.

"Les Dartt," Roxy answered without taking her eyes off Horn's. "He's what you might call a tour guide for the underside of this glitter dome." She waved toward the ceiling in an all-encompassing gesture. "The man's a little odd, but he knows the Strip like the back of his hand." Roxy paused a couple of moments before adding, "He also knows what's going on in the Down Side."

"Down Side?" Horn drew back his head slightly in a gesture that asked for explanation.

"You guys aren't too familiar with the Strip, are you?" Carol jerked her head toward a space somewhere above Horn's left ear.

"I'm going to have to get her home pretty soon," Roxy said, glancing briefly in Carol's direction. "She's a dealer in the casino and she's been under a lot of pressure lately—profit quotas, you know."

Horn didn't know, but he nodded, anyway. "We'd certainly be interested in meeting this Mr. Dartt," he said, wanting to keep Roxy's mind on the thought it had been tracking. "And what's the Down Side?"

"I'll let Les explain it to you," Roxy answered. "He's sitting right over there at the far end of the bar." She nodded toward a lone figure perched on a stool at the last stop on the bamboo-trimmed alcohol freeway. "He's not that cheap, but he has an electrocar and sure as hell knows his way around this god-awful place."

Horn took a long look at Dartt, who was bent over a glass of amber liquid. The man was in his early to mid-forties, and had a scraggly, reddish-colored beard and an untrimmed mustache that made him look like a fur trapper or mineral prospector. His clothes didn't match his physical attributes, however; he was wearing a Spanish-style cowboy hat, a long-sleeved French-cuffed shirt and dark gray parachute pants tucked into highly polished riding boots.

"Should I just go over and introduce myself to him?" Horn asked Roxy.

"I'll take care of it," she said, and stood. Both Horn and Winger got to their feet, too, as the tall redhead grabbed Carol by the arm and pulled the drunken woman up from her chair.

"You need some help with her?" Winger asked, nodding at Carol, who was swaying like a tall reed in a windstorm.

"Thanks," Roxy answered, "but I'm used to this."

"See you around, then," the young cop said.

"More than likely," Roxy answered, but she was staring straight at Horn. He felt as if she were somehow choosing him, and he could only wonder for what.

As Horn watched Roxy stop to talk to Dartt, with Carol hanging shakily on one of her arms, Winger launched into him. "You know," he said, leaning across the table, "every time I pick up on a woman, you cut in." Winger's voice rose in anguished frustration. "And you sure as hell didn't let me down tonight!"

Horn had just taken a swallow of his beer and nearly choked as he broke into laughter. "You're joking, right?" he said, wiping his mouth with a cocktail napkin. Winger's glare told him he wasn't. "What do you mean 'every time'?" Horn asked. "I hate to be the one to break it to you, partner, but Roxy was the one giving *me* the eye."

"You've done the same damn thing before," Winger said.

"Let me say this," Horn stated with mock sincerity. "I can understand why you're so upset, but there's nothing I can do about it. I have that effect on women. Call it one of the hazards of being my partner."

Winger's expression slowly changed from one of diluted anger to a sloppy grin.

"You two been breathing nitrous oxide, or what?"

Horn looked up and saw Les Dartt beside their table. He motioned toward a seat. "Please, Mr. Dartt, sit down." He held out his hand, which Dartt took as he lowered himself into a chair. "I'm Max Horn, and this is my partner, Stu Winger." Winger also shook hands with their new guest.

"Roxy says you two are cops from New York City." Dartt raised his eyebrows into the shadow beneath the brim of his hat.

"Yeah, we are," Horn answered. "And we realize that doesn't carry any particular weight up here. Our mission is to pick up one man and take him back with us. Roxy said you might be able to help us locate him."

"Maybe," Dartt said, leaning back in his chair. He studied Horn and Winger from beneath the leather brim.

"What are you drinking, Mr. Dartt?" Winger asked, beckoning the waitress.

"Whiskey. Bourbon, straight up. And you can call me Les."

Dartt wasn't a big man, but he was husky like a fullback. Crow's-feet fanned out from the corners of pale green eyes that almost looked reptilian. Horn noticed Dartt didn't avoid making eye contact and sensed that they could trust him.

"I'm curious about this electrocar business," Winger said as he handed the waitress another credit wafer. "Roxy was telling us you had one. She made it sound like something out of the ordinary."

"I guess it is, up here," Dartt answered. "You may have noticed the streets aren't exactly jammed with driving machines. If you want to get anywhere on the Strip—and the place isn't exactly small—you gotta take one of the few junk heap taxicabs, a slower-than-shit trolley the Strip's dippy commission runs, or you hire someone like me. I've got one of the early Douglas experimentals they sent up here before the ban. It'll do a 150 klicks in the ditches."

"Ban? Ditches? What the hell are you talking about?" Winger picked up his beer and drank.

Dartt took a sip of the whiskey the waitress had placed in front of him, then held up the glass. "Thanks," he said. "Good shit. Now let me answer your questions." He placed the glass on the table and pulled a thin cigar from a pocket on the sleeve of his shirt, drawing it under his nose before placing it between his lips. "The commission banned the import of all vehicles about a year and a half ago. They said they didn't want the place turning into a goddamn orbiting salvage." Dartt pulled a lighter from the same sleeve pocket and lit the cigar. He blew a smoke ring toward the ceiling before continuing. "The ditches are what we run in on the Down Side. The streets aren't worth shit, so you can't get any speed up, know what I mean?"

"What the hell are the ditches?" Winger asked for the second time. "I mean, it doesn't rain here."

Dartt laughed hoarsely. "The ditches," he answered when his laughter subsided, "are like the plates of this floating crap table." He held his hands out flat and butted them together. "It's like where they joined them together—you know, the seams." Dartt took a drag on his cigar, inhaled deeply, then took a big swallow of whiskey. "I'll tell you what they remind me of. You know those humongous concrete aqueducts that run all over Los Angeles? Well, they're like those. And sometimes they can be a motherfucker to run in."

"You mentioned the Down Side," Horn said. "Roxy mentioned it, too. What is it?"

"It's the belly of this neon snake." Dartt waved his hand in a slow arc, the cigar between his fingers making a little smoke trail as he swung his arm. "If you two are looking for someone on the run, you ain't going to find him on this end of the Strip." He leaned over the table and looked from Horn to Winger, then back to Horn. "You're going to find him on the Down Side. And that's just what it is, *down,* way down." He leaned back in his chair and smiled, exposing wide teeth like a beaver's.

"What's your rate?" Horn asked, intrigued by the man's explanation.

"I charge six hundred a day plus expenses," Dartt answered, his face suddenly expressionless.

"We'll pay four hundred and you cover your own expenses," Horn told him. "We won't be leaving the Strip."

Dartt said nothing for several seconds, then a lopsided grin crept across his face. He ran his hand through his red beard. "All right," he drawled, "but it's got to be in Blue Scrip or that Chinese shit that's tied to gold."

Horn laughed. "Okay," he said, "four-fifty, but in good old American electrocash." He pulled a five-hundred-credit wafer out of one of his jacket pockets and tossed it across the table. "Here's a retainer. We got a deal?"

Dartt picked up the thin piece of plastic and tapped it on the table, turning it over in his hand, hitting each edge as he studied Horn's face. "What's the guy's name?" he finally asked.

"Jack Rohde," Winger put in, surprising Horn. "A big Texan in his fifties, balding, likes to gamble."

"No doubt," Dartt said, suddenly standing. He slipped the wafer into a pant pocket and held out his hand to Horn. "Deal." He grabbed Horn's hand and held it firmly, then slowly moved his eyes down to the black leather glove.

Horn pulled his hand away. "Your call," he said. "What's next?"

"Meet me here tomorrow evening. Early, around six. I'll find Rohde for you." He rolled his eyes toward Winger. "After that you're on your own."

CHAPTER TEN

MARK SHARKEY'S KNEES were shaking beneath the table as he watched the man he'd been tracking for the past ten days turn over a second queen. He silently cursed himself for being so stupid as to get roped into the game, but at the time he'd figured it was a slick way of getting close enough to the man to nail him. Now he was stuck in a situation that was making his mind ache.

He knew if he tried to pull out his Mag and walk the guy out at gunpoint, he'd be dead before he reached the door. The other four players sitting around the green felt table were obviously pals of his target, and they were all packing weapons, mostly large caliber, from what Sharkey could tell by the size of the bulges beneath their shirts and jackets. To make matters worse, he was losing his ass. They'd only been playing for a little more than an hour, and the low-rent bounty hunter had already lost more than half his bankroll, which consisted of every last credit of his operating capital. He feared he would end up dead or broke or both.

"Your pair of kings bets. What're you goin' to do?" Jack Rohde asked, his eyelids drooping lazily and his voice doing a slow Texas roll.

"Oh, I fold," Sharkey answered nervously, turning his face cards over. The look on Rohde's face sent stabs of fear into his chest. He had a sneaking suspicion that the gambler knew who or what he really was and was toying with him like a cat with a broken-winged bird. Sweat ran down his sides, and he imagined the next words Rohde would speak—something to the effect of *the son of a bitch is the guy trying to nail my ass. Let him have it boys!* After which Rohde and the other four would pull out their automatic cannons and turn his body into a heap of lead-poisoned dog food.

Sharkey's heart raced as Rohde shook his head slowly. "Shit, son," the big man drawled. "You got me and everyone else beat. Why the hell are you foldin'?"

"Well, this *is* seven-card stud, right?" Sharkey picked up the glass of straight vodka next to his dwindling stack of credit wafers and downed the contents in one swallow.

"Right," Rohde answered. "You got four more cards comin'."

"That's what I mean," Sharkey said weakly, wishing he had another glass of the Russian potato juice to dump down his spitless throat. "Look at you—" he nodded at Rohde's cards and ran a hand through his short black hair "—a pair of queens and you have four more chances to pick up another. No one else is showing a queen." Sharkey gestured at the cards in front of the other players as a flush of embarrassment spread across his face.

Rohde laughed. He looked at the other players around the table, then returned his attention to Sharkey. "You're kiddin', right? Is this some new way of bluffin'?" He broke into a wheezing laugh, and the others followed his lead, hooting and slapping the table as though they'd just heard the joke of the week.

Sharkey watched Rohde take a long drag on his cigarette and blow the smoke into the thick cloud that hung over the table like poison gas. The son of a bitch is dicking with my mind, he thought. "I guess I'm just out of my league," Sharkey said, raising his hands and shrugging.

"I think you're out of more than just your league," Rohde said, his laughter finally subsiding. "You ought to stick to bingo or checkers. I don't know why you even

bothered gettin' into this game.'' The other men broke into
fresh cackles of laughter, but Rohde's face stayed sober this
time, his eyes boring in on Sharkey's.

"Shit," Sharkey stammered, fighting panic. He squeezed
his arm against his side to reassure himself that the Mag was
still hanging under his sweat-soaked armpit. Another pang
of fear plowed through his guts as he watched Rohde's eyes
follow the involuntary movement. "I . . . I don't even know
how to play bingo, let alone this shit," he said almost urgently, regretting the words as soon as he'd spoken them.
Sweat poured down his unshaven face in tiny rivers, and he
knew the bullet-headed Texan was watching the panic
winding in his eyes like snakes.

"I can see that," Rohde said. "The way you been playin',
I doubt if you know whether your asshole was drilled or
punched."

Once again the other four men erupted in laughter, and
Sharkey glanced around nervously. He licked his lips and
eyed the only door in and out of the dingy back room card
parlor. He shifted his eyes back to Rohde, and felt his heart
drop like a glob of wet mud. The big Texan was now aiming the ugly black barrel of an autoloading dart pistol
straight at his chest. He hadn't seen Rohde make the slightest move for the weapon. It was as though he'd pulled it out
of the deck of cards in front of him—a deadly demonstration of sleight of hand.

"Hey, I wasn't cheating," Sharkey said weakly, his voice
squeaking like an unoiled hinge. He held up his shaking
hands and tried to work up some spit in his mouth. "Honest to God, man—"

"Now that's pretty funny." Rohde nodded at a big Asian-
looking guy to his left and then at Sharkey. The man immediately got up and moved behind Sharkey's chair, then
reached down across his chest and extracted the big Mag-

num. He tossed it into the center of the table on top of a pile of credit wafers.

"You say you ain't much of a gambler, but you sure as hell bet your life with that thing," Rohde said, chuckling. He looked up at the Asian. "See what else he's got in there, Kane."

Kane reached into Sharkey's jacket and fished around, finally pulling out and tossing onto the table a crushed package of cigarettes, a disposable lighter, several small-denomination credit wafers, a plastic card key that had The Sand Dollar—Room 156 stamped on it, and a folded piece of paper stuck beneath the clip of a ballpoint pen.

Sharkey felt the chunk of mud that had replaced his heart finally hit the dirty metal floor that was miles below his seat. He watched Rohde poke through the articles with the barrel of the dart pistol until it came to rest on the piece of paper.

"This looks familiar," the Texan drawled as he pulled the paper from beneath the clip and unfolded it with his free hand.

"Shit, Jack," the Asian said, staring over Sharkey's shoulder. "That looks just like you."

"Not bad for a compu-image," Rohde said, looking up at Sharkey. "Read what this says." He waved the barrel of the pistol from Sharkey's eyes to the standard computer-generated form issued by the FBI.

Sharkey swallowed hard. "Listen, Mr. Rohde, I wasn't out to pick up the reward, no shit."

Rohde laughed again, his shoulders heaving as he wheezed. Finally, he said, "You better read the son of a bitch, boy. This little peashooter is loaded with razor tips, and at this range...well, it'll ventilate your lowlife ass pretty darn proper."

Sharkey forced his eyes down to the twenty-first-century equivalent of the Wanted poster and cleared his throat.

"Wanted, Jack Rohde. Interstate and possibly near-space flight to avoid prosecution. Height, six-ten. Weight two-forty. Age, fifty-three. Heavy gambler, known to fre-quent...goddamn!" He looked up from the paper, his voice cut with fear. "Ain't that enough?"

"Not quite." Rohde tapped the gun barrel on the last line on the page. At some earlier time Sharkey had circled it and written exclamation points next to it.

"Ah, shit!" Sharkey whined. "Why the hell don't you get it over with and shoot me?"

"Read it!" Rohde shouted. Suddenly he leaned forward and slapped the barrel of the pistol across the side of Sharkey's head. The force of the blow sent a shower of sweat into the face of the man sitting on Sharkey's right.

"Godamn it, Jack," the player complained, wiping his face with his shirtsleeve.

"I'm sorry," Rohde said, sounding sincere. He reached into a jacket pocket, pulled out a handkerchief and handed it to the man. "Here, Phil. Honest, I didn't know the bas-tard's head was waterlogged."

Sharkey knew the blow must have hurt, but he didn't seem to feel it. Fear had numbed his body, making his head feel thick, as though he'd been megadosed with painkillers. Everything was numb except his mind. It was racing around inside a death maze, wondering how long the big man was going to play with him before pulling the trigger and blow-ing him away like so much confetti.

"Now read it, punk," Rohde ordered.

Sharkey forced his lips to form the words. "Reward, twenty-five thousand, electrocash, tax free." He looked up at Rohde and realized that the big gambler had just made him announce the price on his head in front of four men who didn't exactly look like pillars of society. Sharkey fig-ured Rohde was either very stupid, very gutsy or better friends with the men than he'd believed. The sleazy bounty hunter felt a new respect for the gambler, in spite of his state of terror.

"Now this puts you out of your league," Rohde said, leaning back in his chair and seeming to relax slightly. "Who the hell are you, anyway?"

"I told you before, Mark . . . Mark Sharkey."

"No, not that, you dipshit." Rohde waved the pistol. "Are you an independent, are you workin' for someone or what? Is there anyone else hangin' around outside or in that bar waitin' to help your lame ass out?"

"No, sir," Sharkey answered. "I work alone."

"Well, that's real funny," Rohde said without laughing. "You know, you don't get this ree-ward unless you get me to the Feds alive. You do understand that, don't you?" he asked, raising his drooping eyelids slightly.

"Yeah, I know it." Sharkey felt his entire body vibrate. He wished like hell he had a drink. On impulse he blurted, "Listen, you're probably going to kill me, so how about a drink?" He paused, then added, "And a smoke." He figured he had nothing to lose.

For a few seconds a blank expression hung on Rohde's face. "Huh?" he said. Then he seemed to snap out of his momentary stupor. "A drink? Shit, why not? Kane, would you mind fillin' the man's glass?" The Asian picked up a bottle of Siberland vodka from a cart to one side of the card table and poured the booze into Sharkey's glass. "Help yourself to the smokes." Rohde nodded toward the pack of Goldtones.

Sharkey picked up the glass and drained half of it in one swallow before reaching for the cigarettes and lighter. He thought about making a grab for the Magnum, but figured he might as well prolong his life till he finished his last smoke and the rest of the liquor that was roiling its heat in the pit of his stomach.

"Now I just want to make sure of a couple of things," Rohde said, speaking softly. "You're not lyin' to me about being alone, are you, boy?"

"No. No, sir," Sharkey answered as he lit one of the bent cigarettes. He inhaled deeply. "I'm not lying to you, Mr. Rohde. I work alone." He held up his hand, the cigarette jammed between two fingers as though he were pledging an oath.

"Well, that's where we got a problem," Rohde said, leaning forward and resting his forearms on the table. "Last night someone tried to take me out in back of a joint about a mile from here. There was more than one . . . of you."

"No, no," Sharkey answered, panic causing his nerves to jump crazily in spite of the soothing effects of the vodka. "That was me, but it wasn't *all* me."

"What? It wasn't all you? That makes about as much sense as the career you've chosen, which is no sense at all. You don't even look like a man-tracker. You look more like some stringhead who just crawled out of a manhole."

Sharkey felt a pang of embarrassment. He knew he didn't exactly fit the bill of a professional bounty hunter. He'd been hitting the booze pretty hard lately and was sort of behind in doing his laundry; his wardrobe was on its second rotation since the last time it had been washed. Then the absurdity of this concern hit him and he almost laughed. Here he was about to have a hole sliced through his body by a .357 cartridge-powered razor dart, and he was worried about his appearance.

"I'm telling you the truth," Sharkey said. "I wasn't trying to take you out last night. Those were just warning shots I fired over your head. I'm smart enough to know that you're no use to me dead."

"Then who were the guys on the roof?" Rohde asked. "They sure as hell weren't thinkin' the way you say you were. They hit the guy I was talkin' to like a duck on the water.''

''You gotta believe me when I tell you I don't know who the hell they were.'' Sharkey held up his hands to emphasize his plea. ''There were two of those fuckers on the top of those buildings. They surprised the shit out of me. Honest to God, one of them even shot at me. Mr. Rohde, I ain't lyin'.'' Sharkey grabbed the glass and downed the rest of the liquor. He *was* lying about one of the men shooting at him, but he figured it might make Rohde feel some sort of empathy for him. He could tell by the big man's expression that he was mulling over whether he was hearing the truth.

''Well, now,'' Rohde said, suddenly hefting his large frame up from the seat, ''maybe you're tellin' me the truth and maybe you ain't. The problem is that it don't change the fact that you been trackin' me. Now don't get me wrong—'' he gestured with the dart pistol as if he really wanted Sharkey to understand his position ''—I don't mind anyone makin' a livin'... as long as it's not at my expense. You see, somebody's out to kill me—not just turn me in to the Feds or whoever.'' He picked up the Wanted poster and waved it at Sharkey, then wadded it up and stuffed it into one of his own pockets.

''Why don't you let me take you in?'' Sharkey asked, faint hope blooming in his mind like a sick flower. ''The cops will protect you. You're supposed to be one of them special witnesses, right? You can cut a deal—''

Sharkey's weak brainstorm died out as Rohde's laughter cut short his suggestion. ''You're some kind of comedian, right? The goddamn cops couldn't protect a fence post. Those sons of bitches got me to within one cat hair of the big sleep. You really make me laugh, son, but I've had about all of this funny shit I can take for one night.'' Rohde shifted his eyes to the Asian. ''Want to help me out, Kane?''

"Sure." Kane grabbed Sharkey by the arm and pulled him to his feet.

Rohde scooped up the stack of credit wafers in front of his seat and stuffed them into one of his pockets. "No offense, boys, but hold the hand here and we'll be back in a minute and finish it." He motioned toward the door.

Sharkey felt the barrel of a weapon jab into the small of his back, and he shuffled toward the door, Rohde leading the way. The three men walked through a small smoke-filled bar toward the back exit of the place. Sharkey glanced around, hoping someone would come to his aid, but for the most part the trio was ignored. Those who did look up from their drinks only glanced at the men casually, as though the sight of someone being led out of the place on the leash of a weapon were an everyday occurrence.

Rohde led them into a trash-cluttered alley lit by the dim glow of a single bulb hanging over the door. They walked several yards into the murky darkness before the Texan raised the pistol in his hand. "This is far enough," he said, turning toward Sharkey.

"Want me to do him?" the Asian asked, moving around to Sharkey's side. The skid row bounty hunter felt his knees turn to soft rubber and wondered how long it would be before he lost control of his bowels.

"Sure," Rohde answered. "You got a silencer for that hog leg?" He nodded at the revolver the Asian was holding in his hand.

"Silencer?" He raised his eyebrows and chuckled. "I don't need no silencer down here." He turned his head and nodded toward the dark hole of the alleyway.

Sharkey jumped back and cringed as Rohde suddenly swung the dart pistol up and around, striking the Asian with its butt just behind the left ear.

"Holy shit," Sharkey gasped. The Asian fell, crumpled like a stepped-on paper sack. Sharkey looked up at Rohde just in time to see the black handle of the weapon zeroing in on the side of his head. Stars exploded in his head, and he fell facefirst onto the dirty, simulated asphalt. He watched the big gambler stride away down the alley as his eyelids fluttered crazily, finally closing. For the first time since he'd gotten to the Strip, Sharkey felt warm and safe as he lost consciousness.

CHAPTER ELEVEN

WHEN HORN WALKED OUT of the hotel the next evening, Winger and Les Dartt were waiting for him. Dartt was gesturing toward a machine parked next to the curb that looked like a cross between an automobile and a bobsled. It was slung low, with wide, flat tires, and skirted by a dirty black plastic cowling that gave it an aerodynamic shape similar to a Frisbee. A clear acrylic plastic bubble covered four worn bucket seats laid out in the conventional arrangement. A sliding sunroof built into the top of the bubble was raised on two hydraulic arms, reminding Horn of an aircraft canopy.

"There you are," Winger said as Horn walked up. "Les was just telling me that machines like his are going for as much as a hundred K up here."

"It's the ban, like I said," Dartt said, reaching out and shaking Horn's hand. Horn noticed he didn't look askance at the hand as he had the night before.

"He also tells me he's got a line on Rohde," Winger added.

"I got a line on where he hangs out," Dartt corrected.

Horn noticed that their tour guide had exchanged his hat and loose-fitting shirt for an outfit appropriate for combat. He was wearing a black T-shirt and an old military-style flak jacket. Wrapped around his waist was a web belt from which hung an ancient-looking double-barreled shotgun pistol, a long-barreled, large-caliber revolver and a set of dull green combat *shaken*—death stars, Horn had heard them called.

"Don't you attract a lot of attention dressed like this?" Horn asked motioning toward the weapons that adorned Dartt's belt.

"Shit." Dartt laughed. "This is the Strip." He waved a hand toward the pulsing neon. "As long as you don't pull anything up here, the Outland Strip Security don't bother you. They don't care if you carry around a goddamn cannon as long as you don't pull the trigger. It's kind of an understanding between the SCs and the Down Siders: don't screw up our business and we won't even ask what goes on down there."

"The SCs?" Winger asked.

"Yeah," Dartt answered, "the security cops. You see them every now and then running around in those old blue General Electric vans, but mostly they're on foot in plainclothes, protecting the whales that swim up here to lose their money."

"What are whales?" Winger queried once again.

"Whales, you know, high rollers. The cats who bet one or two hundred thousand a pop." Dartt snapped his fingers. "And if you want me to stand here and explain this shit to you, I hope you know I'm charging you for it." He grinned. "I get paid the same whether we're here or down there." He nodded in the direction of the Down Side.

"Ah, right," Winger said, crawling into one of the back seats of the machine. "Let's go find Mr. Rohde."

Horn got into the seat next to the driver's as Dartt walked around and stepped in. "Better buckle up, boys," he said, pulling a shoulder harness down from behind the seat. The two cops followed suit as Dartt punched a series of buttons on the curved dashboard and the whining hum of an electric engine sounded from a smooth hump in the center of the four seats. He took a strip of red cloth that was hanging over the spokeless steering wheel and tied it around his head. "Ready to roll?" he asked, flipping a toggle switch on the left side of the dash. The plastic bubble dropped over their heads and locked into place with a loud click. Dartt flipped another switch, and a bluish beam of light stretched out in front of the machine.

"Sure, let's go," Winger said over Dartt's shoulder. "Where exactly is it we're going, anyway?"

"We're going to a place called Dingo's, where a couple of my connections have seen Rohde," Dartt answered as he pulled onto the Strip and accelerated around a trolley jammed with people. "It's in the Down Side, so getting there's going to be half the fun."

Horn was amazed at the smooth, quiet ride the electro-car was giving them. "You mind?" He directed his question to Dartt and pointed at the sliding door over their heads.

Dartt glanced up. "No, go ahead."

Horn slid back the opening, and the cool night air washed the inside of the car. He could detect the faint camphor odor that was sometimes characteristic of a synthetic atmosphere, but couldn't help thinking the drive through the forest of neon was almost pleasant. He was impressed with how clean and slick the Strip was. The sidewalks were crowded with people, most of them well-dressed, who strolled beneath the neon glow as though they were mingling at a huge party.

"What did you mean when you said getting there was half the fun?" Winger asked, leaning forward as far as his shoulder harness would allow.

"Well, it's like this," Dartt answered, turning his head slightly. "We got a bunch of crazies in the Down Side who think it's their job to confront anyone and everyone who goes in and out of the place." He chuckled. "They're like self-proclaimed border guards who want a toll when you pass their little outposts. If you pay it, they usually won't hurt you, unless you got something else they might want, like a woman, weapons or a machine.''

"What about the people who work here and live down there?'' Horn asked. "The ones who do a daily commute?''

"They pretty much leave those folks alone,'' Dartt replied. "They hassle the ones going in to find something a little more thrilling than what's offered up here.''

"How come they don't just let you through?'' Horn asked. "You live down there, don't you?''

"Yeah, that's true,'' Dartt said, smiling. "They been trying to get their claws on old Lola here for the past year.''

"Lola,'' Winger murmured, shaking his head.

Dartt pulled off the Strip and onto a narrow boulevard that headed in the direction of the Down Side. He kicked the machine up to a 120 klicks as the casinos and hotels thinned out, giving way to a sprawling area of warehouses and flat buildings that Horn assumed housed the maintenance and other service facilities required to run the Strip.

"You see those lights way up ahead?'' Dartt asked, pointing up the road as the glow from the Strip behind them faded completely.

"Yeah,'' Horn answered.

"That's one of the six ways—checkpoints, if you will—of getting into the Down Side. Now watch this over here.'' Dartt pointed off to the right of the car, where a huge concrete-colored ditch appeared, running parallel to the road. It was V-shaped with a flat bottom twenty yards or more across. The sides sloped at nearly forty-five-degree angles and were covered with wild graffiti. Trash and puddles of what Horn assumed was water covered the floor of the ditch, which was split lengthwise by a huge seam. "This is the way we'll get in,'' Dartt said, looking over his shoulder at Winger, a wild light shining in his eyes. "We run de ditch, mon!'' he added in an exaggerated Jamaican accent.

"Doesn't seem a whole hell of lot different than the way we get into the Bronx, does it, partner?" Winger reached up and slapped Horn on the shoulder.

"Hold on to the cracks of your asses!" Dartt whooped, and suddenly whipped the machine onto a flat drainage trough that angled straight into the ditch. The car went airborne for a moment as it cleared the lip, then jerked wildly as the wide tires hit, digging into the angled side.

Horn found himself leaning heavily sideways as Dartt drove the machine down the ditch, just inches below the curved lip. He looked at Dartt, who was grinning at him as though waiting for Horn to bestow praise. "Don't you ever drive on the flat part?" Horn asked instead.

"Sure," Dartt answered, the mad grin still plastered across his face as though it had been slapped there. He jerked the wheel to the right and whipped the machine down into the bottom of the ditch. Horn felt a sharp bump as they jumped and straddled the seam, Dartt punching up the speed to one-forty on the digital readout. The machine's big engine was wound up like a jet turbine, and its high-pitched whine reverberating against the walls of the ditch reminded Horn of a mach-plus wind tunnel.

"Look at this," Winger shouted over the engine noise, pointing a thumb behind them. A rooster tail of trash and debris following the electric speeder, kicked up a good forty feet above the top edge of the ditch.

Dartt reached up and shut the sliding door, causing the noise level inside the machine to drop considerably. "You like this?" He appeared to be having the time of his life.

"Sure," Horn answered. "You got any other talents I should know about?"

"Well, I can fly," Dartt said matter-of-factly.

Horn felt a twinge of anxiety, wondering if Dartt was referring to some trick he could do with the electrocar.

"I've got a Class 2 license for near-space." Dartt gave Horn the you-should-be-impressed look again. "If you ever have a job on one of the colonies, let me know. We'd have to rent a shuttle, which ain't cheap, but I can fly rings around anyone you want to put me up against."

"I don't doubt it," Horn said. "Hey, what the hell is that?" He pointed ahead. The rusting hulk of a car was turned sideways, directly in their path. Several men were on the walls of the ditch, watching their car approach the makeshift roadblock.

"Holy shit!" Dartt jumped the seam and ran up the right bank, tires squealing on the simulated concrete surface. "Goddamn!" he yelled as the right front of the car struck one of the men scrambling up the side of the ditch. The blow upended him and flipped him over the bubble like a stick figure.

"Don't worry," Dartt said, straightening out the machine and taking it back down to the floor of the ditch. "I've hit harder things than that."

"What the hell was that?" Winger asked.

"A loony roadblock," Dartt answered, waving his hand. "It just means we're now in the Down Side. Hold on." He jerked the wheel to the left and vectored the car up the side of the ditch and into another drainage trough, slowing as he pulled onto a bleak-looking street that ran between rows of mismatched modular buildings.

Horn's first impression was that they were in a ghost colony, for he saw no one. But as they drove, signs of life began to appear. He saw people hanging around in the shadows of dimly lighted doorways over which hung such signs as The Sex Stop, Dread Poker and Maxie's Money Pit.

"This is mostly a flake area," Dartt said, turning onto a wider street lighted sparsely by a couple of ancient streetlamps. "But Dingo's is in what you might call the upscale end of the Down Side." He laughed.

They drove several more blocks before Dartt pulled up behind an odd, jeeplike vehicle parked in front of a large, windowless modular building that resembled a giant, rusting cake box. He raised the bubble and punched in a code on the dashboard that, he explained to Winger, set his machine's audio alarm. Horn got out and stretched and the others joined him. Above them a backlit sign proclaimed the place to be Dingo's Diamondhead.

"You fellows looking for a party?"

Horn turned toward the voice. A streetwalker with a very short skirt and heavy makeup was doing her best to smile seductively at him. Her body said she was in her thirties, but the lines on her face told him she was in her late forties or early fifties. "Not tonight," Horn said. "We're here on business." He couldn't help but think that the woman fitted in with the surroundings—worn down and fading away.

"Your loss," she said, her smile wiped clean by a tired, bored expression. She turned and sauntered down the sidewalk, looking for another potential customer.

"Yo, Henry," Dartt bellowed as he mounted the sidewalk. A short, stumpy man wearing a cracked and grease-stained leather jacket suddenly appeared out of the shadows between Dingo's and the building next to it.

"Hey, the Dartt Man," Henry replied, skipping up and slapping Dartt's open hand.

"Listen, Henry," Dartt said. He pulled a ten-credit wafer out of his pant pocket and put it into the little man's hand. "These two guys and I are going into Dingo's for a while and I want you to watch my car."

"You got it," Henry said excitedly. He took the credit wafer and ran the edge of it up the part of his slicked-back, jet-black hair. "Ding, ding, ding . . . ten big ones, you're all right, Dartt Man." He smiled, exposing a mother lode of gold teeth.

"You got your gun?"

Henry was doing a little dance and stopped at the question. "You bet your ass," he answered, opening up one side of his jacket.

Horn saw what looked like an old CAR-19 automatic rifle with the stock sawed off sticking out of Henry's waistband. It looked ridiculous, he thought, but he pitied whoever might be on the receiving end of the weapon if the little man ever had to use it.

"That's good." Dartt patted Henry on the shoulder. He motioned for Horn and Winger to follow and led the way into the nightclub.

The interior of Dingo's was in sharp contrast to the outside. Green carpet covered the large floor except for a small area in front of an empty bandstand, which was laid with multicolored tile. Several tables were spread out around a semicircular metallic bar situated against the wall opposite the door. Several rows of electronic slot machines and felt-covered poker tables were spread out on the side of the room farthest from the tiny dance floor. The walls were covered with huge framed photographs of stark landscapes in Australia. A little bit of down under on the Down Side, Horn thought, smiling to himself.

"Over here." Dartt motioned toward a table close to the door.

Horn took a seat, noticing the place wasn't exactly teeming with people. There were perhaps forty people in the club, half or more in the area reserved for gambling.

"What're you drinking?" Dartt asked as a slick-chinned young waiter approached the table.

"Beer," Winger answered, and Horn nodded, indicating he'd have the same.

"Three drafts," Dartt said, placing a credit wafer on the man's tray.

"Not too busy, huh?" Horn said to Dartt, who was lighting one of his pencil-thin cigars.

"It's still early," Dartt answered, scanning the sparse crowd. "You going to recognize the cat if he shows?"

"We've seen his file," Horn answered. "He's a little hard to miss."

The waiter returned and placed frosted mugs of foaming brew in front of the three men. Dartt picked his up and said, "Well, don't worry. If your man doesn't show, someone who can tell me where to find him will." He raised the mug and drank, then wiped away the flecks of foam that hung from his mustache with the back of one hand. "Damn, that's good shit." He belched loudly and stuck the cigar between his teeth.

"Where you from, Les?" Winger asked. He also tilted his mug and took a long pull.

"Oklahoma," Dartt answered. His attention was focused on a couple of rough-looking goons who had just walked into the club. "See those gorillas?" he said softly, nodding toward the two men, who were decked out like a couple of throwback gangsters. "They'd probably be out looking for your Texan, but I doubt they can read." He slapped the table and laughed heartily as the two men disappeared into a hallway over which hung a sign: Rest Rooms.

"At least they can read enough to know where to take a whiz," Winger said, and he and Horn joined in the laughter.

Suddenly Dartt's laugh broke off and his face turned to stone as the front door of the joint opened and a man walked in. Horn sized up the newcomer carefully. He was of medium build and was wearing a black beret, dark glasses and at least four days' beard. He headed straight for the bar. "Bingo!" Dartt whispered.

Horn knew the man wasn't Rohde, but he was obviously someone whom Dartt found interesting. He raised his eyebrows. "One of your connections?"

"Not quite," Dartt answered, "but I know him. His name's Sharkey, and he probably *is* tracking your man. He's pretty much a small-timer, heavy drinker. He comes up here about once a year with a fistfull of Wanted sheets. The little gutter dweller can probably give us a good line on where to pick up Rohde. Wait here," he said, getting to his feet. "I'll bring the bastard over to our table."

Dartt walked to the bar and slipped onto the stool next to Sharkey, putting his arm around the man's shoulders. He said something and Sharkey turned his head toward the two cops, then shook it violently. Dartt moved his hand from Sharkey's shoulder and grabbed the back of his neck. He stood and pulled him backward off the stool, and with his other hand grabbed the drink Sharkey had been swilling. He pushed the reluctant man toward his own table, finally shoving him into the seat next to Winger.

"These guys and I want to talk to you, Mark," Dartt said, sitting down on Sharkey's other side. "And up there at the bar you were a regular inconsiderate asshole." He placed the drink in front of Sharkey. "Here, have a shot of this. It'll calm your nerves."

"What the hell do you guys want?" Sharkey whined. Horn half expected the man to burst into tears at any moment. Sharkey picked up the glass in his shaking hand and raised it to his lips, spilling some of the clear liquid over his grimy fingers as he drank.

"You look like you're in pretty rough shape," Dartt said, placing his arm across the back of Sharkey's chair. "Why don't you take off these damn things so my friends here can see how fucked up you really are." Dartt snatched off Sharkey's dark glasses.

"Hey, you son of a bitch!" Sharkey protested weakly, and made an even weaker grab for Dartt's hand.

Dartt tossed the glasses over his shoulder and slapped the back of the man's head. "What's with this beret shit?" he asked. "I've never seen you wear something this dipshit before. Your goddamn ear's all covered up, for chrissake."

Sharkey immediately reached up and grabbed the corners of the felt beret with both hands.

"Come on," Dartt said as though he were admonishing an unruly child. "Don't be a complete jerk." He grabbed a handful of the beret and ripped it off Sharkey's head and out of his hands in a motion that reminded Horn of someone pulling a tablecloth out from under a set of dishes.

"Jesus!" Dartt drew back from Sharkey. "What the hell happened to your ear?"

Horn could see a baseball-size lump behind the man's ear. The hair on that side of his head was crusted with dried blood.

"I had a little accident. Cut me some fucking slack, will ya?" Sharkey's voice was somewhat calmer after the exposure, but his bloodshot eyes kept shifting back and forth between Horn and Winger. He looked like a feeder rat trapped between two boa constrictors.

"Do you know us?" Horn asked, leaning across the table and nodding toward Winger.

"No. I mean . . . Shit. Is this a trick question, or what?" Sharkey had lapsed back into a whine, his voice filled with hopelessness and desperation.

Horn could see that the man was truly confused. "Here," he said, shoving Sharkey's glass toward his hand, "take a drink, take your time." After the man downed several swallows of booze, Horn continued. "You ever seen either one of us before?"

"Seen you?" Sharkey asked nervously. "You mean, with my own eyes?"

"No, he means with your balls, you dim—"

Horn held up a hand, stopping Winger's interruption. "It doesn't really matter," he said calmly, locking onto Sharkey's eyes. "Let me put it this way, why are you afraid of us?"

"You're the two guys who were on top of the buildings, aren't you?" Sharkey asked, cringing as though he expected something big to hammer him at any second. He still kept shifting his eyes back and forth between Horn and Winger, looking like the referee in a tennis match.

It was an answer Horn hadn't expected. "What do you mean?"

"The guys on the roof. You know, the ones trying to take out the Texan."

"Did they get him?" Winger put in quickly.

"Hell, no," Sharkey answered. "But I think they got some bastard who was with him. And then the big son of a bitch put this grapefruit behind my ear after I tracked him to a dump about a mile from here."

"Where's Rohde now?" Horn asked.

Sharkey raised his eyebrows. "So you know his name?" He seemed to be calming down, and reached for his drink.

"Yeah," Horn said. "And the two guys trying to kill him are called the Sthil brothers. Ever hear of them?"

Sharkey's eyes widened and he nodded slowly. "I've heard of them." he turned toward Dartt. "How about another drink?"

Dartt looked over at Horn, who nodded. "Sure buddy," he said, waving at the waiter.

"You're up against some pretty stiff competition," Winger said. "You could wind up getting stiffed."

"That's real funny," Sharkey said, a hint of dryness in his voice. "But the reward on the son of a bitch keeps going up. It started out at like ten grand and now it's up to twenty-five." He felt around inside his jacket pocket for something. "Shit, the bastard took my goddamn Wanted sheet."

"That large a reward isn't going to do you any good if you're dickin' a piece of dirt in some poor man's boneyard, is it?'' Dartt asked. He took a glass of vodka from the waiter's tray and placed it in front of Dartt, who had retrieved his beret and pulled it back over his head and ear. "After your run-in, if you can call it that, with the Sthil brothers, how come you still went after him?"

"Like I said, the money. And, anyway—" he looked around the table "—it's my job. I like it. I tracked Rohde and I got his pattern down. I know where he's going to be and I'll get him. Watch me."

"Sure you will," Dartt said, patting him on the shoulder. "Living on the edge and all that shit is what you're all about. But let me tell you something." He pointed at Winger, then Horn. "These two guys are going to take Rohde in alive."

Sharkey started to say something, but Dartt held up his hand and gave him a look that shut his half-opened mouth like a door with freshly greased hinges. "Don't worry, dipshit." He blew a puff of his cigar smoke into Sharkey's face. "They're not doing it for the goddamn reward. They're cops."

Sharkey looked at Horn, then swiveled his head toward Winger. "Cops, huh?" He turned back to Dartt. "So don't they get the reward if they bring him in?"

"Yeah, I guess so, but that's where your dismal world is starting to look up." Dartt moved his head closer to Sharkey's and spoke as though he were confiding in the man. "I'm going to tell you something, but I need to ask you a question."

Horn wondered what Dartt had up his sleeve. He was obviously leading Sharkey to some conclusion, but Horn hadn't quite figured out what it was. He had to admit he liked Dartt's style. The man knew his way around the street and seemed interested in doing what he'd been hired to do.

"Go ahead," Sharkey said, picking up his drink, "ask away." He took a big swallow of the liquor.

"You said you had Rohde's pattern down." Dartt leaned even closer to Sharkey, as though he were asking him to reveal the secret of the universe. "Do you know where he's going to be? Like tonight?"

Once again Sharkey opened his mouth to speak, and once again Dartt stopped him, only this time it was in a manner that was almost courteous. "Because," he went on, "if you do, and you turn us on to it, these guys will turn you on to the reward, every damn credit."

Winger started to say something, but Horn held up his hand and shook his head slightly. He liked Dartt's idea and even wished he'd thought of it.

Sharkey stared at the table for several seconds before finally raising his head. He looked at Horn. "No shit?" he said simply.

Horn nodded. "You can go with us when we take him in."

"Well," Sharkey said, turning back to Dartt, "I don't know where he is tonight, but I know where he'll be Friday night."

"Okay," Dartt said, "where's that?"

"The Milky Way," Sharkey said, revealing the secret of the universe.

"That's on the Strip," Dartt said, pulling his head back slightly and raising his eyebrows.

"Yeah," Sharkey confirmed. "It's like he's gotta get out of the Down Side and gamble in some place that's clean."

"How long has it taken you to establish this pattern?" Horn asked, knowing Rohde hadn't been on the Strip more than three or four weeks. It was hardly enough time to establish much of a pattern.

"Long enough," Sharkey said to Horn. The alcohol was beginning to make his eyes shine. "Like I said before, it's my job and I—"

"Yeah, we know," Dartt interrupted. "You like it." He turned toward Horn and shrugged, his face screwed into a question mark.

"Hell," Horn said. "Why not?"

CHAPTER TWELVE

BACK AT THE HOTEL, Horn and Winger arranged with Dartt where and when to meet on Friday. Horn headed up to his room then, leaving the young cop and their Down Side guide to check out the Jungle Room. With a little luck—and if what Sharkey had told them was true—they'd have Rohde in cuffs and on a shuttle in less than forty-eight hours. And after they got back to New York, Horn thought, he would make sure he got tagged to pick up Zamora. His mods glitched as he punched the floor button in the elevator and stared at multiple reflections of himself in the mirror-walled box as it rose.

Two floors into its upward journey the elevator stopped and an elderly couple got on. "Shit," the shrunken, gray-haired man suddenly exclaimed as the doors closed and the elevator started up again. "We wanted to go down to the casino."

The woman, who looked so much like the man she could have been his twin, not his wife, put a hand on his arm. "George, watch your language. There's someone else here." She tilted her head toward Horn.

"Oh! I'm sorry...." George shuffled a little and held up his hands. "My wife doesn't like me cursing in front of anyone but her."

Horn had to laugh. "Don't worry," he said as the elevator came to a stop and the door opened. "This is my floor. It'll go down once I get out."

He walked down the plushly carpeted hall, keyed in the lock combination, shoved the door open and froze. A soft mambo was playing in the suite. He wondered if the maid had left the music channel on, but he sensed otherwise. Someone was in the room.

Horn pulled out the 9 mm and thumbed off the safety as he eased himself into the entryway. He fanned what he could see of the suite with the barrel of the weapon. The red beam of the laser sight found no targets. Moving on cat feet, he swung into the main room and pointed the big automatic straight at Roxy Corner's left breast.

The woman was standing beside the king-size bed, one foot on the edge of the mattress, and was rolling a black silk stocking down one of her shapely legs. She casually turned her head and looked at the red dot of the laser. It appeared to be painted on the fabric of her slinky gold nightgown, which clung like a second skin to the hills and valleys of her supple body.

"You sure know how to keep a woman waiting," Roxy said, raising her eyes slowly.

Horn eased off the trigger and the beam disappeared. Mixed feelings of anticlimax, disbelief and anticipation replaced the adrenaline-pumped edge he'd just been riding. He pushed the safety to the on position, reholstered the weapon and looked around the room. A wine bottle in an ice bucket stood on the table near the foot of the bed. Next to it was a tray spread with hors d'oeuvres.

"You were taking quite a chance coming in here like this," Horn said to the woman, who was now sitting on the edge of the bed. "I came close to ruining what looks to be a very nice item of your wardrobe."

Roxy crossed her legs, and an opening in the gown fell away, revealing nearly half the length of her thighs. "Taking chances is what this place is all about," she said, her eyes following Horn as he walked to the other side of the bed.

"So I'm finding out." Horn lifted the bottle of wine out of the bucket and pretended to read the label, then let it slip back into the ice. He was really stalling for time.

Horn didn't quite know what to make of the woman. She was beautiful. She was sexy. She could probably have been throwing bones with her choice of any of the high rollers on the Strip. What was she doing in his room? The cop side of his brain automatically raised a warning flag. His instinct, however, said she represented no danger other than what he held in his eyes. And that was danger of a different sort.

"What are you doing here?" Horn asked bluntly. Then he realized it was a pretty stupid question. Holding up a hand, he corrected, "Why me, is what I meant to ask. To what do I owe this . . . pleasure?"

Roxy smiled, and it wasn't the smile she used to welcome guests at the registration desk. "I thought maybe you'd ask if I provide this service for all the guests."

Horn cocked an eyebrow. "Do you?"

Roxy laughed and got up from the bed. She walked into the hall, closed the door and slid shut the security bolt. "Open the wine," she said, walking back into the room, "and I'll answer your first question."

Horn peeled the heavy foil from around the neck of the bottle of Chablis in the bucket. After using the corkscrew that hung from one handle of the bucket, he filled two glasses with wine and carried them over to the couch where Roxy had taken a seat.

As she took the glass he offered, Roxy nodded to the space on her left. "Sit here beside me."

"In a minute," Horn answered, placing his wineglass on top of the credenza that housed part of the entertainment center and taking off his jacket. He tossed it into a chair, then removed the shoulder holster and hung it over the chair's back. Stretching his left arm and rotating it slightly, he turned toward Roxy and said, "Please excuse me, but

I've been out cruising with your friend Les. That machine of his isn't exactly built for comfort.''

"You mean Lola?'' Roxy laughed lightly and took a sip of her wine, then placed it on the coffee table.

"Yeah,'' Horn answered, picking up his glass. "He did call it Lola.'' He shook his head and chuckled. "Quite a machine, and Les is quite a driver. I'm glad you recommended him.''

"That 'machine,' if you will,'' Roxy said, "is like his woman.''

Horn laughed heartily and took a healthy swallow of wine. It warmed him inside. He suddenly realized, almost as if he'd just awakened into consciousness of the situation, that he was enjoying talking to Roxy. He felt relaxed, calm. He sensed somehow that Roxy was normalizing his existence. It was a strange and compelling feeling. Horn had experienced it before, most recently with Christina Service, but here, now, with this sultry redhead, he felt something more. It was as though reality had become the fantasy. The woman was real, her laugh was real, and the sweet smell of her perfume danced through Horn's senses like a flame in a matchbox. Whatever it was with her, he wanted to prolong it as long as possible. She made him feel alive again.

"I like Les,'' Horn said. "He's a good head.''

"I'll drink to that.'' Roxy picked up her glass and sipped.

"Okay, why me?'' Horn rested an arm on the entertainment center. "It's the question you said you'd answer.''

"Right, why you,'' Roxy said, flipping her head so that the back of the gray leather couch was covered with her flame-colored hair. "Let's just say that you didn't come up here to drown in this neon wasteland. You're real.''

Once again Horn laughed. "I'm a cop,'' he said as if the statement would render her reasoning meaningless. "I'm about as real as . . . hell, this place.'' He waved as if to indicate the entire Strip.

Roxy got up from the couch, walked around behind to a sliding glass door and pulled it open. "Come here," she said, stepping out onto a tiny balcony that overlooked the Strip.

Horn walked out onto the balcony and found Roxy gazing into the multicolored light show that rolled out into the darkness like an electric, serpentine magic carpet. There was a cool breeze blowing, simulated, from the huge ducts that circulated and purified the Strip's air.

"This place is about as far from reality as you can get," she said, turning toward Horn and leaning back against the chrome railing. "Its plastic, it's cheap, it's a facade for greed."

Horn shrugged and looked at the Strip over the woman's shoulders. "Why don't you leave?" he asked, shifting his eyes to hers.

"I plan to," Roxy answered, winding her arms around Horn's neck. She tilted her head up and kissed him long and deeply, probing with her tongue. "You're real," she said, breaking the kiss. "I can feel you, taste you."

Horn noticed Roxy had run her hand down his right arm and had a curious, intrigued look on her face. "Things aren't always what they appear to be," he said, the old excitement stirring in his loins.

"I guess not," Roxy breathed, moving her hand down to his right hand and squeezing it. "Are you a man, a cop, or what?"

Horn turned sideways and leaned against the rail. He pulled off the glove covering his E-mod and held it up for Roxy to see. The lights from the Strip glinted on the titanium, which had been worn so smooth that it shone like living gunmetal. He opened and closed the hand slowly, and a faint electromechanical whir could be heard somewhere beneath the hard metal skin.

"Fascinating," Roxy said, moving her fingers over his hand, her eyes fixed on it as though it were something magical. "The other one?" Her eyes shifted briefly to Horn's left side, then up to his eyes.

"No," he said, a little surprised that the woman seemed taken with the mod instead of withdrawing in revulsion. "My right knee, though."

"I'll see that soon," Roxy said, moving in front of Horn. She kissed him again and took his right hand and placed it at the small of her back. "Hold me," she whispered into his ear, running the wet tip of her tongue across its lobe. Horn squeezed her gently. "Tighter," she said, pressing her body against his.

Horn could feel her soft breasts against his chest as she molded to him. He willed his mod to pull her closer, and she moaned. Immediately he relaxed his grip, but she ran her hands up behind his head and nipped his ear with her teeth.

"No," she said, her lips on his ear, "tighter. I need you to hold me, Max, hard. Squeeze me harder."

Horn flexed his arm to the point where he feared something in Roxy's body might break. Again he relaxed the mod, and she leaned her head back, eyes closed and red lips parted slightly.

"Don't stop," she said hoarsely, running a hand down his chest. "This is the best thing I've felt since I got to this godforsaken place. You're the first breath of fresh air—" Roxy opened her eyes halfway and focused them on Horn's "—the first touch of reality I've had in more than six months."

Horn smiled. "Reality," he murmured, more to himself than to Roxy. He held up his mod behind her. He could see the Strip reflected in his palm. What was it, he wondered, that separated illusion from reality, the past from the future, life from death?

Roxy drew away at last and took his arm. "Come on. Let's have some more wine." She led him into the suite and made him sit on the edge of the bed before walking to the credenza to retrieve his glass. She refilled it, then held it out to him.

"Thanks," he said.

"Take off your shirt," Roxy said, sitting on the bed next to Horn and crossing her legs.

Horn took a swallow of wine and handed her his glass. "Hold this." She set it on the night table, then turned toward Horn, who was pulling his shirt over his head.

"Max, I didn't know it was so..." Roxy's voice trembled with amazement and shock until it trailed off into silence as she took in Horn's upper torso.

With the exception of Horn's right hand, the rest of the E-mod was a flat combat green, covering his entire arm and shoulder. Where the mod joined his own flesh there was an expanse of crisscrossed white scar tissue. Juxtaposed against the rest of his body, the appendage looked like an alien weapon that had been grafted onto the body of a human.

"So ugly?" Horn finished the sentence for her.

"No," Roxy said, once again sitting next to him. She ran her hand up the length of the mod and over the scars where it became a part of his body. Horn felt her hand move across his back and knew she was tracing the scar that had been left by the razor edge of a now-defunct hit man's knife. "No, not ugly," she repeated, moving her fingers down Horn's spine. "Just different . . . sort of crazy."

"That's the best description I've heard," Horn said, turning toward the woman. He put his arm around her waist and drew her to him.

"Wait," Roxy said, pushing away slightly. She unbuttoned the top part of her gown and let it drop from her shoulders, then raised herself and slipped it away from her body. Turning toward Horn, she pushed him onto his back and ran her hands over his chest and around to the back of his neck. She lowered herself against him and touched her lips to his, then kissed him hard, greedily.

Horn ran his modified hand down her back and stroked her buttocks. Roxy moaned softly, moving her right leg across his thighs and rubbing it against him.

"Yes," she breathed as Horn moved his hand over her buttocks again and squeezed. "Harder," she groaned.

Half astride Horn's right leg, Roxy rubbed herself against him in a slow, rhythmic motion. She moved her face to the side of Horn's head and bit his ear, softly at first, then harder as her movements quickened. To his surprise, she soon appeared to swoon with pleasure, digging her fingernails into his neck. She let out a little scream, and a sinuous trembling coursed through her body. Finally she relaxed against him, looking all pink and spent. Then Horn felt her nipples travel across his sweat-slick chest like a couple of smooth pebbles and watched her face appear above his. She smiled seductively as her hair cascaded around his shoulders, framing his picture of her in fiery red.

"You do strange things to my body," she said. "It's crazy. I've never had something like that happen to me before."

"It's all crazy," Horn said as he felt Roxy loosen the rest of his clothing.

"Just relax," she said, half sitting up. In no time they were all smooth slithering skin.

"This is a treat I wasn't expecting," he whispered as Roxy broke a kiss.

"You've only seen the preview," she said, placing a row of kisses down his neck and along his shoulder. She planted kisses everywhere, pausing to squeeze and caress. Horn was mesmerized, feeling as though he were under the influence of a hallucinogenic drug or had opened his eyes on a strange, hidden dimension. Then a wild joy convulsed him, and Horn felt his mechanical parts jerk madly.

He had a crazy thought as his entire body reacted to the sensation; he saw himself whole, his entire body flesh and blood, none of it machine. He held that thought as the orgasm swept over him like a whitecapped wave, racking his body with a pleasure that unrolled itself into the farthest reaches of his existence. Horn thrashed wildly as Roxy drew him into a consciousness that linked him to some vague time in the past, a time he was almost afraid to recall. As the intense pleasure subsided, a comforting warmth spread through him.

"God, that was . . . the best," Horn said to Roxy, finding words inadequate to describe the experience.

"It's only the beginning," she said with a smile as she swung a long leg across his body and straddled him.

Horn leaned back and closed his eyes as her soft femininity enveloped him. He knew it would be a long night.

CHAPTER THIRTEEN

"THIS IS KIND of an out-of-the-way place for a meeting, isn't it, Erwin?" Zamora asked Erwin Rust, who was settled in the corner of a comfortable overstuffed couch, a nearly empty martini glass in one hand.

"Well, shit," Rust drawled gruffly, "you wouldn't come to Vegas, so I thought it'd be fair to meet halfway."

"Halfway to nowhere," Zamora said, chuckling softly and looking around the executive-level private box seat overlooking the historic Indianapolis Motor Speedway.

"How 'bout a drink?" With some effort Rust pulled himself to the edge of the couch and placed his glass on a brass-edged coffee table.

"Scotch on the rocks," Zamora answered before turning to the three men who had entered with him, one of whom was the ubiquitous Leonard. "Take your cousins and have a look around," he said to Leonard, nodding toward the door. "They've probably never seen this place."

"They've probably never heard of it, either," Rust said, struggling to his feet and walking toward a well-stocked bar in the corner of the plush room.

"You're probably right," Zamora said as the three hulking men went out the door. He turned toward the wall of glass that faced the large oval ring of asphalt. "It's kind of dead around here now that the race is over, isn't it?"

"Sure is," Rust answered as he poured himself a fresh martini from a pitcher he'd taken out of a small refrigerator behind the bar. He took a large swallow, then topped up the glass again. "I really don't know why they still run the damn thing. We haven't made any money off our ownership in the place for years."

Then why do you continue the investment? Zamora wondered silently, taking out his cigarettes. He lit one and turned toward Rust, who was walking toward him holding out a martini. Zamora raised his eyebrows at the color of the liquid in the glass, but made no comment. He watched Rust amble back to the bar, where he hoisted his heavy frame onto one of the stools.

Rust picked up his own glass and raised it in a halfhearted toast. "To your health," he said, and drank.

"To yours," Zamora replied, placing his untouched drink on the table. Rust didn't seem to notice. "Where's Tucker Moore?" the Colombian asked.

"Should be here any minute," Rust answered, fishing the olive out of his glass with two of his fat fingers. He turned toward a telemonitor on the wall next to the bar and punched two digits into the flat keyboard. Moments later a guard appeared on the screen. "This is Erwin Rust, in suite G. Has Mr. Moore arrived yet?"

"Ah, yes, sir," the uniformed man answered. "He and two others were here just a minute ago. We sent them up as you requested."

"Thanks," Rust said, punching off the monitor.

Moments later Tucker Moore opened the smoked-glass door and entered the room alone. As usual he was dressed to a T. Zamora wondered where he'd dropped off his escorts.

"Glad you could make it," Rust bellowed. "We were beginning to think you'd gotten lost."

"How the hell could I get lost in a city like Indianapolis, Erwin?" Moore asked, extending his hand to Zamora, who smiled and shook it.

"You fly into Eagle Creek?" Zamora asked, referring to the airpark near the speedway.

"Yes, as a matter of fact, we did," Moore answered. "Flew the old Double Nickel in. And you?"

"We're probably parked next to each other," Zamora said. "Where's your pilot? Swayne, isn't that his name?"

"Wayne" Moore corrected. "He stayed with the aircraft. There's some sort of minor problem with the avionics, and he's getting it taken care of."

Rust slipped off the stool and moved behind the bar. "Tucker, what kind of whiskey you drinking?"

"Just soda, or mineral water if you've got it," Moore answered, straightening his tie. He flicked an imaginary piece of lint off one sleeve and stood in the middle of the room as though waiting for something to happen.

Zamora chuckled silently to himself. He suspected Rust had taken the lead in calling the meeting and that Moore had received an advance briefing. Whatever was coming down, Zamora figured, was supposed to be coming down on him. But it was going to take more than these two, he thought as Rust staggered across the room with a glass of club soda, to do a number on him. Zamora knew Leonard and the two hard-line triggermen they'd brought up from Bogotá could handle Rust's personal guards and the two men Moore had brought with him. He didn't know if Rust had squirreled away reinforcements in case things got out of hand, but from the looks of Rust, he doubted it. The fool probably thinks he can pull whatever bullshit he's trying to pull with just his wit, the Colombian thought.

Zamora lit a fresh cigarette. He resisted the urge to say something and prompt the discourse that would disclose the real reason for the meeting. Rust had told him the three of them needed to meet face-to-face to discuss some new financial circumstances that could "really fuck things up." The information was supposedly too sensitive, too critical to be discussed or transmitted over any electronic medium. Yeah, right, the Colombian had said to himself skeptically.

"Well, what's up?" Moore asked Rust, taking the glass, whose contents had sloshed over the rim during the transfer and were dripping onto the carpet.

Rust grimaced slightly as though he weren't prepared for Moore to ask him the question. "Shit," he said awkwardly, "you two have a seat and let me get my drink."

Moore started toward the couch but hesitated when he saw Zamora wasn't acting on Rust's direction.

"Have a seat," Rust repeated as he weaved sloppily toward the couch with his martini in hand.

Zamora rolled his head around as if he were working out a crick in his heck. "No, thanks," he answered as Rust flopped down in the couch and squinted in the Colombian's direction as though trying to bring his eyes into focus. "The plane ride, you know, I've been sitting too long."

"Me too," Moore said, walking to an armchair and resting one hip on its back as though for a compromise between the other two men.

"Well, shit," Rust said, the liquor slowing even more his naturally slow speech. "I want to have a goddamn meeting and you two won't even sit down with me."

Zamora figured this would be a good time to screw around with Moore's mind. He turned toward him, blowing a stream of smoke toward the ceiling. "Your friend here is too full of...how shall I say, the dog that's biting him, to pull off whatever drama it is you've planned for me." He pointed straight at Moore. "So why don't you pick up the slack and ad lib?"

"What the hell are you talking about?" Moore said, nervousness creeping into his voice like a hairline crack.

"Yeah, goddamn it," Rust barked, trying to take control. "I called this fucking meeting, and by God I'll run the son of a bitch!"

"No problem," Zamora said softly, holding up one hand and shifting his attention to Rust, whose face had turned red. "So, why don't you let me in on the real purpose of this meeting?"

Rust looked puzzled for a few seconds, staring at his martini glass as if it held the answer to the Colombian's question. Then he raised the glass to his lips and downed what was left of the drink.

"What the hell are you trying to do here," Zamora asked incredulously, "make this some kind of asinine game?" He turned and started toward the door.

"Wait," Rust slurred behind him.

Zamora smiled to himself and turned around. "Make it quick. I don't have time to put up with this kind of crap."

"We want out of the VAC," Rust said, resting his forearms on his knees, staring up at the Colombian, his eyes bleary and bloodshot.

"Now wait a second," Moore said, straightening from his relaxed posture against the chair. He held out his hands in a gesture that indicated he wanted things to slow down. "With all due respect, Erwin, we said we were going to *discuss* dissolving the VAC. It hadn't been decided that we wanted out." He turned toward Zamora, his voice taking on an obsequious tone. "At least not by me."

"I see," Zamora said, scratching a corner of his mouth with one of his little fingers.

"Wimp," Rust said disgustedly. He leaned over and grabbed the martini Zamora had set on the table earlier.

"Well," Zamora said, "let's discuss it. What's the problem?"

"More like problems," Rust said, pulling a pair of reading glasses out of his shirt pocket. He put them on and glared at Moore for a moment before reaching around to the side of the couch and bringing out a brown leather briefcase. He placed it on the coffee table, opened it and pulled out a blue folder.

"At least you came prepared," Zamora said. He walked to one of the bar stools and leaned against it.

Rust ignored the remark and opened the folder. "Since the VAC was formed," he said nervously as though reading a script for the first time, "we've continued to lose money. As a matter of fact—" Rust thumbed through several sheets before reaching the one he wanted "—net combined losses have increased eighteen percent, even though we have experienced a slight increase in cash flow." He took off his glasses and pointed them at Zamora as if to add drama to his indictment. "That increase amazes the hell out of me since you've done none of the shit you said you were going to." Rust's face had flushed once more. He dug into the briefcase again, finally pulling out the briefing paper Zamora had supplied at the meeting where they'd formed the consortium. He tossed it toward the Colombian. "You ain't done shit of what you listed there," he said, breathing heavily.

Zamora was mildly surprised that Rust appeared to be sobering up. He was also irritated by the lame and disorganized manner in which the two men were attempting their undercut. Fools, he thought, they really have no idea who they're dealing with. His little demonstration with Taylor at their initial meeting had been for naught, he decided. They obviously hadn't gotten the message the man's death should have conveyed. Zamora looked at Moore, who avoided his eyes like a bird would avoid a cobra's. He addressed Rust, who had picked up the martini and was draining it. "Very well, your concerns may be valid, but considering the short period of time—"

"I knew you'd use that as an excuse," Rust interrupted. "But that only brings home my point that you don't know shit about the gambling business. Let me tell you something." The heavyset man leaned back on the couch and crossed his legs. His voice no longer shook, and he sounded as though he had the meeting totally under his control. "The profits and losses in this trade are calculated by the minute. We got more fucking accountants on our payroll than we got dealers."

"Maybe you'd be better off if they switched roles," Zamora interjected with a laugh.

Rust's jaw dropped and he stared at the Colombian as though he'd just urinated into his soup. "You bastard," he said, pulling at the knot in his tie, which was already so loose it was hanging near the second button of his shirt. The confident tone he had acquired a minute ago was gone again, and he sounded uncertain. "Let me speak for myself," he said, shooting a quick, disconcerting glance at Moore. "I want out of the VAC now. If you don't want to release my holdings amicably, then I'll turn the matter over to my fucking lawyers, and I'll guarantee I'll at least get a freeze put on your use of my assets."

Zamora resisted the urge to take the man's head off right then and there, and forced his voice to remain calm. "Don't you think this discussion is a little premature, Mr. Rust? After all, any discussions relative to breaking up the VAC must include Taylor's widow."

Rust laughed as though he couldn't believe what he'd just heard. "That dizzy bitch'll do whatever the hell you tell her. Don't give me that crap."

"You've been using a great deal of the VAC's rather limited cash assets," Moore remarked tenatively to Zamora. "And frankly, we haven't seen even a start of what you said you were going to accomplish." He nodded toward the paper on the floor.

Zamora was surprised Moore had gotten up enough courage to speak, let alone say what he did. "Give me six more weeks," he said, lighting a cigarette. "If I haven't turned things around by then, I'll voluntarily cancel my portion of the agreement." Zamora took a long drag on the smoke and held it in his lungs for several seconds before exhaling. Eloy Baca had calculated that once they shut down the Outland Strip it would take at least three weeks to generate the cash reserve he needed to conduct the seamy political business of freeing his uncle. Six weeks would be more than enough time.

"I feel obligated to inquire what you've been using the VAC assets for," Moore said, rubbing his short beard.

"I'll tell you what he's been using them for," Rust said, picking up the glass and raising it to his lips before realizing it was empty. He set it back on the table. "He's been financing his efforts to have his old bean counter tracked down and killed." As soon as he said, this, Rust seemed to regret it; he held up his hands and added hastily, "But don't get me wrong—I mean, you gotta do what you gotta do." His pudgy face took on a pained, almost fearful expression.

Zamora chuckled, enjoying Rust's obvious discomfort. "Six weeks, gentlemen. If it doesn't work out, I'll pay back all I've spent with interest."

Rust scratched his head and appeared to be thinking. But Moore said sternly, "I don't think so."

Both Zamora and Rust looked at Moore with surprise written on their faces. The Colombian had never figured on Moore being the one to dig in his heels. He had expected him to follow Rust's lead.

"May I ask you to explain?" Zamora said, grinding out his cigarette in an ashtray on the bar.

"It's pretty simple," Moore said. "The longer we keep you on the payroll, so to speak, the more money we lose. I had a couple of our top marketing people look at your plan—" once again he nodded at the paper on the floor "—and they informed me that most of the strategies you proposed have been tried before at one time or another, perhaps not in an organized way or on as large a scale as you intend, but nonetheless they've been tried."

"Your point?" Zamora asked, lowering his eyelids. He was imagining a target between Moore's eyes.

"My point is that they won't work," Moore answered. "Yours is a treatment that's been proved not to cure."

"That's a good point," Rust said, "a very good point."

As he watched Rust fall off the fence in Moore's direction, Zamora felt disgust for both men. Several Spanish curses floated through his mind as he stood away from the bar stool.

"You seem somewhat surprised, Ruben," Moore said, the flaky confidence now replaced by the real thing. "After all, you don't have a monopoly on dirty work." He walked over to the couch and took a seat next to Rust before completing his explanation. "There's something about the Outland Strip besides the tax avoidance, the weirdness you can get into and so forth. It's like another world up there. People seem to go there in order to get away from the planet. Right, Erwin?" Moore turned and looked at Rust.

"It seems logical to me," Rust answered. His reply had nothing to do with what Moore had been saying, and Zamora wondered if he was stupid or merely drunk.

"Four weeks then," Zamora said. Inwardly he was seething; he wasn't used to being forced into a corner.

Moore looked at Rust, who nodded as if to say he accepted Moore's acting as his spokesman. Moore turned back to Zamora. "Zero weeks. We're sorry," he said, shrugging. A thin smile had crept across his face, causing his eyes to sparkle.

"I'm sorry you had to come to such a—" Zamora, who had stayed on his feet throughout the whole discussion, unbuttoned his suit coat and gestured as though searching for the correct word. "Such a moronic decision," he finally said.

Rust and Moore glanced at each other, then returned their gazes to the Colombian. "What the hell is that supposed to mean?" Rust said gruffly.

Zamora reached inside his coat and withdrew a slim .32-caliber automatic with a sleek gray silencer screwed into its barrel like a death flag. "It means we're going to have to alter your decision, at least temporarily." Zamora watched both men stare at the end of his weapon as he aimed it somewhere between them, at head level.

"You're kidding, right?" Moore looked up at Zamora, the sparkle in his eyes replaced by fear.

Zamora smiled. "My father once told me never to pull out a gun unless I intended to use it. This isn't a prop, and I sure as hell haven't been playing any game. I thought I was being reasonable, but apparently you two had already decided to cut me out, even prior to this useless meeting. Isn't that correct, Erwin?"

Rust flinched as Zamora aimed the weapon at his forehead. "T-take it easy, Ruben," he stammered, holding up his hands. Little beads of sweat had formed across his upper lip, which was quivering noticeably.

"Maybe we can reconsider," Moore said, the panic in his voice making it sound choppy.

"That's funny," Zamora said, keeping the gun aimed at Rust. "We had an agreement, and as far as I'm concerned, both of you tried to screw me out of it."

"But—" was all Moore got out of his mouth before the Colombian cut him off.

"Shut up, goddamn it," Zamora barked. He turned his head slightly toward Moore without taking his eyes off Rust. "Don't make me tell you twice." He eased up a little and lowered his aim in the direction of Rust's heaving chest.

"Please, don't kill us," Rust whined.

"I've got one problem," Zamora said, appearing to be speaking more to himself than to either of the men in front of him. "If I kill both of you, then your respective operations could be suspended temporarily, at least insofar as they contribute to the VAC."

"That's right," Moore said, tiny streams of sweat running down from his temples into his beard.

Zamora ignored him. "However," he said, moving his stare somewhere over the two men's heads, "I can't very well let you both off the hook. You've already proved what your minds can do when fused. Let me put it this way," he said, trying to appear as though he'd just come up with a solution for the problem. "You have to know, Erwin, that Vegas is in much better shape than Atlantic City." Zamora locked onto Rust's eyes, which were bouncing back and forth between him and the door. "Oh, don't worry about your boys out there. Leonard and his two friends will make sure we aren't disturbed. But as I was saying, Atlantic City is really pretty much of a rattrap. The office Mr. Moore gave me in the Taj Mahal is, well, drab. The whole goddamn place is depressing. What is it, Tucker?" Zamora turned toward Moore. "Isn't this the second or third time they rebuilt and opened the dump? Don't answer." He held up the automatic in a gesture that said halt. "They should have left the place buried the first time." He turned back to Rust, aiming the weapon at his shirt pocket. "The point is, Atlantic City is more of a sinkhole than, well, than you two think *I* am."

"I'm not quite following you," Rust croaked, his brow covered with a sheen of perspiration.

"You're not? Well, let's see, can you understand this?" He immediately swung the automatic toward Moore and pulled the trigger.

A muffled pop filled the room as though a pressure valve somewhere had suddenly been released. Moore's head flinched backward, and a small hole appeared directly between his eyes, which rolled up and crossed as his head tilted crazily to one side. Blood started running from his nose and ears as he slumped against Rust, who immediately started crawling toward the end of the couch.

"Son of a bitch!" Rust cried as he tried to push away Moore's body and draw back a blood-covered hand. "Yi, yi, yi," he squealed as he crawled away from Moore, whose eyelids fluttered wildly for several seconds before staying wide open to reveal the man's death stare. Rust pulled himself over the arm of the sofa, smearing it with blood, and tumbled to the floor.

Zamora stepped around the table and pointed the silenced barrel of the .32 at Rust, who was leaning on one elbow trying to wipe the blood off his hand onto the carpet. "As I was saying," he said with a smile. "Atlantic City can freeze for all I'm concerned, but I need Las Vegas. Understand?"

Rust's chest was pumping and his skin had lost all of its color. He managed to stutter. "Sure, sure. Please, God, don't shoot me."

"I'm not going to shoot you," Zamora said, noticing the distaste that he always felt when he watched someone beg. He crouched on one knee and leaned toward Rust, who was unconsciously wiping his hand on the front of his shirt. "But let me tell you this. If you try to pull another foolish stunt like you did here today, I'll have everyone in your family killed."

Rust swallowed hard and nodded slowly, his entire body trembling. He tried to say something, but nothing came from his throat except a pitiful squeak.

"There, that's okay," Zamora said, patting Rust on the shoulder. "Excuse me for a moment." He went to the door, opened it and beckoned to Leonard, who was waiting outside.

"Listen, *compadre,*" Zamora said, putting an arm around Leonard and ushering him into the room. "I want you to have your cousins take care of the two this one brought with him." He pointed the pistol at Moore's body, which was leaking blood down the front of the couch in tiny crimson rivers. "You need to take all three of them out of here in the trunk of whatever they drove here in. They didn't come in a cab, did they?"

"No," Leonard answered. He appeared undisturbed by the sight of the bleeding corpse. "They rented a limo. The two guys you mentioned are hanging around it down by the grandstands."

"Anyone else?" Just to be on the safe side, Zamora kept the weapon trained on Rust, who was now on his knees with his head in his hands.

"No. Just the guys at the main guard gate. One of them patrols every hour or so, but that's it."

"Good," Zamora said. "Have your cousins take care of the two downstairs, then come up and get him." He nodded at Moore's body. "Tell them to drive all three back to the airpark in the limo trunk and wait next to our plane. I'll tell them what to do when we get there."

"What are you going to do?" Rust asked, getting to his feet unsteadily. His face was drawn and weary.

"First, let me remind you that you're an accessory, just as you were with Taylor. Remember that." Zamora pointed the barrel of the .32 at Rust's bulbous nose as though it were an extension of his index finger. "If you try to pull some stupid play like going to the cops, I'm sure they'll want to know why you didn't come clean when Taylor was killed."

"Don't worry," Rust said, holding up his hands in surrender. "All I want to do is get back to Vegas and mind my own business."

"To answer your question, then," Zamora said, smiling at Rust, "we'll pick up Mr. Wayne, the pilot, at the airport and escort the lot of them and their airplane to a little strip this side of Wichita. Then—'' he spoke as though it were a routine procedure ''—we simply blow up their airplane with them in it.''

''On the ground?'' Rust asked.

Zamora laughed. He patted Leonard on the shoulder and said something to him in Spanish before turning to Rust. ''Of course, on the ground. We'll have to get Leonard, here, off the plane first. You see, he'll be riding...how do you say, shotgun.''

''No doubt,'' Rust said, his voice hollow.

Zamora had decided that Rust was no longer apt to do something reckless. He excused himself and left the man alone, while he accompanied Leonard out of the room. ''Listen, *compadre*,'' Zamora said as soon as they were in the hallway. ''As soon as you get in the car, call Eloy. Tell him to get in touch with Sam Tripp. I want that son of a bitch waiting for us at La Guardia—no, make that Teterboro. I know he hasn't had the full week yet to work on it, but have Eloy tell the bastard we urgently need a solution to our problem *now*.''

CHAPTER FOURTEEN

KRINGA WOKE UP to the chain-saw sound of Luther's snoring and a whiskey hangover that was pounding in his head like an out-of-balance flywheel. He propped himself on his elbows and glanced across the fleabag room at his brother. Luther was stretched out on his back, his arms and legs hanging limply over the edges of the narrow cot as though they were broken. His hairy belly rose and fell in time with his snores. Turning his head, Kringa looked on the nightstand next to the bed and, to his disappointment, saw only his cigarettes and an ashtray overflowing with butts.

"Where the hell's that bottle?" he asked himself, leaning over the edge of his cot, fishing on the floor with his hand. "Nope," he said, feeling the stock of his shotgun. "Ah," he sighed, lifting a bottle from the floor. "Goddamn!" he grunted, holding the nearly empty container of Wild River whiskey up to the dim light filtering into the gloom through a cracked transom over the door. "Shit." Less than two inches of amber liquid remained in the bottle, and Kringa knew it wasn't enough to extinguish the smoldering coals behind his eyes.

He groped around in the drawer of the nightstand and finally found a brown pill bottle. Popping open the lid, he poured three large red capsules into his hand. "Damn," he breathed when he saw there were no more. He held the bottle up to the light to make sure there weren't any stuck inside and noticed an orange label that read Do Not Take with Alcohol. "Whatever you say," Kringa said with a chuckle.

He tossed the pill bottle onto the floor and popped the three capsules, then unscrewed the cap on the whiskey, tilted the bottle and drained it in a single gulp.

With a loud groan he swung his legs off the cot and onto the floor, sliding the autoloader out of the way with his foot. He grabbed the package of cigarettes and shook one into his mouth. "Lighter." He felt around on the table and came up empty-handed, then tried his pant pockets, where he finally found a disposable. "Time for breakfast," he said, lighting the cigarette. He immediately lapsed into a coughing fit, which lasted a minute or two.

"Keep it down, goddamn it," Luther growled from across the room. He had rolled over onto his side and covered his ear with a thin, flat pillow.

"Blow it out your ass," Kringa muttered. He lurched to his feet, staggered over to a sink next to the door and spit into it. He placed his cigarette on a little shelf attached to a cracked and filthy mirror over the sink and turned on the single-handled faucet. Taking a deep breath, he stuck his burr head under the stream of water and held it there for a good thirty seconds. "That's better," he said, turning off the water. He did feel better. The pills and the booze were beginning to kick in.

Kringa wiped his face on a rag that hung next to the mirror and picked up his cigarette. He walked back to the open drawer of the nightstand, picked out his wraparound shades and donned them. "Time to get up, Loo-Thor," he said, taking three steps and flipping a switch next to the door. The room was immediately bathed in a bright yellow light that glared down from a single fixture covered in wire mesh and hanging from the center of the ceiling. Luther responded by pulling the dirty pillow over his face.

"Hey, shit," Kringa said as he noticed a flashing red light next to the ancient telemonitor built into the wall near Luther's cot. "Hey, Luther! Goddamn it, wake up. We got a fucking call, for chrissake." He picked up the empty bottle from his cot and tossed it at his brother.

The glass projectile struck Luther on the elbow, and he howled in pain. "I ought to kick your ass," he snarled, tossing off the pillow and rolling to a sitting position. He rubbed his elbow and glared at Kringa through squinting eyes. "What the hell's your problem, dipshit?" he barked. "You looking to shorten your worthless life or what?"

"A call, Luther." Kringa pointed toward the signal light with his thumb. "Get your shit together, will ya?"

"Who the hell's calling us?" Luther stared at the flashing light as if fascinated by it.

"Who the hell do you think?" Kringa spit and walked toward the telemonitor. "You're the one who was stupid enough to tell Zamora where we was staying."

"Shit," Luther said. He stood and hitched up his pants. "Maybe we shouldn't answer it."

"Maybe we shouldn't go back to Earth," Kringa said, punching the answer button on the ancient control panel.

The words Stand By lit up the center of the old CRT, which finally came fully to life with a warning that the registered occupant of the room was responsible for all charges made on the telemonitor during the course of his or her stay. Less than twenty seconds later Ruben Zamora's image flickered onto the screen like a bad dream.

"Damn," Luther whispered under his breath as he pulled a dirty sweatshirt over his head.

"Mr. Z," Kringa said in greeting, trying to sound upbeat.

"Take those damn glasses off," Zamora told him. A hum filtered through the tiny speaker with his voice.

Kringa immediately whipped off the glasses and held them behind his back. He also dropped his cigarette onto the floor and ground it out with the toe of his boot. "Yes, sir," he said, coming to attention. "What can you do for us—I mean, what can we do for you, Mr. Zamora?'' Kringa cringed, wishing he could kick himself in the ass.

"You can tell me you've taken care of Mr. Rohde," Zamora answered.

Kringa felt a lump rise in his throat and glanced over at Luther, who looked pale and even more unkempt than usual. The hair on one side of his head was matted and sticking up like a bunch of dead weeds, making him look more like a skid row derelict than a hired killer.

When it was obvious that Luther wasn't going to help him out by responding to the Colombian, Kringa cleared his throat and said, "We haven't got him yet, but—"

"But what?" Zamora interrupted, his voice calm and measured. "If you haven't got him yet, you're failing, right?"

"Now wait a minute," Kringa said, holding out his hands. "It took us a little while to find the son of a bitch. This place ain't that small, you know." He shuffled nervously and wondered why the hell Luther wasn't taking up the slack.

Zamora lit a cigarette. "If you know where he is, why haven't you taken him out?"

"Well, we don't know where he is at this very minute," Kringa answered, "but we know where he's gonna be come Friday night."

Kringa watched Zamora reach down to a console built into the armrest of his seat and press a button. The speaker went dead and Zamora turned his head. He appeared to be talking to someone out of range of the video senser. After several seconds he released the button and turned back to the screen. "Where were we?" he asked.

"Are you on an airplane?" Luther asked, staring at the telemonitor as though he were mesmerized.

"Shut up!" Kringa barked before answering the Colombian's question. "I was just telling you that we're going to nail him Friday. He's a slick son of a bitch, and to tell you the truth, we ran into a little trouble the other night when we did have a chance to do him.''

"Go on," Zamora said, taking off his glasses and rubbing his eyes.

"Some two-bit bounty hunter got in our way. Apparently the Feds put some measly price on Rohde's head. Now every punk who reads *Man-Tracker* magazine is out to bring the bastard in.'' Kringa was feeling a little more relaxed and decided to light up another smoke. Then he remembered the package was still on the nightstand. He sure as hell didn't want to chance pissing off the Colombian by interrupting their conversation to go grab a smoke. He figured he'd just have to suffer as he watched Zamora light a fresh cigarette from the butt of his last one.

"This Friday night thing," Zamora asked, "how certain are you of pulling it off?''

Kringa looked over at Luther, who was staring at the screen with a glazed look so that he appeared to be almost comatose. What a time for Numb Nuts to go to sleep, Kringa thought, turning back toward the telemonitor.

"Well, Mr. Z," he said, cracking his knuckles loudly, "I'd give it anywhere between a ninety and a ninety-five percent chance of coming off. Me and Luther made contact with a weapons broker yesterday, and we're going down there today to pick up some extra firepower. That should up it to around ninety-eight.'' Kringa had no idea what the probability was of taking out Rohde, but he figured something in the nineties would keep the Colombian calmed down, at least until Friday night.

"That sounds pretty good," Zamora said. "Now listen, there's something, or I should say someone else I want checked out while you're up there.''

"Oh?" Kringa was curious.

"He's a New York City cop. He's been sent up there to bring Rohde back...alive, naturally. He's probably got his partner with him. I want you to kill him." The Colombian leaned toward the screen. "Take Rohde *and* the cop out and I'll triple your fee."

"This cop," Kringa said, his mind registering the sound of electrocash. "Do you know his name?"

Zamora turned his head and spoke in Spanish to someone off the screen. There was a quick exchange of mumbled words before he turned back to Kringa. "His name is Max Horn," Zamora said. "He's a detective from Manhattan. I don't know his partner's name, but take them both out if you can."

"What does he look like?" Kringa asked, "Have you got a hologram or reflective image or anything?"

"No," the Colombian said flatly. "Not even a photograph. Use your street IQ. He's after the same man, so you should be able to figure out who he is, right?"

"Right." Kringa nodded and bit his tongue to keep quiet. What he wanted to tell Zamora was that the Strip was a little larger than a poker chip and that tracking someone in his god-awful slum called the Down Side was like trying to find a rat turd in a hundred-pound sack of black beans.

"But remember," Zamora said, leaning toward the screen, "Rohde is your priority. I want you to call me as soon as you have his ring."

"Ring?" Kringa was puzzled, then he remembered. "Oh, yeah," he said quickly before Zamora had a chance to remind him in his subtle way, "the ring on Rohde's finger. I'll get it for you, Mr. Z. Don't worry about it."

"I won't, but you should," Zamora said, placing his hand on the console. "I don't think I can emphasize enough the importance of what I've hired you to do." The Colombian's face filled the screen. "Your whole purpose in life is to keep Rohde from leaving the Outland Strip alive. You got that?''

"And the cop," Kringa responded, nodding his head soberly.

"And the cop." Zamora leaned back and the screen instantly blanked out.

"Good riddance," Kringa said, giving the finger to the black hole that had swallowed Zamora's image. "And to you, too." He turned toward Luther, who still stood, slack-jawed, staring at the telemonitor. "I ought to—" Kringa raised his open hand, then suddenly remembered he was dying for a cigarette. "Your ass is saved by nicotine," he murmured to the unhearing Luther. He dropped his hand and walked quickly to the nightstand, where he lit a nonfilter Chessman and inhaled deeply.

Kringa felt pretty good now, he realized. The pills and the booze seemed to have cleared his thoughts. He was pleased with the way he'd handled himself in front of the Colombian. He doubted if Luther could have gotten through the conversation without stepping on the man's crank at least seven or eight times. Shoving the pack of smokes into his pocket, he walked back to where his brother was standing, still staring at the telemonitor screen.

"Time to wake up the dog," Kringa said, the cigarette dangling from his lips. He walked behind Luther and placed a doubled-up fist at the base of his skull. "All right," he said, drawing his other arm back, its hand open, "come on, Socrates or Plato or whoever the hell you are, wake the fuck up!" He swung hard and slammed his palm into the end of his fist like a hammer hitting a nail. Luther's head jerked forward, his hair flying out, then springing back like strands of wire.

"What the hell," Luther mumbled as he took a couple of steps forward, his body reacting to the impact to his head

He rubbed the back of his neck and rolled his eyes toward Kringa. "How long was I gone?"

"Too goddamn long. I had to talk to the fucking Mr. Z on my own while you had another out-of-body experience."

"Shit." Luther bent to pull a pack of cigarettes from one of his boots, which stood next to the cot. "What did he want?"

"He wants us to kill a cop who's up here chasing Rohde."

Luther looked confused. "Does he still want us to kill Rohde?"

"Of course," Kringa said, his shoulders slumping. "Did you leave part of your brain out there in...wherever the hell it is you go?" He waved a hand as if to indicate the universe.

"Drop dead," Luther said. He sat on the edge of the cot and pulled on his boots. "How much extra is he going to pay us to do the cop, too?"

For a moment Kringa considered telling Luther a sum less than what the Colombian had offered. But he had a feeling that Luther would know he was lying. He'd also seen what his brother did to others who screwed him over, and he didn't want to chance that. Kringa had heard someone compare his brother in a rage to a crazed rhino on string. And, after all, he figured, the key word was *brother*. If you couldn't trust your brother, who the hell could you trust?

"Three times the fee for Rohde alone," Kringa answered.

"Hot shit." Luther stood and ran his hands through his hair in a useless attempt to flatten it into some kind of order. "You ready to go find that cat with the heat?"

"Yeah," Kringa said. "You ready?"

"Not quite." Luther bent over, pulled a large-caliber handgun from beneath his cot and stuck it in the waistband of his pants. He fished around under the pillow on the cot and retrieved a silver-handled stiletto, which he slipped into one of his boots. "Ready," he said, throwing a loose canvas jacket over his broad shoulders.

The two hired assassins walked out of their low-rent unit and headed down Gravity Street, which cut through the roughest, seediest section of the Down Side. While the Down Side was roughly equivalent to the lawless shadow world of the worst sections of the Bronx, Gravity Street was like the gutter of the place—an open sore zigzagging through a maze of rusting, faded buildings that housed, dangerous people who played out their lives in a world of grim anarchy.

Although it was early in the morning, Kringa and Luther were propositioned three times by worn-out, emaciated hookers and offered a wide selection of drugs by no less than four fixers who hung around in the shadows, their eyes darting up and down the desolate street as though they were hopped-up lab rats. All of this occurred as the brothers walked nine blocks toward an address that Luther had written on his left forearm.

"What the hell is the guy's name?" Kringa asked as he followed his brother into a narrow street strewn with garbage. It smelled like sour milk, and Kringa lit a cigarette in an attempt to combat the stench.

"His name's Barker," Luther answered, pushing up his sleeve and squinting at his arm. "Shit," he muttered to himself, "I'm sure it's around here somewhere." He peered around at the doors and darkened entryways that were strung out randomly.

"What number is it?" Kringa asked, blowing smoke through his nose.

"It ain't a number. It's a symbol," Luther answered, checking his arm again.

"A symbol of what?" Kringa asked, observing that indeed the doors were marked with symbols. There were different patterns of stars, silhouettes of animals and shapes that Kringa figured could have some meaning to a devil worshiper, but he didn't understand them and didn't want to.

"It's a goddamn snake coiled up like it's going to strike," Luther answered. "I think it's a cobra." He looked at Kringa. "You were there last night when they told us. Can't *you* remember?"

"I couldn't even remember the bastard's name." Kringa turned his head and spit. "How the hell do you expect me to remember that he's got a goddamn snake for a house number? Shit! I was drunk."

"There it is," Luther said triumphantly, pointing to a large metal door a little farther down the street. He checked his arm again. "It's a cobra."

"It ain't like no cobra I've seen," Kringa said as the two men walked toward the door. "It looks like somebody on blue line painted it."

The upper two-thirds of the metal plate was covered with the fanned hood of the snake, which wound down to a coiled, scaly tube near the bottom. The painting was stained and fading but still distinct enough to give Kringa the creeps. Where the cobra's eyes, nostrils, mouth and fangs should have been, the geometric pattern of scales blended into a reptilian image of a human face, with eyes like a snake's, a human nose and an open mouth from which curved two long fangs dripping with what was presumably venom.

"You know, I really miss the hell out of New York," Kringa said, staring at the demonic face. He shifted his gaze above the door and noticed a surveillance cam inset into the metal facing, its smooth eye following them as they made their approach. The door, an otherwise smooth piece of metal, contained a single slit in the upper left corner, which Kringa figured was the locking mechanism.

"You'd miss the inside of a garbage truck once you got used to it." Luther laughed loudly, the gravely sound echoing down the street.

As Luther raised his hand to knock, a series of electronic bolts clicked down the face of the door. Seconds later it glided open about a foot and a booming voice rolled out from inside. "The fabulous Sthil brothers . . . please come in."

Kringa followed Luther into a large room that looked like the staging area for a mammoth rummage sale. Junk, boxes and baskets of old clothes, books and household items were scattered everywhere. A path had been cleared through the mess. It led to a closed door at the opposite end of the room, in front of which stood a huge Buddha-like figure holding an electronic device in his hand. An old CRT monitor sat on a table next to him, displaying a view of the street in front of the building.

"That's Barker," Luther said, stepping over a plastic crate filled with empty bottles. "Remember him now?"

"Yeah, vaguely," Kringa answered. He heard the front door close and lock behind him as he followed Luther across the room.

Barker was tall, almost six feet, but he was also fat. Kringa figured he weighed close to three hundred pounds. His long black hair was pulled back in a ponytail, twisted and tied into a knot. Streaks of gray ran through his untrimmed beard and his eyes looked like two polished orbs of onyx. A tent-size sweatshirt with Die Happy stenciled across the front hung from Barker's bulk like a bizarre monk's robe. Actually, Kringa now remembered the man more than vaguely. How do you forget someone the size of a goddamn mountain? he asked himself.

"Barker," Luther said simply, shaking hands with the man.

Kringa reached around his brother and shook Barker's hand, nodding his greeting.

"This way, gentlemen," Barker said, turning. He pressed a button on the small device in his hand and the door behind him swung open, revealing a long, well-lighted room. A garage-type roll-up door was set into the far wall, in front of which a vehicle covered with a brown tarp was parked. A workbench ran along one wall. It was littered with all types of tools, electronic and welding equipment, boxes of junk, vises and spools of wire. Along the opposite wall, boxes, drums and canisters—many with red stickers declaring Explosives—Danger—were stacked to the ceiling. A wide table about twenty feet long ran down the center of the room. It was covered with several oil-stained, ratty blankets under which the lumpy contours of oddly shaped objects could be seen. Kringa smelled Cosmoline and knew the table held what they'd come to see.

"Can I smoke in here?" Luther asked as the door clicked shut behind the three men.

"Sure," Barker growled. He was puffing as though the twelve-step walk from the other room had tired him out.

Kringa reached over and grabbed one of Luther's cigarettes as soon as he'd shaken them out of the pack. "Thanks," he said as Luther sneered.

"I want to point out one thing to you boys before we get down to business," Barker said, shuffling his weight down one side of the table.

"What's that?" Luther asked, moving down the opposite side, with Kringa behind him. He carried his smoldering cigarette between two nicotine-stained fingers.

"It's not that I don't trust you." The big man smiled, his eyes nearly disappearing as his cheeks moved up. "But in my business you need to take certain precautions."

"What're you getting at?" Luther asked, looking around the room.

"Not there," Barker answered. "Up there." He pointed toward the corners of the ceiling, from which hung weapons resembling shotguns, mounted on swivel mechanisms. A glass-faced sensor device hung beneath each weapon, all of which, Kringa noticed, were pointed at him and his brother.

"Nice," Luther said. He moved several steps toward the end of the table.

Kringa watched two of the weapons follow his brother's movements, while the other two remained trained on him. "Why the hell don't they follow you?" he asked, looking across the table at Barker.

"I control the little beggars," Barker answered, chuckling. He held up the small black box in his left hand. "I like to think of them as my Dobermans. But don't be offended," he said quickly, his voice sounding sincere. "It's just that, well, Gravity Street isn't exactly a place you'd want to take your mother to, and in my line of work, security's the byword."

"No need to explain," Luther assured him. "Let's get on with business."

"What type of shit are you looking for?" Barker asked, eyeing first Luther, then Kringa.

"We need to kill somebody who'll most likely be in a crowd," Kringa answered.

Barker raised his busy eyebrows. "How about explosives?" He looked as though he were discussing politics or philosophy instead of the most appropriate device for a murder.

"I don't think so," Luther chimed in. "We don't know the layout, and besides, we'll probably be in the same room with the target. It could be relatively close-range."

"What we need is something that scatters like a shotgun," Kringa said, glancing up nervously at one of the Dobermans, "but hits harder."

"Yeah," Luther agreed enthusiastically. "It's gotta have a hell of a kick. One of the things we were thinking about was if you had some M-79 rounds—"

"What?" Barker interrupted.

"M-79 rounds," Luther repeated. "You know, 40 mm grenades. They come in all—"

"No, no, no," Barker interrupted again, and laughed loudly. "The last time I saw an M-79 was in a goddamn museum. I don't carry crap like that."

Luther turned his head to look at Kringa, who could tell that Barker's comments were getting on his brother's nerves. He hoped Luther wouldn't forget about the four death-dealing fingers pointing in their direction.

"Well, what do you recommend?" Luther asked. His voice sounded like coarse sandpaper being rubbed across rusted metal.

"This, down here." Barker moved toward the end of the table near the vehicle, motioning for the two men to follow. He flipped back one of the blankets to expose an ugly tri-barreled weapon that looked like a marriage of three 10-gauge Bush Cutter shotguns.

"Shit! What is it?" Luther asked, drawing back his head.

"I bought this beauty from a guy in Detroit," Barker answered, hefting the short, heavy-looking weapon. "He had it made for a little job he did somewhere in Africa. Said it would cut a tree in half."

"May I?" Kringa asked, holding out his hands.

"Sure." Barker handed the weapon across the table. "It ain't loaded."

"Of course not," Kringa said. He eyeballed the gun, whose breech mechanism bore a faint resemblance to the short version of a Composite Autoloader. Its black carbon fiber stock was molded into the polished, multichambered firing mechanism under which hung three rectangularly shaped clips that fanned out slightly from one another. The black barrels of the weapon were arranged in a triangular manner—two on bottom, one on top.

"Here's what goes inside it," Barker said, pulling an ammo case from beneath the table and setting it on top. He popped the lid, exposing several hundred rounds of 10-gauge fleshettes. "Razor darts," he said, picking up one of the cylindrical caseless cartridges. "These have double loads and are guaranteed not to misfire." Barker pointed toward the clips. "Each one of those will hold twenty of these." He held up the shell. "You can fire the weapon on semi- or full-auto simply by pressing that switch next to the trigger. But remember, each time it fires, you get three rounds out. It can be a bitch to hold on to."

"Can we test it?" Kringa asked, noticing that Luther had moved around him to the end of the table and appeared to be inching his way toward Barker.

"No, sorry," Barker said, shaking his head. "The deal is, you buy it and if you aren't satisfied, bring it back within twenty-four hours, pay for the spent ammo, and I refund eighty percent of the selling price."

"How much do you want for it?" Kringa asked. A cold feeling congealed in his stomach as he watched Luther out of the corner of one eye. You're gonna get us killed, you crazy son of a bitch, he thought as Luther stopped less than three yards from Barker, lifted the corner of a blanket on the table and peered beneath it. Barker glanced in Luther's direction, but quickly looked back to the weapon, apparently too caught up in the sale to notice that Luther had moved within striking distance.

"I was asking fifteen grand," Barker answered, leaning forward over the table. "But business has been a little slow lately, so I'll let you have it along with five hundred rounds of mil-standard ammo for twelve-five."

"Shit!" Kringa jerked backward as Luther lunged toward Barker like a released spring.

"You son of a—" Barker's voice was cut off as Luther wrapped an arm around the big man's neck and fought to grab the hand holding the controlling mechanism for the Dobermans.

"Kringa! Shoot him," Luther yelled as Barker spun him around and rammed his body against the edge of the workbench.

Kringa tossed the weapon he had in his hands onto the table and reached inside his jacket for his .44, which he aimed in the direction of the struggling men. "I can't get a clear shot!" he shouted. "Turn him around!"

"Hurry!" Luther yelped as Barker swung him against the workbench again.

Kringa glanced up in time to see one of Barker's fat fingers fumbling with a switch on the side of the little box, and he didn't have to guess twice what was going to happen next. "Shit!" he yelled, diving to the floor and rolling beneath the table just as two of the Dobermans exploded. A double shower of steel shot slammed into the simulated concrete floor next to Kringa's prone body, peppering him with chips of the composite material. "Goddamn!" He covered his head with his arms as the pieces ricocheted crazily off the walls and boxes of explosives. At any second he expected the whole lot to cook off and shred him like a head of cabbage. The explosion never came. Instead he heard his brother yelling for help.

Pushing aside a crate of grenades, Kringa rolled over and could see Luther's and Barker's feet engaged in a violent, shuffling dance. "Damn," he said, pulling back the hammer of his automatic. "Maybe this'll help you, Luther." He aimed the barrel of the weapon at one of Barker's enormous feet, which were stuffed into leather sandals, and pulled the trigger.

Barker screamed at the top of his lungs as the chunks of lead ripped away his ankle. His leg went out from under him as though he'd been cut down by a scythe. He crashed to the floor, taking Luther with him. Luther's face slapped against the simulated concrete, sounding like someone hitting water with the flat side of an oar.

In spite of the blow to his face, Luther was immediately up. He took a half step forward and kicked the control box out of Barker's hand. It clattered across the floor and banged into something, which was followed by the sound of the door opening.

"My foot!" Barker wailed like an air raid siren.

Kringa raised the automatic toward the man's head, but it was too late. Luther had whipped the stiletto out of his boot. In one fluid motion he stuck it six inches into the soft flesh beneath Barker's chin. The man's screams were immediately replaced by an awful gurgling as foaming blood poured out of his mouth and nose.

"That'll teach your fat ass," Luther grunted as he backed away from Barker, whose body suddenly began to thrash violently. Just as suddenly the spasms stopped, and the body went limp.

"He's dead," Kringa said, crawling from under the table.

"No shit." Luther reached down and grabbed the handle of the knife. He wiped the blade on Barker's shirt, then straightened and turned toward Kringa, a mad grin covering his face. "I always knew you were the genius of the family."

"Speaking of genius, asshole," Kringa responded, "why didn't you shoot Moby Dick here—" he nodded toward Barker's body "—instead of harpooning the son of a bitch?"

Luther looked confused. "Uh, I dunno."

"You're damn right, you dunno," Kringa said, pushing his weapon back into its holster. He lit a cigarette. "Let's pick out what we want and get the hell out of here."

"I know what I want," Luther said. He turned and walked to the covered machine in front of the garage door and whipped off the tarp. "Wheels."

An old two-seat General Electric Suncruiser squatted on the fake concrete like a streamlined frog. Its green fiberglass shell had faded to the color of dead grass and its acrylic plastic windshield was chipped and cracked as though it had been hit repeatedly with a hammer. The car was a convertible, but its fabric top was missing. Little pieces of green canvas hung from the back edge of the passenger compartment like rag streamers, giving the machine a trashy appearance.

"Shit," Kringa said, walking toward the Suncruiser. "How do you know if the son of a bitch runs?"

"It runs. See." Luther popped a hinged section of the cowling that covered the back of the vehicle. He pointed at a digital charging meter built into a bulkhead over a row of batteries which indicated they were fully charged. "And it looks like the thing's been modified or something. Look." He kicked one of the tires, which were wide enough to pass for lawn rollers. "I bet this little sucker flies."

"Well, let's get our stuff together and try it out," Kringa said, turning back toward the table.

Luther walked the length of the table, pulling off the blankets. He dropped one of them over Barker's head to cover his staring and accusing eyes. "Holy shit," he gasped as he stared at the assortment of weapons covering the metal tabletop. "Christmas came early this year." He started gathering up several electronically sighted automatic rifles.

"Hold it a goddamn minute, Luther." Kringa picked up the three-barreled gun and walked over to the car. "See this?" He waved his hand over the machine, then laid the weapon on the passenger side floor.

"So?" Luther huffed belligerently.

"So, how are you gonna get all that hardware into this golf cart?" Kringa walked back to the table and closed the lid on the ammo case containing the fleshette rounds. "I suggest we take what we need to do the job we came here to do." He carried the case to the car and heaved it into the front seat. "If we take care of that, you'll have enough money to buy ten times this much shit when we're back in New York."

"I suppose you're right," Luther said disappointedly. He released his hold on the rifles and they clattered to the floor.

Kringa walked to the other end of the room and found Barker's control box next to a five-gallon can of solvent. He picked it up and studied it for a moment, then pushed a button labeled Door B. The steel door behind him shut, causing him to jump slightly.

"Don't, goddamn it!" Luther barked from the other end of the room. He pointed toward one of the Dobermans.

"Shit." Kringa felt a chill of dumb fear run down his back. He'd forgotten about the shotgun security system. Very gently he placed the control box on the workbench and breathed a sigh of relief as though he'd just defused a bomb. He picked up the can of solvent and walked toward Luther, who was slipping several white phosphorous grenades into the space behind the driver's seat. "See if you can open the door," he said. "Let's get the hell out of this morgue."

"All right." Luther turned his head and spit. He wiped his mouth on his sleeve and walked to the door. "Like this?" he asked, turning a handle and raising the door.

"Yeah, like that, smartass." Kringa peered out the door into a narrow alley full of dirt and debris. He turned around. "Pull this piece of junk into the alley, and I'll take care of the cleanup."

The electric engine of the car wound to life as Kringa headed for the back of the room. He unscrewed the lid of the solvent and sloshed the flammable liquid across the floor, workbench and table. Working his way toward the front, he made sure everything got a good soaking, including Barker's corpse. As he stepped into the alley, he saw Luther watching over his shoulder from the driver's seat of the Suncruiser. He continued pouring solvent to within fifteen feet of the car before tossing the can to one side.

"Let's move it, boy," Luther said enthusiastically. "I'm itchin' to see how this baby drives."

Kringa picked up a wadded piece of newspaper. He lit a cigarette, then held the lighter to the newspaper. "Rest in peace," he said, tossing the paper into the river of solvent.

CHAPTER FIFTEEN

ELOY BACA WAS WAITING next to the limo when Zamora stepped out of the jet. Even though it was almost midnight the heat was sweltering. It hit Zamora like a hot, wet blanket. "Where's Tripp?" he asked, crawling into the back seat as Eloy opened the door.

"Mr. Tripp is waiting in the Ambassador's Club at the main terminal," Eloy answered.

"Hey, wait," Zamora said as the limo started pulling away. He rolled down the window between the passenger and driver's compartments. "Stop this son of bitch," he ordered. A young Spanish man wearing a tan suit quickly brought the car to a halt. "Who is this guy?" Zamora asked Eloy.

"He's my nephew." Eloy leaned over the seat and told the driver to back up to the plane.

"Tell him we've got other passengers and that I want Leonard to drive," Zamora said.

Eloy relayed the message to his nephew, then turned to his boss. "I'm sorry about that, Ruben. He's just a little nervous, you know."

"Sure, sure, that's okay," Zamora said, patting Eloy on the knee. "We were young once, too, right?" He chuckled lightly as the limo backed up to the jet and stopped.

Leonard got into the driver's seat. "Where to?" he asked over his shoulder.

"The main terminal," Zamora said. "What about your cousins?"

"They're catching a ride with the pilots," he answered.

In the Ambassador's Club Zamora found Tripp sitting on a leather couch and gazing out a large window that overlooked one of the runways. He was immaculately dressed in a gray pinstriped suit and held a tall iced drink in one hand. Zamora watched the man's reflection in the glass and knew that he was watching his and Eloy's approach.

Tripp stood and turned when the two Colombians were no more than ten steps from the couch. "Mr. Zamora," he said, holding out his hand.

Zamora shook it. "What have you got for me?" he asked, dispensing with the usual small talk.

Tripp puckered his lips and looked at the floor for a moment before raising his eyes to Zamora's and smiling. "I've got a solution for your problem, but..." His voice trailed off and his expression turned tentative, as though he'd chosen that particular moment to debate with himself whether he should actually make his proposal to Zamora.

"But what?" Zamora snapped impatiently. "I hired you for your talents, Mr. Tripp. Are you having second thoughts about the job?"

"No, I'm not having second thoughts about the job," Tripp answered calmly, setting his drink on a nearby table. He walked around the couch to where Zamora stood and spoke softly, his face less than six inches from the Colombian's. "I've got doubts about whether you can stomach my solution."

Zamora was dumbfounded. He'd expected the well-dressed fraud artist to say almost anything but what he did. Suddenly the thought that there could actually be something that he couldn't stomach struck him funny. He laughed long and loud. "That's good," he said, his laughter subsiding. "Why don't you tell me about it and I'll decide whether, as you say, I can stomach it?"

"Not here," Tripp said, glancing at his watch. "Anyway, we need to go meet a guy who's integral to the deal."

"Meet where?" Zamora asked, caution flags being hoisted in his brain like sails at a regatta.

"At a bar called Toadie's over by the Meadowlands," Tripp answered. "It's right off Seventeen. Know where it is?"

"Yes, I know where it is. What time are we supposed to meet this friend of yours?"

"In twenty minutes."

"Let's go then," Zamora said, nodding at Eloy to lead the way.

The three men climbed into the back of the limo. Zamora told Leonard where to drive them, speaking in Spanish, and also told him to ring up a couple of his friends and have them head for the place—just in case Tripp's meeting were something more than just a meeting. *"Vaya mas despacio,"* he added before hitting the button that raised the glass between the two sections of the car.

Thirty minutes later they pulled into the crowded parking lot of Toadie's Sports Bar, a long, low, wood-shingled structure. It was open twenty-four hours a day, seven days a week, and was known for its illegal bookmaking activities. Leonard parked and the four men walked into the main area of the establishment, which was a maze of tables clustered around a large semicircular bar. Booths lined the walls and wide-screen video panels were fitted into the corners of the large room so that anyone seated could see at least one of them. A baseball game was on, and Zamora looked up in time to see someone get tagged out at home plate. Several patrons booed loudly.

Zamora directed Leonard to have a seat at the bar in order to keep an eye on things. He'd already noticed Leonard's cousins who'd gone to Indianapolis with them, sitting at a table on the other side of the room and sipping glasses of draft beer. He figured Leonard must have gotten in touch with them through the telelink in the pilots' car. Their presence made him feel a little more comfortable. He also realized he was intrigued by what Tripp had said to him at the airport.

"There he is." Tripp pointed at a booth next to the back wall.

Zamora and Eloy followed Tripp among the tables to the booth in which a middle-aged man was sitting. He had curly, reddish-colored hair, a drooping mustache of the same color and was smoking a thin plastic-tipped cigar. He was dressed in a dark green jogging suit, with Wetstone Engineering embroidered over the upper left chest area in white letters.

"Mr. Zamora and Mr. Baca, this is Nelson Johnson." Tripp put his hand on the man's shoulder. The introductions were followed by handshakes, and Zamora and Eloy sat down in the booth across from Tripp and Johnson.

Tripp leaned across the table, his hands clasped, and was about to say something when a waitress in a short, frilly skirt approached the booth. "Drinks?" she asked, holding the edge of her tray against her stomach.

Motioning toward the others, Tripp pulled a twenty-credit wafer from his inside pocket and placed it on the tray. "Go ahead, gentlemen," he said.

Zamora and Eloy both ordered Scotch on the rocks and Johnson a draft beer. "And I'll have a vodka straight," Tripp said. As the woman walked away, he spoke softly. "Nelson here—" he nodded at Johnson, who was chewing on the tip of his cigar, making it bob in front of his mouth "—is a systems engineer at Wetstone Engineering."

"I've heard of the company," Zamora said. "They mostly do defense contract work, don't they?"

"That's correct," Tripp answered.

"Aren't they located in Los Angeles?" Zamora asked, glancing at Johnson, who appeared to be waiting for Tripp to shut up so he could pitch his wares.

"That's right again," Tripp said. "Nelson flew out here just for this meeting."

"Actually, I'm on vacation," Johnson said, looking up as the waitress brought their drinks. He waited until she departed before continuing. "I work in the Flight Control Section."

Zamora lit a cigarette. "So, what's this all about?" He blew smoke toward the ceiling and picked up his Scotch.

Johnson looked at Tripp. "Want me to go through the whole thing?"

Tripp nodded and leaned back against the imitation leather. "Just like we went through it this morning."

"You guys ever hear of the TRWS?" Johnson asked, pronouncing the acronym, *trues*.

The two Colombians looked at each other. Zamora shrugged and answered. "No, what is it?"

"It stands for Toxic Radioactive Waste Scow, T-R-W-S, *trues*. Sure you haven't heard of it?" Johnson cocked his head to one side, waiting for an answer.

Zamora shrugged without bothering to look at Eloy to see if the explanation had rung any bells. "What you say is meaningless to me. Are you talking about something on a river? A scow?"

Johnson laughed, tilting his head back. He looked at Tripp. "I like these guys," he said, picking up his beer. He turned back to Zamora, smiling. "Let me explain it to you. TRWS Number 12 is up there now—" he pointed toward the ceiling "—going through its preprogrammed sequence to disengage Earth orbit and head for the sun."

"Hmm." Zamora took a sip of his Scotch. "Now I think I know what you're talking about. This is the space-borne waste removal system initiated about ten years ago."

"Twelve to be exact," Johnson said. He seemed pleased that the Colombian now understood what he was attempting to discuss. "TRWS Number 12 represents the twelfth year and the twelfth ship of the program. TRWS is the reason they turned the faucet on for so much nuclear-supplied electricity—there was finally a way to dispose of all the radioactive waste associated with it."

"Probably helped the nuclear weapons business, too," Zamora said, grinding out his cigarette in an ashtray shaped like a toad.

Johnson laughed. "Hell, they would have been burying the shit in our backyards before it slowed that business down."

"Well, what's your point?" Zamora asked, lighting another cigarette. "I know what a TRWS is—at least I've heard of it. What has this got to do with my problem?" He glanced at Tripp, who smiled almost serenely. This better be good, Zamora thought. If it isn't, I'm going to have your ass for breakfast.

"I designed the flight control system for the drone," Johnson answered smugly, leaning back in his seat. "That's what it is." He suddenly leaned forward again as if he'd left out part of his explanation. "It's nothing more than a big-ass drone."

"Okay," Zamora said, speaking now to Tripp. "How does this solve what we discussed? I'd appreciate it if we'd get down to the real issue."

Tripp straightened and the smile vanished from his face. "Certainly, Mr. Zamora." He glanced at the engineer. "Nelson here has been told what we're trying to accomplish, and—correct me if I'm wrong, Nelson—we can reprogram the main flight control computer on the TRWS so that it targets something other than the sun."

"Let me put it another way," Johnson interjected. "Despite what you may think, the flight controls on the bird are highly accurate, as is its navigation system. True, we just program it in the general direction of the sun and launch it. Sort of fire and forget." He chuckled and took a sip of his beer before continuing. "Hell, we're all going to be dead before TRWS Number 1 gets there. Anyway—" Johnson gestured with his hands as he explained "—I can reprogram the system in a couple of hours so that it—let's say, has a target that's a little closer to Earth."

"Like the Outland Strip," Zamora said, his eyelids partly closing to slits.

"That's right," Johnson said. "It'd be a piece of cake."

Zamora felt relief, then elation sweep through his mind. It was as though he'd finally chopped his way through a triple-canopy jungle and could now see clear sky instead of a dense tangle of vines, trees and brush. But he controlled his enthusiasm. The concept sounded innovative, but Zamora had experienced enough false-start schemes in the past to be wary of what his father used to call shooting stars. Zamora laughed to himself as the memory bloomed in the back of his mind. Shooting stars are only good for wishes and false hopes, the old man used to say. It's time to get real.

Right, Zamora thought, let's get real. "I see a couple of problems I'd like you to address."

"Shoot," Johnson responded almost cockily.

Zamora glanced at Tripp. He was wearing a smug smile. Zamora then addressed Johnson. "I have a rather urgent need to take the Strip out of operation. How long would it take to accomplish this so-called reprogramming?"

"That's the beauty of it," Johnson said enthusiastically. "They just started the launch sequence yesterday. That gives us a window of, say, a week to make the changes."

Zamora raised his eyebrows. "A week?"

"A week before the drone is too far gone to catch, let alone program," Johnson clarified. "The thing's already moving during the launch sequence—moving out. I can make the actual changes in two or two and a half hours."

"How do you actually make these changes?"

"That's the kicker," Johnson said. "You have to be *on* the big mother in order to reconfigure the program."

"Is that a problem?" Zamora asked.

Johnson sent Tripp a glance that said, How naive is this guy? He returned his attention to the Colombian. "Let me put it this way. First, you'll need a transatmospheric aircraft that can manage a high Earth orbit."

"That's no problem," Zamora said. "I've got one." He took a drink of his Scotch and lit a fresh cigarette. "I can have it and a pilot ready in less than eight hours."

Once again Johnson glanced at Tripp, only this time his look said, Is this guy joking? Tripp shrugged and sipped his vodka. "No shit?" Johnson asked, turning back toward Zamora.

"I'm very serious about this, Mr. Johnson," Zamora said slowly, his eyes locking onto Johnson's like tractor beams. "I suggest you approach the problem in the same manner—otherwise we're wasting each other's time."

"Agreed," Johnson answered. "If you can get me up there, I can get us into the ship and I can do the job. I've done at least a half dozen on-board checkouts, so I know the access frequencies, the docking procedures, how to activate the flight deck and work station artificial gravity systems, and like I said, I can reprogram the fight controls so that they'll fly the bird to within a hundred yards of any coordinate in the solar system. And that reminds me, I'll need the coordinates and the lunar orbiting profile for the Strip."

Zamora looked at Eloy, who immediately pulled a little electronic notebook out of his suit coat and began pressing the tiny keys. "Once you reprogram the machine," Zamora said, turning toward Johnson again, "and it's on its way toward its target, isn't there some sort of destruct mechanism or override command that can be initiated from Earth?"

"Yes," Johnson said. "But I've thought of a way around that. The destruct mechanism is programmed through the main computer, so I can disable it when I make the other changes. However, it's highly unlikely that anyone would initiate the destruct sequences between here and the moon."

"Why not?"

"Well, the destruct mechanism is meant to be used if the bird loses its track to the sun, and then the plan calls for it to be destroyed at least somewhere on the other side of Mars. They sure as hell don't want a cloud of nearly nine million tons of radioactive waste and toxic shit floating around Earth for the next million years. I'm sure it wouldn't be blown. But I'll disable the system, anyway, just in case. As for the ability to override and make course corrections, I can take care of that, too."

"What's to keep the military, or whoever, from flying up and undoing your handiwork?" Zamora asked, satisfied with Johnson's answer so far.

"That's easy," the engineer answered. "The launch sequence is a process that takes the scow out of orbit and then ignites the big engine. By the time that occurs it'll be too late to catch it, even with one of the Air Force's little Earth Stars. The moon isn't that close, you know."

Zamora took a deep drag of his cigarette. "You said a minute ago that this barge carries nine million tons of radioactive garbage. It has to be a big goddamn ship."

Johnson laughed. "Flying garbage truck is more like it," he said, pulling the cigar out of his mouth and looking at its mutilated plastic tip. "But you're right. It's one big sombitch." He put the cigar back in the corner of his mouth and picked up a brown folder from the seat beside him. "Want to see what it looks like?" he asked, placing the folder on the table.

"Sure," Zamora answered.

Johnson opened the folder and took out a panoramic shot of something that looked like a rusted, arrowhead-shape monolith. It was an actual photograph, and Zamora could see an old cargo shuttle positioned near the point of the scow, looking like a bee hovering in front of some mutant beast.

"It's as big as the Glick Tower," the Colombian said, referring to one of the largest skyscrapers in Manhattan. He was impressed by the size of the scow. "It looks like a mass of transport containers jammed together almost haphazardly." He looked at the engineer, who was draining his beer.

"You got that right," Johnson answered, setting the glass on the table. "They just build the thing around one of the old nuke impulse drivers. Number 12 happened to come out looking like a wedge. The others looked sort of like...well, like what they are, a mass of shit." The engineer laughed. "Aerodynamics are pretty meaningless when you get up there." He pointed toward the ceiling with his thumb.

Zamora was fascinated by the mass and ugliness of the machine. It was like a strange mix of a prehistoric creature and a gigantic, rusted chunk of dead metal. "What do they do," Zamora asked, "burn the engine once and let it go on momentum?"

"No," Johnson said, obviously enjoying the discussion. "The beauty of TRWS is that the actual waste it's carrying fuels the engine. It can burn damn near forever. Hell, maybe it does burn forever. Who knows?" He shrugged.

"So far you've answered my questions satisfactorily," Zamora said, leaning back in the seat. "Now let me ask you, to use your own terminology, the real kicker."

"Ask away," Johnson said, raising his hand to summon the waitress, who steered toward the booth. Without checking to see if anyone else wanted another drink, he ordered for everyone.

Zamora waited until the waitress had left before he spoke. "Why are you willing to do this?"

"Well, that's the last problem to address, isn't it?" Johnson smiled, but it was a slightly nervous smile. One corner of his right eye twitched involuntarily.

"I'm afraid I don't follow," the Colombian said, noticing that Tripp also seemed a little edgy now. He wondered what the two men had up their sleeves.

"My incentive is my fee, of course," Johnson explained. Just then the waitress returned with the fresh drinks. He pulled a credit wafer out of a waistband pocket of his pants and placed it on her tray, telling her to keep the change.

Once again Zamora waited until the waitress was out of earshot before speaking. But he wasn't ready to talk about money yet. He decided to twist a few more of the engineer's brain cells first. "What exactly will happen when the scow rams the Strip?"

Johnson hesitated for a moment, then glanced at Tripp, who ignored him. "Well, it'll probably go right through it," he answered, turning back to Zamora. His edginess seemed to abate temporarily, as though talking about the scow and what it could do had a calming effect on his nerves. "I don't have any idea what the Strip is made of, but by the time TRWS gets there it'll be moving like a son of a bitch. It'll probably punch straight through the Strip...like a ten-penny nail hitting a potato chip." Johnson chuckled as he picked up the fresh glass of beer.

"You know," Zamora said, watching Johnson's face intently to see how he was going to react, "at any given time, there are at least four, maybe even five hundred thousand people on the resort. Does it matter that they'll all probably die?"

Johnson did a double take. He stared at the Colombian as though he'd just been told his winning lottery ticket was a counterfeit. His mouth opened to speak, but no words came out.

Zamora looked at Tripp, who was staring straight at him with a look on his face that said, Shit, the bastard can't be that stupid.

"I guess I never really thought about it," Johnson said numbly. He was staring at a place somewhere over Zamora's left shoulder. "Maybe I assumed it would be evacuated or something like that. I don't think I realized there would be so many—"

"You kill one or you kill a hundred," Tripp interrupted, surprising Zamora. "The crime's the same."

"Yeah, but *five hundred thousand?* For chrissake, Sam—" Johnson turned to face Tripp "—goddamn it, this is mass murder."

"Keep your voice down," Tripp cautioned, putting his arm around the engineer's shoulders. "Let me remind you of something. Remember that job you helped me with four years ago?" Johnson didn't react to Tripp's question. "The one where we did a number on the flight controls of that Hansford Industries research shuttle." Tripp slipped his arm around Johnson's neck in a headlock and drew the man's face close to his. "Let me remind you," he went on calmly. "There were thirty-six people on that ship, and you had a direct hand in burning each and every one of them to death. You get cold feet on me now, and I'll make sure all of those marked-up schematics and drawings you sold me get shipped straight to the FBI. You want me to do that?"

Johnson shook his head as much as he could given the stranglehold Tripp had on him. "No," he said with a look that told Zamora he'd resigned himself to whatever fate Tripp had cast his way.

"Good," Tripp said, relaxing his grip. "Besides, this gentleman—" he nodded at Zamora "—is going to make you a rich man."

Tripp released his grip on Johnson completely and picked up his vodka. "He's asking a million and a half," Tripp said before downing the clear liquid in one swallow. "Half before he does the job and half after. Isn't that right, Nelson?" He looked at Johnson, who nodded like an automaton.

Zamora figured he'd just heard what the two men had been ready to pull before Johnson's mind got derailed by Zamora's making him face up to the deaths involved in the plan. Tripp would probably get at least a third of whatever fee he was able to negotiate for the engineer. "Done," Zamora said without hesitation, causing Eloy to look at him with surprise.

"Good," Tripp said. He looked at his watch. "Can we conclude this meeting now? It's getting late."

"Not quite yet," Zamora said, holding up a finger. "We've got a little logistics problem to solve. Can you leave tomorrow night?" he asked, directing his question to Johnson.

"What, Thursday?" Johnson asked, seeming surprised that Zamora had addressed him.

"Yes," Zamora answered. "By my estimates, that should put the scow on the target, so to speak, sometime Sunday."

Johnson stared at the wall above Zamora's head for several seconds, apparently calculating the times in his head. "That's pretty close. But I guess I can be ready to leave tomorrow night."

"Good," Zamora said. Tripp is a genius and doesn't even know it, he thought. Not only would taking out the Outland Strip solve the financial problems of the VAC almost instantaneously, but it would also add some timely insurance for the job he'd hired the so far unimpressive Sthil brothers to do. Rohde would be guaranteed dead as would the cop, Horn. Zamora liked it; he had to force himself to remain cautiously optimistic rather than jump for joy.

"Are you driving, Mr. Johnson?" Zamora asked.

Johnson looked puzzled. "Driving?"

"Did you drive here, or did you come in a cab?"

"Oh, I drove," Johnson answered. "Rental car."

"Can you give Mr. Tripp a ride back to his place?" Zamora asked, glancing at Tripp, who had a wary look on his face.

Johnson shrugged. "Sure."

"Where are you staying?"

"At the Hilton near Lincoln Center."

"Are you registered under your real name?" Zamora asked.

"Sure," Johnson answered, as though he had no idea of why he might do otherwise.

"We'll arrange to have you picked up tomorrow evening," Zamora said, holding his hand across the table. Johnson hesitated for a second, then shook it.

"And may I ask you to do one small favor for me?" Zamora asked politely.

"I guess so."

"Could you give me just two minutes alone with Mr. Tripp before you take him home?"

"Yeah," Johnson answered, sliding out of the booth. "I've got to go to the head. I'll be back shortly."

As soon as the engineer had walked off, Zamora leaned across the table. "Listen to me, Mr. Tripp," he said, his voice like a straight razor. "You don't let Johnson out of your sight until he gets on the goddamn shuttle tomorrow night. Do you understand?" Before Tripp could respond, Zamora went on. "I want you to spend the night with the son of a bitch. I don't give a damn what you have to do, but if he doesn't come through with this, you're the one I'll hold responsible."

"He'll do it," Tripp said defensively. "The jerk acted the same way before the last job."

"I couldn't care less," Zamora said, waving his hand as though casting off Tripp's assurances. "What I'm telling you is that I want to see your face when Johnson walks up the ramp of my shuttle. Understand?"

Tripp appeared disturbed for a moment, but answered, "No problem. I'll be at the hotel, too."

"Good," Zamora said, lighting a cigarette. "I knew I could count on you, Sam Tripp."

CHAPTER SIXTEEN

EARLY FRIDAY EVENING Les Dartt backed the Douglas into an area reserved for electrocars a block away from the main entrance of the Milky Way Casino. Horn looked around and counted no more than a dozen other vehicles. From the number of people milling around the sidewalk in front of the place, however, he knew it would be crowded. He felt a little wave of anxiety as he imagined the effects on innocent bystanders of an exchange of gunfire inside the casino. But he forced the thought from his head, knowing they would have to play it by ear. He hoped they could just wait Rohde out and follow him when he left, making the arrest on the street.

Dartt popped the bubble on the machine and he, Horn and Winger crawled out to be greeted by a blue-uniformed security guard. "You gentlemen staying long?" the guard asked, addressing Dartt, who was keying a code into a panel next to the bubble.

"Maybe," Dartt answered. He pulled a fifty-credit wafer out of his jacket pocket and handed it to the guard. "It's forty for twelve hours, isn't it?"

"Yes, sir," the guard answered.

"Well, you keep the difference," Dartt said placing the wafer in the man's hand.

"Don't worry about your machine, sir," the guard said, pocketing the wafer. "It'll be safe with me." Horn noticed a long-barreled automatic hanging beneath the man's blue blazer. Dartt motioned for Horn and Winger to follow and led the way toward the sidewalk that ran in front of the luxurious casino.

The neon facades that lined the strip were going full tilt as they walked down the crowded sidewalk. Horn had the impression that he was inside a gigantic electronic kaleidoscope instead of one of the most popular gambling resorts of the twenty-first century. He looked up and could see billions of stars stretching to infinity. Triangular-shaped sections in the roof added to the kaleidoscopic effect. Horn noticed the bright blue ball that was Earth hanging far away in the vastness. The thought that he lived there, one of millions on a tiny, round chunk of matter in the middle of infinity, made Horn feel more like a speck of dust than a human. Yet here he was in a crowd of others, all with some sense of their existence painted in their minds like abstract art trying to match reality.

Horn shook off such thoughts, deciding it was best to leave the contemplation of existence to preachers, philosophers and bullshitters. He grabbed Winger by the arm and motioned for Dartt to pull up in front of a nightclub that had a sign posted across its double doors declaring it to be closed for remodeling. "Once we get inside the place," Horn said to the two men, "I want you to spread out. Keep me in sight, though. I'll give you your cues if there's any action to be taken. You said a balcony runs completely around the casino floor, right?" He directed his question at Dartt, who nodded. "I'll find a spot somewhere on the balcony where you can see me. Once we've ID'd Rohde, don't get too close to him. I hope to wait until he leaves the casino before we snatch him. Got it?"

"Got it," Winger said, turning his back toward the sidewalk. He adjusted the machine pistol hanging beneath his arm before shaking his arms and running his fingers through his short hair. "How do I look?" he asked, grinning.

"You look like the first week of a bad haircut," Horn answered, returning the grin.

He glanced at Dartt, who was dressed in a black leather suit, some kind of reptile-skinned boots and a frilly, tuxedo-style white shirt. Horn watched him roll one of the little cigars from one side of his mouth to the other. He could tell from the bulges beneath the leather jacket that the man was carrying the revolver and shotgun pistol he'd seen the night they checked out the Down Side.

"You don't have to help us make the collar, you know," Horn said.

A sly sort of smile crossed Dartt's face. "Hell, I know that. But old Sharkey doesn't trust cops, and he offered me a cut of the reward if I make sure you guys kept your word about him getting it."

Horn laughed. "I should have figured. Let's go."

The Milky Way Casino was a large, round place with two levels: a huge open area on the main floor and an upper-level balcony that ran completely around the inside of the structure, fronting a wide variety of shops, restaurants, bars, private gambling rooms and a glitzy whorehouse called Christie's Palace. Holographs of scantily clad women walked around in front of the arched doorway, seductively inviting passersby to come inside and sample the wares.

Taking it all in from just inside the long row of glass double doors that comprised the main entrance, Horn was amazed at the size of the casino. The layout reminded him of a huge shopping mall that had been converted into a gambling and amusement park. A multicar monorail ran from a long platform off the balcony down and completely around the casino in a long spiral. A number of escalators also provided access to the upper level.

"What time did Sharkey say he usually gets here?" Horn asked Dartt.

Pulling back a sleeve, Dartt glanced at his watch. "Probably be another hour at least."

"Spread out then, take your time and get a feel for the place. Winger, check out the other exits. I'm going to be right up there." He pointed across and up to an open area bar bordering the balcony railing. Tables were situated so that the patrons had a view of the casino floor. "I'll try to find a table right next to the railing." Winger and Dartt nodded and faded into the sea of people spread out across the casino, crowding around long rows of electronic slots, fan-shaped blackjack and crap tables and roulette wheels.

Horn headed for the monorail and boarded a car just before its sliding doors closed. He scanned the crowd as the machine spiraled upward, noticing that the people were a little more diverse than at the Orion. There were the high rollers—whales, as Dartt had called them—flashing huge stacks of large-denomination credit wafers as well as an occasional piece of the coveted blue scrip. Horn spotted a mega whale, an immaculately dressed man wearing a turban who lost a six-inch stack of ten-grand credits on one roll of the dice. It didn't seem to faze him in the least. Among the whales and their pilot fish of long-legged bombshells and flashily dressed hustlers who looked and talked like used car salesmen were the run-of-the-mill gamblers who sat at the tables or pulled the handles as if they had been trained to do so.

Horn noticed that many in the crowd were dressed like him and Winger in a sort of street jungle camou that was functional, not flashy—a fact that made him feel a little more at ease. He figured they were from the Down Side, or at least from the fringes of the Strip, and had come into town like miners on a Saturday night to party and forget, at least for a while, about whatever it was they did for a living.

It made sense that Rohde would venture out to the Strip when it was the most crowded and when he would be least likely to stand out. And, after seeing some of the joints that served gamblers in the Down Side, Horn could understand why Rohde would want to chance visiting the Strip once a week at least.

A good-looking waitress in a skintight spandex jumpsuit led Horn to a table next to the railing from which he could see almost the entire floor of the casino. He ordered a beer, tipping the woman generously, and settled back to do what cops did more than almost anything else—wait. Across the casino he could see Winger moving down a row of brightly lit electronic slots, stopping occasionally to pull a handle, but mostly surveying the crowd. It was good to know he could trust the young cop to keep a cool head in case something went wrong. Horn wasn't as sure about Dartt, although from what he'd seen so far, the man seemed dependable and streetwise enough that he wouldn't panic if someone pulled a gun.

Horn thanked the waitress as she placed the beer and a basket of mixed nuts on the table in front of him. He took a sip of the beer, wondering idly if Rohde would still roll over on the Colombian when they did finally bring him in. That thought led Horn's mind to the events that had launched him on the chase in the first place—Kelso's death and Rohde's escape—and he felt remorse stab through his heart like a sliver of cold blue steel. He suddenly chuckled sadly, remembering one time when he and Kelso were girding up their courage to enter the assistant district attorney's office for one of her patented ass-chewings. "How can the meat refuse the grinder?" the little police captain had asked sardonically before opening the door to Service's office.

Horn forced the memories from his mind, cursing himself for allowing his thoughts to drift from the task at hand. He focused his eyes on the crowd below and began a sys-

tematic sweep of the faces, picking up Dartt, who was seated
at a five-credit blackjack table. Dartt gave a little salute as
their eyes locked briefly. Horn acknowledged him with a
nod, then allowed his visual radar to move on, looking for
the big, balding man, the key to Ruben Zamora. A thread
of comfort, albeit a thin one, lay in the fact that even if
Rohde wouldn't roll over, the Colombian was bound to
come after him. One way or the other, sooner or later, Horn
knew he would find out the details behind Kelso's death,
and when he did, all those responsible would die as violently as Kelso had. It wasn't much of a consolation, but it
was better than nothing.

A movement out of place in the crowd caught Horn's eye.
He focused in on Winger, who was standing at the end of a
row of slots, waving his hand in front of his chest. Horn
nodded to indicate that he'd seen him, and his partner motioned with his head toward one of the crap tables twenty
yards away.

The tall, hulking form of Jack Rohde was unmistakable,
even though this was the first time Horn had seen him in the
flesh. His smooth, shiny, bullet-shaped head reflected the
lights of the casino as he bent over the table to place a bet.
Horn's heart rate quickened as Rohde turned toward a tall
blond woman in a red dress and held out his clenched hand
for her to kiss before leaning back over the table and rolling the dice. Rohde, the ghost gambler, out from the shadow
world of the Down Side to shoot craps beneath the bright
lights of the Strip.

Horn felt like a hunter spying his prey for the first time,
and studied the man, who stood head and shoulders above
most of those in the crowd. He was wearing a tan sport coat
over a bright flower-patterned shirt, whose collar was arranged over the neck and lapels of the sport coat. His slacks
were brown, with one leg hung up on the top of one of his
high, intricately carved western boots. If it hadn't been for

his size, Horn thought, Rohde would have looked like any other tourist up from the Lone Star State to play with some of his fossil fuel and ranching money.

Horn leaned back in his chair and watched the big man play. He saw that Dartt, still at the blackjack table, had changed his seat to the other side and was watching Rohde as he played. Horn munched some nuts from the basket, sipped his beer and watched Rohde play. The Texan was on a lucky streak, and a crowd of other gamblers and hangers-on began to gather around his table, placing bets and yelling and whooping each time he threw the dice. The stacks of credit wafers in front of Rohde grew each time he rolled. A cigarette dangled from one side of his mouth, and a wide grin seemed permanently fixed across his face. He did a little dance with the blonde as another stack of wafers were shoved across the table toward him.

Enjoy it while you can, Horn thought.

Then someone behind him dropped a glass, and the sound of it shattering across the tile floor caused him to jump. He turned his head, and as he did, a loud, cracking explosion filled the casino like a sonic boom. Horn dived to the floor, automatically drawing the 9 mm from his shoulder holster. Screams and curses split the air as another boom reverberated through the place. Horn looked down just in time to see Rohde's blond companion get hit; the upper portion of her body was shredded like a tomato tossed into the spinning blades of a high-speed turbine, and she was knocked across the table as though she were a betting wafer someone had tossed idly onto the green felt. Blood spattered over several bystanders, who were stumbling over one another in an effort to escape the killing zone. Horn saw Rohde's head disappear beneath the table just as the person who had been standing behind him was laid low by another shot.

Horn's eyes swept the balcony on the other side of the casino, where he calculated the shots had come from, and

he spotted the source of the gunfire at once. A wiry-haired
man was leaning over the railing, aiming an unfamiliar-
looking weapon at the crap table. Horn squeezed the laser
sight of his 9 mm to life and willed it toward the man, but
never got the chance to follow it with a bullet, for the sound
of Winger's little machine pistol firing aroused another
outbreak of screams. Sparks flew off the metal rail in front
of the gunman as Horn's partner sprayed the area with a
stream of Teflon-coated lead. The enemy took a leap and a
roll to one side and disappeared, but Horn knew he hadn't
been hit.

Suddenly another automatic weapon opened up to the
right of Horn. Several electronic slots next to Winger exploded in a shower of glass and sparks like an abbreviated
fireworks display. The young cop dived to the other side of
the machines, while Horn brought the 9 mm around as
though it were connected to his eyes. Less than thirty yards
away a tall, slender man whose shaved head resembled a
bare skull was standing next to the rail firing, the muzzle of
his weapon flashing like a death strobe. Horn squeezed the
trigger of his 9 mm without waiting for the laser to paint its
target. His shot slammed into a support column next to the
man, who immediately spun in his direction, whipping the
smoking barrel of the automatic rifle around, too.

Horn dived for cover behind a wooden vending cart
loaded with cigarettes and magazines, just as the man's
weapon barked like a rabid dog. The cart shook and almost disintegrated as the bullets hosed it down, splintering
the wood and scattering its wares across the floor. Horn
crawled to one end and whipped the 9 mm around the corner of the cart, firing three quick shots in the direction of the
gunman.

The automatic suddenly ceased firing. In the ensuing
quiet Horn could hear someone over a loudspeaker re-
questing everyone to remain calm and to exit the casino in

an orderly manner. Horn crawled slowly forward, expecting to hear the automatic's death rattle again at any second. Sweat ran down his face. He peered around the end of the bullet-riddled cart but saw only a large, potted palm tree where the man had last been standing. While Horn stared in amazement, an arm appeared from behind the trunk of the tree and flung something across the floor in the direction of the cart.

"Goddamn!" Horn yelled as he recognized the object skipping across the tile in a crazy slow motion. It was a grenade. His blood turned to ice water as the grenade came to rest less than three feet from his head. Out of instinct Horn dropped his automatic and grabbed the smooth, neat little death egg. Its triggering mechanism had popped out, and he could hear a mechanical whir from beneath its dull green shell. Just as Horn swung back his arm, he saw the gun-wielding man break cover and run, his head lowered like an Olympic sprinter. Horn flexed his modified arm and flung the grenade after the man, who was disappearing around the gradual curve of the balcony.

The grenade exploded outside the windowed walls of a restaurant called Miguel's. The entire front of the place blew apart as though a killer earthquake had just struck. Horn covered his head as shrapnel and pieces of the tile floor whizzed by his body like angry bees. When he raised his head, he could hear screams of pain and panic coming from inside the restaurant. He grabbed his 9 mm and headed after the gunman.

Horn raced flat out, knowing he was apt to run into the lead spray from the man's automatic at any moment. However, he had a hunch the gunman was making an attempt to hook up with the guy on the other side of the casino who had started it all by firing the cannon, or whatever the hell it was. Horn finally caught a glimpse of his quarry and fired on the run, his shot ricocheting harmlessly off the door-jamb of a barbership.

"Damn," Horn whispered, breathing hard as he finally gave up the footrace. He moved to the railing and surveyed the floor of the casino, which was nearly empty except for several people cowering behind the rows of slot machines and two or three overturned blackjack tables. "Winger!" he yelled. Almost immediately his partner's head appeared between two rows of slots.

Horn pointed toward the crap table where the blond woman still lay draped across the green surface like a piece of roadkill. He mouthed, "Is he still there?"

Winger bent to take a look, then raised his head and nodded. He also held up his machine pistol and pointed at it with his left hand, which Horn took to mean that Rohde had a weapon.

Horn looked across the smoke-filled casino and watched as the monorail began its automatic descent. He reached into his jacket and pulled out a fresh clip as the cars moved around the wall toward him, dropping as they went. "Here goes nothing," he said aloud as he released the old clip from the butt of the automatic, letting it fall to the floor. He jammed the fresh one into the weapon's handle and crawled over the railing, hooking his right arm over the polished metal tube.

"Cover me!" Horn yelled as the cars moved directly under him. He released his grip on the rail and dropped to the roof of the lead car, where his right leg penetrated the thin fiberglass. "Shit!" he screamed, startled. He tried to jerk his leg out, but it was stuck. His left leg was splayed painfully to one side.

Horn's attention was suddenly drawn to a man who had popped up from behind an overturned blackjack table and was pointing the long barrel of a large-caliber handgun somewhere above it. Just as the weapon fired, he realized it was Dartt. In the next instant came the staccato sound of the automatic that had originally opened up on Winger, and a line of bullet holes appeared in the top of the car less than a foot to Horn's side. He craned his neck, but couldn't see anything. Dartt's weapon barked three more times.

"Watch it, Horn!" Dartt yelled, crouching behind the table. "He's still up there somewhere."

Yeah, and here I am a goddamn sitting duck, Horn thought. He figured he'd better get the hell off the top of the car before he rode it straight to his death. Then the boom of the original gunman's weapon filled the casino like pressurized air, and Horn heard the front of the car come apart as though it had been hit by several hundred rounds at the same time. He heard Winger's machine pistol open up, too, and saw the wire-haired man dance away from the railing. Horn could have sworn he was smiling.

"I've had enough of this shit," Horn said, passing the 9 mm to his left hand. Raising his right fist into the air, he brought it down on top of the car next to his leg. The fiberglass splintered like balsa wood. Horn's weight suddenly shifted, and he realized he was falling. "Damn," he yelped painfully as he landed on his hip between two padded bench seats inside the car. He pulled himself to his feet and felt a burning sensation in the calf of his right leg. Reaching down, he pulled the ugly razor point of a fleshette round out of his leg and felt a warm trickle of blood flow over his skin. He looked around and noticed hundreds of the deadly little darts scattered across the floor of the car.

"So that's what the son of a bitch is shooting out of his cannon," Horn muttered, following the trail of razor-edged darts to the other end of the car, where his eyes fell upon the mutiliated body of a man in his early twenties. He was sprawled on the seat at the back of the car, his face and upper chest resembling a crowded pincushion. Blood ran down from the darts sticking out of his body in one wide stream, covering his shirt and pants and the floor around his feet with the crimson stain of death.

Horn jerked his eyes away from the grim sight and looked out the sliding door of the car. It was still nearly twenty feet off the floor of the casino and just moving into a position where it was closest to the crap table under which Rohde was hiding. Without bothering to try sliding the door open, Horn cocked his right leg and slammed the flat of his foot into the locking mechanism, ripping the entire door off the side of the car. It flew to the floor like a windblown sheet of newspaper and slammed into a roulette table. Without hesitating, Horn jumped, positioning himself so that most of his weight would land on his right leg. He hit hard and rolled forward just as the cannon fired again, the fleshettes slamming into the tile behind him in a hailstorm of metal death.

Winger's machine pistol erupted and Dartt's big revolver cracked as Horn scrambled to the end of the crap table. Suddenly a hand reached out from under the table and fired a snub-nosed handgun inches from Horn's face. He jerked back, feeling the heat from the muzzle-flash.

He thinks I'm trying to nail him, Horn thought, suddenly standing. He drove his right fist down, straight through the pass line, and grabbed something. Rohde yelled out in pain and Horn peered through the hole. He saw a flash of gunmetal, released his grip on whatever it was he'd been holding and grabbed the gun, ripping it out of the hole and tossing it away in one blurred motion.

"You son of a bitch!" Rohde screamed from beneath the table. "You damn near ripped off my goddamn—"

The chattering of the skull-headed man's machine gun cut off Rohde's curses. Horn felt a sledgehammer blow slam into his right shoulder, spinning him around. He raised the 9 mm and fired two shots at the gunman, who instantly faded away from the railing. Horn dropped to the floor and crawled around to the side of the table just as the fleshette gun exploded again, driving its swarm of razor darts into the end of the crap table where he'd just been standing.

Horn rolled under the table just in time to see Rohde, a crazed and desperate look on his sweating face, swing down a short-bladed knife. Automatically Horn raised his right arm, and Rohde's wrist slammed into the titanium appendage like a stick of wood hitting a three-hundred-pound anvil.

"Oh, shit," Rohde moaned in pain. The knife fell onto Horn's chest. He grabbed it and flung it across the floor.

"Listen to me, asshole," Horn said, grabbing Rohde by one of his lapels and jerking him forward until their faces were inches apart, "I'm not trying to kill you. Get that through your head." He shook the man a couple of times to emphasize his point.

The fleshette gun cracked again, followed by the sound of breaking glass and ripping metal. Horn figured Winger was now the cannon man's target. He could hear the young cop cursing wildly as the machine pistol opened up again.

"Who the hell are you, then?" Rohde drawled, amazing Horn with his slowness of speech.

"I'm a cop," he answered. "I'm taking you back to New York."

Rohde looked dumbfounded for several seconds then broke into a fit of wheezing laughter, his eyes turning into narrow slits as his cheeks rode up on his face. Horn wondered if the big man might be choking instead of reacting to Horn's answer as though it were the funniest joke he'd ever heard.

"You gotta be shittin' me for sure," Rohde said, his chest still heaving.

"If I weren't a cop, you'd be dead meat," Horn said, staring into the Texan's eyes. "Your old boss has a price on your head that makes the Feds' reward look like pocket

change. And *he* wants your ass dead.'' Horn released hi
grip and allowed the man to pull away.

''Well, who in hell else is out there?'' Rohde asked so
berly. ''And can I have my goddamn gun back?''

''A couple of heavy hitters who're trying to nail you
ass,'' Horn answered, popping the clip on the 9 mm. He
glanced at the line of bullets that still covered more than half
the length of the clip and jammed it back into the weapon'
handle. ''And I don't know where the hell your gun is.
threw it out there somewhere.'' He nodded to the side.

''You want me to stay cool?'' Rohde raised his drooping
eyelids in mock astonishment. ''We're in hell, boy,'' he said,
lowering his voice, his expression deadpan. ''We're both
gonna burn.''

''Not if I can help it,'' Horn said, turning away from the
Texan. ''Hey, Les!'' he yelled in the direction of Dartt'
overturned table.

Dartt's answer was drowned out by another volley of
gunfire that lasted five or six seconds before dying out
Horn watched the table slide around until he could see
Dartt, who was crouched on one knee. Horn pointed in the
direction of the main entrance, then mimed steering a ca
with his hands. ''We'll cover you,'' he barked. Dartt gave
him a thumbs-up and got into a sloppy version of a run
ner's get-set position.

''Goddamn, boy, you been hit.'' Horn heard Rohde'
voice behind him, then felt the man's fingers on his shoul
der. ''Hey, there ain't no blood. What the hell is—''

Ignoring Rohde, Horn yelled at the top of his lungs.
''Winger! Cover fire, now!'' In the same instant he rolled
from under the table and rose to one knee, firing at the rail
ing where he'd last seen the skull. Out of the corner of one
eye he saw Dartt break for the front of the casino, his arms
and legs pumping wildly. Winger's machine pistol began its

deadly music as Dartt hurdled a fallen slot machine and disappeared behind a section of partitions used for keno.

The fleshette gun fired somewhere off to Horn's right and he ducked, raising his right arm as the darts slammed into the table and the body of the dead woman. He felt one of the metal bees ricochet off his forearm, its angry whine blowing past his left ear like a bullet.

Horn rolled back under the table and pushed Rohde toward the other side. "Let's go," he said, shoving hard. "It's time to get the hell out of here."

"I'm for that," Rohde said, sliding his big body toward the perimeter of the table.

"You see where my partner is?" Horn asked, pointing over Rohde's shoulder toward the rows of slot machines. The short barrel of Winger's weapon could be seen sticking out from the gap.

"Yeah," Rohde answered, looking worriedly over his shoulder at Horn. "That's a hell of a long way, ain't it?"

"You just haul ass when I give you the word, understand?"

Rohde swallowed hard. "Shit," he muttered. "I wish I had my damn gun."

Horn ignored him. "Winger!" he bellowed. "Give us some cover—we're coming your way. Go!" He followed Rohde's mass out from under the table and scrambled to his feet. He was surprised at how fast the Texan moved as they ran through a gauntlet of tables, overturned slot machines and other debris produced by the firefight, finally rounding the end of the row of slots and diving into Winger's little hiding place.

"Nice of you to drop in," the young cop said, grinning as he shoved a fresh clip into the machine pistol.

"They didn't fire," Horn said. The only weapon he'd heard during their little sprint was Winger's.

"They must be moving," his partner said, turning in the direction of the main doors. "Let's get out of here."

Winger led the way between two rows of super slots that rose a good three feet over their heads, their gaudy come-on lights still flashing carnival-like in the hazy gunsmoke. The trio hadn't gone ten yards before a metallic bang sounded on top of one of the slots. A grenade landed on the carpeted floor less than ten feet in front of Winger, who froze, staring at it as though it were a coiled snake.

Horn moved quickly, shouldering his way around Rohde and shoving his partner to one side. Instead of trying to snatch the thing up, he kicked with his right foot and watched it bounce along the carpet, banging against one row of slots like a misshapen, metallic golf ball. It exploded in a flash of light, driving Horn backward into Winger, who in turn fell against Rohde. The big man kept them all from falling down.

"Let's go," Horn said. He shook his head, trying to alleviate the painful ringing caused by the explosion. They're on the floor, he thought as he led the way toward the entrance.

Then, something in the part of Horn's brain that was reserved for hunches, feelings, superstitions and shadows of an extra sense, told him to do something inconsistent with the course his rational mind and police training would have him take. "Shit," he muttered to himself. He knew that giving in to that urge, however ambiguous, had saved his life more than once.

Horn pulled up and placed his right shoulder against the front of one of the slot machines, pushing with his body and flexing his mods at the same time. The metal frame of the machine creaked as it pulled four machines on either side of it into a tilting position. Horn figured they were connected somehow. He gave a final shove, and the double section of slots toppled over into the next aisle.

"Whoa! Goddamn!" Someone on the other side of the machines yelped like a dog hit with a strap. "Luther!"

"Come on," Horn ordered, motioning with his head. He took off at a run, figuring their stalkers would be slowed, at least for a moment.

Exiting the row of slots, Horn sprinted for the bank of sliding glass doors that would get them out of the casino. He could hear Winger and Rohde grunting and huffing behind him. The doors were closed and Horn slowed, giving them time to open. As they began their agonizingly slow movement, the fleshette cannon cooked off somewhere behind them like a rocket launcher. Horn cringed as four of the ten-foot-wide doors blew out, scattering glass and strips of metal into the middle of the street.

Horn stepped through one of the frames, glass crunching beneath his boots, and swung to his right. A crowd of people across the street raised a cheer as the three men ran up the street toward Dartt, who was backing the Douglas toward them, its top raised like the plastic cover of an egg cooker.

"Hurry, goddamn it!" Dartt urged as the three men scrambled into the machine.

Horn shoved Rohde into the seat behind Dartt and took the one next to the big Texan as Winger covered their six o'clocks. "Go," he yelled as the young cop stepped over the cowling into the seat next to Dartt. The big electric engine whined, and the Douglas accelerated down the synthetic asphalt.

"Shit!" Winger yelled, jerking his arm out of the way as the bubble snapped into place.

"What the hell!" Dartt screamed as a section of plastic just above and to the left of his head exploded, splintering and breaking away from the bubble as though it had been violently bitten off by an invisible beast.

The electrocar slid sickeningly sideways. Horn grunted as Rohde's body hit him like a proverbial ton of bricks. He could see Dartt fighting with the wheel of the machine as it spun out of control. Then, suddenly, the Douglas accelerated. The machine's engine strained loudly, and Horn's body was pressed back into the worn seat by the force. An overheated smell wafted into his nostrils. Horn's head jerked back and then forward when the rear wheels bounced as though they'd just hit a field of land mines, and the nose of the vehicle pitched up.

As Horn looked out through the bubble in front of the car, he wondered if his perception had been impaired. The street looked different now as a tall mass blurred crazily to the right of the speeding machine. He felt disoriented, as though he'd just gone through a dizzying series of aerobatics. Then he saw Winger rise from his seat, slide back the sunroof and stick the upper part of his body through the slot in the acrylic plastic.

Horn's heart froze in the middle of a beat. He flashed back to the sight of his previous partner, Dan Riddle, leaning out of the Buick, firing the autoloading shotgun at a two-eyed monster that had the young cop's picture injected into its death program like an incurable virus.

"Riddle!" Horn screamed, grabbing for Winger's waist. "Hey, snap out of it!"

A voice jolted in from the periphery of Horn's consciousness as a heavy hand smacked into the side of his face, knocking his head sideways. He shook his head, and the entire situation erupted in his mind with a sudden, violent clarity.

Horn realized they were moving down the sidewalk in the opposite direction from the one they'd started in. He looked up. Winger was aiming his machine pistol in the direction of the street. Turning his head slightly, Horn could see the crowd of people who had cheered their exodus from the

Milky Way, scattering like roaches from strong light as the Douglas sucked up the sidewalk, its engine screaming like a tortured banshee. He glanced to his left and saw the skull-headed gunman crouched in the center of the street, aiming the automatic rifle in a vector through which the electrocar was destined to pass.

"Get down!" Dartt howled as the rapid popping of the skull's weapon echoed between the buildings on the Strip.

Horn heard Winger's machine pistol answer and looked up in time to see his partner firing the dangerous little weapon just as the left side of the plastic bubble was stitched with a line of the skull man's bullets. Ducking his head, Horn figured Winger was a goner, and his mods jerked violently. He was oblivious of the tiny shards of plastic peppering the left side of his face as the machine blazed through the free-fire zone and the gunfire died away.

"Holy shit!" Rohde said, his drawl filling the inside of the aerated bubble. "You're still alive!"

Horn looked up as Winger was pulling himself back into the body of the speedster. Relief spread through Horn's mind, as though he'd just awakened from a nightmare; the tightness in his chest vanished. He couldn't believe that his partner hadn't been cut in half by the stream of lead.

"I missed the son of a bitch!" Winger said disgustedly as he flopped into the seat next to Dartt. "I can't believe it. I had the son of a bitch dead on."

"No doubt," Dartt answered, raising his voice above the whistling of the wind blowing through the holes in the canopy.

Suddenly Horn remembered his discussion with Christina Service and realized who the two hitters had to be. "Those guys were the Sthil brothers," he said to Rohde, who looked puzzled. "Friends of your former boss, Zamora." The Texan's puzzled look faded to one that said, It figures.

"Hey, goddamn it!" Winger snapped, apparently figuring out where they were. "You're on the freaking sidewalk. What the hell are you trying to prove?"

"Sorry," Dartt answered, jerking the wheel hard over and launching the machine off the sidewalk and back into the street.

Horn watched the colored lights of the Strip blur as Dartt pushed the machine hard, its digital readout pegging their speed at a 138 klicks.

"You're a cop, right?"

Horn turned to Rohde, who was speaking as though his lips and tongue had been injected with anesthetic. "I told you I was," he answered as the lights of the Strip began to fade.

"Are *you* a cop?" Rohde asked, placing a hand on Dartt's shoulder.

"Hell, no!" Dartt answered over his shoulder. "Are you an asshole?" he asked, laughing as he whipped the Douglas around a slow-moving trolley.

Rohde tapped Winger on the shoulder. "*You're* a cop, right?"

"Yeah, one of New York's finest," Winger answered tiredly. "I'm a cop, just like him." He pointed a thumb at Horn.

"Well, don't take this the wrong way, fellas," Rohde said, fishing a cigarette out of one of his jacket pockets and sticking it between his lips. "But could I see some ID, please?"

CHAPTER SEVENTEEN

ZAMORA WAS PLEASED with the way things were going. Tripp had done as he said he would and delivered Johnson to the airport on time. The high-priced fixer had even managed to accept the little surprise Zamora sprung on him by insisting he accompany them. "I can't even believe *you're* going," Tripp had protested vehemently, but the hulking form of Leonard standing behind him offered sufficient persuasion for Tripp to board the shuttle.

Originally Zamora hadn't intended to participate in the sabotage personally. But too many things had been going wrong during the past years. The cash reserves he'd managed to squirrel away from the latter days of his family's drug empire had diminished, his father had taken the secret of where he'd hidden the bulk of the family fortune to a maximum-security prison and then to his grave.

The question of whether his father had told his uncle where the fortune was stashed ate constantly at Zamora's brain like a disease. He had convinced himself that of the two uncles who had been convicted and sent to the Pennsylvania prison with his father, Ernesto was the more likely to have been the confidant. And, he rationalized, his father had been ill long enough to know he wasn't going to make it out of the prison alive and should pass on the family secret to at least one of the two relatives who were allowed to communicate with him. Each night as he engaged in his ritualistic bout with insomnia, which he usually lost, Zamora would persuade himself anew that Ernesto was now the keeper of the key to a fortune. That fortune had been built over the course of twenty years, thanks to the insane love some humans held for a white powder that made them feel like gods instead of the animals they were. The Colombian regretted that those days were gone, but there were other ways to exploit the human animal. He only needed capital, and lots of it. The VAC would provide the bankroll, Ernesto would provide the entire bank and Zamora would provide the brain to use them to the benefit of all concerned.

"Isn't it beautiful out here?" Zamora gestured toward one of the oval-shaped windows of the shuttle, beyond which stretched the infinite, star-drenched darkness. "Aren't you glad now that you came?" He spoke across the narrow aisle to Tripp, who looked as though he would have preferred to be sitting in hell than where he was.

"Let me put it this way," Tripp answered, hesitating as if thinking twice about what he was going to say. "I had other plans for the weekend," he finally answered, turning his head toward the window next to his seat.

Zamora laughed to himself and thought, I bet you did. "Well, enjoy the trip now that you're here. I'll have you and Mr. Johnson back in the States before you know it."

Johnson emerged from the cockpit, looking like a kid in the proverbial candy store. Zamora concluded that whatever reservations the engineer had had earlier over killing half a million people had been dissolved in the excitement of their dark mission. A million and a half dollars in electrocash didn't hurt, either. Money, Zamora said to himself once again, could put any conscience to sleep.

"The pilot says we're making the approach to Number 12," Johnson said. "I've asked him to rotate the shuttle ninety degrees so that you can have a look at her."

Zamora was conscious that the shuttle was slowly pivoting and looked out his window as the TRWS came into view.

It was even more massive than it had seemed in the photograph Johnson had shown him. It was also uglier than the photograph had indicated. He was impressed. He wondered how the machine would look from the Outland Strip as it approached on its death vector.

"How do we dock to the thing?" Zamora asked Johnson, who was looking over his shoulder.

"See that slit up by the nose?" the engineer asked, pointing toward the front of the scow.

Zamora picked out what looked like the doors of a small airplane hangar. "That's the docking bay?"

"Yeah," Johnson said. "I gave the pilot the frequencies to open the door and engage the artificial gravity. Do you see that funny bump right near the tip of the nose?" Again he pointed over the Colombian's shoulder at a domelike structure at the front and on top of the craft.

"Yes."

"That's the flight deck, if you want to call it that." Johnson chuckled. "That's where everything that runs the big bird is located—the central computer, the flight controls, the reactor controls, environment, everything. We call it the skull, because it houses the virtual brain of the machine."

"You said it would take you two hours to reprogram the system?" Zamora said, looking at his watch.

"Two and a half," Johnson answered. "No more than three. It depends on how many security loops I have to go through before the computer lets me bring up the real program."

Zamora noticed that the shuttle was turning around in preparation to enter the docking bay. He looked out the window and watched the dirty metal sides of the TRWS sweep by as they entered the belly of the ugly flying beast and landed. Zamora felt the landing more than he heard it;

the only sound was a loud hydraulic whine, which he assumed to be the docking bay doors closing behind them.

"It'll just take a couple of minutes for the place to pressurize, then we can get out," Johnson said, popping open a small overhead compartment. He took out a worn leather briefcase and moved toward the crew door near the front of the shuttle.

"Coming, Mr. Tripp?" Zamora said, rising from his seat. He looked farther back in the passenger compartment and motioned for Leonard to follow as the crew door was opened, creating the sound of a slight decompression inside the shuttle.

The Colombian followed Johnson down the short flight of stairs to the dirty, oil-stained floor of the docking bay. He could hear a low, resonant rumbling coming from somewhere deep within the bowels of the machine.

The docking bay was large, capable of holding four or five shuttles the size of Zamora's little Citation. It was built to be functional; its metal walls were dirty and discolored, and the ceiling of the hangarlike bay was actually the bottom of one of the waste containers that made up the bulk of the scow's structure. Some sort of jellylike substance oozed from the seams in the rusted metal and dripped to the floor in several places.

"Yeah, it's time for this baby to head out," Johnson said, staring up at the ceiling with Zamora. "There's no telling what that shit is that's dripping, so don't get it on you. You guys ready?" he asked, turning toward Tripp and Leonard, who had just exited the shuttle.

"Mr. Wotring is going to stay with the plane," Leonard said, referring to their pilot. "He says he needs to calibrate one of the sensors."

"Very well," Zamora said, turning to the engineer. "Lead the way, Mr. Johnson."

The four men followed Johnson across the metal decking and up a few steps. He unlocked a pressure-sealed door, saying, "You'll get your exercise here," and headed up more stairs. Made from a crisscrossed metal mesh, they switched back several times in a narrow shaft at least five stories high.

Zamora looked up. The stairs ended at a large landing with another pressure-sealed door. If they were headed for the interior of what was termed the skull, Zamora mused, then they were about to reach it by a climb up the inside of the creature's spine. He put his hand on the cold railing. He could feel the vibration he was hearing. It was as though the TRWS were alive.

After two flights the Colombian stopped to catch his breath. He waved the others on. Leonard wanted to hang back with him, but Zamora told him to keep an eye on Johnson and Tripp. He lit a cigarette and waited until the three men passed through the door at the top of the stairs, then reached inside his suit coat and took out a little Hauer Arms .32-caliber automatic. The sleek weapon was loaded with twelve fiberglass-tipped bullets designed to break apart once they hit something. He didn't want to risk blowing a hole through someone and having the same bullet pierce the shell that was separating them from the vacuum of space. He had made sure that Leonard, too, had loaded his Magnum with the same type of ammunition, and had told him not to use it unless it was absolutely necessary. Charging the chamber, Zamora flipped off the safety and pushed the pistol back into the holster beneath his coat.

Zamora was breathing hard when he reached the landing at the top, and paused for a minute to compose himself before entering the control center. He pulled out a handkerchief and wiped the sweat from his brow, then lit a fresh cigarette from the butt of his old one before grinding it out on the handrail. He tossed the dead butt down the stairwell, straightened his tie and stepped through the doorway.

"Hey!" Tripp said as Zamora stopped in the middle of the large room and looked round. "You're not supposed to smoke in here. Is he, Nelson?" He turned toward Johnson, who was hard-inputted to a console that curved around nearly a third of the dome-shaped flight deck.

Johnson turned toward them. He pulled one of his plastic-tipped cigars out of his shirt pocket and stuck it between his teeth. "I don't care if he smokes. I don't care if he shits on the floor." The engineer laughed in a high-pitched giggle. "The FAA isn't exactly in control up here."

Zamora thought the room looked more like a bunker than the control center for the massive drone. The ceiling and walls were covered with a beige-colored, urethanelike foam, and the aluminum-tiled floor was scuffed and dirty, giving the place the feel of a remote outpost or scientific station. A narrow window about two feet high curved around the circumference of the flight deck. Through its transparent slit he could see the brown, irregular back of the scow stretching out behind them like the skin of a desert-dwelling reptile. Ahead, and to either side, Zamora saw only space. He wondered what the Outland Strip would look like when it filled the windshield.

Zamora motioned toward a padded bench. "Let's have a seat, Mr. Tripp, and let Mr. Johnson earn his fee while we relax." He looked over his shoulder as he sat down and saw that Leonard had taken a position near the door. "I wonder if there's anything to drink in this place—I see there's at least one convenience." Zamora chuckled and pointed to a low door marked Rest Room.

"I won't relax until we get back to New York," Tripp confessed, perching on the edge of the bench.

"You know, Mr. Tripp," Zamora said, grinding out his cigarette on the floor with the toe of his hand-sewn dress boot, "I'm somewhat surprised by your...nervousness.

Certainly you've been on ... how shall I say, hairier excursions.''

Tripp looked at the Colombian as though he were trying to sell him a thousand acres of swampland for a building site. "Frankly, you have a reputation for leaving a number of your business associates floating in a river, that's all.''

"Oh, so that's it!'' Zamora laughed heartily. "That's funny, Sam Tripp. You think something like that might be in store for you?''

"I don't know what I think,'' Tripp answered. "But I sure as hell didn't count on taking this little ride up here with you and the others.''

"Let me explain why I insisted you come,'' Zamora said, sounding almost polite. "Last night, when Mr. Johnson almost balked at the deal, I was very impressed by your ability to persuade him to accept the situation for what it was. You and I are in similar types of business, Mr. Tripp.'' The Colombian took out his cigarettes and lit yet another. "We both know it's wasted energy to dwell on the unfortunate side effects of some of our operations. Since you were the one who proposed we use Mr. Johnson's services, I thought it your responsibility to come along and, if he gets cold feet again, make certain he carries out the task he agreed to perform. But perhaps I was unnecessarily concerned. Look at him.'' Zamora nodded at Johnson, who was bent over the console running his fingertips over a touch-activated screen displaying a schematic. He appeared oblivious of everything but the screen in front of his face. "He seems happy to do his part.''

"What would you expect from an engineer?'' Tripp asked. He no longer looked so nervous. "I imagine the million in electrocash erased most of his concern.''

"A million and a half,'' Zamora corrected, watching Tripp grimace ever so slightly.

"Whatever," Tripp said casually as he stood. "If you'll excuse me..." He nodded toward the rest room sign.

"By all means," Zamora answered, blowing smoke toward the ceiling as Tripp retired to the rest room.

The Colombian walked over to Johnson, who had donned an optical interface unit and was busy inputting the coordinates for the Outland Strip. "How's it going?" Zamora asked.

"Fine," the engineer said without taking his eyes off the screen. "I'll be done in thirty minutes."

"Thirty minutes?" Zamora was surprised. "I thought you said it would take three or four hours?"

"That's correct," Johnson answered, "but I managed to macro out all of the bullshit security algorithms. When I get done with these nav changes, I'm going to program in some new acceleration values that'll get this hummer launched in about half the time it would normally take." He looked around briefly and smiled. "I just want to make sure you get your money's worth," he said, and turned back to the screen.

"Good," Zamora said. "I'm impressed." His heart rate quickened, in anticipation not only of the scow's being driven through the Strip like a gigantic spearhead, but also of what would take place on the flight deck within the next hour.

Tripp came out of the rest room, and Zamora walked toward him, meeting him near the center of the room. "This should make you happy."

"What?" Tripp asked suspiciously.

"Your engineer says he'll be done in thirty minutes. We'll be leaving sooner than originally anticipated."

"Good." Tripp seemed relieved, as though Zamora's news had dispelled most of his anxiety.

Zamora lit a fresh cigarette. While Johnson hovered over the console like an orchestra conductor over his music, Zamora and Tripp stood in the center of the flight deck discussing a couple of jobs the Colombian had contrived. In exactly twenty-seven minutes the engineer unplugged the HI from the back of his neck and pulled the optical interface unit from his head.

"It's done," Johnson said, turning around. "All the data is locked in and—" he looked at his watch "—in approximately thirty-two hours the Outland Strip will no longer exist."

Zamora clapped his hands. "Bravo! You have just made me a very happy man, Mr. Johnson."

"Glad to be of service," he answered, walking toward the two men. "I think now is the proper time to ask you about payment of my fee."

"Certainly," Zamora said, taking a step backward. "In anticipation of your success, and of yours—" he nodded at Tripp "—I brought both your fees with me." Zamora started to put his hand inside his suit coat, but stopped, his eyes sparkling like diamonds. He held it up, open palm toward the two men. "You will take blue scrip instead of electrocash, won't you?"

Johnson broke into laughter, as did Tripp, though somewhat more tentatively. "You gotta be shitting me," the engineer said, his cigar protruding from one corner of his mouth. "Blue scrip is better than gold...hell, it's better than sex!"

"I'm glad you think so," Zamora smiled and moved his hand inside the coat. "I've decided to give you both a bonus, too." He pulled out the .32 and aimed it from the waist at a spot between the two men. "How about a trip to the Outland Strip?"

Johnson's mouth dropped open like a trapdoor, his eyes fixed on the weapon as though it was the last thing he'd ever expected to see. "Hey, hey, g-goddamn it," he stuttered, "what the hell's going on here?" He looked at Tripp, who was slowly shaking his head, his eyes fixed on the Colombian's face.

"When you travel in the jungle," Zamora said almost cheerfully, "sooner or later you're going to have to step over a snake. You can only hope it is sleeping when you do." He laughed.

"You're a snake, all right," Tripp said, his voice strangely resolute, and he took a step toward the Colombian.

Zamora immediately backed away, swinging up the weapon and aiming it at the man's forehead. "Don't do anything stupid," he said, nodding to Leonard, who had his big Magnum out and was aiming it at the side of Tripp's head, "or I'll make it painful for you."

"You can't kill me," Johnson whined. He seemed on the verge of tears.

"Why not?" Zamora asked. "You just pulled the trigger on five hundred thousand people and they don't even know it."

"You don't even have to pay me, please." Johnson fell to his knees and began sobbing, his face in his hands.

Zamora aimed the Hauer at the gap between the engineer's little fingers and pulled the trigger. Johnson's head snapped back as though it had been slapped hard by an invisible hand. His blood-covered hands dropped away, revealing a round red hole where the bridge of his nose had been. His head fell forward, leading his upper body to a sickening thud on the metal floor.

The Colombian started to swing the pistol toward Tripp, but suddenly found himself flying backward. Tripp had launched himself forward, his body crashing into Zamora's chest and knocking him to the floor. The .32 clattered across the metal tile behind and to his right. "Leonard!" he gasped. "Shoot the son of a bitch!"

Zamora felt Tripp jerk him over so that he blocked Leonard's line of fire just as his bodyguard's Magnum cooked off, filling the inside of the flight deck with sudden pressure. The bullet ricocheted off the aluminum floor, and he felt a sharp pain in one leg as though it had been stuck with several splinters. "Leonard!" he yelled again.

"I can't get a clear shot," Leonard cried.

Zamora managed to look down and could see Leonard moving up toward his and Tripp's tangled legs. "For God's sake . . ." Then one of Tripp's legs kicked out in a blur, up-ending Leonard. In the same instant Tripp released his grip around Zamora's chest. The Colombian rolled over, searching the floor for the Hauer. Running footsteps pounded on the floor behind him, and Zamora whipped his head around just in time to see Tripp disappear out the door.

"Goddamn it!" Zamora got to his feet, ignoring the pain in his leg. He looked at Leonard, who was struggling to get his bulk off the floor, and pointed toward the exit. "Go get the son of a bitch!" he screamed. Leonard hustled after Tripp, who could be heard pounding down the stairs.

The Colombian cursed himself for not shooting Tripp first. He should have remembered that anyone with experience in killing would himself be harder to kill. He spotted his little automatic next to the padded bench and moved toward it, suddenly realizing he was limping. "Damn," he said, looking down at his left leg. The pant leg above his boot was soaked in blood.

Zamora forced the pain from his mind, determined to retrieve his weapon. Replacing pain was a mixture of rage and fear. Tripp was, after all, heading toward the only means of escape from the TRWS. Zamora picked up the .32 and willed his legs to break into a shuffling run toward the door. Echoing up the stairwell came Leonard's shouts in Spanish, followed by the resounding boom of his Magnum. Suddenly Zamora's legs flew out from under him and his head and back slammed against the floor. For a crazy second he wondered if Johnson had somehow regained consciousness and reached out to trip him. He looked around and realized he'd slipped in the dead man's blood.

It took Zamora a good five minutes to limp down the stairs, his anger growing with each step. He peered through the crack in the door that opened onto the docking bay and could see Leonard crouched near the nose of the shuttle peering toward a round, open hatchlike door that was stenciled Engine Access. Zamora started to move into the hangar, but something made him stop. He watched Leonard rise slowly and move cautiously toward the hatch, the Magnum held high next to his head, pointing at the roof.

Zamora took a step over the threshold and watched in amazement as legs appeared on the other side of the shuttle. Tripp was sprinting after Leonard, who spun around just as Tripp hit him with a cross-body block. The two men fell onto the grimy floor and slid a couple of feet before coming to a stop in a wild tangle of arms and legs. Zamora moved toward them, limping down the short span of steps to the hangar floor, aiming the .32 at the struggling bodies. Somehow Leonard's weapon suddenly fired, and the sound cracked in the hangar like thunder near the point of a lightning strike. The Colombian crouched instinctively as the bullet slammed into the ceiling overhead, punching a hole through the rotting metal. Looking up, Zamora saw a tiny stream of liquid fall from the smoking point of impact. "Shit," he said, and resumed his lurching run toward the two men. A sharp odor filled his nostrils as he steered around the little puddle that was forming beneath the hole. Ahead he could see Leonard holding up the Magnum, both of Tripp's hands latched onto his big wrist like the jaws of a mongoose on the neck of a writhing cobra.

"I hope this hurts," Zamora said, pulling the trigger of the Hauer, unconcerned that he might hit Leonard. The little weapon kicked slightly in his hand, and a small hole appeared just below Tripp's right shoulder. Tripp screamed in agony. He released his grip on Leonard's wrist and, pain-racked, rolled over into a fetal position.

"Let me finish off the son of a bitch," Leonard said, scrambling to his feet and pointing the barrel of his weapon at the back of Tripp's head.

"Hold it," Zamora ordered, raising his left hand to stop him. "I don't want the bastard to die that fast." He shuffled forward a couple of steps and smacked the side of the automatic across Tripp's right ear. "Look at me, you son of a bitch."

Tripp rolled his eyes up toward the Colombian, his face the color of a dirty bed sheet. "Go ahead and kill me," he moaned.

"What the hell!" The pilot, Wotring, suddenly emerged from the shuttle and walked up behind the three men.

Zamora turned toward him. Wotring was wearing a bright orange flight suit, his short gray hair flattened from the headgear he'd been wearing. "Where the hell have you been?" the Colombian asked. "Why weren't you out here helping Leonard?"

"Jesus!" Wotring said, holding up his hands, his voice defensive. "I heard the shooting and closed the crew door, and it's a good thing I did. That bastard tried to get in." He pointed at Tripp, whose face was now ashen. "I figured it was best to protect our ride." He raised his eyebrows and jerked a thumb toward the shuttle.

Zamora nodded. "At least someone was using his brain." He turned to Tripp and spit on him.

"What the hell happened, anyway?" Wotring asked.

Zamora ignored the question and addressed Leonard. "Drag the son of a bitch over here." He pointed at the puddle of foul liquid that was dripping more heavily now from the bullet hole in the ceiling. "Let's give the man a bath."

"No!" Tripp cried, his eyes wide with horror as he stared at the dripping gunk. It had formed a milky pool approximately four feet in diameter, and little wisps of white vapor roiled up from it like smoke from a witch's brew.

"Looks like some sort of acid," Zamora said, his eyes burning. He backed away several steps from the noisome puddle and pulled out a cigarette. "Drag his ass over here," he repeated before lighting it, "and don't make me tell you a third time."

Leonard tried to grab one of Tripp's ankles with his free hand, but the man kicked down, slamming a shoe across his knuckles. "Damn!" the big bodyguard yelped in pain, jerking his hand away. He kicked Tripp hard on the blood-soaked shoulder where Zamora had shot him. "I'll teach you a lesson, asshole," Leonard huffed, kicking him again, this time in the back of the head.

Tripp screamed and clasped his hands over his head as Leonard managed to seize one of his wrists. The Colombian bodyguard dragged him across the floor like a sack of garbage and flung him into the seeping pool of mystery milk.

Zamora watched in grim fascination as Tripp thrashed around in the liquid as though several hundred volts of raw electricity were being pumped through his body. His screams became a high-pitched wail as his clothes began to smolder. He rolled over, unintentionally putting his face right under the source of the liquid, and almost instantly the skin melted away, exposing blood-painted areas of his skull and the sickly orbs of his eyeballs.

"Watch out," Zamora said calmly to Leonard and the pilot, stepping back as Tripp's grotesque form rolled again. The dying man crawled across the hangar floor, his dissolving body leaving a trail smeared across the dirty metal. After advancing less than five yards, the body slumped into smoking heap, screams giving way to a gurgling death rattle.

"Just in time," Leonard said. He pointed at the ceiling with the barrel of his Magnum.

Zamora looked up. The stream of liquid had tapered off to a slow drip. "Let's get the hell out of here," he said, taking a deep drag of his cigarette. He motioned toward the shuttle with the automatic before sticking it back in its holster.

Wotring took three steps toward the machine and froze. He turned slowly toward Zamora, looking worried. "I hope Johnson's still up there," he said, pointing toward the stairs.

"He's up there all right," Zamora assured him, puzzled by the pilot's concern.

"That's good," Wotring said, "because I don't know how to open this son of a bitch." He waved toward the massive doors of the docking bay.

Zamora's stomach dropped into a deep, dark pit. He thought for a moment that the artificial gravity system had malfunctioned. "What do you mean?" he asked, his spit drying up inside his mouth as though it had been blowtorched. "I thought Johnson gave you the frequencies for all of that crap."

"He gave me the ones to open doors and initiate the gravity field," Wotring answered, his face pale. "He didn't give me their counterparts."

"This is not a good time to be making jokes, Mr. Wotring," Zamora said, his mind racing like an out-of-control roller coaster.

"Hell, it's no joke!" The pilot shook his head in shocked amazement.

Zamora looked around. Icy fingers gripped his throat, reducing his claustrophobic breathing to shallow gasps. He forced himself to concentrate, driving fear from his mind by sheer willpower. "Maybe you use the same frequencies," he said weakly.

"I doubt it," Wotring said with a shake of his head. "I've never heard of a command telemetry signal causing the inverse response just because it's repeated."

"Well, have you got any goddamn better ideas?" Zamora snapped, trying to keep the desperation out of his voice. Without waiting for the pilot to respond, he turned to Leonard. "Get your ass up there and see if Johnson's got a pulse."

"But, boss," Leonard protested, "you shot him in the—"

"I know where the hell I shot him!" Zamora screamed. He could feel his heart jumping around in his chest, and it reminded him unpleasantly of Tripp's body flopping in the death pool a few minutes earlier. "Now just get your ass up there and wait for us. If he's alive, make him tell you how to get out of here."

Leonard immediately took off up the stairs, holstering his Magnum as he ran. "Come on," Zamora said as the bodyguard disappeared through the doorway of the stairwell. "You're going to try the same frequencies. Hey, wait a second," he said, grabbing the sleeve of Wotring's flight suit. "How did you close the damn things after we landed?"

"Sensors," the pilot answered, jerking his arm away. "They close automatically."

"Shit," Zamora breathed. He followed Wotring up and into the cockpit of the shuttle, oblivious of the burning pain as he dragged his injured leg along, but aware that blood had filled his boot, causing a squishing sound as he hobbled up the narrow, ladderlike steps. "Don't start the engines," he said as the pilot brought up the electrical system and activated the closure of the crew door. "Just try the command. If the doors open, start the engines then."

Wotring looked up at Zamora, who was leaning over his seat. "If this does happen to work," he said, his face grim, "your friend Leonard is going to bite the big one."

"Just shut up and try it," Zamora said, praying to himself that it would work.

Wotring punched a series of numbers into a small control panel inset in a console next to his seat. "Here goes," he said, punching the initiate key. "It didn't work," he said after a couple of seconds. "I told you it wouldn't."

"How the hell do you know?" Zamora said, panic eating away at the vestiges of his rational thought process. "I know we didn't hear anything, but look, you can't see the goddamn things.... They could be open!" He leaned forward and craned his neck, trying to look behind the shuttle through the cockpit's side window.

"This is how I know." Wotring pointed at a digital readout on the panel display in front of him. "The pressure outside is still the same as it is in here." He turned his head toward Zamora, who was staring at the screen as though he'd just read his own obituary. "Looks like we're trapped."

"Open the goddamn crew door," the Colombian ordered. "We're going upstairs, Johnson said the central computer controlled everything, so *you* should be able to figure out how to get us the hell out of here."

Wotring tilted his head and laughed. "I'm a goddamn pilot, for chrissake, not an engineer!" He turned sideways in his seat and spoke to Zamora's back. "I suggest you let me send out a Code Zebra distress signal, and we sit tight until someone who knows how to open up this junk heap comes up here and springs us."

Zamora reached under his suit coat and pulled out the automatic. He swung around and jammed the barrel under Wotring's nose, tilting his head back with it until the pilot was looking straight up into his face. "Listen to me, you idiot," he grated, resisting the temptation to squeeze the trigger. "This goddamn scow is going to ram a hole straight through the Outland Strip in about thirty-six hours. Now I suggest we go up to the control center and try to figure a way to get out of here before that happens. Does that make sense to you?"

Wotring slowly moved his hand up to a switch on the instrument panel and opened the crew door. "Not much on the whole damn trip makes sense to me," he said, his voice hollow and flat.

"Any more insolent remarks from you," Zamora said, straightening and pulling the gun away from the pilot's face, "and you'll eat the barrel of this son of a bitch." With his sweat-drenched face twisted into a hideous mask, he threw back his head and broke into manic laughter.

CHAPTER EIGHTEEN

FROM THE OUTSIDE Les Dartt's little hideaway in the Down Side looked like a rusting wreck in salvage. It was just one of dozens of nondescript, slump-roofed, modular buildings jammed together on a trash-littered street called Moonrise Boulevard. Horn got a different impression of the place, however, after Dartt pushed the button of an opener on the dash of the Douglas speedster and the reinforced garage doors on the street side of the building rolled open. Inside he could see a clean, brightly lit and well-organized area that reminded him of the inside of a fire station.

Dartt popped the bubble as the door closed behind them, then parked next to a large rubber cord hanging from a hook on the wall. One end ran into a junction box with a digital control panel built into its metal face.

"Everybody out. We're home," Dartt said, unstrapping his harness and getting out of the machine. He popped a cover over the right wheel well and grabbed the plug end of the cord hanging on the wall. "Fill her up," he said, plugging the cord into the car before turning and punching a button on the panel that was labeled Quick Charge.

Horn crawled out of the car and looked around. The end of the room opposite the garage area was obviously Dartt's living quarters. There was a single bed, two olive drab steamer-type trunks and a wooden chair in one corner next to an open door that led to a small bathroom. The other side of the room was set up as a combination kitchen, dining room and study. A section of the wall was covered with shelves stuffed with books. There were also several boxes of books stacked neatly on the floor in front of the shelves. A small table with two chairs sat in front of a narrow counter that held a single sink and an old microwave. Under the counter were cabinets and next to it was a small green refrigerator that had red letters stenciled across its door, spelling out Medical Supplies Only.

"Looks like your place," Winger said, slapping Horn on the shoulder, "only clean." He laughed and rubbed the stubble on his chin.

"You boys want a beer?" Dartt asked, walking toward the kitchen area. He pulled a couple of six packs of Rushmore out of the refrigerator.

Winger looked at his watch. "Seven a.m. . . . sure," he said, grinning. Dartt handed him a can and Winger popped the top.

"You got anything to go with this?" Rohde asked, accepting a can of beer.

"You mean something to eat?" Dartt asked.

"No, something stronger than beer." Rohde chuckled and squinted his eyes before taking a sip. He acted as though the liquid would burn his lips. "Whiskey," he drawled, wiping his mouth with the back of his hand. "I need something to give this frog piss a little kick."

Dartt hesitated, staring at the big Texan while handing a beer to Horn. He set he remaining cans on the table, then opened a cupboard door and fished around inside. Finally he pulled out a half-filled fifth of generic-label whiskey. "How's this?" he asked, holding it out to Rohde.

"Hot damn!" The big gambler grabbed the bottle by its neck. "Old No Name, my favorite." He took a long, healthy swallow of his beer, then uncapped the whiskey and poured a large measure of the amber liquid into the can. "Now this'll hit the spot." He raised the can to his lips and drank.

"Shit," Winger muttered, shaking his head. He walked to the refrigerator and grabbed the handle. "May I?" he asked Dartt.

"Sure, help yourself," Dartt answered, popping a beer for himself. He turned toward Horn, who was leaning against the Douglas, sipping his beer. "Let me change my clothes first, then I'll call up the commercial shuttles and find out when the next flights out are scheduled."

"You have a telemonitor?" Horn asked, looking around the room.

"It's right behind you."

Horn looked at the wall behind him. An old black-screened CRT telemonitor was built into the wall next to a fading poster announcing the Long Beach, California Grand Prix of 2022. "Mind if I call the States?" he asked as Dartt walked toward his bed, pulling off the leather jacket.

"Go ahead," he said. "I've got a tap into a satellite feed. Call Mars if you want to."

Horn stretched. He felt stiff and sore and knew the aches and pains would get worse as the adrenaline worked up during the firefight continued to fade.

"Want some of this, partner?" Winger asked. He was slicing cheese from a half wheel he'd found in the refrigerator. Horn shook his head. "How about you, dice man?" the young cop asked Rohde, who was busy pouring whiskey into another beer.

The Texan set the whiskey bottle on the counter. "Sure," he said, then picked up a large slice and stuffed it into his mouth.

Horn chuckled and walked around to the telemonitor. He punched on the power to the screen and waited patiently for the dead eye to flicker back to life. When it finally lit up, Horn entered the code for Christina Service's office. A bright Stand By prompt flashed on the screen. Horn leaned against the Douglas and took another swallow of his beer.

It tasted good, the alcohol was warming his body, making him feel sleepy.

The face of a woman with glasses and a severe hairstyle appeared on the screen. "This is the district attorney's office," she said, her voice nasal and grating. "How may I direct your call?"

"Assistant D.A. Service, please," Horn said. He took a drink of beer and noticed the disapproving look on the woman's face.

"May I tell Ms. Service who's calling?" she asked, looking as though she'd just been sucking on a particularly sour lemon.

"Yeah," Horn said, stifling a belch. "Tell her it's Detective Horn, Manhattan West." The screen went back to standby mode.

A few seconds later Christina Service's image filled the screen, her ice-blue eyes burning directly at the camera lens that Horn knew was situated over her monitor. "Max, where the hell are you?" she demanded urgently.

"The Strip," he answered. "Just having breakfast." Horn drained the beer can and immediately wished he had another.

"I mean *where* on the Strip?" she asked, ignoring Horn's tired attempt at humor.

"We're at a guy's house in a section of the place called the Down Side. We got Rohde."

Service's eyebrows shot up a fraction of an inch. "Is he—"

"Alive? Sure he is. Rohde," he said, turning toward the Texan, "come over here."

Rohde finished loading cheese and crackers on a plate, picked up his doctored beer from the counter and walked over next to Horn. As he took a bite of two crackers sandwiching a piece of cheese, the crackers broke and crumbs rolled down the front of his shirt. "Damn," he said, and looked up at the screen.

Horn gestured toward the big Texan. "This is Jack Rohde."

"Who's she?" Rohde asked.

"I'm the assistant district attorney for the City of New York," she answered.

Rohde had been relaxed since their safe arrival at Dartt's home, but now the full significance of his presence there accompanied by the two police officers seemed to sink in. With it came memories of the last time he had been in police custody, the attempt on his life, and his escape from both police and his boss-turned-enemy, Ruben Zamora.

"Wait a minute," he said. His voice was sober and he pointed a finger at the screen. "Did the cop die? I never did hear." Horn detected genuine concern in the man's voice.

"What are you talking about?" Service asked, glaring at Rohde.

"Pull in your claws, lady," Rohde said, his face long and sad. "I'm talkin' about that little police captain who was takin' me to the hearin' when we got hit. Kelso was his name."

"He's dead," Horn said. The reminder of Kelso's death erased the warm, relaxed feeling he'd been enjoying just seconds earlier.

"I'm sorry to hear that," Rohde said. "He seemed like an okay guy just doin' his job. He treated me like a human being, which can't be said of all cops."

Horn reached up and punched the mute button on the telemonitor's ancient control panel. Now they couldn't hear Service and she couldn't hear them. "How did you escape, anyway?"

"Just lucky, I guess," the Texan answered, shaking his head.

"How the hell do I know whoever killed Kelso wasn't helping you escape?" Horn asked, confronting Rohde with a question he needed an answer to.

"Shit," Rohde said, swallowing hard. "Those were Zamora's goons." He shook his head. "I see what you're gettin' at and you're dead wrong, boy. Those bastards were tryin' to kill me, not help me escape. That little po-lease captain saved my ass." Rohde's voice had risen almost to an angry yell. "Man, I didn't have a goddamn thing to do with his death or his driver's. You can't pin that kind of rap on me." He looked straight into Horn's eyes and his voice dropped. "Listen, son, they just happened to be in the wrong place at the wrong time, that's all—just plain got dealt a cold hand."

Horn knew the big man was telling the truth. His account of how things had come down jibed with what he'd suspected. But part of his brain—the cop part—had had to hear it from the man's own lips.

His eyes drifted up to Service's image on the screen, and he jerked his head back in surprise. He had meant to tune her out for only a brief exchange. Instead he had become totally involved in the grim digression with Rohde and had forgotten all about getting back to the assistant D.A. He decided to hold off for now on asking the Texan about Zamora.

"Better put her back on the horn, boy," Rohde drawled, and gave his wheezy chuckle. "She looks plenty pissed to me."

Horn punched the button to restore the sound, and Service's voice blared out from the speaker. "Goddamn it Max..." she barked, her eyes throwing cold blue knives. Horn braced himself for a full-blown ass-chewing, but it never came. She appeared to will her anger to subside, and when she spoke again her voice was controlled and measured. "If you'll excuse us, Mr. Rohde..." she said, nodding at the Texan.

"Why sure, darlin'," Rohde drawled, and walked back to replenish his blend of beer and whiskey.

"We've got a very serious problem," Service said as soon as Rohde was out of range. "I don't have a lot of details, but here's the situation. The Department of Energy has lost control of one of their space-launched waste receptacles."

"So?" Horn said. He wondered why Service was telling him this. "What's that got to do with what's going on up here? Why don't they just blow it up?"

"Max, shut up," Service said simply. "You may be able to help in this situation. There's not much time, so I need you to listen. And you, too, Detective Winger."

Unnoticed by Horn, Winger had approached the screen when Rohde left. He appeared mesmerized by the sight of the assistant D.A.

Horn was slightly taken aback by the woman's direct approach, but he could tell by her tone that she was serious. Winger took out his notebook and pen as Horn said, "Go ahead. I'm all ears."

"The thing they lost control of is big, Max. It's one of those Toxic and Radioactive Waste Scows." Horn could see she was reading from something below the screen. "They started the program ten or twelve years ago, remember?" Service looked up. "It was a big deal back then."

"Yeah, I remember. The things are as big as buildings and they're launched into deep space, right? I thought it was a pretty good idea."

"They're launched toward the sun," Service corrected, "but that doesn't matter. What does matter is that the one launched this week is off course and heading straight for the place you're standing on. The Feds tell us that in less than eighteen hours it's going to ram the Outland Strip and they can't do anything to stop it."

"You gotta be shittin' us!" Winger blurted out, then looked embarrassed at his lapse.

Horn ignored his partner's outburst. "What the hell happened to the thing?"

"They don't know. There's speculation that there was some kind of catastrophic failure of the guidance system, but I think it's pretty damn coincidental that of the infinite number of vectors available for it to take, it's on a near-perfect trajectory to take out the resort. Doesn't it sound funny to you, Max, considering what you've been doing up there?"

"I don't know if *funny*'s the right word," Horn answered, looking over at Rohde, who was intent on a conversation he and Dartt were having. "What about the military?" he asked, turning back to the screen. "Can't they catch the damn thing, or at least take it out with a missile?"

"There isn't time," Service answered. "Besides the guidance problem, the thing apparently has a malfunction in its throttle system. It's accelerating at about twice its normal rate. The Air Force can't launch anything in time to catch it, including missiles."

"If it does hit, how much damage can it do?" Winger interjected.

"It'll destroy everything, Detective Winger," she answered. "Everyone who can't get off the resort will die."

"How the hell can it do that much damage?" Winger asked skeptically. "This place is huge."

"This barge is larger than one of the Twin Towers," Service said, sounding irritated. "It's filled with millions of tons of radioactive and toxic waste that will probably saturate anything it strikes, not to mention the fact that it's got a nuclear engine burning like a Roman candle somewhere in the middle of all—"

"I get the picture," Winger said, holding up a hand.

"Back to the military, or the government, hell..." Horn shrugged in frustration. "They must have *something* flying in this area, and surely whoever built the damn thing can tell them how to shut it down. You said there were how many hours to play with?"

"Eighteen," Service replied. "And to address your other contentions, we're in the process of contacting the officials of Wetstone Engineering in Los Angeles. They designed and built the thing—"

"Wait a minute," Horn interrupted. "You said *we* are in the process of contacting Wetstone Engineering. How come you've involved in this?"

"That brings me to the point you just made—that there has to be something in the area. There's *someone,* Max," she said solemnly. "It's you."

Horn was struck dumb for several seconds. He looped what he'd just heard through his mind over and over before it finally registered. "Hell, I don't have a shuttle," he spoke slowly, his tongue feeling as if it had been anesthetized. "I only flew one once and it was all automatic. I didn't even land it. They recovered us with a..." Horn's voice trailed off and he looked across the room at Dartt, who had changed into a paramilitary camou outfit. There was a click in Horn's mind, and he remembered Dartt saying something about being qualified or licensed to fly shuttles. Dartt had bragged about how hot a pilot he was. Maybe you're going to get a chance to prove it, Horn thought, turning back to Service. "Sorry about that," he said. "Even if we can get to the thing before it reaches here—what makes you so sure we can derail it, even if someone manages to tell us how?"

Winger spoke up again, surprising Horn, "If it's something like changing a couple of lines of code, I could probably handle it. I'm sure Wetstone can give us some pretty detailed instructions on what we need to do, maybe even a play-by-play, in real time.''

"We'll give it a shot," Horn said with determination. He realized he no longer felt tired. The old magic of his adrenaline was pumping through his veins like fresh blood. "If Wetstone can't come up with a technical solution, maybe we can try something else," he added, even though he had no idea what that might be. He almost laughed when he thought of something the size of a standard business-class shuttle trying to physically nudge off course a ship the size that Service had described. The picture of a gnat trying to turn a charging water buffalo came to mind. Service gave him a worried look, but she didn't comment on what he had to admit was probably false bravado on his part.

"Let us get back to you once we solve our first problem," Horn said. For one crazy moment he wanted to say something more personal to the blond woman on the screen. An endearment came to his lips, but he swallowed it back. He had to admit, though, that he felt something more than respect for her, something that he couldn't define. It made him uncomfortable—yet in an oddly pleasant way.

"What do you mean, your first problem?" Service asked.

"We've got to beg, borrow or steal a shuttle," Horn answered. "Otherwise we can't get there from here."

Service frowned. "How long do you think it'll take you to get off the Strip?"

"I don't know—a couple of hours maybe." Horn was only guessing. He had no idea what the chances were of getting their hands on a shuttle, let alone how long it would take.

"Well, listen," Service said, rubbing her brow with a fingertip, "when you're ready to launch, or whatever it is you do, get back to us and hopefully we'll have the Wetstone people tied into the net by then."

"Any news on the Colombian?" Horn asked, remembering their earlier conversation.

Service looked puzzled. "What?"

"The Colombian," Horn said. "Zamora. Where is he?"

"Oh, yes." The assistant D.A. nodded. "I got a report less than an hour ago that he's disappeared. The FBI had an agent on him up until yesterday, and he apparently left LaGuardia with a flight plan to Sydney, Australia." Service shrugged. "They never landed in Sydney."

"Say no more." Horn held up a hand. "Talk to you in a couple of hours."

"Goodbye, Max," Service said, "and good luck." The screen faded to read Transmission Completed, then went dark.

For some strange reason Horn wished Service hadn't tacked "good luck" onto the end of her goodbye. He didn't want to think that he needed luck to do the job.

"I told you she likes you," Winger said.

Horn turned toward his partner, who was grinning. "Huh?"

"The Barracuda." Winger gave Horn a playful jab on the arm. "She has the hots for you. You don't think I missed the *Max* this, and *Max* that, and *goodbye, Max,* because I sure as hell am gonna miss that wild palooka of yours." The young cop laughed crazily and patted Horn on one cheek.

"You're so full of shit, Winger," Horn said, pushing his partner's hand away, "you need to register your brain with the sewer department. Let's go, partner. We've got to find ourselves a shuttle."

Just then a loud hammering could be heard on the door. Everyone froze, looking around with a "who the hell could that be" expression on their faces. Dartt pulled the long-barreled revolver from beneath the camouflage jacket he was wearing and moved past Horn to the door.

Horn was about to pull the 9 mm out of its holster in order to give Dartt some backup when something so strange
happened that it sent chills down his back. Instead of his
mods glitching as they sometimes did in reaction to a stim-
ulus, Horn felt his entire body glitch. He'd just *thought*
about reaching inside his jacket and extracting the big automatic when he looked and saw it already in his hand,
hammer cocked. His mod had extracted the weapon of *its
own* volition, not his.

"Yeah, who the hell is it?" Dartt demanded, jerking
Horn out of his brief detachment from what was going on,
and he looked up. Dartt was peering through a tiny peep-
hole in the door.

"It's me, Sharkey," someone yelled on the other side.
"Let me in, Dartt. Your neighborhood sucks."

"Oh, shit," Dartt said to Horn. "It's him, God's alba-
tross."

Horn shrugged, and Dartt pushed a button next to the
door, raising it a couple of feet before stopping it. "Get your
ass in here. You've got two seconds," he barked.

The scurvy body of Mark Sharkey appeared beneath the
door as he scrambled into the garage area like a giant roach.
He was wearing black engineer's boots, black pants and a
dirty white dress shirt. A frayed gray flight jacket hung from
his shoulders like the rag it was. Horn noticed that the little
bounty hunter had replaced the beret with a bright red scarf
that was tied around his head gypsy-style, covering the
wound Rohde had pistol-whipped into his head.

Dartt closed the door as Sharkey got to his feet. "What
are you trying to do," he asked, "win the perpetual bad
penny award? How the hell did you find my place, anyway?"

"Shit," Sharkey answered, "tracking fools like you is
how I make my living." He looked around the room and his
eyes lit up when they landed on Rohde. "You got the big son

of a bitch. Damn good deal.'' He clapped his hands once and pointed at the Texan. ''Got ya, sucker.'' Sharkey blew Rohde a kiss and gave a high-pitched titter.

''Well, if it isn't the famous Mark Sharkey, bounty hunter extraordinaire,'' Rohde drawled, walking toward Sharkey. He was smiling and seemed to be on the verge of laughter. ''You nailed any other desperadoes lately...besides me?'' Rohde wheezed out a restrained version of his snorting laugh, then calmed himself by taking a long pull on the beer can in his hand.

Horn caught Dartt's attention and motioned him to follow to a corner of the room away from the others. ''Listen,'' he said, ''you told me you can pilot a shuttle. Is that right?''

''That's right,'' Dartt answered. ''Commercial, military, I can fly damn near anything as long as it's got English or intersymbol nomenclature on the instruments.''

''You want to expand the scope of your contract with me?'' Horn asked.

Dartt took out one of his little cigars and lit it, never taking his eyes off Horn's. ''I couldn't help overhearing most of what you and the woman were talking about.'' He lowered his eyelids slightly. ''I can get you up to the scow, but we'll probably have to steal a shuttle.''

''Why is that?'' Horn asked. ''I figured we could rent one.''

''You could,'' Dartt said, ''but they almost always require a twenty-four-hour background and credit check—unless, of course, you're a regular customer.''

''Well, that I'm not. But maybe we could commandeer one if I flashed my badge.''

Dartt laughed. ''Hardly.'' He pulled back his jacket and nodded at the worn grip of his pistol. ''We could commandeer one if we flashed this.''

"What about getting one of the casino owners to bail us one?" Horn asked. "I'm sure if we explained the situation, they'd be willing to help."

"I don't think you've got time, cop," Dartt said, blowing smoke toward the ceiling. "What'd the woman say—eighteen hours? I don't know how close the damn thing is, but the more time we dick around trying to get a shuttle legit, the less time you're going to have to do whatever it is you need to do once I get you there."

"Then you'll do it?"

"Yeah, but it won't be cheap." Dartt smiled. "Ten thousand, fixed price and no negotiating."

"Done," Horn said. He was still trying to shake the weird, almost numb sensation that had overcome him minutes earlier when he discovered the 9 mm in his modified hand. He concentrated on getting on with what Dartt had emphasized—saving time.

"Then let's get our asses over to the main shuttle port and pick out something I've been itching to fly." Dartt smiled and clasped his hands together, cracking his knuckles. "One problem, though," he said without concern in his voice. "We'll have to go on to Earth once you fix this garbage scow, or whatever the hell it is. I won't be able to come back here, especially if we have to appropriate a flying machine."

"Makes sense to me," Horn said. "We'll take Rohde—"

"And me," Sharkey interrupted, a rank smile on his face.

Both men turned and looked at the gutter-based man hunter, who had walked up to where they were standing without their noticing.

"Shit," Dartt said, a sardonic smile creeping across his face. "We wouldn't take you to a dog fight."

"Wait a minute." Sharkey held up his hands and turned to Horn. "You said I could go with you when you took this guy in." He pointed at Rohde. "You're not going to stiff me on the goddamn reward, are you?'' The little man lowered his eyebrows and worked up a look that almost passed for mean.

"I did say that," Horn acknowledged. He looked at Dartt and shrugged.

Dartt shook his head, but couldn't suppress a rueful grin. "All right, you can come along, you little bastard, but you'll have to ride the hump," he said, referring to the rise between the four seats of the electrocar, which housed the big engine.

"I don't mind," Sharkey said, smiling victoriously.

"You look like a fool with that silly smile," Dartt said, walking to the Douglas and unplugging its power source.

"You'll probably look like a fool when you die," Sharkey jabbed back.

"Shit, let's get out of here," Dartt yelled, climbing into the driver's seat. He activated the door opener and wound up the machine as the others crawled over the cowling: Winger in the front with Dartt, Horn and Rohde in the back and Sharkey sitting up above the others as though he were riding a camel. The bounty hunter had to bend over slightly as Dartt lowered and locked the bubble.

"How long will it take us to get to the shuttle port?" Horn asked as Dartt backed out of his bungalow and closed the door before heading up Moonrise.

"Twenty, thirty minutes," Dartt answered, pulling onto a wider, trash-littered street that paralleled one of the ditches. "Depends on whether or not we have to toe-dance with any of the loonies, down there." He nodded toward the ditch on his left.

"It's kind of early for them, isn't it?" Winger asked.

"Time has no meaning on the Strip," Dartt said, kicking up the speed of the machine, "especially if you're crazy." He turned his head toward Sharkey. "Time doesn't mean shit to you, does it?" he asked, laughing.

Just as Dartt was returning his eyes to the road, something slammed into the side of the bubble, just behind and above Horn's head. A millisecond later came an explosion like a sonic boom to the right of the car. Everyone ducked simultaneously, and Dartt jammed the foot feed to the floor. At the sound Horn flashed back to the casino and remembered the fleshette gun wielded by the wire-haired man.

"Shit!" Winger yelled. "There they are!" He pointed at a faded green convertible that was screaming out of an alley in an attempt to intercept the Douglas. The young cop pulled out is machine pistol and jerked back the sliding mechanism, charging the chamber. "It's the same two assholes who were at the Milky Way," he said, sliding back the sunroof and rising toward it.

"Watch it," Horn yelled, grabbing the back of his partner's jacket and pulling him down just as an automatic weapon opened up, stitching a line of splintered holes across the upper part of the bubble.

Horn swung his head around as the attacking vehicle slid into the street right behind them, white smoke coming off its tires like roiling thunderheads. The man whose burr head looked like a skull was at the wheel of the death machine, holding the same automatic rifle he'd been using in the casino. Its muzzle flashed as the weapon jacked itself up into the air, its lead flying harmlessly over their heads. Horn shifted his sight to the wire-haired man, who looked like a demonic biker in his wraparound goggles. He sported a mangy-looking goatee that Horn hadn't noticed during the turmoil at the Milky Way. He was fumbling with the fleshette gun; Horn knew they would be in deep shit if he got off a shot at the range they were now tracking.

"Now! Give it to them!" Horn shouted, shoving Winger up through the open sunroof.

The young cop sprayed the car behind them, and pieces of fiberglass flew from the body of the machine as it swerved sharply in an attempt to get out of the line of fire.

Rohde slapped Dartt on the shoulder. "Come on, boy. Step on it." He looked at Horn, his face pale and worried. "Let me have a gun."

Horn figured the man had a right to defend himself. "Give him your Magnum," he told Winger, who had dropped back into the passenger compartment and was changing the clip in his machine pistol.

"Him?" Winger tilted his head at Rohde. The young cop's face was flushed and his eyes were wild.

Horn nodded. Winger pulled out his .44 and tossed it into the Texan's lap. Rohde opened his mouth and started to say something but was interrupted as the fleshette gun cooked off again. It sounded as though it had been fired point-blank directly behind the Douglas. Horn seemed to feel, as well as hear, the nasty little darts slam into the back of the machine. He wondered what would happen if they pierced the batteries.

"Goddamn!" Dartt yelled, looking over his shoulder. "That may be a piece of shit they're driving, but it's a hot piece of shit." He accelerated to almost 130 and managed to put a little space between the two cars.

"Whoa," Dartt yelled, grabbing Winger's jacket as the cop tried to crawl back up through the sunroof. "Everybody hold on," he ordered. "I can't lose these bastards on the street, so let's see how good they are in the ditch."

Horn felt his stomach rise in his throat and had a crazy sensation of weightlessness as Dartt cranked the wheel over hard and cut through a sickeningly steep drainage slip that was filled with garbage and other debris. Horn's body was pressed hard into the seat, then jerked violently sideways so that his head banged into the plastic bubble. When he looked up, they were in the ditch, trash blowing out behind the Douglas as if a tornado were cutting through a landfill. Dartt was laughing crazily and slamming one hand on the top of the padded steering wheel as though he'd just pulled the escape of the century.

"I think you lost them, hoss," Rohde said, turning his head and peering behind the car. He was holding the Mag, barrel up, next to one ear. Suddenly he whipped it out, slapping Sharkey across the side of the head. The little bounty hunter screamed in pain and fell against Dartt, who lost control of the speeding machine for a moment. It swerved up one bank of the ditch and rode the lip in a dangerous speed wobble as Dartt fought for control.

Horn grabbed the collar of Sharkey's jacket, jerking him off Dartt. He jammed the little man into the small space between him and Rohde, as though he were stuffing a rag into a crack.

"You son of a bitch," Dartt yelled as he brought the machine back down from the side of the ditch into its flat bottom. He reached back and tried to slap Sharkey, but quickly gave up as the Douglas slammed into a metal garbage can. He had to latch both hands on the wheel as the can flipped over the top of the car and bounced off the rear cowling.

"Why the hell did you do that?" Winger asked Rohde, who was glaring at Sharkey as if he wanted to seriously hurt the man.

"I should have killed you when I had the chance," the Texan said to Sharkey, ignoring Winger's question.

"What the fuck did I do?" Sharkey squeaked.

"The two guys in the car must have followed your ass to Dartt's place." In spite of Rohde's anger, his voice still rolled slowly out of his mouth like a snake shedding its skin.

Horn realized the Texan was probably right, but he could have killed them all by trying to punish Sharkey inside the car at such an inopportune moment. "Pull a stunt like that again and I'll take the weapon," he told Rohde.

"Don't worry," Rohde responded. "I won't hit the son of a bitch again. At least not until we get the hell out of here."

"Shit," Dartt said, "I don't like the looks of this." He slowed the Douglas and pointed at an overpass about five hundred yards ahead. "I forgot about this son of a bitch."

"What's wrong?" Winger asked, peering through the scarred bubble.

"You can't tell if anyone's on that overpass," Dartt explained. "I almost bought it here one night when one of the loonies dropped a bowling ball from the damn thing."

"A bowling ball?" Winger laughed in wild amazement. "You gotta be kidding,"

"Hell, I'm not kidding." Dartt glanced at the young cop and grinned, apparently infected by Winger's sense of humor. "Well, there's only one way to handle this little problem," Dartt said, pressing the foot feed to the floor.

The Douglas accelerated quickly, its engine winding up like a jet as the wash of rubbish boiled up behind it. Horn was surprised to see Sharkey wriggle free from between the seats and pull an ancient, sawed-off double-barreled shotgun from beneath his jacket. Its stock had been replaced with a pistol grip wrapped with friction tape.

"What the hell are you going to do with that popgun?" Rohde wheezed.

"Show you guys how to ride shotgun," Sharkey answered, pulling himself from between the seats and rising through the sunroof.

"You don't want to do that," Horn said, wondering what the bounty hunter was trying to prove. He figured he must be trying to dispel the washed-out gutter image that was more or less his trademark.

He started to reach for the back of Sharkey's jacket to pull him down but froze as Winger yelled and pointed at the overpass. "Goddamn it, Les, they're up there."

"Shit." The word was jerked from Dartt's mouth as he swung the Douglas onto the left bank of the ditch, its tires squealing like four wild pigs.

"Whoa," Winger screamed, crossing his arms in front of his face as a ball of fire erupted from the lip of the overpass.

They were within thirty yards of passing under the structure. Horn could see the wire-haired man in a prone position, the weird-looking fleshette gun kicking up and smoke billowing out following the explosive muzzle-flash. He looked up at Sharkey just in time to see the man's upper body disintegrate as though it had exploded from within. Fist-size pieces of flesh, suspended in a red cloud of blood, were torn away in the slipstream. The rest of his body remained lodged in the Douglas as it flew beneath the overpass like a rocket.

As soon as they cleared the bridge, Horn heard the pop of the skull's automatic rifle open up behind them. Everyone instinctively ducked, except what was left of Sharkey, which appeared to be caught on the lip of the sunroof. Acrylic plastic splintered, and Horn felt himself thrown to the left as Dartt whipped the Douglas down from the bank again and onto the floor of the ditch. Dartt slowed the machine then, swearing as he wiped away Sharkey's blood, which had spattered across one of his pant legs.

"You better haul ass, son," Rohde said, raising his voice above the high-pitched whine of the engine. He was half turned in his seat to look out the rear. "Believe it or not, them sons of bitches are behind us and closin'."

"You gotta be shitting me," Dartt yelled incredulously, glancing over his shoulder. He reached around Sharkey's blood-soaked legs, slapped Winger's arm and pointed a thumb at the remains of the bounty hunter. "Throw him out. We got too much weight—that's why I can't outrun the bastards."

Without hesitating, the young cop grabbed Sharkey by the waist, hoisted what was left of the body through the sunroof and let it slide backward off the bubble. A red smear was left on the bullet-riddled plastic. The body rolled through the trash and under the wheels of their attackers' machine, which bounced only slightly, as though it had hit a shallow pothole.

"What the hell is this?" Horn groaned. The ditch had begun to narrow rapidly, causing the Douglas to rise from the floor, straddling the gap.

"I don't know," Dartt answered. "I've never been down this section. But our shit's in a sling if we get knocked off this track."

Horn could see what Dartt was talking about. The ditch had already narrowed to little more than the width of the car, and there was now a good twenty feet beneath them and the trash-covered floor. There was no way off the track without going in sideways and winding up in the shape of a taco.

"Look out," Rohde yelled, ducking his head and covering it with his arms.

The explosion of the fleshette gun sounded so close that for a moment Horn thought the electrocar's batteries had overheated and blown apart. He crouched as a tight pattern of the deadly metal darts ripped through the back and out the front of the bubble, leaving two holes. A rush of wind immediately whipped through the inside of the car, whistling loudly. And Winger screamed, clutching his left shoulder.

Horn turned around as best he could in the narrow seat and aimed the 9 mm out through the hole. He suddenly experienced the same bizarre feeling he'd had back in Dartt's bungalow when the big automatic had just appeared in his modified hand. He couldn't remember drawing the weapon. It was as though he expected it to be there, a natural extension of the odd configuration of flesh and machine that was called his body.

Shaking these distracting thoughts from his head, Horn concentrated on drawing a bead on the wire-haired man, who was setting up for another shot with the fleshette gun. Horn squeezed the trigger without attempting to use the laser and saw a chunk of fiberglass on the front of the car fly off and into the face of the driver, who nearly lost control of the machine. It rode crazily up one lip of the bank, like a circus clown car. Horn could have sworn no more than an inch of tread was keeping the car from slipping into the ditch like a wedge in a crack. He pulled the trigger four more times. The two men ducked as the front of the car exploded in a shower of faded green fiberglass. The attackers dropped back out of range, but Horn knew it wouldn't be for long.

"You got any grenades?" Horn asked Winger, who had straightened in his seat. He could see one of the ugly little razor darts sticking out of his partner's shoulder. Winger's face was twisted in pain. "No," he answered between clenched teeth, "sorry."

"Shit," Horn said aloud, looking back through the hole in the rear of the bubble. The attacking machine was moving up again, and the wire-haired man was bringing the business end of the fleshette gun to bear on the rear of the Douglas. An idea broke loose from the periphery of Horn's mind and floated into focus, and he turned toward the front of the car. "Pop the bubble," he told Dartt.

"What?" Dartt managed a quick glance at Horn. Dartt's face was beaded with sweat, in spite of the gale-force wind blowing through the inside of the machine. "Are you fucking crazy?"

"Pop it," Horn repeated.

Dartt turned his head toward Horn again, this time flashing a smile of understanding. "You got it," he said, reaching toward the dash.

Horn looked behind them just as the locks of the bubble snapped open and the leading edge of acrylic plastic popped up and hooked the wall of air that the Douglas was now piercing at more than 130 kilometers an hour. There was a fleeting sound of metal ripping, then the bubble was gone. Horn felt his head pushed toward the rear of the machine as the dome flipped end over end straight into the nose of the car behind them. It broke in half, flying over and under the machine, which lurched sideways, its rear end sliding into the crack in a shower of sparks. Horn saw the fleshette gun fly from the wire-haired man's hands as the machine did a washboard bounce, then cartwheeled and jammed violently to a stop.

"Shee-it," Rohde said as a brown cloud of dust and trash caught up with the crashed vehicle and enveloped it.

Horn thought he saw movement in the wreckage as it receded in the distance. He broke his stare from the odd vision and turned toward Winger as Dartt brought the speed of the Douglas down. Before his partner had time to take a breath, Horn transferred the 9 mm to his left hand and reached up with his right, grabbing and extracting the dart from Winger's shoulder in one blurred motion.

Winger grunted painfully. "Don't touch the son of a bitch," he said to Horn, his face pale.

"You mean this?" Horn held up the dart, its razor edges slick with his partner's blood.

The young cop stared at the ugly projectile in Horn's hand for several seconds before a lopsided grin spread across his face. A moment later his skin turned ashen, his eyes rolled back in his head and he slumped sideways in a dead faint.

"He'll be all right," Rohde drawled as Horn tossed the dart out of the electrocar. "You did the boy a favor."

"No doubt," Horn answered. He noticed that Dartt had slowed almost to a stop and was pulling onto some kind of metal grating. "Where the hell are we?" he asked the driver.

"Shit! I don't believe it," Dartt answered, wheeling the Douglas onto a narrow street. "We're out of the Down Side...and if I'm not mistaken, the shuttle port is less than ten blocks from here."

"Still think you can get us a ride?" Horn asked, stuffing his handkerchief inside Winger's jacket, directly over the wound.

Dartt glanced around and smiled. "After this shit—" he raised his reddish eyebrows "—it'll be a piece of cake."

CHAPTER NINETEEN

HORN LEANED INTO the narrow aisle of the Rutan business-class shuttle and yelled, "Hey partner, get back here. It's Service again."

Winger emerged through the open cockpit door; he'd been talking to Dartt, who was behind the controls. He settled into the seat next to Horn, where they faced Christina Service's image on the panel display built into the bulkhead in front of Horn's seat.

"Gentlemen," Service said, "I'm afraid they haven't been able to locate the Wetstone engineer. He's on vacation and can't be found anywhere. They're trying to get hold of the guy's backup, just in case."

"What do we do in the meantime?" Horn asked, looking at his watch. "We should be intercepting the damn thing in less than thirty minutes."

"Just maintain the last heading we gave you. That will get you in visual range," she answered.

Horn fixed his eyes on the woman's. "Don't you think it's about time you leveled with us?"

"What do you mean?"

"What I mean is, when you first put us on this intercept vector, it was supposed to take a little longer than seven hours to reach the scow. Since then you've given us four course corrections and the flying time is half the original estimate. Whatever the hell's going on, Christina," Horn said in his best "don't give me any bullshit" voice, "we have a right to know."

Service rubbed her ice-blue eyes, which were rimmed with red circles of weariness. "The Wetstone people told me not to tell you, but to hell with them. The scow has definitely been sabotaged. And since we talked earlier when you were on the Strip, they've figured out that the throttle has been put in some sort of loop that has caused the engine to run away."

Horn shook his head. "Run away?"

"Well, something like that," Service answered. "It's accelerating out of control. It's speed keeps increasing and they can't slow it down."

"Holy shit," Winger breathed.

Horn held up a hand to silence his partner. "So? We still have time to get there and change its course—that is, if you can get hold of the engineer who can tell us how to do that."

"There's no need for sarcasm, Detective," Service said, her voice edgy. "The reason they didn't want me to tell you about the throttle problem is because the drone wasn't designed to travel at any speed above a slow crawl. They say the whole thing could shake apart at any minute."

"If it does, then at least the Strip will be out of danger," Winger interjected.

"Not really," Service said, shifting her gaze to Winger. "All the waste containers that make up this ship will still be flying at the same speed when it breaks apart. The Strip will get hit one way or the other. But some of Wetstone's technical people think it could hold together long enough to make it past Mars."

"If its present course is altered," Horn added.

"That's correct," Service said, lowering her voice. "I think you have to take the chance, Max. I just wanted you to know the risks."

"I appreciate that." Horn suddenly felt something warm stir inside him as the woman's aura seemed to touch him.

But the moment was gone as quickly as it had come, blown away by Winger's voice.

"Listen, Ms. Service," the young cop said, "if you don't find the guy who can tell us how to steer this thing away, this little excursion is going to count for nothing."

"You're absolutely right," Service responded, forgoing a reminder to Winger that he was repeating the obvious. Then she said, "Just a moment, please." She turned away to speak to someone off the screen for a minute or two, then returned to Horn and Winger. "I've just been told the chief engineer from Wetstone, a man called Nelson Johnson, is now considered to be a 'missing person,' and it seems likely he's involved in the sabotage, either voluntarily or through some kind of foul play. His backup, a Mr. Strohacker, is supposed to be on his sailboat, somewhere. The Coast Guard has been sent to pick him up, and we can then link you directly with their cutter. We should be hearing from them any minute."

"If we get there in thirty minutes," Winger said, thinking out loud, "that doesn't to give us much time to make the changes."

"Exactly one hour and thirteen minutes," Service said bluntly.

"Holy shit," Winger said again. This time Horn didn't raise his hand.

"By the way," Service asked, "where's Jack Rohde?"

"He's in the back, sleeping," Horn answered. He didn't tell her that the big Texan had discovered the shuttle's minibar shortly after they launched and had promptly drunk himself into a stupor.

"And whose shuttle are you using?" she asked. "Did you hire one?"

"We rented it." Horn figured he wasn't too far from the truth. The only difference was that Dartt had used his Magnum instead of a credit card.

"I'll make sure you're reimbursed," Service said. "Which reminds me, Wetstone says they're going to pay a substantial reward if you pull this off."

"Substantial?" Winger grunted. "Probably a hell of lot less than what they'll pay out to settle the lawsuits if the scow does ram the Strip."

"True," she said, appearing to mull something over in her mind. "That probably has a lot to do with why they didn't want me to tell you about the throttle."

"I've got a visual," Dartt yelled excitedly from the cockpit. "And it's one big son of a bitch."

Adrenaline surged in Horn's bloodstream. "Get back to us when you get this Strohacker guy on the wire," he said to Service. "I'll make sure someone stands by the link on this end." Service nodded and the transmission ended.

Winger was already heading for the cockpit. Horn, too, squeezed into the cramped space and looked out through the curved window at a brown spearhead that was rapidly filling the view.

"Goddamn!" Winger exclaimed. "The son of a bitch must be a mile long."

"At least," Dartt said, flipping off the full-authority autopilot and assuming manual control of the little ship. "Let's take a little survey of this dinosaur." He touched one of the screens on the instrument panel and upped the shuttle's speed. His other hand pushed a side arm controller, and the needle nose of the shuttle pitched down toward the droned scow.

Horn felt as if he were on a crazy carnival ride as Dartt flew within five hundred yards of the jagged, pointed nose of the TRWS before whipping the shuttle up and racing down its length.

Winger broke out in a thrill-laced laugh that was almost a giggle. "Damn it, Dartt," the young cop said when he'd brought his outburst under control, "you weren't kidding when you said you could fly."

"I can fly better than anybody living or dead," Dartt said, pulling up and over a particularly large section of waste containers in a maneuver that caused Horn's stomach to drop. "Watch this," the pilot said when they reached the end of the scow. He jerked the grip of the controller, brought the ship around, rolling inverted and punching up the throttle, and raced back up the length of the scow.

"Find the docking port," Horn ordered as they cleared the nose and Dartt righted the shuttle.

"Well, this is the control deck, I'm sure of that," Dartt said, swinging the shuttle around a circular dome on the nose. "Wait a minute. What the hell was that?" he suddenly barked, taking the bird in dangerously close to the bump that perched like a smooth wart on the nose. "Goddamn it, I saw somebody, or something, moving in there."

"You're full of shit," Winger immediately responded. "I didn't see anything."

Dartt glared at Winger. "You better watch who the hell you're saying is full of shit, cop," he snapped. "I know what the hell I saw."

"Sorry," Winger said sheepishly.

"Watch it," Horn cautioned. The nose of the shuttle drifted within yards of a stained conex that stuck out from the mass of containers clustered around the dome.

"Shit," Dartt gasped, jerking the controller back and to one side. The shuttle did a ninety-degree nose-up, then spun to one side in a sort of pivot, missing the obstacle by inches. "That's right, sweetheart," Dartt said, rolling gently away from the nose of the scow.

"Find the docking bay," Horn repeated, placing his gloved right hand on Dartt's shoulder.

"You got it, boss." Dartt brought the shuttle around in a half circle, transversing the side of the droned scow just below and behind the dome. "There it is," he said seconds later, pointing through the cockpit window at the huge rectangular doors built into the maze of waste containers. He turned to Horn. "But I swear I saw something moving in there."

"We'll find out soon enough," Horn answered. "You've got the frequencies. Open it up."

Dartt punched a series of numbers into a data entry panel below the glare shield. Seconds later the massive doors pulled apart, revealing the interior of the docking bay. A black Citation shuttle sat in the center of the hangar like a sleeping cockroach.

"What'd I tell you?" Dartt said. He looked at Horn as if waiting for instructions.

"Take it in," Horn said, nodding toward the jawlike doors. "You know how to pressurize the thing, right?"

"Environment, gravity, your woman friend gave me all the codes, but I don't think I'll need to initiate the gravity," Dartt said as he eased the shuttle down and into the bay next to the jet-black Citation.

Horn understood what Dartt meant; without the artificially induced gravity field, the other machine would have been floating.

"Doors are closing automatically," Dartt said, turning the shuttle slightly to one side before allowing it to settle on the metallic floor. "Pressure and environment coming up." He punched another series of numbers into the panel. "She said it would take four or five minutes before we could get out," Dartt reminded them, shutting down the shuttle's engines. "What's the plan?"

"Where the hell are we?"

Horn turned around with a start at the sound of Rohde's voice. The Texan, who was peering over Winger's shoulder, looked puzzled.

"The waiting room in hell," Dartt said. He motioned toward the cavernous hangar. "I bet we can go right in."

"Think that guy will mind us taking his place in line?" Rohde asked, pointing out the window at the grotesque lump that was the remains of Sam Tripp.

"Jesus!" Dartt gasped. "Is that a man?"

"It ain't no beast, son. Those rags you see were its clothes," Rohde drawled, laughing as if pleased by Dartt's discomfort.

"Let's cut the crap and see what's going on," Horn said. He motioned for Rohde and Winger to clear the way.

"I'm with you," Winger said, pulling the machine pistol from beneath his jacket, grimacing slightly as he raised his left arm. He pulled back the slide and checked the chamber of the weapon.

"You're forgetting one thing," Horn said. "You—"

"Oh, you mean this?" Winger said, interrupting Horn. He looked around at the bloodstain on his jacket shoulder. "It's not bad. No shit. It'd be different if it were my right . . ."

"I'm not talking about your shoulder," Horn said, extracting the 9 mm and checking its clip. "You're supposed to get the dump from Wetstone on how to change the course of this machine." He gestured with the automatic, indicating the scow. "You gotta stay here, partner."

"Shit!" Winger's voice revealed his disappointment and frustration.

"But don't worry," Horn said, grinning. "I'm leaving Mr. Rohde here to keep you company."

"I'm dropping the side door," Dartt said before Winger could respond to Horn's sarcastic consolation.

There was a sound like steam being released as the door came open. Horn was immediately aware of a sharp, acrid odor that made his eyes burn slightly and his throat close up involuntarily.

"Well, tell me what you want me to do once the Wet-stone transmission comes through, and then hurry up and get the hell out before this shit gasses us," Winger said, screwing up his face in reaction to the odor.

"We're going up to check out the control room," Horn said. "I'm sure that's the access over there." He pointed at a hatchlike door at the top of a few steps. "Once they tell you how to turn this bastard, get your ass up there."

"Listen, partner," Winger said, "wouldn't the de-compression have asphyxiated anyone in here when we opened the doors?"

"Maybe. But the door over there—" he nodded toward the stairs "—looks like some sort of pressure hatch. Notice that it's closed."

"Let me go with you," Winger said. "Dartt can stay and talk to the engineering guy."

"Forget it," Horn said, and addressed Dartt. "Come on, Les, let's check out this ghost you saw." He swung back to Winger. "And, anyway, you're the one who told Service you could handle it, remember?"

"Don't remind me," Winger said, stepping back to let Horn and Dartt exit the shuttle.

Horn and Dartt approached the mass of melted flesh and bone curled like a misshapen pretzel on the dirty metal floor. Their footsteps echoed strangely in the docking bay. Horn was surer by the minute that something or someone was waiting for him in the bowels of the big machine. He could feel a distinct, low-frequency vibration coming through the floor.

"Pretty grim," Dartt said, pulling the long-barreled re-volver from its holster.

"What about the bird?" Horn asked, pointing at the Ci-tation. "The door's closed. Does that mean someone's in it?"

"Not necessarily," Dartt said. "See that little panel inset next to the door? You can close it and lock it up from the outside. But it would have been a perfect place to be when we popped the big doors. Want me to try and open it up?"

"No," Horn answered, motioning for Dartt to follow as he headed for the stairs. "There's nobody in there." Somehow he knew that whoever was in the scow was above them in the dome-shaped control room. Horn didn't understand how he knew it—he just did—and he accepted the information without questioning it.

There was a slight hiss as Horn unlatched the door and the pressure between the docking bay and the stairwell evened out. "Look at this!" Dartt said, pointing at a smeared trail of blood leading up the stairs.

Horn didn't comment but climbed steadily, two steps at a time. He was feeling great. His adrenaline had pumped up his perception to a fine edge as well as his body. He was aware of his E-mods in that he wasn't aware of them; they seemed as natural a part of his body as his flesh-and-blood appendages, and they had tuned in to the part of Horn's mind, the *cop* part, that was raising a big red flag in front of his face. It warned that he was about to cross into the death zone, and so he felt very much alive.

"Wait," Dartt breathed as Horn reached the landing at the top of the stairs. His chest was heaving, and beads of sweat had formed across his wrinkled brow. "Give me a chance to catch my breath before you pop that thing." He nodded toward a door similar to the one at the bottom of the stairwell.

The run up the stairs hadn't altered Horn's breathing in the slightest. He saw no reason to delay just on Dartt's account, so he pulled down the lever on the oval door.

There was another hissing sound as the latches released and Horn pulled the door open, stepping into the control room. The red beam of his laser sight automatically painted a spot on the chest of a slightly built man standing in the middle of the room. He looked like a South American. Out of the corner of one eye, Horn could see another man, in an orange flight suit. "Cover that one, Les," he ordered, pointing with his left hand.

"No need for the weapons, gentlemen," the South American said. "There's been enough killing here for one day."

Horn took a swift glance at the body on the floor near the slight man, splayed out in a pool of blood. The South American was standing with his hands in the pockets of his suit coat, a strange smile etched across his face.

"You're Zamora."

The man didn't deny it. "And who might you be?"

"Horn, Max Horn."

A look of surprise and uncertainty passed across the Colombian's face like a shadow. "The cop, right?"

"The cop..." Horn repeated. "Right." He noticed the blood soaking the lower part of Zamora's pant leg. "Have an accident?" He motioned toward Dartt, who was frisking the man in the flight suit. "Who's that?" he asked.

"That's the man who flies the black Citation downstairs," Zamora answered. "We were just getting ready to leave, and now that you're here, I guess we can. Which of you has the codes to open the big doors?"

Horn laughed. "You mean you locked yourselves in here?"

"I guess you could say that." Zamora chuckled. "Pretty funny, yes? But now that you're here, well, think of yourself as our key. Now that's pretty funny too. Right, Leonard?" Zamora craned his neck and looked over Horn's shoulder.

"Shit," Horn breathed as he turned and stared at the hulking form of Leonard, who was aiming a large-caliber weapon at the middle of his back. How could I have been so stupid? he thought, noticing now the open door of the rest room.

"Drop your weapons, both of you," Zamora snapped. "Kill the first one who hesitates," he ordered Leonard.

Horn let the 9 mm slip from his hand and glanced over at Dartt, who placed the Magnum on the floor.

"That's better," Zamora said, his voice suddenly relaxed, calm. With his left hand he extracted a pack of cigarettes from his coat pocket. He shook one out, stuck it between his lips and pulled out a lighter. "Now, we're going to go downstairs, get in the Citation and head for Earth. If you're cooperative, I might let you live." He lit the cigarette and inhaled deeply, squinting as the smoke curled up in front of his face.

"Your idea of cooperation, no doubt, is for someone not to scream when you put a bullet through his head," someone drawled from the doorway. The Colombian's face turned ashen as he whirled and saw Jack Rohde.

"Drop the gun, Leonard," Rohde said. "Or don't drop it and give me a reason to blow a hole through your worthless body."

Leonard dropped his weapon as Rohde stepped through the doorway. He had Winger's pistol trained on the big bodyguard, who was staring at Zamora as though waiting for instructions.

"Long time no see, *señor*." Rohde laughed. The word *señor* took three or four seconds to roll off his tongue. "When are you going to get it through your head, Ruben, that I ain't the easiest guy in the world to kill?"

"I should have had you in New York," Zamora spat, glaring at the Texan.

"You had two cops killed instead of me," Rohde said, his wheezing laugh stopping abruptly as though it had been cut off with a switch.

Zamora shrugged. "This one will make three," he said, nodding at Horn. "Only this time, Jack, you'll be dead, too."

Horn jumped as the right pocket of Zamora's suit coat exploded in a muzzle-flash of shredded fabric and white smoke. He swung around and saw Rohde bend over double as the bullet struck him square in the stomach.

"You son of a bitch," the Texan groaned, falling to his knees. The Magnum clattered to the floor.

Horn took one step toward Zamora and spun, kicking out with his right foot, aiming for the Colombian's chest. He felt his modified knee flex as the bottom of his boot slammed into Zamora's left breast, knocking him backward violently as though he'd been struck with a wrecking ball.

"Horn, watch out," Dartt yelled.

Horn pivoted in time to see Leonard's big arm swing wildly toward his head. Before he could dodge it a flash of light burst in front of his eyes and he found himself on the floor, his cheek pressed against the vibrating metal. Across the room he could see Dartt struggling with Zamora's pilot, both men wrestling for control of Dartt's weapon.

Out of the corner of one eye Horn saw a blur. It was Leonard's shoe, swinging toward his face like a sledgehammer. Horn raised his right arm, and the big man's shin cracked across the titanium forearm like a piece of wood.

Leonard's scream filled the control room as Horn staggered to his feet, shaking his head in an attempt to regain some of his senses. Leonard had fallen into a sitting position and was clutching the area above his shin, moaning in pain. Horn's head cleared and he moved toward the fallen man, something like rage, only more controlled, cleaner, welling up inside him. His modified arm cocked itself sideways in a pure, machine motion that bore no resemblance to the movement of a human appendage. He neither willed nor resisted the inclination of the E-mod as it shot out in an arc and drilled its titanium fist into Leonard's soft temple. Horn heard bone shatter as the bodyguard's head snapped sideways, lying across his shoulder. Leonard's dead eyes rolled up into his head and he fell backward, his arms bouncing as they smacked the floor.

At that moment the orange-suited pilot succeeded in ripping the pistol away from Dartt. He slammed its butt across the side of Dartt's head and knocked him unconscious to the floor. Horn took eight quick steps and clotheslined the pilot just as he was aiming the pistol at Dartt. The blow knocked the man over Dartt's body and headfirst into one of the control consoles. Horn grabbed him by the collar, jerked him backward like a rag doll and spun him around. Blood poured from a cut over one of the man's eyes, and his nose was twisted sharply to one side, obviously broken. Horn felt something jab into his stomach and looked down, surprised to see the pistol still gripped in the pilot's hand. He slapped his right hand down and hooked his fingers around the barrel of the weapon, jerking up just as it exploded between them. Horn turned, raising his arm across his face as the bullet hit the pilot directly under the chin, then blew off the top of his head in a gruesome fountain of blood and brain.

Spinning around as the pilot toppled across the console, Horn surveyed the control room. There were five bodies on the floor, but Zamora was gone. "Damn," Horn said. He picked up his 9 mm and walked toward Rohde, who lay curled up just inside the door in a pool of his own blood. Crouching, Horn used his teeth to pull off the glove on his left hand and laid two fingers across the Texan's neck. At the same time he looked over and saw Dartt's chest rising and falling. "At least he's alive," Horn said aloud.

"Damn right I'm alive," Rohde groaned.

"Shit!" Horn gasped, startled. "I guess you are."

"Did you get the son of a bitch?" the dying Texan asked, rolling his eyes toward Horn.

"Not yet."

"What the hell are you waiting for? Go get the bastard." Rohde choked and began coughing as blood foamed out of his mouth and nose.

"Take it easy," Horn said, patting the man on the shoulder. "You'll be okay." He realized how ludicrous his words were and felt a stab of helplessness as blood covered the floor around Rohde's head.

"One favor, cop," the Texan said, controlling his cough for the moment.

"Sure," Horn said, nodding. "Anything."

"Do me," Rohde moaned. "The pain's worse than..." He coughed again, a gurgling sound.

Horn didn't have to ask Rohde what he meant. He forced himself to rise to his feet, though he felt numb. Looking down at the Texan's pleading eyes, he slowly lowered the 9 mm, activated the laser and aimed it at the man's left temple. He waited for the mod to pull the trigger the rest of the way, but nothing happened. A cold sweat broke out across his forehead, and he wondered what the hell was going on.

"Please," Rohde begged, his death rattle more pronounced.

Horn released the trigger and the beam disappeared. He backed away from Rohde and looked down at Winger's Magnum, his mind floating somewhere outside his body. Not conscious of having made the decision, Horn slid the weapon toward Rohde with the side of his boot.

"Thanks, hoss," the Texan breathed as Horn stepped over him and went out the door.

Horn heard the Magnum fire its mercy shot as he bounded down the last flight of stairs and ducked through the door into the docking bay. He froze and raised the automatic as the door to the shuttle popped open. Relief re-placed the anxiety in his mind as Winger came down the steps and ran toward him, the machine pistol dangling in his right hand.

"I couldn't stop Rohde from leaving," Winger said rapidly, his voice excited. "I was right in the middle of getting the word from this Strohacker at Wetstone when he made the slip. Sorry."

"That's okay," Horn said. "Can you make the changes?"

"Yeah, they're pretty simple," Winger answered. "He even gave me a code that would get me into the master co-ordinate bank without going through all the security protocol. It should take me less than fifteen minutes."

"Do it," Horn said, looking around. He wondered if Zamora had boarded the Citation.

"Oh, by the way—" Winger pointed across the floor to the door that accessed the engine room "—the guy you're looking for went in there. I watched him from the cockpit. You must have got him in the leg because he's limping like a bastard. He's got a gun, too."

"You get going," Horn said, shoving Winger toward the shuttle. "I'll take care of him."

Horn slipped through the door to the engine room and peered around cautiously. He fanned the red beam of the laser sight across a narrow catwalk that stretched thirty yards across a gap between two massive waste containers. Under the catwalk was a pit filled with corroding metal drums over which a steel netting was stretched. Noxious fumes leaked up from the drums in wisps of yellow vapor, causing Horn's eyes to water. Another door across the catwalk was standing open several inches, and a loud rumbling like thunder rolled out from behind the door, the ship vibrating in time with its beat.

Moving across the catwalk, Horn realized how oppressively hot it was. The huge containers were radiating heat like a furnace. Sweat ran down his back as though it were coming from a faucet, and he stopped at the door long enough to strip off his jacket.

Inside the brightly lit engine compartment was another long catwalk that ran across the round, curved tops of the engine's three main reactors. He could see it vibrating as though the ship were passing through some strange turbulence. Horn took two steps onto the metal grid and froze at the sound of Zamora's voice behind him.

"This looks like a good place for a cop to die," the Colombian said.

Horn turned around slowly. Zamora stepped through the door behind him, an insane smile spread across his sweat-drenched face. His little automatic was pointed directly at Horn's head.

"Where the hell did you come from?" Horn asked, baffled as to how the man could have been behind him. "My partner said he saw you come in here."

"I saw the fool watching me as soon as I entered the docking bay," Zamora said, never taking his eyes off Horn's. "I let him watch me come in here, then after his face disappeared from your ship's window, I doubled back to the Citation. I was on the starboard wing resting my leg, waiting for you to come trotting by." The Colombian laughed. "If you move an inch, I'll blow a hole in your head big enough to see through," he warned. "Now drop your gun."

"Why should I?" Horn asked, the rage he'd felt in the control room returning, sweeping through his mind like a cold wind. "You're going to kill me one way or another."

Zamora grinned. "You're not as stupid as most of your brothers in blue."

"Just like you did Dick Kelso," Horn went on, ignoring the Colombian's remark.

Zamora raised his eyebrows. "Dick who?"

"One of the cops you had killed the first time you tried to nail Rohde," Horn answered. "He was a friend of mine." A picture of the police captain flashed in Horn's mind, and he felt his mods flex involuntarily.

"Too bad," Zamora said, mock pity hanging on his words. "Like my father used to say, 'Fools die.'" He laughed.

Horn eased his body forward ever so slightly, following the lead of his mods, which seemed to have a track on the Colombian.

"I said don't move," Zamora hissed.

"Go ahead and get it over with," Horn said calmly, his mods spinning up like death gyros.

For a moment Zamora looked confused, then the composed madness returned to his eyes. "All right, then die."

Horn's right foot was already slamming into the Colombian's midsection when he pulled the trigger. The blow caused the weapon to drop, and the bullet ricocheted off Horn's modified shoulder, its fiberglass tip exploding in a shower of splinters that peppered the side of his face like shrapnel. He screamed in agony and staggered sideways as one of the shards drove itself nearly an inch into his right eye. His mods jerked crazily as the pain filled his head. His right leg went out from under him and his body hit the catwalk. He fought the pain and rolled over onto his back, forcing his left eye open. Zamora's blurred form staggered in front of him, pointing the automatic at his chest. Zamora was clutching his stomach with his left hand and his chest was heaving.

"You son of a bitch," the Colombian said, his face twisted into a hideous sneer. "I hope that hurts. I want you to be in a lot of pain when you drop into hell."

Horn looked around desperately for his 9 mm. His stomach dropped as he saw it lying between Zamora's feet.

"Too late, cop," Zamora said, the sneer changing to a smile. "You're dead—"

Horn's mods glitched in anticipation of the bullet slamming into his body, but instead he saw Zamora's head jerk forward suddenly as if it had been hit with a maul. The entire top of his head came off, and he fell forward, slamming facedown on the catwalk, his blood dripping through the metal gird onto the gleaming dome of one of the reactors.

"Are you all right?" The voice was Winger's.

He stepped through the doorway, the barrel of his machine pistol smoking. Dartt followed, and the two men stepped over Zamora's body.

"Holy shit!" Winger breathed. "What the hell happened to your face? Goddamn! Did you catch a bullet?" The young cop sounded on the verge of panic.

"No," Horn said, his eye burning like a live coal. He was leaning on his left elbow, covering his right eye with his modified hand. "I caught some fragments in my eye. I think it's gone."

"Looks like you caught them all across the side of your face," Winger said, crouching. "Let me see." He grabbed Horn's hand and pulled it gently away from the eye. "Oh, man! Partner, I think you're right." Winger's voice was filled with empathy. "It's pretty grim."

Horn looked up at Winger. He realized his rage was gone, replaced by an inner peace. "Don't worry." He smiled at the young cop. "I'm sure it's something Dr. August can take care of. I owe you one, partner."

"Let's get the hell out of here," Dartt urged. He took Horn's left arm and helped him to his feet. "We got this goddamn thing turned away from the Strip, but it feels like it could fall apart any second."

Horn let Dartt and Winger lead him to the engine room door, then pulled his arm away. "Wait," he said, walking back toward Zamora. He leaned down and picked up the 9 mm, pausing to look at the Colombian. Responsible for the deaths of so many, Zamora had overreached himself with the killing of Dick Kelso. Nemesis in the shape of Max Horn had hunted him down.

The TRWS would carry its toxic cargo—and the remains of six bad men—deep into space. And Horn and his partner could go home.

Horn turned to Winger and Dartt. "Yeah, let's beat it out of here. Dr. August has fixed me up once, and I want to see if he can make me into another man again." He flexed his glove-covered mod thoughtfully. "Maybe he'll give me second sight."

GOLD EAGLE

GOLD EAGLE action/adventure books are now available in stores each month at a new time.

Look for The Executioner and GOLD EAGLE's new miniseries: SURVIVAL 2000, SOLDIERS OF WAR, TIME WARRIORS and AGENTS on the 16th of every month in your favorite retail outlet.

We hope that this new schedule is convenient for you. Please note that there may be slight variations in on-sale dates in your area due to differences in shipping and handling.

GEDATES

AGENTS

The action-packed new series of the DEA.... Sudden death is a way of life at the drug-enforcement administration—in an endless full-frontal assault on America's toughest war: drugs. For Miami-based maverick Jack Fowler, it's a war he'll fight to the end.

TRIGGER PULL

PAUL MALONE

In TRIGGER PULL, a narc's murder puts Fowler on a one-man vengeance trail of Miami cops on the take and a Bahamian kingpin. Stalked by Colombian gunmen and a hit team of Metro-Dade's finest, Fowler brings the players together in a win-or-lose game where survival depends on the pull of a trigger.

THE MEDELLÍN TRILOGY
THE EXECUTIONER®

Message to Medellín: The Executioner and his warriors are primed for the biggest showdown in the cocaine wars—and are determined to win!

Don't miss The Medellín Trilogy—a three-book action drama that pits THE EXECUTIONER, PHOENIX FORCE and ABLE TEAM against the biggest narco barons and cocaine cowboys in South America. The cocaine crackdown begins in May in THE EXECUTIONER #149: *Blood Rules,* continues in June in the longer 352-page Mack Bolan novel *Evil Kingdom* and concludes in July in THE EXECUTIONER #151: *Message to Medellín.*

Look for the special banner on each explosive book in The Medellín Trilogy and make sure you don't miss an episode of this awesome new battle in The Executioner's everlasting war!

In the Deathlands,
everyone and everything is fair game,
but only the strongest survive....

JAMES AXLER

DEATH LANDS

Latitude Zero

Heading west toward the nearest gateway, Ryan Cawdor and his band
of post-holocaust survivors are trapped in a nightmare when a deal
necessary for their survival pits them against Ryan's oldest enemy—a
sadistic, ruthless man who would stop at nothing to get his hands on
Ryan Cawdor.